WHITE LINEN

About the Author

Martin Howe is a journalist who has worked for the BBC, Channel 4 and a news agency in Washington DC. He writes literary fiction as an escape from the constraints of factual news. White Linen is his first novel.

www.mbhowe.com

WHITE LINEN

MARTIN HOWE

Matador
9 Priory Business Park,
Wistow Road, Kibworth Beauchamp,
Leicestershire. LE8 0RX
Tel: 0116 279 2299
Email: books@troubador.co.uk
Web: www.troubador.co.uk/matador
Twitter: @matadorbooks

ISBN 978 1789015 966

British Library Cataloguing in Publication Data.
A catalogue record for this book is available from the British Library.

Printed and bound in Great Britain by 4edge Limited
Typeset in 11pt Minion Pro by Troubador Publishing Ltd, Leicester, UK

Matador is an imprint of Troubador Publishing Ltd

For Clare

MRS BREEN: Mr Bloom! You down here in the haunts of sin! I caught you nicely! Scamp!

BLOOM: (Hurriedly.) Not so loud my name. Whatever do you think me? Don't give me away. Walls have hears. How do you do? Its ages since I. You're looking splendid. Absolutely it. Seasonable weather we are having this time of year. Black refracts heat. Short cut home here. Interesting quarter. Rescue of fallen women Magdalen asylum. I am the secretary...

MRS BREEN: (Holds up a finger.) Now don't tell a big fib! I know somebody won't like that. O just wait till I see Molly! (Slily.) Account for yourself this very minute or woe betide you!

Ulysses – James Joyce

Foreword

White Linen is the fictional account of five women who were forced to work for most of their lives in a Magdalen laundry in Ireland. These institutions were attached to convents and took their name from Mary Magdalene, the prostitute, who repented her sins in time to witness the resurrection of Christ. They were set up in the nineteenth century by the Catholic church in Britain and Ireland to "tidy away" problem women and girls. Most were unmarried mothers who had been rejected by their families, but there were also orphans, the wayward, those unfit to look after themselves and the plain unlucky. They were victims of a society which judged by strict moral codes of behaviour, sanctioned by the Church. For those women that transgressed these moral boundaries, the price was heavy. They were often confined for a lifetime of unpaid labour, rejected by and cut off from their families and communities. In the late 1960s the women were finally allowed to leave the convents, but by then it was too late for many of them. They had known no other life and were ill-prepared for the outside world. Often they elected to stay within the safe walls of the convent. As the Twentieth Century drew to a close, the role of the Madgalen laundries was increasingly questioned. From the 1980s the Catholic Church found itself beset by a number of scandals involving the children of bishops and priests, allegations of cruelty and child abuse and concerns over adoption policies. The pressure to modernize was intense.

The Magdalen laundries were gradually closed down – the last one in Ireland shut on October 25th 1996 – leaving the Church with the problem of what to do with the many women in their care.

Chapter 1

The Laundry, Convent of our Lady of Mercy at the
Magdalen Asylum, Dublin – August 1995

The sun was almost directly overhead. Light streamed through
the skylights, patterning the floor of the laundry into an irregular
grid, that shimmered as clouds of steam rose slowly from the
boilers and presses. By mid-morning the high-ceilinged hall was
filled with air so heavy with moisture it had a physical presence. It
lay like a blanket over the thirty-two working women, restricting
their movements and stifling conversation. The heavy fog, laced
with the cutting fragrance of soap, the scything chemical blasts
of bleach and the cloying taste of starch, moved around and
over the women unaided by any natural drafts, influenced by an
energy uniquely its own.

The laundry was strangely silent, the only sounds – the
occasional hiss of escaping steam, the dripping of condensation
onto stone-flagged floors – distant and inconsequential. Voices
were seldom heard and when they were, they appeared muffled
and out of place.

It was a scene of intense physical labour, carried out with
an economy of effort. A line of six women stood hunched over

steaming sinks below the tall windows, which lined one wall. They appeared barely to move and yet they worked for hours on end scrubbing clean clothes too delicate for the boilers, the piles of damp washing growing imperceptibly beside them on the wooden draining boards.

In the centre of the hall other women stood in squares of vivid sunlight ironing lethargically, sweat glistening on their arms and faces. Occasionally, one would stop to mop her brow and glance upwards, but seemed incapable of moving out of the fierce glare. They appeared unconcerned by the intermittent hissing of the two presses close beside them, the steam billowing outwards as the boards gaped open and the pressure was released.

Soiled whites bubbled away in three large copper vats that stood in a line at one end of the long narrow building. Their burnished sides streamed with water that dripped steadily onto the feet of the women, who would step forward in pairs at regular intervals to lift the heavy metal lids and stir the murky foaming liquid with long wooden paddles. They would rub their faces with the back of their hands as they moved back, blinking through bloodshot eyes, to resume their places on the wooden bench pressed up against the damp green-painted wall.

Regaining her breath after this manoeuvre, one of the women called out a warning to another group bent double over a series of smaller basins, brimming with water.

"This lot's nearly done so. You'd better be getting a move on with your rinsing there."

Several of the women looked up. Their hair where it had escaped from head scarves was plastered to sweating faces, the fronts of their overalls were drenched and their bare arms red-raw from constant immersion in cold water.

There was exasperation in the voice of the tall, big-boned woman, who spoke up in reply, but nothing more. It was all too routine to get bothered about. Barbara had worked with most of the others at the laundry for over forty years and such exchanges had become commonplace, and for the most part, jovial.

"Jesus, will you give over, Maeve? You can talk. You only look to be halfway through to me."

She nodded at the pile of bulging laundry bags heaped haphazardly beside the steaming copper cauldrons.

"It's not us who's holding things up, Barbara," replied Maeve in virtuous tones. A slim pale-faced woman, her brown hair scraped back and held tightly by a green headscarf, she shook her head as she spoke. "Sure we can only go as fast as the slowest one here."

"And that seems to be Margaret at the moment. Where is she? She should have been in by now to take out those clean sheets. There'll be no room left soon."

Maeve, who was usually on the receiving end of Margaret's jibes, enjoyed it when she could for once criticize her tormentor.

"You know her, she'll be taking it easy outside somewhere. Not pulling her weight. As usual."

Behind them, a round-faced woman stood silently mop in hand. Her skin was red and blotchy; white overalls darkened between the shoulder blades by sweat and damply matched under each arm, whenever she raised a hand to the perspiration running into her eyes and tickling the end of her nose. But she was smiling, almost hugging the mop to herself in obvious delight.

"Doris, have you seen Margaret?" Maeve asked her.

She held her beatific smile while shaking her head vigorously.

"No Maeve, not recently. She's gone missing, I suppose?"

"As usual."

"She'll be back soon. I'm just off to make the tea."

Doris had been happy all morning, had in fact been happy for several weeks, ever since they had given her new duties in the laundry. Father Michael, the Convent's confessor, had quietly explained that she had done an excellent job for many years, for which he and the Church were extremely grateful, but there came a time when everyone needed to row back a bit and take it easy. He had been so careful – not like him at all really – to reassure her that there was still plenty of work to be done, emphatic that she was not being pushed aside and ignored. Doris had protested of course, mildly and without any conviction. The priest had needed few words to brush her objections aside. To be honest, it was amazing to her that her own silent wishes had come true. The Church had long since ceased to surprise her, the dazzlements of her youth now only a distant memory. But a priest fulfilling a banal act of pastoral care had brought those old ecstatic feelings back to life, rekindling in Doris a belief in the miraculous she had believed lost forever.

Outside, the lines of damp washing hung limply in the oppressive heat. The stillness was unbroken, even the sparrows that usually flocked noisily around the eaves of the laundry were silent. A skinny, hatchet-faced woman with strands of dyed blonde hair protruding from beneath her tattered headscarf had given up pegging out white shirts and was sitting on an upturned wicker basket in the shade of the towering convent wall, staring lethargically at the dusty ground at her feet. Margaret was feeling deeply envious of Doris – of all people – and she could hardly believe it. It wasn't fair. If only she herself got on better with Father Michael, she could have gone and asked him if she could stop doing all this and retire as well. On days like today it really was unbearable. And there was Doris swanning around with her broom, with just a bit of sweeping and mopping up to do, and maybe make the odd cup of tea. The rest of the time she could sit inside in the cool with her feet up. She always was the lucky one. It just wasn't fair.

Margaret glanced at her watch. It was almost eleven, break time, and she was gasping for her tea. That's if Madame Doris hadn't grown too fucking grand in her semi-retirement to put the kettle on. Margaret levered herself to her feet, noticed a run in her lisle stocking and swore viciously to herself.

"You wouldn't wish this heat on anybody, even your worst enemy, would you?"

Doris muttered the words aloud as she peered blindly out through the kitchen window into the glare. She closed her eyes against the searing light, burning images of yellow and orange illuminating the lidded darkness, and decided she wasn't so sure. Maybe Margaret deserved it, the only one in all these years here she could say that about. There had been many heated words and rows that ended in tears, women she had barely spoken to again even though they had lived closely together for years, but there had been no one like Margaret. There was a tenacity and relentlessness about her that meant she never gave up. It was as if she was fighting a war that would only be won when she had defeated everybody else, but she was the only one who knew that hostilities had been declared. Friend or foe meant nothing to her in the endless campaign.

Doris' release from the laundry – her miracle – had had an almost physical effect on her. Her body was relaxing and lightening. She felt years younger, even though she knew this was pure vanity and, for the first time in ages, was actually looking to the future with something approaching eagerness. She had escaped from the worst of the work not a moment too soon. Doris had never been overly concerned about her appearance, to the despair of many of her friends who had urged her not to let things go. It was all right for them, but for Doris her plump body and round face, her tight curly hair and the glasses she had worn since childhood offered little in the way of inspiration. There was only one thing she had once secretly prided herself on and that was her hands. As a girl she had seen her long thin fingers and manicured nails as the only sign on an otherwise uninspiring exterior of inner elegance. Working in the laundry had ruined them. They were so painful some days, red-raw, "like meat on a slab" as Barbara would often say. "Occupational hazard, love, grin and bear it." She tried, oh, how she tried. It was the flaking skin and the tender, stinging patches beneath that worried Doris most; they seemed permanent these days.

The patch of skin between the second and third knuckles on her left hand would itch and itch, then suddenly the skin would peel and lift in diaphanous, papery sheets and the wound would weep tears of clear, salty liquid. The pain would suddenly intensify and deepen, paralysing the muscles of her hand. It was sometimes difficult to pick anything up for a day or two. The feeling – seemingly impervious to any medicament – would never completely disappear. It was present in the benighted hours of the early morning, present in the bright sunlight of a Sunday afternoon, present even in competition with the searing heat of a steaming cup of tea. The pain was ever present.

Then it would seem to ebb as the blistering on the inner wrist of her right hand flared, bubbled and burst into stinging life, the pale near transparent skin between her index and second fingers on the same hand would redden and stiffen, shackling movement as surely as the bandages that Dr O'Grady would occasionally bind her with. And so it went on. Doris hoped her hands could yet be saved. With miracles, she supposed, anything was possible.

She started suddenly as she noticed the clock on the wall. If she wasn't careful she'd be late with their elevenses, and then what would Margaret say?

* * *

Father Michael was nervous, a rare condition for him, and he hated it. What use was a nervous priest, after all? It shouldn't happen to someone who dealt in certainties. Nerves, one Bishop had told him, were a sign of humanity, but try as he might he could only see them as weakness. This speech was going to be difficult, he knew, but he should be able to cope. He shuddered at the thought that his feelings might have anything to do with the fact that he had known some of these women for years. Pure sentimentality. It was more probably a slight attack of sunstroke.

He braced himself as he walked up to the laundry with his visitors. A spring loaded door pull kept the entrance permanently shut to protect the convent building from the worst ravages of the humidity and the chemicals. The Reverend Mother of the Convent of our Lady of Mercy at the Magdalen Asylum, Sister Beatrice, had agreed to meet them there at eleven o'clock sharp, but she was late. That was not like her and the priest thought she was probably already inside. He reached across and opened the door, then stepped back almost immediately, a raised hand shielding his eyes as a cloud of warm air rolled into the corridor and temporarily blinded him.

"All that's missing, don't you think, is the roar. With all this steam you could be entering a dragon's lair."

Father Michael turned and smiled at his visitors. He had said it all many times before. He could be even more risqué, depending on who was with him, and start talking about the infernal gases belching out of his own personal Hades.

"All that's missing is the flicker of the eternal flames and the whiff of sulphur and you could be entering hell on earth."

This usually managed to raise a laugh, but the dragon seemed the right metaphor for the present company and didn't let him down. Councillor Anderson, who was anxiously rubbing the front of her steamed up glasses with a pale pink handkerchief, smiled faintly. Her companion, a Mr Purvis, clerk to the Council, was grinning broadly. He was enjoying the discomfort of the officious, demanding councillor – his boss – and would have been only too happy to have left her standing there, blinded by the steam. Then Father Michael took pity, something he felt himself rather good at. Much as he liked to lash out at weakness, and often did, it was more often of the moral and spiritual kind rather than the physical. He took her arm.

"This way, Mrs Anderson. I think Sister Beatrice must be inside."

They disappeared into the swirling mist followed by a disappointed Mr Purvis.

"Ah, Sister, you're here ahead of us."

A tall thin figure, dressed in the traditional black habit, turned to meet them. The nun's narrow face was grimly set, her startling blue eyes hooded and barely open. She nodded in their direction. Father Michael had known her for many years and had rarely seen her look so bleak. He supposed it could be the heat, which was unbearable, but he feared not. This damn business was affecting everybody.

"Sister Beatrice, I believe you know Mrs Anderson from the Council…"

As the two women shook hands, Father Michael ran a finger along the inside of his dog collar and glanced around the apparently empty laundry.

"… and this is her colleague, Mr Purvis. Where is everybody? I thought they would be here."

"They're on a tea break".

The priest leaned forward. He could barely hear what Sister Beatrice was saying, which was again unusual. He took care not to appear disrespectful by moving too close. They got on well, but were not friends.

"Sorry, Sister?"

"They're next door in the refectory, having a cup of tea".

"Good, good. It'll be cooler in there, I trust".

"It is, Father."

The priest cleared his throat.

"Then shall we go through?"

* * *

Doris was looking at her hands and thinking maybe she would have to go and see the doctor again when the Reverend Mother, Father Michael and two people she didn't recognize walked into the room. All heads turned to look at them as they shuffled their way to places behind the high table, scraping chairs as they went. Glancing at each other as if anxious to keep in time, they all sat down in a row. The women, many still red faced and sweat stained, had just finished their tea and biscuits and the dirty crockery was being passed down the long tables to be placed in green plastic washing up bowls, before being carried out to the kitchen. That would be Doris' job from now on; they had used to take it in turns.

It was very unusual for their priest or anyone else to come into the refectory during breaks. He was often here on a Sunday, but then that was the best meal of the week. Something must be afoot. What with this and all the rumours lately, the room fell silent almost immediately. Father Michael got to his feet and banged unnecessarily hard on the top of the table.

"Sisters, this concerns you only indirectly, so feel free to excuse yourselves".

He nodded at a couple of nuns who had been reading at one of the side tables. His voice sounded faint and distant to Doris, and she hoped he would speak up as the hall had very high ceilings and sounds could easily get lost. Many was the time she had nodded off after a good meal as one of the nuns read indistinctly from the Bible, the reassuring drone lulling, soothing, easing her towards sleep.

"Father?"

"I have an important…"

"Father … Father?"

"Yes, Daisy, what is it?"

"You couldn't say that again, could you? The old hearing's not what it was."

"Sorry, Daisy, I never seem to get it right in here, do I?"

He laughed, but sounded distinctly uncomfortable.

"Ladies, the two people up here you don't know are Mrs Anderson and Mr Purvis. They are from the local Council."

The thirty-two laundry women in the hall exchanged glances. Michael clasped his hands across his stomach and looked over the heads of his expectant audience, careful not to meet their eyes.

"I've known you all for a good many years and what I have to say gives me very little pleasure. Believe me when I say I have done everything in my power to resist this decision. It is not something I would ever support. In fact, not to put too fine a point on it, I think it is positively misguided. But, and I've said this many times to you all, "Make the most of any situation you find yourself in and God will make the most of you." Very true in this case, for me personally as much as for you. I've searched my soul in the hours since I heard this news and genuinely believe I can now see some good in it. Some of you will be shocked when you hear what I have to say, but please hear me out as your interests really have been looked after. I would never be party to anything that was not…"

His voice cracked. Deliberately he swallowed hard, letting them wait. He felt the warm satisfaction of knowing once again that the old magic was not going to let him down. He had the words, he had the emotional range and control, he had his audience eating out of his hand. They were waiting on his every word now.

"I have not let you down," he finished, modestly hanging his head.

The Reverend Mother seemed to underline his words by nodding her own and looking from side to side, sweeping the upturned faces in front of her with calm unsmiling eyes.

"A decision has been made by the diocese and the City Council about the future of the laundry. In a few months it will close."

There was an audible gasp, heads turned and voices whispered. The priest paused an instant, before waving for silence.

"I know, I know … it was a shock to me too. You all know how much I've enjoyed working with you in the laundry. I did everything I could to try and persuade them to keep going with it, but I'm afraid there was a clear majority against me."

His voice faltered. Once again the priest was surprised how emotional he felt about it all. Maybe, he surmised, it was the sight of all those aged faces looking up at him, some bemused, some befuddled, most trusting, that had touched him. And maybe it was something else entirely – the prospect of actually living in his prudently purchased "retirement cottage" in Galway, comfortable – luxurious even – though it was. He shook his head to clear the troubling thoughts and went on.

"I couldn't make them change their minds. The laundry is to close."

"What's to happen to us?"

Irritated, he searched the room for the source of the voice that had interrupted him, just as he was getting into his stride. Nobody moved.

"Sorry, I missed that? Come on, speak up."

An arm rose slowly into the air, mid-way down the hall. The priest strained to make out who it was in the dim yellowing light.

"Ah, Morag, speak up, there's a love".

"If the laundry closes, what will happen to us?"

For the first time Doris, who was sitting more or less opposite Morag on the same long table, understood the seriousness of what was going on. Closing the laundry? Where would she live? What would she do? Things had just seemed to be working out for her at last, she had her new role, but for how long now? Morag, who had partly raised herself from her seat, sat back down again. Doris looked around in panic.

"Look, I'll be coming to that."

Michael glanced at Reverend Mother beside him and raised his eyebrows. Sister Beatrice stared straight ahead and resolutely refused to meet his gaze.

"Now, where was I? Ah, yes. The powers that be claim we are hopelessly outdated and nowhere near as efficient as some of the newcomers."

Mrs Anderson shifted uncomfortably in her seat and Mr Purvis smirked, beginning to enjoy himself. The priest seemed to have forgotten they were there, or else didn't care. In this company the councillor's hands were tied, she would have to take what was coming. Father Michael answered only to a higher body from now on.

"Of course I asked what about the quality of our washes, our high standards of ironing, the personal service? To no avail. All they were interested in was the bottom line. I wanted to refurbish the laundry, before they closed it down on health and safety grounds. I wanted to modernize. Get in new machines that would cope with three times the amount of work in less time. It wasn't right that you should labour on in these conditions. At a bare minimum you deserved better ventilation. But what did they do? They refused to stump up any extra money. Refurbishment was not the answer, apparently. Economically, it didn't make sense. The commercial laundries were better equipped and could provide a much more competitive service."

Father Michael laughed bitterly.

"And so, Ladies, hard cash is what it boils down to – if you'll pardon the pun. Blow the fact that there's been a laundry at this convent for a hundred and fifty years. That all across the country there have been church laundries – Magdalen laundries, call them what you will – since time immemorial, a haven for the unfortunate and the fallen. Who else but the Church would have done that, I ask you? Alas that argument means nothing to the Council."

He drew out his handkerchief and waved it dramatically in the air.

"I despair, I really do."

Then he blew his nose and wiped his sweating face. There were audible sobs from his audience and he realized belatedly that some of the women were genuinely frightened.

"Ladies, come on now, what do you take me for? Rest assured you'll all be taken care of. I know we could do without all this unnecessary upheaval, but it'll be for the best in the end, I'm sure."

Every eye was fixed unwaveringly upon him and he shifted his feet slightly.

"Believe me, please. This is not the time for detailed explanations, but everyone will be looked after. Hasn't the Church always taken care of you?"

Now that wasn't always true, thought Doris in one of those increasingly rare moments when shards of memory broke through the confused surface of her consciousness with a shocking clarity. She wanted to challenge the priest and willed herself to put up her hand. She needed to call out that she didn't believe him. She could see in her mind's eye the faces turning towards her, the smiles, the looks of encouragement, the words of support egging her on, the smug expression of the priest dissolving before her, the gaping mouth, his astonishment. The moment was hers, but her knees were trapped under the table by the long bench she was sitting on, made immobile by the weight of the others. Doris struggled briefly to get up as the rim cut into her leg. Sitting on her right Maeve looked askance at her efforts to move. It was so out of character for Doris to push herself forward.

"She must be desperate so", thought Maeve, and pulled a sympathetic face.

"Ok, let me fill you in as best...".

Doris' time had passed.

"..I can. There is going to be reassessment of your needs. Sounds complicated, but it isn't. You will be able to say what you would like to do. Those who want to stay here will be able to."

A number of heads nodded around the hall.

"Others will be able to leave and set up home outside on their own or with their families. There will be lots of help and no one, I repeat no one, will be forced to do anything they don't want to."

"But what will we do if the laundry is gone?"

Morag was standing up this time. A lock of curling red hair had worked itself loose from the hair net she always wore and was hanging across her face. She brushed it away as she spoke.

"I couldn't stand having nothing to do."

"Don't you worry about that. It's already being sorted out by Mrs Anderson here and Mr Purvis. There will be work available at the Council's Occupational Therapy department. As I understand it, some of you will be packing "Spick and Span Cleaning Bags" on contract. Other firms are being approached. Isn't that right, Mrs Anderson?"

She nodded and smiled. Her voice carried clearly to the back of the hall.

"I will be talking to all of you over the coming weeks about what you would like to do. Together with the Church authorities, I'm sure we'll be able to satisfy everyone here. Believe me, no stone will be left unturned. Despite the way we've been painted here, the council is not a heartless body. We do care about your welfare. Father Michael, please continue."

The priest forced himself to smile at her before addressing the laundry women.

"Any more questions before I let you get on with your duties?"

"I've got a question."

A tall raw-boned woman he recognized as Barbara someone or other, got to her feet and squared her shoulders angrily.

"How dare you stand up there and tell us our lives are to change forever. It's not fair."

Her voice was fractured and charged with emotion. She banged the table with one fist. Doris knew her friend had a fiery temperament, but she had never seen her like this.

"What am I going to do? I've been here years – it's all the home I've got. And now you bastards are taking it away, damn you to hell!"

Without waiting for a reply, she fled from the room. Sunlight briefly flooded through the open door, together with sounds from the distant street. Then with a thud the door closed, the light dimmed and silence fell, an audible quiet that cried out for punctuation. Everyone in the refectory listened. Then finally the full stop came as a car door slammed shut outside with a percussive clap, an engine started, someone called out, and for a second the sounds of the street seemed to fill the enclosed hall. Then they were submerged, drowned out by the shuffling feet, the coughs and creaking benches as everyone turned once again to face Father Michael, who assumed his most long-suffering expression and clasped his hands before him.

"I think a prayer would be appropriate at a time like this."

He took a prayer book from his jacket pocket and looked out over the sea of greying heads, already meekly bowing in response.

"Lord, hear our prayers on this momentous day. For many of us gathered here before you, this is a time of profound change. Our lives will never be the same again. Many of us are moving on to a new station of life. Embarking on a journey that for some is into the unknown. For others who are staying behind, many of the old familiar faces will have gone. It will be as much a new journey for them as for the others who are leaving. So it is with sadness in my heart that I say farewell to so many old friends. But I know we will all meet again in a higher place at an appointed time. Let us dwell not on the end of an era, but ask God for happiness in the new one.

Amen."

Chapter 2

*The Snug – March 1996 – five
past twelve in the afternoon*

Doris was confused. But then, for the last few months, everything had been confused. Ever since Father Michael had dropped his bombshell about the laundry closing, she'd been unsure what exactly was going on. Take today for example. Here she was, sitting in the Coach and Horses on a Friday – a Friday lunchtime. That had never happened before. If it was a Saturday, that would be different. She'd been here on a Saturday before, sat and watched the horses on that screen high above the bar. Football on there now, best she could tell. It was so high up that even with her glasses on it sometimes wouldn't come into focus. But then it was the company, wasn't it, that made coming to the Coach and Horses so much fun? "The craic" as Lily used to say. God, how she missed Lily.

Doris looked round as if Father or Reverend Mother might hear her thoughts. Blasphemous thoughts, she knew that all right. Clear as a bell. For a second her mind was blank. Almost imperceptibly the lines on her forehead drew closer together, then relaxed – points breaking free in a thaw. Margaret had always been so rude about the lines on her face. "Clapham Junction" she called them. She could talk. Come to think of it, Margaret was always going on about Doris' appearance; the grey hair – thinning now – the short-sightedness, her stocky build and the fact that she wasn't as tall as the rest of them. Margaret never seemed to give up. Doris suddenly remembered – Father and Mother wouldn't be around anymore. Never would be again. They had made that perfectly clear this morning when they had said their goodbyes. Patiently, as always, but Doris had been sure there had been an edge. She decided Father Michael must have been tired. He was getting on, you had to remember that. Weren't they all! Doris smiled. She liked to think of everyone growing older – "a community of increasing decrepitudes", as Barbara put it. She was a one with the words, but then she did make people laugh.

Barbara, Margaret, Maeve, Lily and Doris, the Famous Five. They were all here now, bar Lily, who'd left years ago, sitting in the snug, smiling, laughing and sipping their drinks. Barbara was the only one smoking, but then she was always smoking. A cigarette never seemed to leave her lips, even when she was talking, which was often in her case. It appeared to have kept her young, the drifting smoke caressing a strong face remarkably untouched by the years, a complexion as unblemished and vibrant as it had been in her youth. Grey barely flecked her wavy auburn hair, which she wore short. Her sparkling eyes were beacons now in the dim smoky light, her excitement barely contained, charging the atmosphere, rallying her friends. It had always been the same since Doris had first met her ages before. Barbara had always given them strength, kept them going, held them together. They were all here now because of her. She'd suggested a last drink, a final get together in the Coach and Horses, before they went their separate ways – Barbara to live with her sister, Doris to her niece's, Margaret and Maeve to stay at the Convent. The only one missing was Lily. She was gone. Had just left some years before, had left the Convent with no word of goodbye. Doris still hoped that one day she would find out why.

Barbara was at the bar, getting in the next round of drinks. They always sent her, as she was the tallest, had not seemed to shrink and bend as much as the rest of them. She had a loud voice and was not afraid to use it. She could always make herself heard above the hubbub, even when the horses were running. Barbara liked the "gee-gees" but always said, "I'll make the sacrifice, as a good Catholic, I'll get them in. I don't mind missing the action".

If anyone picked up on her blasphemy, it would be Maeve, sitting on the opposite side of the beer-spattered table from Doris, with her hands clasped neatly in her lap. She was still wearing her neatly knotted headscarf, even though they'd been inside for over a quarter of an hour, a grey cardigan draped over her shoulders. She was the only one of them who had bothered to hang her green overcoat on the peg in the corner, taking care to place her neatly folded belt in one of the pockets. The others had slung their coats over the backs of the chairs when they arrived.

Maeve suddenly gave an involuntary shiver and slightly hunched her body. She always felt the cold something Margaret teased her endlessly about, saying loudly that if only she wore stockings and not the knitted knee socks she was so fond of, then she'd have no problem. She turned her pale thin face to stare once again through the steamed up window at the crystal blue sky beyond. She'd already said, "At least it's a good day for it," several times and looked as if she was about to say it again.

Hurry up with those drinks, thought Doris.

Maeve didn't approve of the horses; didn't really like to drink either. She was an ostentatiously good Catholic, who should have been a nun; could have been one if she'd put her mind to it, or that's what they had all thought. But when she was younger she had suffered from horrible mind-numbing depression and had harmed herself on a number of occasions. She never really stood a chance after that. The Reverend Mother had said kind things, but she knew it would never happen. And there was always Margaret, who was not one to let anything pass unremarked upon.

Hard-faced Margaret was a woman who had not softened with time, had not folded or slackened but had set like concrete, then imperceptibly fissured and crumbled as over the years the chill that never left her took its toll. These outward signs of an inner pain she wanted kept hidden filled Margaret with a quiet desperation. Make-up and hair dye had become her shield. She grabbed minutes, away she thought from prying eyes, to moisturise and smooth over, but Doris had noticed and was strangely satisfied. When they were young Margaret had used her ruby red lipsticks, blue eyeliner and black mascara to flaunt her beauty in front of her plainer friend. Now she used them simply to hide her age. They were finally equal, a fact which would have horrified Margaret if Doris had ever had the nerve to tell her.

Now she was in the Ladies. Couldn't hold her drink, Margaret couldn't, not in the waterworks department anyway. It was one of the few things Doris could use to get back at her. Margaret was so rude sometimes – often when Doris thought about it she wondered why she put up with it, why they were friends with her. She did so again as she twirled a beer mat between her scarred thumb and middle finger, but forgot to answer her own question as she stared dreamily at the flickering screen. They weren't going anywhere, the Famous Five, not yet anyway. They were to have one last drink together, one final lunchtime in the Coach and Horses. On a Friday this time, but who cared about that?

"Jim there says he's just heard they're closing us down. He sounds real sorry we're going. Asked who was going to do his dirty washing now. These are on him. Real nice of him, though it's not as if we haven't spent enough in here over the years, is it?"

Barbara carefully placed two half-pint glasses filled to the brim with Guinness on the table.

"Look, steady as a rock. I haven't spilled a drop".

She turned and moved in her stately way through the lunchtime crowd that was spilling from the public bar into the snug. Jim handed her two more glasses through a small wood framed glass door, one of three, that formed part of a mahogany screen blocking off the bar from the snug. He smiled then disappeared, flicking the door shut with practised ease. It spun round several times, the reds and golds of the upturned whisky bottles glinting diffusely through the dappled surface of the glass, before it settled gently into place.

The smoke floated lazily upwards, mingling imperceptibly with the haze that hung like a pale shroud over their heads. For a moment they were all silent. Barbara, sitting now, her head resting back against the dark wooden panelling of the snug, inhaled deeply to recapture some of the escaping smoke, disturbing as she did so the eddies spiralling into the smog. Her one vice. Wrong she knew, but how she loved it. Barbara sipped her Guinness, then took a long drag on her cigarette, half-closed her eyes and inwardly sighed with pleasure.

It had not always been like this, of course. There had been times when she couldn't get hold of a cigarette for weeks on end. Reverend Mother had always been strict and when she was younger hadn't allowed smoking anywhere. If she caught you there was hell to pay. Early to bed, chores in the kitchen, cleaning up in the laundry on your knees without any cushions, beatings – they had hurt. Broken her nose once, given her intermittent nose bleeds for years afterwards, always at night, the sheets stained red in the morning, nostrils crusted almost closed. Breathing was often difficult. The cold water chapping her hands as she pounded the sheets in the white enamelled bath, the pink tinged water spiralling away, gurgling down the plug hole. A bitter taste in her mouth, that even bi-carbonate would never quite wash away. Reverend Mother was the difficult one right enough. She had it in for Barbara over her smoking, that was for sure, but what could she do? She'd craved her cigarettes, more than she craved the nuns' approbation. Barbara had decided that long ago. It made things easier, knowing which way you would go if it ever came to the crunch. It never quite did, of course, but she was clear in her own mind. It definitely helped that she was gobby, not afraid to have a go and say what she thought. Mother didn't like confrontation, preferred to keep it all private and personal. She backed away from public rows.

"I'm not a brawler like you, not a street fighter", she'd once told Barbara, "I'll see you later in my room. Now calm down."

She'd been beaten across the calves with a ruler that time, if she recalled rightly. She'd vowed to remember it all – it wasn't right – but it had happened so often she was losing count and now it was over. The laundry was closed and she was leaving forever. From now on it would be all the cigarettes she could afford, whenever she wanted. Bliss. So long as her sister Bernice didn't mind. Strange that she hadn't a clue what her own sister thought, but then she hardly knew her.

Doris watched Barbara as she smoked. She really was her best friend, kind as could be most of the time. Doris glanced around to check no one was looking, but Maeve and Margaret were laughing away, paying no attention to her. It used to be Lily, of course, she thought to herself. Still would be if she hadn't gone away. Tears began to well up in Doris's eyes, as they always did whenever she thought of Lily. She wiped them quickly away, but too late for gimlet eyed Margaret.

"Getting all gushy, are we, Dottie? Trust you".

"Oh, come on, I bet we all will be by the end of the day. After all, we won't be seeing each other for a while".

"Not me, Barbara love, you won't see me weeping any tears, I can assure you of that. How much do you want to bet?"

"Oh, Margaret, give over, will you?"

"Come on, Barbara, money where your mouth is."

"We all know you never pay your debts. It's just not worth it."

"I do so."

"It would be the first time then."

It was Barbara to the rescue yet again. Doris smiled kindly.

"Penny for them, Dot."

"I was just, I don't know, just…"

"You were what, Doris?"

Margaret never could miss an opportunity to poke fun.

"I was just thinking about when we first came here. It was a long time ago and this is the end of it, isn't it?"

"It is in one sense, Doris, but some of us are staying on and you can come to visit any time, not like the old days. We'll still see each other."

Maeve was trying to remain level-headed, but felt anything but as soon as she had spoken. She'd been feeling very depressed lately every time she thought about what was to happen to them all. In fact she had started taking her stronger pills again just to get to sleep. She knew it wasn't good, but it would pass, it was only for a while, just to get her over these next few weeks. Things would settle down.

"It won't be the same though, will it? I'll be miles away. I don't know how often they'll bring me back here, even if I ask them to. I don't know them really. We've only spoken on the phone".

Barbara patted her on the hand.

"It won't be the same, Doris, we all know that. But we're good friends, we'll keep in touch, I know we will. Bernice has told me she always fancies a trip up to Dublin any old time, so I'll be coming and we can probably pick you up on the way. My sister has a grand big car – never seen nothing like it in my life. It's got leather seats, place to put your drinks, newspaper racks. I couldn't believe it that day she took me out for a drive. I must have told you about it?"

"You sure did, Barbara, never stopped telling us, if I remember rightly."

For once Margaret was smiling, her mouth a thin envious carmine slash.

"Dead jealous I was, I can tell you. Still am."

"I came here in 1951. How many years is that?" asked Barbara.

"Let me see. It's over forty".

"Exactly forty five. That's a long time. All very different then. I should know, I was only a few years behind you, Doris. We must be the oldest?"

Barbara looked quizzically across the table at Maeve and Margaret. She knew the answer but was equally certain Margaret would argue and was determined to let her know she was having none of that nonsense. It was funny standing up to Margaret now, when it didn't really matter. Maeve looked close to tears.

Barbara couldn't really believe it. Years and years with these people and they'd never really talked about it before: how they came to be here in this place, living and working on top of each other, day in day out. It had just never come up even though they'd talked about everything under the sun. They all liked a good chat. This bar had seen some times! There had frequently been laughter, tears running down their cheeks. Often the four of them had returned late to the Convent over the road, they'd been having such a fine time. Got them into trouble more than once and been kept in the next Saturday, but it had been worth it.

Memory was a strange thing, though. She'd been sure she could remember everything, but looking at them now she wasn't sure they were the same people she'd been with all these years. It wasn't just that they looked different – older naturally, greyer and with more lines – they were different. Different people. If she didn't know it was impossible, if she didn't believe it was a sin to say it, think it even, she would say their very souls had changed.

Doris was not the same person she had met those forty odd years ago. She was a simpler, purer, cleaner version now, closer to God, Barbara was sure, than some of the so-called sisters who'd lorded it over them all these years. And Margaret was the opposite. She was more wicked, more venal, with never a good word to say about anyone or anything. Maeve, on the other hand, had always aspired to saintliness but had singularly failed and was only now starting to understand that it wasn't everything, there were other things in life besides ritual observance and meek obedience.

She did love them, though, they were her family. Barbara shivered. She suddenly felt very sad. She knew why they had rarely talked about it, why she'd kept quiet: fear. That's what had gnawed its way into their very souls, corroding away from the inside until only the barest shell remained and even that was cracking for some of them. All that was left was bloody emptiness, a vacuum. Barbara knew nature didn't like that, but then what had been natural about any of their lives? She didn't like it either and this could be their last chance to fill it with something, anything. Or if not even that, then maybe paper over some of the cracks.

"Barbara, why are you looking so upset? I thought you were happy about all this?" Margaret probed.

"I never get upset, Margaret, you know me well enough."

"You never cry, we all know that. Never have all the time I've known you," put in Maeve, "Not like me."

"The last time I did was Spring 1951 – the year they took my baby George from me."

"That was his name? You've never talked much about him".

"I know, Doris, I know."

As Barbara stood up, she came to a decision.

"I'll tell you all about it when I get back from the Ladies."

Chapter 3

Barbara's round – September 1950

Patrick's hands were cold, almost icy to the touch. This struck Barbara as strange, it had been boiling hot on the dance floor, they'd danced and held each other close. They'd both been sweating and had to stop to cool down and have a drink. Dandelion and burdock, of course. No alcohol allowed for the children. They were very strict about these things in Ballymena – a right-living place. The music had been intoxicating and she'd really not drunk that much. Patrick was different though, his elder brother Stephen had brought a hip flask of whisky with him and both of them kept slipping out into the cloakroom for a "swift one", as he softly whispered to her; for a "jimmy" as he called out loudly for all to hear. Barbara found it funny at the time and she kept sneaking the odd sip from her father's glass, abandoned on a side table.

He was the worse for wear, as usual, and his head was slumped on his wife's chest as the pair manoeuvred sedately around the dance floor. After years of practice they managed to avoid colliding with any of the other dancers; were famous for it. That very night she had already overheard Mrs O'Flaherty pointing her parents out to Mrs James, who was never far from her side, with a sly nudge in the ribs and the words, "The Mullens sure know how to enjoy themselves on the dance floor, don't they? Not sure how much she enjoys it when they get back home, not if what I've heard is true".

Mrs James nodded knowingly, but said nothing. Her round, fleshy face was flushed as it glanced unsmiling in Barbara's direction.

"The daughter's following their example, if looks are to be believed. That's the third or fourth time I've seen her taking a drink over there. No wonder that Patrick is all over her."

"I know, I know, someone should have a word. Maybe I'll mention it to Father Mackie, he'll know what to do. They won't like it, but you can't just stand by, can you?"

"No, no, you can't"

"And just let things happen, it isn't right. She was such a lovely girl when she was younger, all that long reddish brown hair, so thick and wavy. Why she has to wear it up like she does, I'll never know".

Barbara reached up and tucked a loose strand of hair tightly beneath one of her hair grips. She checked to see if all else was well, and then slid away to find Patrick.

She'd giggled and struggled to get away from him when he'd slipped his hands beneath her blouse. They were so cold and she'd always been ticklish around her waist, beneath her rib cage, across her ever-so slightly convex belly. It was her weak spot. All her family knew that. Her brother was merciless. Her sister invariably fell back on it whenever she was losing the wrestling matches they used to have when she was small, on the big double bed in the bedroom upstairs at the front of the house. Her piercing shrieks would finally bring her mother to the bottom of the stairs, yelling. "What are you two up to up there? It sounds like you're killing each other. You'll have the neighbours round if you don't keep it down."

Patrick had only gripped her more firmly and pushed her back against the pile of potato sacks that were stacked untidily in one corner of the small outhouse round the back from Dacey's dance hall.

"They'll soon warm up, you're very hot to the touch".

He exhaled heavily and she smelled the whiskey on his breath. It was faintly sweet, aromatic like newly mown grass, not like the stale rank animal odour of her father's breath when she used to climb into her parent's bed of a morning. He would always snort in her direction, spraying a jet of foul warm air over her, before turning on his side and trying to ignore them, leaving her and her mother to cuddle sweetly together. Barbara could never remember her mother's breath smelling of anything.

"Hold me, Patrick, give me a cuddle".

His grip tightened. The weight of his body bore down more heavily on her chest, making it difficult for her to breathe. She pushed up slightly with both her hands, which until then had been lying Madonna like across her chest. His right hand slipped up under the edge of her bra, pushing the loose cup up and over her breast. The clasp cut painfully into her back as the strap tightened. Barbara tried to move to make herself more comfortable, Patrick responded by pushing down more forcefully, thrusting his lower body. She opened her legs.

"Kiss me, Patrick".

He mumbled something close to her left ear, his breath warm on her neck. She had begun to perspire, but didn't feel at all hot, sweat was prickling the skin on her forehead and temples. A beam of light from the hall next door forced its way through a crack at the top of the partly closed door and spotted an old paint tin, high on a shelf covered in cobwebs. The last time she had lain like this with Patrick she had been able to watch the stars, picking them out: the Great Bear, the Plough, Orion, his belt – they'd laughed about that; Patrick had wanted to take his belt off that time but she hadn't let him. She knew all the constellations, she had been happy then, it had been a beautiful night. They hadn't got into trouble for staying out just a little later than they should. Patrick had looked so handsome, his dark wavy hair perfectly in place, the blue eyes which she loved devouring only her, his mouth all over hers. She'd never been kissed like that before, had never been at the centre of another person's attention like that, the focus of someone's adoration. It had been one of those perfect days, which did sometimes happen, she knew that now. This time there was nothing to look at except that yellowy ray shimmering overhead. It was very dark. Patrick had been right, no one would come looking for them here.

"Kiss me Patrick, like you did last time".

She could feel his hand sliding up the outside of her leg, pushing the hem of her skirt ahead of it. Her floral party skirt, all reds, yellows and greens, was getting a little small for her now, tight around the hips and waist, but she loved it so. Her grandmother had made it for her, for her fourteenth birthday.

"You'll have to make the next one yourself, love. My hands aren't what they were".

"Yes, don't expect me to help you either," her mother had chipped in. "It'll do you good, you need the practice."

Patrick was having difficulty lifting her skirt any higher, the material trapped between their bodies. Briefly he caressed her upper thigh, then suddenly he rolled over onto Barbara's right leg, freeing the skirt, allowing him to pull it upwards and out of the way. She felt the breath of air waft across her inner thighs as she winced at the weight of Patrick's body pressing heavily down on her leg. His hair rubbed gently across her face. She could smell the brilliantine he used to keep it in place, mingled with sweat and cigarette smoke. She loved it and could never get enough of it. It was just one of the things she had liked about Patrick, who was always so kind and considerate. A "real gentleman" as her mother used to say.

The pressure on her leg grew increasingly unbearable as he fumbled with the buttons on his trousers. He undid every single one and began to undo his belt, before losing patience and reaching inside. He then rolled back between Barbara's legs. Relieved she bent both her legs, bringing them up tight against his waist in an effort to ease the circulation in her crushed leg. Encouraged, he reached down and began to search for a way past the cotton barrier of her blue knickers. His groping fingers felt to be everywhere and very large.

"Why don't you blow in my ear like you did before?"

Once, only the week before, he had asked if he could put his hand down there and "have a feel". She had teased him by saying he could have a look, but only if he showed her his first. He had looked very disappointed. Said he'd seen lots of girls, but hadn't ever touched one. That was what he really wanted. Please, Barbara. Who had he seen was what she'd wanted to know? Turned out it was only his sister and she was younger than Barbara, so probably didn't have much to show. Finally they had agreed, he would touch hers, then she could touch his.

It was a bright sunny afternoon. They had climbed the hill at the back of the park and crawled unseen into a dense thicket of bracken. It grew everywhere and no one would find them there if they searched all day. Patrick rolled around to create a small clearing, then Barbara lay back on the damp smelling crushed plants and stared up at the blindingly bright blue sky. She screwed up her eyes and imagined herself to be lying on an operating table, the surgeon's light shining fiercely into her face. Opening just one eye she looked up at Patrick, his face in darkness, his head surrounded by a halo of flaring yellow, and asked him, "You will be gentle with me, won't you, doctor?"

He had laughed like she had never heard anyone laugh before. A pure abandoned sound of joyous existence, unfiltered through any of the awful realities of life.

"Be quiet, Patrick, someone will hear us", she'd said, laughing herself. "And that would spoil everything."

She had loved him in that instant and would have let him do anything he asked. In fact he'd asked for nothing more, simply stuck to the deal they had agreed. Well, more or less. After he had calmed down, he lay beside her, kissed her gently on the lips, then raising himself on one elbow slid his hand under her skirt, hesitated briefly then slightly pulled down her knickers and rested his hand on her bush of wiry red hair. They kissed for what seemed like hours and his hand barely moved; Barbara was so happy she forgot about his side of the bargain until they were preparing to crawl back out into the wide world beyond their little clearing. Then he'd looked so happy too she didn't want to spoil things by bringing it all up again. So she left it. She didn't care really, there'd be plenty of time for that, or so she'd thought. He would bring it up again, of course, but that wasn't until much later.

The gusset of her blue knickers was loose fitting – her mother always said she should get everything plenty big enough with lots of room to grow into it – and Patrick pulled it aside and began to probe roughly with one of his fingers. Inexperienced he took several minutes of breathing heavily into her neck before his persistence paid off and he thrust his finger inside her. Barbara barely had time to react to the sharp stabbing pain before it was followed by one more excruciating and fundamental.

"Please, Patrick, no".

She imagined him draining himself into her, giving her everything that was vital. She knew she was pregnant as soon as he rolled off her. She lay there, her legs akimbo, it was too dark to feel ashamed, and felt herself overflowing with what she imagined was the essence of life. She ached with the physicality of it, and with the growing fear that what they had done was a sin they would have to pay for in some way, but it didn't feel wrong. If she'd thought about it at all she had believed she would make her life with Patrick. He stood before her now, somewhere in the shadows, buttoning himself up, dusting himself down and muttering, "Are you all right, Barbara, are you all right?" over and over again.

"Come back, Patrick, lie down here with me".

He stopped.

"We can't, they'll be missing us back inside".

Barbara could imagine the look of horrified amazement on his face as she heard the anxiety in his voice.

"Please, just a few minutes more. No one will notice, they're all having too good a time".

"Barbara".

It was half plea, half threat. She lay back, closed her legs and rolled over on her side before curling up in a tight ball, clasping her hands between her thighs. For the first time she noticed the stale organic smell of earth, rotting vegetation and damp hessian.

"Ma will notice. Oh, God".

"I'll be seeing you inside".

Purging everything in an instant, light flooded the dark interior of the tool shed as Patrick dragged open the broken hinged door, cursing. Barbara sat bolt upright, tugging her skirt violently over her knees. Briefly touching her hair, she tried to brush the dried mud from the sleeves of her cardigan. The door was pulled only partly shut before Patrick gave up and ran, or so it sounded, back to the anonymity of the bustling hall. The band must have been taking a break earlier for Barbara clearly heard music for the first time, a cheer and then clapping. The sound of people, her people, enjoying themselves. There was no hurry. She gently placed a hand on her stomach. It felt strange to her, taut, a dull pain like indigestion.

"Don't be silly love, a spoonful of Milk of Magnesia will soon sort that out. You wait and see".

Barbara was always getting an upset stomach; she couldn't eat like the others, sometimes just felt full up. She had grown used to her mother's cures – the silty residue Milk of Magnesia left on the tongue, the fishy slime of cod-liver oil. Often they didn't make any difference. She hadn't the heart to say, it was the only time she got her mother's undivided attention and sometimes she would get a day off school. That was wonderful, hours alone with your mother, baking, washing, mending clothes. Nothing seemed like a chore on days like that.

A mirror… but where would she find a mirror? There was no way she could go back into the dance looking like this, yet she couldn't go home either, it was too early, they would miss her. It suddenly felt very cold sitting on the ground. Shivering, she got to her feet and stretched her cardigan tightly across her chest then looked around her. There was very little to see: the sacks, what appeared to be an old lawnmower, the shelves of paint cans, all different sizes, plant pots, a rake.

So this was it, not how she had imagined it at all. She took a few steps towards the door.

"You can always tell a girl that's done it by the way she walks".

A cruel taunt she'd heard many times in the playground. The boys seemed to take it as a Gospel truth, the girls weren't so sure; the sensible ones said it couldn't be true. Barbara had thought, well, maybe. It certainly didn't feel any different now. Messy, yes, but not different. She took a few steps back towards the potato sacks and sat down. Always a practical girl Barbara carefully checked her hair, tucking loose ends back into place, took off her cardigan and picked off all the stalks she could see then shook it wildly in the air. The dust tickled her nose but she didn't sneeze, which pleased her. Finally, she got to her feet. Her head was aching and she was beginning to feel she might be going to be sick. A drink of water would see her right. Her skirt felt fine to her, creased and a little damp, but in the crush of the dance floor, who would notice?

At the entrance she stopped. The pain in her stomach was getting worse, cramps now. She winced slightly and held on to the old door for support. Outside there was no one to be seen. The air felt fresh on her face, cooling, reviving. She'd been close to tears, but now she was doing something she felt better. The Ladies room was on the same side of the hall as the shed, but closer to the road. It could be reached through the side door of the building, there would be no need to go anywhere near the dance floor until she felt ready.

The hallway was empty, Barbara felt strangely calm, almost happy as she walked to the green door with the slightly askew brass lady with a long crinoline skirt and parasol. Swinging it open, she saw her friend Maureen standing in front of the long wall length mirror, re-touching her lipstick. Stunned, for the first time unsure what to do, Barbara stopped. Maureen merely glanced up, smiled and returned to her make-up.

"It's marvellous, Barbara, isn't it? I've been dancing with Peter – three times!"

She pursed her lips, touched them briefly with a forefinger, then seemed satisfied.

"Who'd have believed it, eh, Barbara? Three times and he's promised me again. Sian'll be mad when she hears. She'll be livid. It serves her right, though, never treated him properly."

Maureen was searching in her handbag for her perfume as Barbara slipped into one of the cubicles and gratefully closed the door. She suddenly felt very cold. To her dismay she noticed a small bloodstain on her skirt. She took off her cardigan and hung it on the peg on the back of the door, then she undid her skirt and stepped out of it. She shivered, turned and lifted the toilet seat before bending forward and dipping the soiled corner of her skirt into the bowl. Wisps of smoky red floated across the surface. Barbara stared at them, mesmerized, then seconds later rubbed furiously at the mark with both her hands. The water turned pink. Satisfied she stood up, wringing out the sodden material, carelessly splashing the rim of the toilet and the concrete floor. They'd be thinking a man had been in here. That'd get the tongues wagging. Smoothing out the skirt, she hung it up, then lowered the seat and sat down to wait. Her stomach ached, a throbbing now with intermittent stabbing pains, knifing sideways into the top of her thighs. She rocked gently back and forth.

"Barbara, Barbara are you still in here?"

It was Maureen.

"Yes, I'm still here".

"You sound poorly to me. Are you all right?"

"I am, Maureen."

She had a burning need to give some sort of explanation, anything to make her friend go away. She'd known Maureen forever, even liked her most of the time, but she was not the person Barbara wanted to talk to now, not the person who could help. It was Patrick, she wanted. If he loved her, needed her, wanted to kiss her like he had done that time, then all this didn't matter, everything would be fine.

"It's my time, Maureen. Typical isn't it? Never regular like you. I'm feeling it a bit, you know, like I do. I'll be all right soon. Leave me be. And, Maureen, thanks".

Too intoxicated with thoughts of Peter to pay that much attention, Maureen happily went back to the dance. It was only later that it occurred to her that everything Barbara had told her had been a lie.

Barbara inspected her skirt. It was still damp, but the bloodstain was gone, and the pattern hid the rest. She stepped into it, did up the button and the zip, then twisted it round her waist until the seam ran straight down her back. Breathing in hard to flatten her stomach, she tucked in her blouse and slipped on her cardigan. Glancing over her shoulder, Barbara noticed the pinkish water slopping gently in the bowl, she reached for the chain and flushed the lavatory, then she left the cubicle. A splash of cold water on the face, a long searching stare into the mirror – she didn't look too bad, if she was honest – a reassuring touch to her hair and she was ready.

Camille Paisley passed Barbara in the corridor without a word, only a nod. The music was louder now, people were cheering and through the glass portholes on the swing doors it looked as if everyone was on their feet, clapping and dancing.

"It must be late, I've only just made it back in time".

The clock on the far side of the hall was invisible through the darkened smoke laden air. She looked around but there was no one to ask. The hot damp atmosphere, tobacco, alcohol and sweat-saturated, was overpoweringly physical, stopping Barbara in mid step as she pushed open the doors. Her stomach heaved, a bile heavy infusion filled her throat and mouth. Gagging she stepped aside into the shadows where she stood and watched the swirling dancers. Feeling calmer she circled the room, moving in that small ill-defined space between the dancers and the exuberant spectators. Her mother's face, flushed with streaked lipstick inches from her, her hot breath full in the face. "Barbara love, having a good time? Da's sitting this one out". And she was gone. Maureen emerged from the crowd, Peter looming behind, eyes half-closed in a drunken reverie.

"You OK now?"

Ten to eleven. Ten minutes to go. The last dance soon. He couldn't have gone. He'd said he'd see her inside. There was her brother. He might know where he was, they were good friends.

"Barbara, make an old man very happy and have this dance with me, will you?"

"Sorry, Mr Barraclough, I've promised this one".

"Ah, to be sure you have, a pretty little thing like you".

"Ladies and gentlemen, please take your partners for the last dance".

Patrick was standing in a dingy corner of the dance hall furthest from the stage. He was talking animatedly to two boys from the village, Mike Driscoll and John Doyle. They were listening intently, their bodies leaning in towards Patrick, their faces close to his. Patrick held a silver hip flask in his hands. He took a sip and handed it to the others, a look of elation on his pale face. They each swigged briefly from the flask then handed it back. Patrick never once stopped talking. All three, up on the dance floor for most of the evening, now showed no interest in the last dance. A number of girls glanced wistfully in their direction, then disappeared into the throng. Barbara emerged seconds after the last one had turned away and moved slowly towards the three engaged boys. No one noticed her.

"Patrick."

They turned as one, broad grins on their faces, Mike Driscoll looked her up and down.

"A drink, Barbara?"

***

Barbara had been right, she was pregnant. Regular as clockwork, she'd waited all day on the day she was due, expecting nothing to happen and it didn't. The same the next day, just in case. Again nothing. There was an inevitability about it that she accepted. She was pregnant, expecting, and she was just fifteen. Not that much younger than her mother when she got married. True, she hadn't had Frank until she was nearly eighteen, but then they had always said Barbara was advanced for her age. She thanked God that her mother had long ago given up keeping a check on her daughters' periods, like she used to. It had taken a while, Barbara being her oldest girl.

Patrick had more or less ignored her since the night of the dance. It was so hurtful when they had been so happy together. Deep down she secretly believed that once he knew she was expecting his baby, everything would be different. He would change, remember the good things they'd done together, the sweet words he had said about her, about them, the two of them. If nothing else she was sure he would face up to his responsibilities. How often had she heard her mother or father or some other adult say that? They would make sure Patrick did the right thing in the end. They did love each other after all. It wouldn't be hard. Men were never great ones for showing what they really felt. Ma always said that.

"Just look at your father. Never once told me he loved me, never since the day he got me up the aisle. Lost without me he would be though, completely lost".

People had babies all the time. If you worked it out, and she and Pauline and Maureen had, many seemed to be born soon after couples got married. People were vague about it, but no one seemed to mind. Everyone was happy. Why should she and Patrick be any different?

It was difficult to know how to tell him, he was so busy on the family farm, never free in the evenings like before. Whenever Barbara did see him he was always with Mike and John or some of the other local boys, never alone. And he stopped asking to take her out at the weekends.

"You and Patrick had a row, have you? He always used to be around here with his tongue hanging to his knees. What have you said to him, Barbara? You and your wicked words. I've told you to be careful – most men won't take it, especially from a girl."

"I've said nothing, Ma."

"Well, you must have done something – he seemed very keen to me".

"Oh Ma, leave it, will you?"

"Never mind, love, lots more fish in the sea. Lots better than young Patrick, I wouldn't mind betting."

"But I love him, Ma".

"Barbara, don't say such a thing! How do you know what love is at your age? You're still a girl. That sort of talk leads to trouble, you mark my words. I don't want you setting young Bernice a bad example either, you know how she looks up to you. So you hush up about such things till you know what you're talking about.

**

He hadn't loved her. Barbara had never seen anybody so angry. Calling her all those names and blaming her. Saying she'd led him on, that she had done it on purpose just to trap him and he had tried to stop her. The most hurtful thing was when he'd said. "How can you be sure it's mine?" Knowing her as he did, he couldn't be too sure. Then the threats. If she told anybody he would beat her, and even worse. The hatred in his eyes. Blind screaming rage at one moment; it was a wonder nobody heard him. Except her, of course. They were only in the field at the back of his house, but his Ma had the wireless on loud like she often did. Then he turned calm and calculating; she'd have to go away, get rid of it. After all, it happened all the time, her friends would know what she should do. The hissed insults and her bent figure crying under the hedge, inconsolable.

"Get away from me, you whore!"

She'd run away then, her body heaving uncontrollably, but there had been no tears. She had felt an arid, desolate grief that provided no relief but left her strangely in control. She was careful. No one had an inkling, of that she was sure. Her baby was growing inside her, it was changing her forever. Like a cuckoo, she thought, unwelcome, but she loved it for what it was, hated it for what it was doing to her, the destruction of all that was intimate and close to her. It was the hatred, the desire to hurt herself and it, him, her, that drove Barbara to Father Mackie. She was frightened, it seemed so wrong to feel this way about something so "innocent". The word had to be coaxed into life, caressed like the baby it was, for she didn't believe it, not deep down, not cross your heart and hope to die deep down. It was fear that was born that afternoon with Patrick, not love, and it drained her dry. Years later Barbara was to talk about being "a wanderer in a desert of love", a phrase she used often, but increasingly without meaning.

That had been Tuesday. On Wednesday he was out. On Thursday helping his Dad on the farm. Friday: "I don't think he wants to see you Barbara. Is everything right with you?" By Saturday Barbara was starting to feel self-conscious about her body. Was she starting to show? Bernice would never notice, even though they shared a room, but Ma ... you never knew with her. On Sunday she saw Father Mackie after mass.

"A special word, if I may, Father?"

"To be sure, child. Give me a minute, will you?"

In the end the priest had not really said anything, just listened. No penance to speak of, just a long silence.

"Your mother and father, do they know?"

"No, Father".

"And the boy, does he?"

"Yes, Father."

"Does he want you and the baby?"

"I don't know, Father".

"Who is he, child?"

"I'd rather not say."

Barbara had liked going to confession. She'd always felt secure, the door closing in on a twilight world that smelled of beeswax and maybe tobacco smoke or lilies of the valley. Then the dull gleam of the highly polished dark wood as the grille slid open to reveal Father Mackie's silhouette leaning towards her, the easy flow of the words, the ritual repetition of phrases long familiar, the rhythmic cadences of the priest's voice. It was usually so reassuring. It had never before seemed threatening.

"I'll ask you again – who is he?"

"Father, I..."

"Barbara, I'll not be messing with you. Tell me who he is."

The tone was authoritative, as he'd intended. The parish priest in full spate, in his element, but there was cruelty present as well and Barbara felt it. It was a physical entity there in the confessional, sucking the oxygen from the small space around her, drawing the air from her body. She felt herself deflating like a punctured tyre on a lonely road. She could barely breathe, let alone speak but Father Mackie was relentless. His face appeared full on in the grille. She imagined him gripping the bars.

"Barbara, tell me".

"Father".

Her voice faltered and she needed to relieve herself, more than anything else in the world.

"Barbara, I'm losing patience".

"I need to go, Father".

"Barbara!"

Father Mackie thought he liked women, He enjoyed their company and had been tempted in his youth, even seriously questioned his vows for a period. But it had all resolved itself in his mind into a question of temptation. Not an original thought, but it helped him when he realized that what was on offer didn't really appeal to him. He didn't honestly like the idea of physical intimacy with a woman, and saw no need for a lifelong association with a female. He felt himself more at home in the companionship of men, his fellow priests, who were honest, open and uncomplicated. Nothing to do with the uninhibited messiness of temptation, down that route lay, at the very least, complication, at the worst, disaster. He'd seen it time and time again.

"Pure lust, was it?"

"Father?"

"I said, pure lust, was it?"

The angry, growing self-righteousness in his voice was slurring his words.

"Patrick."

"What was that? Speak up."

"Patrick."

"Patrick who?"

"Patrick Whelan."

"Good God."

He was speaking to himself now, thinking in a reverie of his own about the swirling currents of scandal and recrimination that were about to be unleashed on his parish. What did he know about these people, really know, and how they would react? What would they do? And, more importantly, what should he do?

"I might have guessed".

"Father, I love him".

"You do what? Don't talk to me about love, a girl of your age. You should have been loving your mother and father, your sisters and brothers. Not some young man. Love is an indulgence. But you'll learn that."

"But I do …"

Barbara was close to tears, but they never came. Her body was weeping inwardly at the bitterness of his tone, but her anguish extinguished all outward emotion. She sat there, her hands on her knees, staring straight ahead.

"Do the Whelans know?"

"I…I don't know".

"You mean you don't know whether Patrick's said anything to them? Knowing the boy, I would think not. Has he owned up to it?"

"Father?"

"Is it your word against his?"

"We did it, Father. We did it behind Dacey's".

"Don't you speak like that in here. Don't you say such things in my confessional. Get out".

"But it's true, Father. Patrick and me – we love each other. It'll be all right".

"Go on, get out. I'll deal with this mess".

"You won't say anything, will you, Father?"

***

Tuesday, a full week since her meeting with Patrick. Barbara was lying in bed; she'd come up early. She'd not been feeling well; sick in the stomach, probably something she'd eaten. The last few evenings had been strange. Lucky for her there had been no problem in the morning because even Bernice, snoring gently over in the corner by the window, would have noticed that. But in the night it was different. It was the pains in her stomach and she was so nervous, shaking and barely sleeping. The creaking of the old house, the wind in the apple tree outside, rattling the sash window when it blew in from the south, the patter of rain on the glass. The sounds, all so familiar to her, were now ghosts, haunting rather than comforting, frightening rather than soothing. Her only companions.

There were voices downstairs. One of them was Father, half shouting, being restrained. He sounded angry. There was crying, that had to be Mother. Barbara leant forward in bed, propping herself up on her elbows, and listened. It had always been hard to eavesdrop on her parents downstairs; the house was too solidly built. You had to creep to the top of the stairs from where you could hear clearly as long as all the doors were open. When she was younger she often used to sit there listening for hours, shivering in her night-dress. Sometimes Bernice would join her and then go to sleep, cradled in her arms. She had felt daring but safe, had never learnt anything in particular, but it had thrilled her nonetheless. This night she didn't want to leave the safety of her bed. She knew it was about her and she didn't feel brave or safe. Things went quiet downstairs; it sounded as if everybody was whispering, a faint hubbub of voices. Bernice turned over in her bed, her blankets gliding silently to the floor. Oh, to be so innocent again.

Life before Patrick, was there such a thing? Barbara was no longer sure. The instant it all changed seemed to her so infinitesimally short and imprecise that it couldn't possibly have existed at all, so nothing was really different. It was all just the same as it had always been. Nothing had happened that was not going to happen. Life before Patrick was just a preparation for life now. There was no before or after. There was no Patrick.

The stairs creaked, then creaked again. Somebody was on their way up. They were trying to be quiet, creeping around. Whoever it was stopped on the landing. There was whispering. Barbara lay back and closed her eyes. The door opened and he came in.

"Barbara."

A stage whisper. Bernice stirred. The curtains billowed in the draft, the cool air an elixir to the airless, anxious Barbara.

"Barbara, get up."

She didn't recognize the voice and she didn't want to move.

"Barbara".

She opened her eyes. There was barely any light from downstairs, but the outline in the doorway was unmistakable, the closely cropped hair, the protruding ears.

"Father?"

"Yes, now get up."

The priest stood on the threshold of the room, one hand on the door-jamb, the other holding the doorknob, unwilling to move any further towards Barbara's bed. Bernice muttered something in her sleep and rolled onto her back. Her breathing instantly rasping and irregular.

"Why, Father, what time is it?"

"That's nothing to you. Now get up and get dressed."

"Get dressed? Why?"

Father Mackie sighed irascibly.

"Is something wrong?"

"It most certainly is, young lady, and you know full well what it is."

Barbara was sitting up but clutching on to her bed-clothes, holding them tightly around her neck.

"Please, Father. I don't like this."

"I don't care. You should have thought of that much earlier. Now don't make me go and fetch your Mother, she's upset enough as it is."

"I was going to tell her … I was. I was going to."

"But you didn't, did you? Now come on."

Father Mackie stood staring into the room as Barbara pushed back her blankets and swung her bare legs off the bed. Her night-dress was crumpled around her waist, but still he didn't look away. She tried half-heartedly to cover herself, then slumped forward with her head in her hands. She could barely talk, she was so short of breath.

"You, you told her, you told her, didn't you?"

"It's something you should have done a long time ago. A mother has a right to know. It's shameful what you've done."

"I've done nothing."

"You could have fooled me, if what I've been hearing is true, now get up."

For the first time the priest spoke without whispering and his presence seemed to grow, blocking the doorway, expanding into her room, overwhelming her territory with a force she was powerless to resist. Occupying her mind, her body and placing her baby under siege. It was a total rout.

"Where are we going, Father?"

"Get dressed first, you'll soon find out."

Barbara stood up and began to unbutton her night-dress. She was about to pull it over her head when she glanced at the priest. He stared back unmoving from the doorway, then suddenly seemed to come to himself.

"Wait. I'll see you downstairs. Don't be long".

The door was dragged shut. The night-dress fell at Barbara's feet and she sat naked on her bed, her hands cradling her belly.

"Baby doll, what have I done?"

***

Her parents were both standing when she came into the parlour. She couldn't look into their faces, but kept her head down, staring at the floor. Father Mackie was over by the fireplace. She could see his black scuffed shoes. He was tapping his right foot and seemed agitated. The only person sitting down and the only person Barbara could see clearly was a nun she'd never set eyes on before. The Sister didn't look up when Barbara came in, but she appeared to be praying, her hands clasped firmly in her lap and her lips moving rapidly, but silently.

A coal flared in the grate, crackling and spitting a glowing ember onto the stone hearth. The fire slumped, sending a host of sparks swirling up the chimney. Someone had set the fire again this evening. It should have been damped down by now, dead to the eye, but burning deep within. It was usually her job to rake it out in the early dawn and set it alight.

Father Mackie coughed, but said nothing. The routine was familiar, he knew he had to take the lead. Parents were notoriously unpredictable and Mullen here was on a short fuse at the best of times – but he suddenly felt very tired. It wasn't the hour, he didn't need that much sleep usually, it was, briefly, his resolve. It wasn't that he felt sorry for Barbara, he wasn't that sort of man at all. He just wished he didn't have to deal with yet another case of human weakness, another example of errant womankind, another bloody silly little mess. Anger brought him round and he coughed again as if to place in parentheses his own brief wavering from the dutiful path.

He stared at the slight bowed figure in front of him – her long auburn hair hanging loose, her face hidden – and noticed that Barbara had done up her green cardigan and missed the bottom button, so that she looked pathetically misshapen. Her floral dress hung limply to just below her knees and the priest thought he detected a slight tremor running through the faded material. He sighed.

"What have you to say for yourself, young lady?"

The bubble of restraint burst and the room filled with movement. Barbara's father advanced menacingly towards his daughter, muttering incomprehensibly, only to be held back by the priest's extended hand.

"Liam."

He reluctantly gave way, glancing venomously at Father Mackie as he retreated. Barbara's mother collapsed sobbing into her father's worn leather armchair next to the fire, something she would never have dared do in normal circumstances, her head in her hands. She couldn't look at her daughter, unlike her husband who never took his eyes off her, except when he glanced angrily at the priest.

"Come on, Barbara it's no good playing dumb, everyone here knows".

Father Mackie's voice was even paced and calm. Barbara understood they all knew, but was still shocked to hear it so baldly stated. A child seemed so much more than simply the knowledge of its existence. She knew of her child and she knew her child. She loved her parents and knew they should know about their grandchild – it came surprisingly easy to her – she knew they should love it as they had loved her. But they were not behaving like her parents, like grandparents. They were abandoning her and the child to this man who had betrayed her. Why was he expecting her to talk to him? She'd done that already, she should be talking to them. The nun filled her with dread, another outsider who should not be there.

Angrier now, she could tell, the priest left the refuge of the fireplace and, bending his knees, grasped both her arms and shook her roughly.

"Barbara, keeping quiet will not do you any good. I've heard some disturbing things about you that don't quite fit with what you told me. I need to hear your side of it, do you understand?"

Her head bowed, she said nothing. Father Mackie's breath smelled of whisky.

"Let me at her, Father, I'll soon get it out of her."

Liam Mullen towered above the priest and his daughter, already unbuckling his belt.

"No, Liam, please! Let me do this my way".

49

"Father, the little hussy is laughing at us. Can't you see that? I know my daughter, just look at her".

His fury growing, Barbara's father hovered behind the priest, his agitated bulk an oppressive presence that Father Mackie could happily have done without. Even though he liked to involve the parents on these occasions, this man with his reputation for violence, his coarseness and intermittent attendance at Mass, was someone the priest devoutly wished was elsewhere. Liam Mullen's normally florid complexion was now radiating a purple heat and sweaty rankness that was rapidly filling the stuffy room. He was perspiring heavily and his grubby white work shirt was damply stained. His pale blue eyes were filling with angry tears, the stinging salt causing him to blink erratically and often. His hands, released from clutching his belt buckle, were now running agitatedly through his greasy thinning hair.

"Problem is, Liam, I don't think you know her at all. So please leave it to me. Why don't you get a breath of fresh air?"

Liam stiffened, his fists clenched, but he stepped back.

"Thank you. Now Barbara, please. We'll stay here all night if needs be. You'll have to talk to us in the end, believe me".

The menace in his voice was unmistakable, but she continued to resist him. Even though they were allies against her Father, she stayed silent, while offering up what was to be her last ever prayer asking Jesus to forgive her insolence. They were after her baby, she knew that, but she wouldn't let them have it. It was hers. It was only as an afterthought that she conjured up Patrick – where was he? – then he was gone. If I want to have the baby, I will. I'll get married. After all he's mine, mine, mine! She vowed.

Father Mackie had let go of her arms. He had felt the tremors, thinking, it won't be long now. She'd crack like they all did. He stared at her, trying to gaze into her eyes, engage her, ensnare her.

The nun said her first words, surprising everyone with the deepness of their tone.

"Would you like to sit here, Father? There's plenty of room".

"No, thank you, Sister, I'm just fine as I am."

Sister Lavinia, from the Convent of St Lucretia and St Bernadette, found these situations embarrassing and would have much preferred to have been somewhere else. Unlike some of her peers she didn't relish this side of her vocational work, which to her distress was becoming increasingly common. The shouting and anguish left her strangely unmoved. The sympathy and sensitive touch others, particularly her Mother Superior, saw in her dealings with these girls was feigned, mere play-acting. It amused Lavinia that this should be the case. She didn't have to try very hard and all were taken in. Reverend Mother would not hear a word about Lavinia working in a different field and now she had stopped protesting.

"Lavinia, it's God's gift. The girls trust you, I trust you. You are just the person to deal with these…" for a moment Reverend Mother had been lost for words, "… these problems".

The problems, sinners the lot of them, were all little fools. Lavinia believed the girls should never be in the mess they were in the first place. It was all down to their own moral failure, to weakness and a lack of spiritual depth. She could not understand how it could happen if they had been raised properly, just couldn't see how a God fearing child would even contemplate having anything to do with a boy in that way. For Lavinia the parents undoubtedly bore some responsibility, but in the main, and she had seen a good many such cases, it was the girls themselves who were the problem. They were selfish, self-centred, fixated on their own bodies, feigning a godliness and religious sensibility that scarcely stood up to even the most superficial scrutiny. And they ended up emotional wrecks, rarely able to face up to the consequences of what they had done. "Boys," as Sister Lavinia always referred to them on the rare occasions she needed to, were never seen as the problem. They were not around in the cases she had to deal with.

Thinking about it as she now sat on the Mullens' sofa, listening to the feeble admonishments of Father Mackie, it was amazing that she got on so well with her charges, that they seemed to see her as some sort of "friend". She smiled at the frightened girl as the priest thundered ineffectually on.

"Barbara, if you won't talk to us then I will talk to you," he declared. "I have spoken to Patrick."

She looked up. It was the first time his name had been mentioned and it shocked her to have him brought into this sordid little encounter. It was not at all surprising that Father Mackie had spoken to him really but she had felt so alone. Now maybe there was some hope.

"Ah, I've got your attention now, I see."

Barbara quickly looked down and noticed her feet were bare. Without thinking she turned to leave.

"Stay where you are, young lady. Don't you dare turn your back on me when I'm talking".

"Get back in here. Don't you leave. Wait till I get my hands on you. The shame of it all – a daughter of mine."

Her father's inarticulate growling brought Barbara to a halt.

"I was only going to fetch my shoes," she said mildly.

Her Mother, silent until then, sobbed loudly and fumbled in the front pocket of her floral apron for her handkerchief.

"See what you've caused, after all your Ma's done for you."

The grandfather clock in the hallway struck a quarter to. A familiar comforting sound, edged now with menace. Barbara resignedly turned back into the room and prepared to face whatever they had in store for her.

"I need the truth from you," the priest insisted.

The ticking of the clock and the crackling of the coals, overlaid with the heavy, wheezing breaths of Barbara's Father, were all that could be heard. Shadows flitting behind the dark heavy figures silhouetted in the deep orange glow were all she could see, the pale insipid yellow light from the single bulb overhead barely making any impression. The room seemed to be filling in around Barbara, all the familiar spaces occupied by things and shapes unknown.

"I told you the truth."

"I'm afraid you most certainly did not, young lady."

Barbara was confused. She thought they all knew. He had said they'd been told. For a brief relieved moment she thought this was about something else. She had no idea what it could be, a broken window maybe. But, no it was about the baby.

"I did, Father."

"How can you lie to a priest you, you… after how we've brought you up?"

"Liam, please. I'll do the talking if you don't mind."

Barbara's Mother was sobbing quietly in her chair, the occasional tear streaking her face, leaving a silvery scar across her cheeks. Enlivened by the tragedy unfolding before her, her normally lined face shone with a ruddy radiance, a distant echo of a once youthful exuberance. Liam, turning to his wife for reassurance he didn't really want or need, momentarily blinked in astonishment at a sight only dimly remembered. It had been a long time since he had thought his wife beautiful, nowadays never thought of her in those terms, but he did think Barbara was a pretty girl, always had done. It looked like Barbara, twenty years on, was now sitting in his armchair and it stopped him in his tracks. His wife had always been "one for the lads" in her younger days and it had driven him mad with jealousy at the time. He had won out it was true, but it had been a close run thing with Brendan Flaherty. He had suffered horribly and he hadn't forgotten. Like mother, like daughter. His anger surged and he knew that if the priest and the nun hadn't been there he would have hit his wife, hard.

"Barbara, let's stop this here. I know you did not."

Father Mackie was unable to hide his growing irritation.

"I don't understand, Father."

"What don't you understand?"

"What you want me to say?"

"The truth, that's all. It's that simple."

"Father, I told you the truth..."

Nobody said a thing.

"... in the confessional."

Barbara's voice could barely be heard. Father Mackie sighed heavily.

"I'm losing patience."

"Tell us the truth and confess your sins. It'll be much better in the long run". Sister Lavinia's exasperated voice silenced the priest. "Tell us, it's late."

They couldn't want her to repeat it again if they all knew. There was nothing really to say except, "I'm having Patrick's baby."

The truth, plainly spoken, shocked all but Barbara who felt relieved. Now they could get on with their lives. These people would go and she could get back to her warm bed. She had never really liked sharing a bedroom with Bernice, had envied Maureen who had just brothers and so had a room to herself, but now it seemed the most wonderful, enticing place in the whole world. She would happily live with Bernice forever more.

"Barbara".

The incredulous tone of the priest's voice puzzled her. She had been expecting, if not quite congratulations, at least some sign of pleasure at it all being sorted out.

"Barbara, look at me."

A brief glance and her universe collapsed.

"You're a wicked girl. I never thought I'd hear myself say it but you are."

He coughed.

"What you told us is not the whole truth and you know it. You're having a baby, that much I believe."

"I am, Father, I swear".

"Quiet! I know that, but whose, that is the question?"

It was incomprehensible to Barbara that there could be any doubt.

"Patrick, it's his."

"How can you be so sure, young lady? Behaving as you do?"

"It's Patrick's, I know it is. He'll tell you."

"But that's just it, Barbara, his story doesn't tally with yours."

For a moment Barbara didn't understand, then sickeningly she realized what all the drama was about. She understood why Patrick had barely spoken to her since she had told him.

"He's a liar, Father. I swear. Oh, God."

She sank limply to the floor, wringing her hands. She felt cold. Her mother spoke for the first time, signalling Barbara's utter rejection.

"Don't use words like that in my house. How could you, how could you? You're no daughter of mine".

"He's a liar."

"That's exactly the word he uses about you."

"But he is, Father. I'm telling the truth".

"I'd like to believe you, Barbara, I really would, but Patrick tells a very different story."

"A very different story."

Barbara's father was standing behind the priest, mimicking him unconsciously almost word for word. He could now be clearly heard, surprising everyone in the room including himself.

"Please, Liam, give me a little room here. This is difficult enough without you perching on my shoulder. Please now, back up a bit, why don't you? Sit with your wife, she looks as if she could do with a bit of support."

Eileen Mullen was sitting bolt upright in the armchair, her face pale, her tears now dry. Her hands were clasped together in her lap, fingers twitching almost in time to the beating of her heart. She stared straight at Barbara – a malevolent look that would become Barbara's abiding memory of her mother in the years to come, until at some imprecise time it became her only one.

"Sorry, Father."

"Better still, Liam, why don't you go and fix us a cup of tea? We're going to need it."

Liam looked aghast at the Priest, finding it increasingly difficult to understand anything that was being said in his own house. Frowning, he turned to his wife.

"You heard the man. Fix us some tea, will you?"

Eileen didn't move, just swallowed hard and continued to stare at her daughter, slumped on the ground in front of her.

"You hear me, woman?"

Liam clenched his fists and stepped back towards his wife. She barely flinched as he hit the arm of the chair – a cloud of dust rose explosively into the air – and he snarled at her, his forehead touching hers.

"Listen to me woman, will you".

The dust billowing around their faces caused him to sneeze and her faint smile made him angrier still.

"You do as I say."

He glared at his impassive wife searching vainly for words that could satisfy the rage that was consuming him. Sneezing again, he wiped the mucus from his face and then hit his wife hard on the side of her head.

"That'll teach you. You, you."

Eileen lurched forward, sobbing, clutching her head.

"Dad, no!"

Barbara leapt to her feet and tried to grab her Father, but was held back by Father Mackie, who had also placed a hand on her Father's shoulder.

"Liam, no. There's a good man. That'll get us nowhere."

Sister Lavinia was also on her feet and spotting the poker lying in the hearth she edged slowly towards it. Nobody in the room, even those who knew him well, could be certain what Liam Mullen would do next.

"Let go of me, Father. Nobody lays a hand on Liam Mullen, not even me local priest".

He grabbed Father Mackie's arm and drew him close.

"Do you hear me, Father? I'll not be messed with. This is my house, you hear and she's my daughter – the little whore. I'll deal with her now."

Frightened, Father Mackie smelled the hot stale damp breath, felt the closeness of his rank body and stared into the tear-laden bloodshot blue eyes that seemed focussed inches inside his own head, and trembled. Anticipation of the blow, the shattering pain, the cracking of teeth, the taste of blood was too much for the man who, for the first time in his life, had lost control of the situation. All the trauma he had ever witnessed had been under his command. Even when he had occasionally been affected by the suffering of those around him, he had never been uncertain how to go on, how to bring the proceedings to a conclusion, nothing had prepared him for someone else taking over. He was afraid of violence. He and his brother knew that, but he didn't want anyone else to know. Liam was not a coward; stupid, but not a coward. He could be exposed by this man, an ignorant farm labourer could bring him to his knees, all because of his stupid, stupid, little daughter. Father Mackie couldn't bear it and he cried with genuine tears of regret. Regret for a life that seemed devoid of any true emotion – at least Barbara's father cared about something – regret for his own deceit, a hidden life lived without any real contact. But most of all regret for his own dishonesty, to his family, his parishioners – his flock – and to himself.

Sister Lavinia looked on in disgust – men – she'd seen many cry in her time, but never a priest. She had been about to step in on his side, support him, but now she held back, fascinated to discover how things would work out. The collapse of faith, the end of the belief in yourself and God, she had seen it in the Convent, young girls enticed by love and the idea of self-sacrifice, unashamedly giving themselves to one man for ever, slowly breaking on the hard rock of constant, daily grinding devotion. There were tears then, tormented words, the anguish of the weak, the feeble-minded, the cowards. She had seen them running away, trying to escape from themselves, the suicide attempts. Grim truths which only made Lavinia even more certain of her own faith. Human frailty was not something she willingly acknowledged in others and certainly not in herself. It was just her luck that she came across so much of it.

Eileen was now sitting bolt upright again, her right hand cupped gently over a violently purple bruise spreading over the side of her face. She was no longer staring at her daughter but looking up at the weeping priest. She was willing her husband to hit him, then she could be certain of his damnation. Hitting your wife and children had never seemed quite enough to Eileen to guarantee anything for eternity. Now she held her breath.

Barbara, forgetting her mother for a moment, looked askance at the priest, his body heaving as he sobbed, her father still holding the collar of his jacket, silent and nonplussed. The focus had shifted and she was relieved, she felt as if the rest of the world had stopped and she could quietly slip away back to her own life, where without a care she would live happily ever after. It would turn out that Patrick had just been having a bit of fun and that he loved her after all, that he loved their baby and they would get married and settle down not far from here. And that would be that. She stepped back – time failed to follow her – she turned and reached for the door.

Liam Mullen could think clearly at last. A crying priest, that was a joke. Men never cried. His wife was insolent, she always had been, he could sort her out later. It was a time for decisions. He let go of Father Mackie's jacket and the priest's body seemed to drop away and grow smaller. The nun would say and do nothing, he was not afraid of her, she was just another woman, the curse of his life.

"Where are you going?"

Time caught up with Barbara and she stopped dead. Her head was suddenly yanked violently backwards, as her Father grabbed her hair. Screaming, she fell over, her body pivoting on her heels. Crashing painfully to the floor, she tried to get to her feet, but her Father held her fast and she came to rest sitting at his feet with her head tilted upwards, staring into his twisted red face. His other hand slowly unbuckled his belt.

"You wouldn't let our weaning priest there tell you, so I will".

The brown belt lengthened before Barbara's eyes, its brass buckle clasped firmly in her Father's fist. His arm was fully extended before the belt came loose from his trousers. For a second it swayed in the air before dropping down and brushing her lap. It was still for a moment then as he spoke it lifted slowly upwards, passing close to her face – she could smell the warm leather – as her Father slowly wound the belt around his hand.

"Patrick told the priest here everything and he's told us. He says it wasn't just him. You were… you were doing it with everyone. You little … "

Arcing down, the belt cut into her side. She flailed helplessly with her hands desperately trying to catch hold of it before it could rise again. She felt the dull surge of pain, gasped through gritted teeth and clung on to the belt first with one hand, then the other.

"Let go, now!"

Spreading his arms apart, almost as casually as he would stretch after a nap in the afternoon, her father hauled Barbara's head back, ripping her hair while forcing the belt from her grip. The prickly pain across her forehead and the hot searing sensation in her fingers and palms brought tears to her eyes. She cried out, an unintelligible animal sound that reverberated around the dingy room, hall and stairway and then was echoed on the landing where her brothers and sister huddled, listening. Once again the belt arced overhead, this time catching the dusty lampshade as it sped downwards. Crazed shadows danced around the walls as the belt lashed Barbara across her shoulders and back.

"He said you were well known to many of the boys around here."

Her Father was breathing heavily, finding it difficult to articulate the words he so desperately wanted to say.

"He said you were…"

He hit Barbara again, this time across the arms waving in front of her face. Blood seeped instantly crimson from her knuckles. He hit her again across her back, the leather tip catching her just below her right eye. Barbara clutched her face, muttering inaudibly.

"No, no."

"He said you did it with anyone who asked. He said it could be anyone's. The shame of it."

Uncertain for the first time, his arm raised, body poised, Liam looked down at his daughter as she cowered at his feet. He saw the blood.

"Liam, please."

Father Mackie stood with his arms outstretched. Liam lashed out one more time before flinging his daughter to the floor.

"Get her out of my sight. I never want to see the little whore again."

He then calmly unwound the belt from his hand, wrapped it round his waist, fastened the buckle and strode from the room.

Movement could be heard upstairs, then just the ticking of the clock, the crackle of the fire, Barbara's rasping breathing and the quiet sobbing of her mother. Sister Lavinia took charge.

"Are you all right, Barbara?"

Tentatively the nun approached the collapsed girl, knelt beside her, leant the poker against the side of the sofa, then reached out and gently touched Barbara on the shoulder. A brief spasm was the only reaction, an imperceptible contraction of the body.

"He's gone, Barbara. You're safe now. This is Sister Lavinia".

Once again that gentle touch, this time lingering seconds longer.

"Come on, sit up and let me take a look at you."

"It hurts".

The nun leant closer to Barbara and patted her softly on the back.

"I know, come on, let me see. It's probably not as bad as it seems. Move your hands, let me take a look."

Father Mackie, downcast and deeply embarrassed, thrust a clean handkerchief into her hand and then retreated to the fireplace where he stood, bowed head resting on his folded arms, staring into the flames.

Barbara felt too scared to move. Her body ached and her mouth felt full, immovable, swollen shut. It was impossible to speak even if she had wanted to. And she didn't. It was speaking that had got her into this mess but speaking certainly wouldn't get her out of it. She knew, Barbara knew. It was inevitable. Eyes closed – Father Mackie in his white flowing robes, standing, arms outstretched, hands grasping the wooden rail of the pulpit.

"Gather ye all the little children, bring them unto me. There is nothing more sacred than the sanctity of life."

Stained glass reds, greens, blues and gold, so much gold. Flickering candles, piles of tormented off-white wax, sputtering trails of smoke streaming upwards. Her aching knees. Mary. Those were tears, weren't they?

"Barbara you should get up now."

It was Father Mackie.

"That's enough for now. Your prayers'll have been heard, believe me. It's a lovely day out".

She hadn't been praying, that had been the funny thing. She had intended to, had even started mouthing the familiar phrases. She had been top of the class at Religious Instruction, had felt confident she knew what to do, had expected to hear and feel something – an answer – but the words had meant nothing. Absolutely nothing. She was going to be a mother, that was what was important, she was going to have a baby. Her stomach knotted; she knelt there in the cold chapel thinking of her own childhood, too scared to move, the icy air chilling the sweat on her legs, arms and face. Dolls with grubby faces, a push-chair, Bernice sitting there wrapped in a blanket, baked beans for tea, all four of them huddled round the table in the scullery, laughing.

"Barbara is everything all right with you? Is there something you want to tell me?"

And she had told him.

Barbara moaned and tried to get up.

"Here, let me help you."

Sister Lavinia shifted round behind Barbara, grasped her arms and lifted her gently into a sitting position, her back against the sofa.

"Where does it hurt?"

Barbara stared incredulously at the nun.

"Everywhere I suppose?"

Lavinia laughed as Barbara nodded weakly.

"I should have guessed. Anywhere hurt more than the others?"

Barbara touched her swollen face.

"Here, let me see."

Barbara slipped unwittingly, unwillingly, under the charming influence of Sister Lavinia. Her natural talents overcoming her own personal hostility to everyone in the room; the calm reassuring voice, warm gentle hands, the appropriate words, never failed her.

The flicker of a smile on Barbara's face was all Eileen Mullen needed. She sat up in her chair, wiped the moisture from her face with her apron, straightened it across her lap then stood up. Staggering slightly she moved towards Barbara, who looked hopefully up at her, leant forward, touched her daughter fleetingly on the head and then walked out of her life for ever.

"Don't worry Barbara", Sister Lavinia whispered conspiratorially into her ear – it tickled – "you don't have to stay here, you're coming with me".

Barbara didn't cry then and never cried again, never ever shed a tear. Her own Mother was horrified, that she could have given birth to and raised such a heartless, cruel little... She could never quite bring herself to say, "bitch". Her Father had no such qualms.

***

Barbara stayed with the nuns of the St Lucretia and St Bernadette Convent in Athlone for the remaining six months of her confinement. Sister Lavinia became her best friend and confidante. Barbara gave birth to a little boy – six pounds, eight ounces – in St Mary's hospital in the town. She was in labour for fifteen hours, it had been touch and go at times, but finally George was born. She saw him briefly – a red creased bawling face, thick matted black hair, flailing wrinkled arms – then he was gone. Sister Lavinia was with her the whole time. The girl slept for a few hours, then was woken by her friend.

She felt dazed, a fuzziness in the head that she couldn't explain given the momentous significance these brief minutes were to assume in her life. She remembered everything but through a gauze – white, hazy and imprecise. She was helped to sit up, many arms it seemed only too eager to help, her night-gown was unbuttoned and flung open, her heavy breasts felt the chill air, her nipples hard. A tightly wrapped bundle was handed to her – George – with his shiny curls protruding. He had been crying, but was now quiet, his mouth open, he looked at her through brown unfocussed eyes. She smelled the soap the nuns had used to wash him and felt the struggling limbs through the layers of linen and wool. Barbara was confused. She held him at arms length.

"He's hungry Barbara. He wants to feed."

Sister Lavinia's voice sounded reassuring, but meant nothing to Barbara. She had seen her Mother feed her younger sister and brother, but hesitated. George began to cry and Barbara panicked, looking desperately at the women surrounding her bed. Briefly lucid, she realized that they would know nothing. They were mere impostors in the game of regenerating life, could have no idea, just circling crows feeding on the carrion of the afterbirth. If only her Mother were here. The crying grew louder, more insistent, the struggling more urgent.

"You must feed him, Barbara".

She looked up, but could see nothing.

"Put him there."

It was one of the other nuns who Barbara had never met but had seen around the convent, her voice was clinically pure – irresistible, yet horrible in its emotionless authority.

"It's natural. Baby will know what to do, to be sure."

Barbara wanted to cry and maybe would have done if she'd been alone and could have kept such a lapse secret.

"Go on, do it."

Vowing again never to cry, she looked down at her son and felt nothing she could identify as a feeling or an opinion, except the faint stirring of an attraction that being almost physical in the grip it exerted over her, she put down to the over exertions of the birth, still only hours away.

"Hold him Barbara, hug him".

It was Lavinia, at least she sounded sensible and well-meaning. Desperate to do something, Barbara gently brought the bundle towards her and squeezed it against her chest. The woollen blanket felt harsh against her skin, but brought some warmth. The crying stopped – Barbara felt relieved, then happy – but only momentarily. The wailing began again. A hand appeared, cradled George's head, guiding it to her nipple. The mouth closed, warm, moist and hard. Silence. Barbara smiled. It felt the most natural thing in the world to her now, holding and feeding her child. Just the two of them. She would never close her eyes again, because this was beautiful, George was beautiful, she knew, even though all she could see was his dark iridescent hair plastered sweatily to the side of his face and a rivulet of warm milk escaping from the side of his mouth.

Her baby shifted and the pain was excruciating. She had never been the victim of such a personal assault before, even when her father had beaten her, he had never got as close as this. She had always known when he was in a foul mood and was going to hit her, this was unexpected.

"Jesus, Mary and Joseph, that hurts!"

The nuns drew back, shocked out of their routine. One crossed herself. Barbara screamed, almost dropping George onto the blankets draped in front of her, and then clutched her breast. The wailing began again.

"He bit me... the little bugger bit me! Look, he almost drew blood."

Suddenly self-conscious she covered herself with her night-dress.

"Watch your mouth, Barbara, remember where you are."

"But he bit me."

The pain was still intense. Her infant had brought the full force of his jaws to bear on his mother's sensitive nipple.

"They do that, you know. They're learning as well. It's all new to them, just like it is for you".

"And how exactly do you know that, tell me? This hurts, really hurts."

"Barbara, now stop this, we're only here to help you..."

"You should have thought about all this a lot earlier if you're not prepared to put up with a little pain".

Lavinia's stern admonishment of her charge was interrupted by the icy tones of Sister Claudette, who had little patience with the women who passed through the Convent, all of them needing help and all receiving it, yet all so ungrateful. Lavinia and she were close, but sometimes Lavinia was just too tolerant and it made her friend angry, particularly as she was certain Lavinia privately felt much as she did. Just listen to the little brat.

"Sister, please, let me deal with this. Barbara's had a difficult delivery. She'll come round, won't you, Barbara?"

Lavinia smiled what she knew from experience was her most winning smile and then scooped up the screaming child. It wouldn't do to have him kicked onto the floor in a fit of pique, now would it? she thought, as she handed him back to Barbara.

"Try again, will you. It will get better, believe me. We've all seen it many times."

She held the child's head as he eagerly searched for the breast with his hot little mouth. Barbara sensed the alternating waves of warmth and rage that washed over her from the lively little body she reluctantly grasped to her chest. The biting pain again, but this time she only winced and took gulps of air deep into her lungs.

"He's hurting me."

"I know, I know."

Sister Lavinia stroked her wavy hair, for the first time showing physical affection for the young woman she had spent months of her life barely apart from. Only too aware of accusations of "particular friendships", jealous taunts that could divide a convent and wreck a community, Lavinia was scrupulous in her conduct with her charges. Never touching, never giving any personal details about herself, never getting close and only rarely letting her guard slip – on this occasion out of irritation with Claudette. It would never happen again with Barbara. After all, she was very nearly out of Lavinia's hands. One brief moment of reassurance wouldn't hurt.

The numbing pain suddenly eased as George finally latched on properly and started to suck, his small fists kneading the side of her breasts. Barbara's milk was flowing and George was drinking furiously, his brow furrowed in concentration, his cheeks pumping like small bellows. She ran a finger gingerly across his forehead and brushed a dank curl of hair behind his ear. She knew he liked it, she knew he knew she was his mother, but the poor thing was so hungry, just look at him.

"Barbara."

Someone was calling her, someone was speaking to her. What did they want?

"Barbara."

Her baby was feeding and her baby loved her, what did anything else matter?

"Barbara."

Couldn't they see she was busy, tied up, just like her grandma with something important, something that couldn't be interrupted, not for anything in the world. Why couldn't they see that?

"Barbara, look at me."

Why, of course, it was her Mother. She sounded like that, it was her Mother. Barbara hadn't seen her in such a long time and of course she hadn't met George yet. She wanted to see the baby, her grandson, that's why. Was Da with her? Barbara looked up to see Sister Lavinia leaning over her, the mole on her right cheek clear and distinct. She seemed unhappy.

"Where's my Mother?"

"She's not here, Barbara. You know she's not."

"But she was calling me."

"That was me, Barbara."

"I heard her voice. It was just like her."

"It was me."

Barbara turned back to her baby.

"I was just going to suggest you try the other one."

Barbara looked up puzzled, the communion with her baby broken. For the first time in ages Lavinia flushed embarrassed at the growing intimacy. She'd had this conversation many times before, with many a silly girl ignorant of even the most basic facts, but Barbara seemed so dependent on her, so adrift, so unaware. Lavinia was surprised at the pity she felt for the girl and didn't like it one bit.

"The other breast. You have two, you know. That one must be dry by now. He's a hungry little chap."

The other breast. It made Barbara smile to think she had forgotten about it. As a girl she had been proud of her breasts.

She had been the first in her class to develop any, the first to have a proper bra. Her school friends had been jealous and she had been very happy.

"I suppose I have", she said dreamily. "Well I never."

Barbara eased George gently from her left breast, a fine milk spray suddenly bathing his face, causing him to grimace then almost instantly cry. His mother was amazed. That was her breast, that was her milk dripping from her baby's chin, she could see it, she could smell it and she had even felt it.

"There, there, it won't be long now."

Carefully she lifted the baby up into the air, he felt light, yet substantial, and turned him over. Instantly he latched on to her other nipple, but this time painlessly, there was just the insistent powerful sucking that would drain her dry.

***

The hours passed for Barbara dozing in an armchair pushed up against the window of her small room. Her view a glimpse of lawn, shrubbery, a wall, then green fields and hedgerows rolling to a distant hazy horizon. There was a house, smoke drifting from its chimney, standing starkly silhouetted against the sky – no one ever seemed to go in or come out – but one day there had been white sheets billowing on a clothesline – the wind strong, the weather overcast. They disappeared while Barbara fed George. Feeding and changing nappies occupied most of her time and when the baby slept in the small crib the nuns had brought in for him, she rested limply in the chair, a blanket pulled up to her chin, watching as the sun, rain, wind, moon and stars played themselves out across her rarely changing view.

Things were going to be all right.

If Barbara thought anything, it was that. There was a symmetry about everything now and she would stare at George slumbering and fight the pleasurable, almost overbearing impulse she had to pick him up and hug him. She knew she mustn't, he needed his sleep and would be cross if woken up. Yet unable to sit still she would lean over, smell his milky head that was like sweet hay freshly damp from the rain – experience for a moment an overwhelming sense of absence, of needing to be elsewhere, of wanting to be home – and then kiss him gently on the cheek before slumping back contentedly into her chair. The blanket was at her feet and she would lean over, bending awkwardly between the crib and the chair to reach it. Her back ached, but she believed it was a small price to pay for so much happiness, and she would smile. Such feelings of elation took hold often now and Barbara would always think of her Grandmother laughing away her rude, childlike questions about why she looked so old.

"I've had so much fun in my life and I've laughed so much my face has fair cracked open, but it's been worth it Barbara, believe me. If you have half as much happiness as I've had, you'll have a delicious time."

As she spoke her creased face would dissolve into a wonderful smile. Barbara could remember that look in such vivid detail, even though her Grandmother had been dead for nearly ten years. It made her happy to think of it. Things were going to be fine and Sister Lavinia was being very kind. The nuns were doing so much for her. Then, exhausted, her mind would clear and she would stare out of the window, the smoke from the cottage a vertical pencil line in a bright cloud-laden sky.

Four days almost to the hour since George was born – Barbara worked this out later – they came. She would describe it to her friends in the "Coach and Horses" many years on, on the day when she felt able to talk about it, felt certain they wouldn't laugh, finally felt the need to tell someone – as just like the descriptions she had read of the condemned prisoner's last moments on earth. Dawn breaking with an eruption of light along the far horizon, the woman had been up. She'd had a restless night and was staring out of the window. Then the footsteps in the corridor, the whispers, the cell door suddenly flung open, the strong arms dragging the prisoner to her feet, the large hand, smelling of vanilla, placed roughly across her mouth, the stifled screams, the terror as the other door opened and her life passed through and away.

Barbara couldn't finish her story without breaking off, breathless but dry-eyed. That touched Doris, Maeve, and even Margaret deeply. She would pause for a moment and then with a sigh continue, her voice cracked and raw.

"I never saw him again, never, ever. They just took him away without a word. Just took him, can you believe it?"

Everyone shook their heads. There was nothing they could say.

There had been a man standing in the background. He never laid a hand on Barbara, it was just the women, the nuns – Sister Lavinia, at the head of them. She had grabbed George. Try as she might Barbara could not remember the look on the nun's face as she'd stolen her baby, even though they had stared at each other for what had seemed like an age – in her mind it was a blank space framed by white linen. Lavinia had remained faceless ever since, even though Barbara was certain she would recognize her if they met again. Indeed to this day she scrutinized every new nun who came to the Convent.

The man in the dark suit had then stepped forward. Barbara lashed out and struck his body a heavy painful blow. The hypodermic syringe he was carrying spun through the air and shattered against the wall, leaving a dark stain on the whitewash.

"Blast", the man hissed, grasping his shoulder. "You'll have to restrain her while I ready another one."

He turned and left the room. Sisters Bernadette and Mary tightened their grip on her arms, upper body and mouth, forcing Barbara back onto the bed. She was barely able to breathe as she lashed out with her feet. Twisting and turning she tried to look into their faces, her hazel green eyes blazing with hatred and anger, but they averted their gaze. The doctor returned, open leather bag in hand. He placed it at an angle across two sides of George's crib, reached inside and lifted out another syringe. Holding it upright in his right hand, he rummaged around in the bag until he found the bottle of sedative. Then with Barbara looking on horrified he filled the syringe, deliberately cleared the air bubbles – a fountain of liquid beads cascaded through the air – returned the bottle to the bag and turned towards the three women, locked in a grim statuesque immobility.

"Have you got a good hold on her?"

Bernadette glanced at Mary then nodded. The doctor appeared uncertain for a moment then lurched forward, sitting heavily on Barbara's legs, catching her by surprise. He was a heavy man and she felt her knees were about to pop apart like the legs on a cooked chicken at Sunday lunch. He roughly pushed up her night gown and plunged the needle into her upper thigh. Barbara's body convulsed at the sudden sharp pain then crumpled back onto the bed, exhausted. The doctor pulled down her gown and stood up. Barbara barely noticed as she slipped into an idiot state, one from which, she would joke many years later to Doris, Maeve and Margaret, she had never come out of. She wanted to scream and yell for help, cry out for her baby, but as the hand slipped from her mouth she found she was incapable of making the slightest sound.

***

"Barbara, Barbara are you awake?"

It was Sister Constance. She usually worked in the Convent garden, summer and winter. Barbara had never known her work indoors. For that reason Barbara knew without even opening her eyes that it had not been a dream. She was a childless mother. Her womb ached, her muscles were stiff and her breasts were full, but she had no baby. Her child was an orphan. She was bereft.

"Barbara, Barbara it's time to get up. There are things to do."

With eyes still shut, Barbara couldn't imagine what needed doing.

"Come on now I have your breakfast, eat it up, there's a good girl."

Barbara sat bolt upright in bed, startling Sister Constance who almost dropped the tray she was carrying, and opened her eyes deliberately. As she expected the crib was gone, there was no sign of her baby, of George, and the room looked larger and tidier. But what she had not expected was to see her clothes and few belongings neatly packed into her battered blue suitcase, which was lying open on the floor by the door.

"Where am I going?" she asked grimly, sensing that the sister had done this many times before. She refused to ask the obvious question, the only question there was to be asked, about George.

Sister Constance was unmoved, thinking only of her anemones and the clipping that needed doing, humanity was far too complicated for her. She was ideally qualified for the only indoor work she ever did.

"Away. It'll be for the best. Now eat up, you'll need all your strength. It's quite a journey."

Barbara couldn't think anymore, her head ached, and she knew all she believed she'd ever need to know.

"I'm tired. I want to sleep."

"No you don't dear. You've already had over a day in bed. Getting up and getting going is the best thing for you now."

Constance's matter of fact indifference almost won Barbara over and she found herself pushing back the bed-clothes, sliding her legs over the edge of the mattress and searching for her slippers under the bed with her feet. The cold dampness across her chest brought her to her senses and she stared at the old, slightly hunched woman in front of her, with her brown watery eyes gazing somewhere way past Barbara, and finally lost patience. It would amuse Barbara later that she had coughed before she had let go, purposefully holding herself back for a few seconds, hanging on albeit briefly to her old life. The cough seemed to surprise Constance, her mind wasn't on the job at all, Barbara imagined she looked around as if searching for a handkerchief. She was not looking at Barbara when the blow fell flatly across the side of her head, her false teeth, never the best fitting, slid from her mouth and disappeared under the bed. The tray dropped from her hands, helped on its way by a downward blow from Barbara, porridge and hot tea spilled outwards, scalding Barbara's bare feet as cup and bowl shattered on the painted wooden boards. It was several seconds before the thin metal tray, embossed with the bright red OXO emblem, rattled itself to stillness. Sister Constance stood in front of Barbara, her collapsed face fixed in a look of utter astonishment, her left hand clasped to her jaw. Without hesitation Barbara pushed her violently backwards screaming at the top of her voice for her to get out and leave her alone.

"I never want to see any of you ever again."

She tripped and stumbled forward, her knees coming to rest in a pool of congealing porridge and breathlessly let out a chilling, anguished scream, before, dry-eyed, she offered up one final desperate prayer for forgiveness.

The nuns hesitated when they rushed into the room some minutes later, seeing Barbara apparently on her knees in prayer. Maybe Sister Constance had been exaggerating, but the disorder in the room suggested otherwise. They stood crowded together in the doorway reluctant to interrupt anyone, even someone as forsaken as Barbara, in their communion with God. Sister Constance, no longer in shock but angry, egged them on vengefully from behind.

"She looks so peaceful, maybe we should leave her. Mother Superior will know what to do."

"She's a wicked one, I tell you. She hit me. Here on the side of my face. I've never been so humiliated in all my born years."

"But Sister she's praying. There's hope for her yet to be sure".

Barbara stayed on her knees and kept her eyes closed. She was aware of people in the doorway, was aware of the mutterings, but she was not listening to them. All she could hear was the baby crying in her head. She was wondering where it was, it didn't sound like her baby, like her George, but it sounded hungry and she could feed it, keep it happy until its mother came back. With a great effort and after much searching she went to it and picked it up and placed it at her breast; it began feeding immediately. Barbara knew it was a little girl, but was afraid to look at her face, just kept staring at the trees that grew all around, she was afraid the little girl would look like her.

"There may be hope for her, but not here."

The nuns drew back from the doorway, almost stood to attention, as the Mother Superior approached down the corridor.

"Sister Constance get yourself off to the infirmary and get your face looked at. Now what is going on?"

Sister John of Montrose towered above the nuns as they looked uncertainly one to the other then, as if choreographed, looked up at her. At nearly six foot tall the Mother Superior in her black robes appeared to float in the air, her whole manner of walking a gentle rolling bob that was unhurried but certain.

There had never been any issue with who exercised authority in this Convent, it rested easily on her shoulders. John smiled and her pale eyes gleamed out of a shadowed face, her hands which had been clasped together as she approached, now parted in a gesture of openness, welcoming information. Sister Constance was about to blurt out her story, then appeared to think better of it and walked slowly off down the corridor, clutching her swollen face and muttering softly to herself.

"Won't someone tell me why there has been all this commotion and why you've all abandoned your duties and are clustered around this door?"

"Mother."

Sister Martha, a young novice hesitantly spoke out, as much from the fact that she stood in front of the Mother Superior and was directly in her gaze as from any desire to push herself forward.

"It seems that the Mullen girl attacked Sister Constance when she brought her breakfast."

Martha bobbed slightly as she ran out of things to say.

"Attacked, what precisely do you mean?"

Martha's face flushed and the Mother Superior glanced at some of the more senior nuns standing silently behind her.

"Hmmmm?"

"It would appear she was slapped and then pushed, Mother. She's very upset."

"I'm sure she is, wouldn't you be after what she's been through?"

Instantly the nun grew flustered and uncertain.

"It's, it's never happened to her before in forty odd years."

"Sister Constance, God bless her, is a tough old woman. She'll survive."

Seeing the shocked looks on their faces, the Mother Superior gently placated them with one of the time-honoured platitudes of her vocation.

"She was after all only carrying out God's will. Please let me through. I must have a word with young Barbara Mullen before she leaves us."

As the Mother Superior entered the room, Barbara was still on her knees. Her breasts tingled. Feeding had become such a pleasure, you quickly forgot, Barbara found, about the pain you sometimes felt as unfettered jaws clamped hungrily onto your breasts. George in his eagerness used, at the beginning, to bite hard on to the pale brown bumpy ring that surrounded her nipples, causing her to gasp out loud and leaving red welts that stung for the hours that he slept. But her new baby had fed well and was now asleep in her lap. You mustn't disturb her. Such thoughts reminded Barbara that she had asked for some cream to rub on her sore breasts – her Mother swore by Germoline – but nothing had come, even though she had mentioned it several times and Lavinia had said she would try and get her some. Maybe she wouldn't have to ask again. This new baby was such a good feeder – a real demon – she wouldn't cause any problems. It was true what they said, girls are much better than boys, seemed happier with the world, picked things up quicker. Sleeping like a dream, one mustn't wake her or there'd be hell to pay.

The Mother Superior saw the kneeling figure, hands clasped as if in prayer, eyes closed, lips moving and like the others hesitated, bowing to a higher authority. Turning she faced the other nuns who had crowded into the room and ushered them away with her hands. Seeing them hesitate she silently mouthed words of assurance and then motioned for the door to be closed behind them. She stood silently watching the young woman in front of her, her hands also clasped and offered up a prayer of her own – a prayer to bring hope and dispel despair, briefly she wondered if it was for her then dismissed the idea. That was too ridiculous. Barbara sensed a change in the atmosphere of the room, a dislocation, a cooling, but heard nothing and kept her eyes shut. Curiosity, self-preservation, an interest in the world meant nothing to her now. She had a baby to feed and clothe and nurture. That was all she wanted to do and that would take time. She could feel the baby's heart beat against her chest, fluttering faster than she would have thought possible. It made her wonder if she was still alive, her heart was so sluggish in comparison, and for the first time Barbara understood what it was like to be old. A heart slowing until finally, like her Grandma's, it stops. A broken heart running down until, sooner rather than later, it beats its last and ceases to be. It could stop now for all she cared, except she had her baby. Where would she be without her? A discomforting thought. Her knees were hurting, the hard wooden floor unforgiving. She shifted sideways, but there was only temporary relief. The Mother Superior who had been watching hawk-like seized her moment.

"Barbara."

It was like a door slamming.

"Shhhhh."

"Barbara, we must talk."

Why was that woman shouting?

"Shhhh, you'll wake the baby."

Sister John lowered her voice.

"Barbara, that's what we must talk about."

"The baby, if you wake her I'll never forgive you."

Barbara's voice was getting louder, more strident. The Mother Superior heard the hysterical pitch of the words vibrating in the air, instinctively her tone changed to match it and to mollify.

"Barbara, sit down please, there's a good girl. We need to have a chat."

Then, as an afterthought.

"The baby is fast asleep. It looks like nothing will wake her."

Barbara shifted uncertainly on her knees, but didn't get up. Her baby was soundly asleep that much was true, she could hear her snuffling breaths – of contentment – maybe if they kept their voices down no harm would be done.

"Barbara shall I help you up?"

Barbara let her head fall back, biting her upper lip; she stared at the picture of the Virgin Mary on the wall above her bed. Her breath escaped through a clenched slit of a mouth, moaning gently the air seemed to drain from her body. Savouring the light-headed drowsiness, Barbara watched as the image of the Virgin passed in and out of focus, the yellowy-gold halo lazily spinning on an uneven axis around her head. Barbara smiled. It was miraculous.

"You're a real miracle worker pet."

The vision disappeared with the fresh air flooding into her lungs. Exhausted she nodded her assent.

Sister John sighed to herself, she felt she had been here before. She did see Lavinia's point sometimes, but it was certainly God's will that the nun and her too on occasions had to deal with these girls. In this particular case, so far so good. A hand on the shoulder, Barbara's body started, even though she had been expecting the contact and no longer cared.

"Here let me help you up. Why don't you take your chair in the window? I'll sit here on the bed."

Barbara moved stiffly to her familiar seat, cradling shadows in her arms. Once she had settled she looked up at the Mother Superior and smiled beatifically. Sister John was stunned; she had never seen anything so beautiful. Barbara was a pretty girl with her brown auburn tinted curls, clear skin, freckles and pale hazel green eyes, but you would never have called her beautiful. Now her face shone with a fresh ruddy health that seemed both innocent and knowing. She looked, John thought, like a girl on the cusp of womanhood realizing for the first time the joys that lay ahead, but still like a child oblivious to the dangers and pitfalls. The Mother Superior hoped, would even pray a little later, that it was so, but coldly she knew it was not to be. She felt guilty in a routine sort of way, always did, that somehow these girls, her girls if the truth be told, had been let down. They all seemed so unaware of the potentials for sin. Where were their mothers, fathers, priests? What had they taught them? What sort of example had they set? Look at Barbara here – pretty beyond imagining and the picture of innocence – if not the serpent in the Garden of Eden then she'd certainly been bitten by it. John smiled. It amused her how pedestrian her mind could be at just the times when her vocation demanded something more stirring, more uplifting, more spiritual. The familiar old biblical clichés were not really good enough, Barbara deserved better, they all did.

"Shall we pray, Barbara?"

She had not intended to pursue this course, but to talk in reasonable and practical terms about the immediate future, about what was going to happen, where Barbara was going, and who would meet her. There would be no mention of her histrionic behaviour, certainly no mention of what had just happened here, no mention of the baby – that was a hard and fast rule, even if they asked over and over again – and most definitely no appeals to God, the Virgin Mary or the Saints. No prayers, for Sister John had found through long experience that in almost all cases at this particular time it was usually singularly inappropriate. So it proved to be, but she was feeling selfish and largely indifferent to the emotions of her charge. John had been a nun for over thirty years, had never dreamt of being anything else, would never have acknowledged anything so spiritually weak, so sinful, as a crisis of faith. But her calling, once so ecstatically pure, so focussed on helping and doing good for others that her own sympathies and ideas had been extinguished by her love for God, for her Church and indeed in the beginning for mankind itself, had mutated into a more personal self-serving relationship between Sister John and God. Womankind was a particular casualty, for Sister John had long ago ceased to think of herself as a woman and she had never bothered much about men. As a conduit for sin woman seemed particularly well suited and John was forever aghast at how little she understood these girls that passed through her hands. It had all seemed so simple to her. At one time she had seen it as a challenge that others found it all so difficult, now it was an irritation. It was simple, it was not difficult.

"Let us pray".

Barbara's beatific smile solidified, her ashen skin stretched taught across her cheekbones, then, as the brightness in her eyes dimmed, her face began to sag and crumple. Her arms dropped lifelessly into her lap and she watched helpless and terrified as her baby, wrapped in its blanket, slid slowly away from her, before slipping off her legs and plunging to the floor. The bundle bounced once on her feet, hit the wooden boards and rolled under the bed. There was silence, where there should have been cries and screams, but Barbara's baby was no more and Barbara was mute.

The Virgin Mary gazed down at Sister John's upturned face, but yielded nothing. Forgiveness was not on offer, not now, but maybe later. John glanced at the silent figure opposite then eased herself onto her knees, loosening her habit as she did so.

Struck down and struck dumb Barbara meekly followed, struggling out of the deep sagging armchair and dropping painfully to her knees. She winced and her eyes filled with tears, but she did not cry out. Sister John placed her hands together and raised them slowly and deliberately until they came to rest inches away from her face. Her lips began to move in silent prayer. Copying the nun's every movement, Barbara clasped her hands together and raised them shakily towards her face, her mouth opening and closing; then the mirror seemed to crack and she clutched her head in her hands and lunged forward, her body crashing to the floor. Lying prostrate in front of the praying Sister John, she silently sobbed, mouthing her pain and anger into the unforgiving wooden boards pressed against her cheek, but she remained dry-eyed for even then the tears failed to flow.

"Lord, grant me the strength to do thy will.
Give me the strength to serve as a guide
to your sinful daughter lying before you.
Give me the strength to carry out your bidding and help
her back on to the road to righteousness.
Amen."

The Mother Superior waited for Barbara to pick herself up from the floor, but after ten minutes and several increasingly desperate pleas for her to get to her feet capped by a petulant threat to pull herself together or else, she gave up and left the room. Sister Lavinia was standing alone in the corridor.

"It's no use trying to talk to her, they'll have to do that in Dublin. They'll have plenty of time after all. Is the driver ready?"

"He's been outside for a while."

"Give her another half an hour then walk her to the car any way you can."

"You want me to do it?"

"It may help, but who knows?"

Sister John dismissed further questions with a wave of her hand and glided away down the hall.

***

The air smelled smoky and heavy with autumnal decay after the stuffy antiseptic air of the Convent. It chilled her sweating face and soothed her clammy body. Barbara shivered and eased her damp cotton blouse away from her chest with her hand. It felt icy on her skin. She pulled her green cardigan tightly around her body and crossed her arms corpse-like over her aching breasts. Two nuns walked either side of her exerting firm pressure in the small of her back – one of them was Sister Lavinia, but Barbara could no longer recognize her, could barely remember her.

Ahead a small portly man in a brown tweed suit and flat cap carried her small blue plastic suitcase in one hand and the overcoat she had refused to wear in the other. He was breathing heavily, even though the Convent driveway rose only slightly in the quarter of a mile it took to reach the gates and the main road. His breath rose in tightly spaced clouds, one after the other, appearing to Barbara to issue from the top of his head and reminding her of the steam trains puffing their way up the incline outside Ballymena at 3.15 every day of her childhood, except Sundays. "No vehicles in the grounds after dark", the Mother Superior was very strict about that. The truth was departures were always better if they happened out of sight, less disturbing that way for the others.

It was a clear night. You could almost touch the stars. Barbara quickly picked out the Plough – her favourite, somehow nothing could go wrong once she had seen that – and Orion, his belt buckle glittering brightly. They were all there. Her Grandfather had known every sign of the Zodiac. They would lie on their backs in the field behind his house and he would point to the heavens and make up stories. There were so many constellations he never ran out of tales to tell. Barbara would lie there holding his hand staring upwards making up new shapes – joining the dots – looking for strange animals, faces, even words.

"You're mad, you two," her Grandmother's voice would ring out through the still night air, strong and clear, used to filling the vast empty spaces of Saint Julian's from her place in the choir, and undaunted by the emptiness of the heavens.

"The ground is awful damp. You'll both catch your deaths. You should know better Fred. Come in now, it's way past the girl's bedtime."

Barbara could hear her now, hear her Grandfather's snigger, feel the warmth of his body as they snuggled together, co-conspirators, hidden deep in their grassy bower shrouded by the darkness.

"Just a few more minutes, eh, then we'd better be going in or she'll do for me."

Then he would laugh and Barbara would too, the long grass would shake and tickle their noses and they would laugh some more. Then hand in hand they would walk across the meadow to the cottage, a lamp flickering in one of the windows. It was all so cosily familiar: a cup of cocoa in front of the fire wrapped in a blanket, the sleepy climb up steep stairs, tucked in so tight you could hardly breath, the fleeting peck on the forehead and then dreams.

Not tonight though, Barbara, you're not going in tonight, you're looking for George. He's up there somewhere, you know he is. Barbara scanned the firmament, her eyes moving in wide arcs across the sky, her head barely moving. She didn't want her captors to know what she was doing. She had to be very careful.

The car, a small black Ford, was parked outside the Convent gates. The driver had already loaded her suitcase and coat into the boot and was standing wearily beside one of the open side doors. His breathing slightly more regular now, his breath hanging in dense clouds around his head, he looked less like a steam train, more like a man smoking a cigarette and exhaling the smoke slowly and deliberately.

"Your hackney awaits. In you go, Miss."

The interior smelled of leather, the seats felt cold against her legs, her body bristled against the firm pressure on her back and shoulders that had shoved her inside. The door slammed shut and was locked. The driver's door opened and Lavinia's head appeared, unsmiling.

"Goodbye, Barbara. God bless."

Then she was gone, to be replaced by the dark bulk of the driver who moved around in his seat for several interminable seconds before settling and calling out a familiar farewell to the nuns, who were already padlocking the Convent gates. He then closed his door.

"Where to?"

For a brief sparkling moment Barbara believed him. She rose up from the back seat as if her body were inflating, only to collapse back as his cruel, broken toothed smile punctured her optimism. He turned back and started the engine, calling out to her over the noise.

"Don't go getting any ideas now. I'm not in the mood for any nonsense."

He pulled out into the deserted road without a glance behind him, the headlights feebly piercing the darkness ahead.

"Where you're going, you won't be getting out for a good while so I'd just lie back and get used to it if I was you."

Dark shapes of buildings passed by the windows, lifeless and inanimate.

"It's nothing to do with me. I just move you lot around. So no trouble there's a good girl."

They were out in the countryside now. Everything seemed lighter, airier, but Barbara could see nothing clearly.

"What did you do then to get yourself in this fix?"

Another car passed in the opposite direction, its headlights blinding, the beams sweeping across the roof of the taxi, spotlighting a ragged tear in the fabric, then darkness.

"Don't want to tell me, but I bet I can guess."

He shifted in his seat and the car swerved.

"You were a naughty girl, weren't you? Out playing with the boys and you got more than you bargained for?"

Barbara wished she could escape, fade away, but for the first time in ages she was only too vibrantly in the present.

"Did it feel good when he touched you? I bet you didn't get undressed, did you? Did he just take your knickers off? Did he?"

She hadn't thought of Patrick in a long time. Now she could taste the beer on his breath, smell the damp earth of that shed, feel his hands mauling her breasts – they had never been the same since, aching, sensitive to the touch, changing shape – his body pressing down squeezing the breath from hers.

"How long did it take? Quick, was it? I bet you wanted more?"

Barbara's full breasts felt taut, her bra was already damp. She could bear no more of this man and covered her ears with her hands and pushed herself deep into the car seat in a vain attempt to get as far away from him as she could. Shutting her eyes just brought back images of Patrick, his face inches from hers, blowing hot air over her in rasping blasts, red and overheated, so she kept them open and stared at the pallid darkened world outside. The words continued but indistinct and far away, they would never hurt her again. People could say what they wanted, she was long past caring. She was travelling with the stars, far away, searching, looking for her son.

It was Barbara's first visit to Dublin. By night the city seemed vast, bulky and alive. At this early hour there were only a few people about, but there were lights, cars, milk floats and a cat. Barbara saw it clearly, bright eyes caught in the headlights, her driver saw it too and swerved towards it, then it was gone. Tall buildings disappeared into the dark, streets narrowed then opened out, and there were traffic lights. Stop. The satisfaction at sitting still, while the driver cursed. Cramped terraced streets closed in, left then right, a high brick wall loomed, braking hard, the wheels skidding slightly on the cobbles before lurching forward to halt before high wooden gates with a black iron grille at head height.

"Stay there. I hope they're expecting us. I'm not hanging around."

The door slammed and Barbara sighed with relief. She heard the heavy knocker rap twice, three times and watched as her driver rocked anxiously from foot to foot, looked furtively up and down the street and then hurried to a nearby lamp-post placed close against the wall, unzipped himself and urinated gushingly against the brickwork. He returned, wagging his finger at Barbara just as the grille in the gate opened and a face appeared.

"Barbara Mullen for you. It was one difficult journey, I'm telling you."

But the face had already disappeared and the gate was opening. Another nun. Barbara clasped her forehead in her hand and shook her head. The car door was unlocked and swung open.

"Get out."

The driver stared at her long pale legs as she got out; her dress – tight across a stomach still slightly distended from the birth – had rucked up under her during the journey and she was forced to push it down as she stood up.

"I ought to tell on you", he whispered as she passed by him.

"Hello, dear, I'm Sister Monica and this is Doris Blaney."

Barbara turned to look at a curly headed young woman, wearing thin-rimmed round glasses and dressed in ordinary clothes.

"She'll look after you over the next few days. She's been here a few years so knows all the ropes, don't you, Doris?"

Doris smiled and nodded, slipped off her glasses and extended her hand towards Barbara.

"Pleased to meet you."

They shook hands tentatively, their fingers barely touching.

"Yes, welcome to the Convent of our Lady of Mercy at the Magdalen Asylum. You'll soon feel at home. Could you take the bag through there, Mr Granger? Thank you. Is that all you have?"

Barbara nodded.

"Never mind, we have plenty of spare clothes. If you need anything. Doris'll show you in the morning."

The driver stood in the doorway, framed in a gold aura from the street lamp outside.

"Is that all then, Sister, 'cause I'd like to be off?"

"It is, Mr Granger, thank you very much."

"You should watch that one, Sister, you really should."

"Pardon me?"

An engine turned over, headlights shone briefly into the hallway, then the car pulled away.

"What could he mean, Barbara?"

The street and Convent were quiet, except for the ticking of a tall grandfather clock standing at the bottom of the stairs.

"Never mind that now. The Reverend Mother will see you in the morning to welcome you properly. She'll tell you all about how we work here and what's expected of you. I'm sure you'll fit into convent life. Now bed, I think. You look exhausted. Doris will show you the way".

Sister Monica nodded at Barbara, took a large key from the pocket of her habit, swung the heavy door shut and threw the two iron bolts, then turned the lock.

"That's done then. Good night, God bless you."

"This way."

Doris picked up her bag and led the way up the dimly lit stairs. Barbara meekly followed. This place smelled just like the other one, an overbearing slightly rank mixture of floor polish, incense and bleach. It even looked the same with its gleaming wooden floors, dark brown wooden panelled walls, statues of the Virgin Mary, pictures of Jesus everywhere you looked. Barbara was close to despair, tired and hungry, her head throbbing, her breasts full and painful, the front of her blouse drenched.

"Here we are."

Doris was pointing the way into a small room, much like the one she had just left, a narrow single bed, a bedside table with lamp and Bible, a chair, chest of drawers, a rug and a crucifix on the wall.

"Home from home", she muttered as she sat down on the bed.

"Oh, you won't have this for long", Doris said perkily, "this is just for the new girls, you know, to settle in. Then it's the dorm with the rest of us, I'm afraid."

Barbara dropped her head and sniffed loudly.

"Oh, it's not that bad really", Doris hastily added, "They're a good lot in the main. A few oddities but then, aren't there always? Here, let me help you; you look just about done in. Things always look better in the morning. They'll let you sleep in, because you arrived so late."

Barbara looked at Doris and smiled weakly.

"Don't worry about me, I don't need a lot of sleep. I've got an easy shift in the laundry so it won't be at all bad. They always do that when a new one is due in."

Barbara nodded, happy to be dealing with someone who wasn't a nun, even if she wasn't paying any attention to what the other girl did or said.

"Do you have a night-dress? Is it all right if I have a look?"

Returning with a freshly laundered linen night gown, she bent down and undid Barbara's shoes, placing them neatly under the bed. Then she unbuttoned her cardigan, which was damp to the touch. The blouse underneath was darkly stained with milk and Doris stared open-mouthed for a moment before, sensing no resistance from Barbara, she proceeded to undo the tiny mother-of-pearl buttons and slip the soaking garment from her shoulders.

Barbara's full breasts strained against the cotton straps of her bra. Red weal's marked where the material had cut into her then chafed against her skin as she had tried in vain to make herself more comfortable during the journey. Kneeling beside Barbara, Doris reached round and touched the clasp on her back, then hesitated. Barbara sat passively, like a weary child waiting for a parent to undress her and safely tuck her up in bed. The sopping wet bra peeled easily off Barbara's skin revealing an etching of itself marked in flaming red lines. The skin was damp and mottled and looked rough to the touch, her nipples were erect and milky. The air was heavy with the bittersweet smell of the dairy.

"That looks painful," Doris whispered. She reached over and gently, ever so slightly, lifted one of the breasts with her forefinger. It felt far heavier to the touch than she had expected. The brown nipple was slightly upturned and pointing at Doris, she could clearly see the forked fissure at its end, beaded with milk. Barbara appeared indifferent to everything that was going on.

Encouraged Doris cupped the breast in the palm of her hand and leant forward, taking the nipple gently into her mouth. Nose pressed tightly against Barbara's bulging breast she could smell sweat and the faintly rancid odour of old milk. The taste was of salt as Doris ran her tongue along and around the nipple. In trepidation she took a deep breath then began to suck. At first nothing then her mouth filled with warm milk and she almost retched, as much from surprise as from horror at what was happening. Deliberately she swallowed, not wishing to offend her new found friend, and was pleasantly surprised. The taste was not unlike what she was used to, more watery perhaps, sweeter in a way, but at the exact temperature of her body it felt like she was soaking it up and absorbing it through every pore rather than drinking it. Effortlessly her mouth seemed to fill again and again. Barbara let out a long sigh and cradled Doris's head in her arms. Stopping briefly to take a breath, Doris felt the fine milk spray tickling her nose and giggled silently to herself – if her family could see her now – before Barbara eased her gently back into position. The second breast followed naturally from the first and then the two women briefly fell asleep together on the bed. Doris roused herself less than an hour later and slipped back to her dormitory just before the nuns began silently trailing to the chapel for early morning prayers.

Barbara awoke soon after Doris had left. Climbing wearily from her bed she wrapped a blanket around herself and went and stood at the window to watch. A faint glow was visible high in the sky in front of her, below it pitch darkness. It felt to her as if she was trapped in a hole staring upwards, the distant light, her rescuers growing ever closer. She cradled her breasts in her arms and swayed back and forth, humming gently, seeking comfort while she waited. To her horror the dawn brought no relief, for as the sun rose Barbara saw that she had been mistaken. The blackness that had pressed in on her was permanent. There was no chance of ever escaping over the high unyielding walls of the Convent.

There was a rustle at the door and she turned to see a face peering in at her, eyes blinking behind circular steel rimmed glasses, curly brown hair uncrushed.

"You're awake."

Barbara could only stare, dazed by her lack of sleep.

"Remember me? It's Doris."

Barbara nodded.

"I have to get up early to open up the laundry and get things going. Thought I'd check in on you on my way down. You all right?"

"What time is it?"

"Just after six. The others come down at half past. They all expect a cup when they do. There's hell to pay if it's not ready."

Doris laughed, a deep-throated chuckle that Barbara warmed to. It seemed to hang in the air, dispelling the gloom, and as it died away they could hear the sound of a horse drawn milk float on the cobbles outside, the chink of bottles and the rattle of crates.

"Go back to bed, Barbara, you need the rest. They won't be calling on you, a new girl, today."

"No, I can't sleep. Can I come with you?"

"If you want, but there's no need. I can sneak you up a cup. They won't notice if I'm quick".

"Please can I come with you?"

Companionship suddenly seemed to be the only thing that Barbara wanted, the thought of being alone in the room was unbearable.

"If you want. I can show you the ropes."

"What do I wear?"

"The dressing gown'll do. I'll get you your overalls when we've got everything going."

The laundry was bitterly cold early in the morning. Summer or winter the first one down always shivered involuntarily as she hurried across the stone flag stones, her slippers slapping noisily, her dressing gown billowing upwards in the icy draft that blew the length of the narrow high-ceilinged room. For three years Doris had been doing just that, taking it in turns with the others to drag herself out of bed, hurry along dingy corridors, down steep flights of stairs to open up the laundry. Light the fire. Stoke up the boilers. Put on the kettle for that first cup of tea in the morning. It was better when there were two of them, but that rarely happened. Maybe Barbara would be happy to do that?

Stopping in the entrance to the laundry, her breath misting the air in front of her, Barbara stared aghast at the silent machinery.

"Doris, is this where I'll be working?"

"Yes. Didn't you know?"

She shook her head.

"We all work here. Six days a week."

"Sisters as well?"

Doris couldn't help laughing.

"No. They never do anything down here. A couple of them keep an eye on us and another, Sister Helen, looks after all the deliveries. There's prayers in the morning before we start and sometimes they make us sing hymns during the day, but that's all."

"What will I be doing?"

"It depends. Probably ironing or pegging out. That's what they usually put the new ones on. Till they get the hang of it. Then it's the boilers. That's what I'm on. You'll have no trouble sleeping after that".

She laughed again, then noticed the bleak expression on Barbara's face.

"It's not too horrible, believe me. I know it looks frightening now. When I first saw it I thought it was like something out of Dickens. But you get used to it, even if it takes a little time. I have."

Barbara felt she could hardly breathe. For the first time she understood what her life was going to be from now on, she understood her sentence and it was almost too much to bear. Doris moved closer and clasped Barbara in her arms. For a brief moment the two young women recaptured the intimacy of the night before, then they turned away from each other and began to work.

Barbara had loved Doris ever since, throughout their forty-five years together in the Convent they had been the best of friends, but she had never let Doris touch her like that again.

Chapter 4

The Snug – March 1996 – twenty to one

"Don't say it, Barbara."

"Don't say what, Doris?"

"Don't say you've never cried. Never have and never will".

Smiling, Doris sipped the foamy dregs from her empty glass of stout and then wiped her lips with the back of her liver-spotted hand. Barbara feigned indignation then laughed out loud.

"But it's true. I never have."

"And you never will", chorused Doris and Margaret, sitting across the small table from her. Only Maeve was strangely quiet, a quizzical look on her face.

"Go on, you daft buggers. I'm proud of that, I really am."

"We know you are", said Margaret snidely. "You've told us all often enough".

"But I think it's really something. I feel like I got back at them, you know, kept my pride. It's important." Barbara's voice trailed off, then suddenly she shot back angrily, "But of course you wouldn't understand, would you, Margaret? Never had anything like that happen to you."

"Don't you take that tone with me, just because you…".

"Come on, you two, not on our last day," Doris pleaded, a hand on each woman's arm.

"I know what you mean, I understand."

Maeve spoke quietly, but everyone had heard. Her face was flushed and slightly sweaty, she looked miserable beneath her pudding basin crown of dark brown hair. She had just removed her green headscarf and her hair, the envy of her friends, thick and healthy with barely a trace of grey, was tousled and sticking out awkwardly over her ears. She would have been mortified if she had known. She prided herself on always looking neat and tidy and would have instantly rushed to the Ladies, comb in hand even before the door had swung shut behind her.

Presentable, was how Maeve saw herself. Contained, constrained, buttoned up, was how she came across to the others. A young psychiatrist called in to treat her depression had scribbled in the margins of his notes in pencil the words "uptight and anally retentive", followed by "nth degree". He had meant to rub them out later, but had been distracted, and they remained there to this day, cruelly prejudicing everyone who had cause to glance through her records. For Maeve was not going anywhere. Maeve was staying on at the Convent. She had a job with occupational therapy, she was luckier in that respect than most of the others, but of her close companions only Margaret was also staying on. And she didn't really like Margaret, no one did. The others were going. Leaving for fresh starts. Doris, who she'd known for ages and always been friends with, was going to her niece's, but worst of all Barbara was leaving to live with her sister. She was glad for her, of course, but it didn't really bear thinking about and Maeve was doing her best to avoid doing just that. Maeve started to cry.

"We know you understand, Maeve."

Doris placed an arm round her shoulders.

"I know why it's important, Barbara," Maeve pleaded.

"I know you do, pet."

She patted Maeve's hand.

"Crying is important for some people, too, you know."

"I know, Maeve, but I just never felt like it and then it became a thing with me. Never could after I realized that. If you can't cry about a thing like that, then you won't cry about anything, I reckon. It's not as if I've got any family to cry about either."

"What about your sister, Bernice?"

Doris and Margaret spoke as one, surprising each other at the previously unnoticed similarity in the tone of their voices. Barbara seemed genuinely shocked at what she herself had said.

"Holy Mother of God, how could I forget about her?"

She crossed herself.

"I never stopped crying. It seemed like for years".

They all looked at Maeve, who was wiping her nose with a handkerchief, her face damp and blotchy.

"Suppose I've never really stopped, if the truth be known".

The door to the snug opened, the hubbub of the public bar clear and distracting, and all four turned as one to look, Doris leaning forward on the table for balance. Barbara leapt to her feet, almost overturning her beer glass. Margaret caught and steadied it, smiling at her feat of dexterity in spite of herself.

"Bernice."

Nodding cursorily at Margaret, Barbara squeezed past Doris and embraced a slightly younger woman, dressed in a black fur coat and grinning happily. A florid man in a dark suit with a bright red tie and pink shirt stood behind her, his body at an angle, hanging back apparently embarrassed at the anticipated rush of female emotion.

"Barbara, how are you? They said we'd find you in here."

"I told you I'd be in here."

"I know you did. Only teasing."

They hugged again, before kissing each other on the cheek.

"It's good to see you again, Bernie."

"You too, Babs. Aren't you going to introduce us?"

"Oh, yes, sorry."

They had never seen Barbara looking so happy, her face radiantly lined, her teeth unnaturally white in the dim yellow light. Arm in arm, she introduced her sister and her sister's husband to her friends, her smile never dimming.

"I'll be living with them outside Dublin, isn't that grand? You can all come and visit, isn't that right, Bernice?"

Her sister nodded and smiled. It really was too good to be true and Barbara still couldn't believe her luck.

Everything had seemed to happen without her having to do a thing. The Church authorities had written secretly to all the known relatives of the laundry women to let them know about the closure and that their relatives were free to leave the Convent if alternate living arrangements for them could be made. There were not as many letters to send as Father Michael had been expecting and only a small number of relatives had replied, among them Barbara's sister, Bernice. She had not seen or heard of her elder sister since that day she'd left in the early fifties. But she had never forgotten her and always missed her. So on one otherwise unexceptionable day Father Michael had asked Barbara in a whisper if she would like to meet someone, someone a little bit special, later that night in the Reverend Mother's parlour.

"Not a word to anyone, mind. We wouldn't want the other ladies asking too many questions and getting their hopes raised, now would we? If it gets out I'll have to call it all off. I'll give you a shout for special duties later".

They were barely able to talk at their first meeting – tongue-tied, hands clasped tightly together – but with the silent chaperone, Sister Amelia, ever watchful, the two sisters had begun to rebuild their long fractured relationship at a number of secret meetings. With the fire crackling in the grate, pots of piping hot tea and chocolate biscuits, they had talked about every detail of their lives. And then finally one night when Sister Amelia had slipped out for a moment, leaving them for once alone, Bernice had said she had never been able to have children and asked about the baby.

"George, he was called George," Barbara had told her. She didn't mind, after all it was right that he should be with them, he was family after all. Bernice began to cry but Barbara remained dry-eyed even as the sisters hugged each other.

"Good to meet you all, Barbara's told me so much about you," her sister said now. "It's a shame but I'm afraid we can't stay. Sorry, but if we leave it much later the roads will be terrible and we mustn't be late."

Bernice shrugged her shoulders and glanced at her husband, who had managed to squeeze himself in against the far wall of the snug and was looking distinctly uncomfortable.

"I've arranged a little surprise for you, a homecoming party. Some relatives you won't have seen for a while..."

For the first time since she had been reunited with her sister Barbara felt doubtful; she didn't know whether Bernice was joking or not.

"... and some of my best friends, who can't wait to meet you. I've told them so much about you."

Bernice moved towards the door, signalling to her husband to do the same. Barbara followed them.

"Nice to have met you all."

Margaret, Maeve and Doris all nodded and mumbled their assent but stayed seated, dazed by the realization that this was finally the moment they had all been dreading.

"We'll wait outside while you say your good-byes. The car's across the street. Don't be long now, Barbara, will you?"

The couple edged their way out, Bernice's husband raising

his hand to the women as he passed and the snug door closed once again on their small time-honoured world. There was a fleeting silence then Barbara, dry-eyed, dragged each of her friends to their feet and hugged them, whispered, "I love you, good-bye," and rushed out.

Maeve fingered the empty cigarette packet lying on the table, it was growing increasingly soggy as the cardboard soaked up a spillage of Guinness. Margaret bit her lip and stared at the light shining through the little coloured glass doors on the bar with tears in her eyes. Doris sat quietly. Barbara was gone. Lily and now Barbara, they were all leaving.

The door opened, all three looked up with tear streaked faces. It was Barbara again damp-eyed and flushed.

"I'll see you all soon."

She reached over and touched Doris gently on the cheek, and was gone again. With a sigh Maeve picked up the sodden packet. She carefully avoided the drips that splashed onto the wet table top – Guinness would stain her grey woollen cardigan – and placed it carefully on top of the overflowing ashtray, extinguishing Barbara's final cigarette which, despite being crushed and broken, had been sending a powerful column of smoke high into the air. Red lipstick, an extravagance she had only taken to lately, marked each of Barbara's stubs, singling them out from the earlier heap of saliva stained roll-ups. As Maeve pressed down distastefully on the damp cardboard a small cloud of grey ash erupted over the rim of the ashtray, floated for an instant, before the pale flecks of dust began to settle across the liquid surface shimmering on the dark blue table top. Without thinking Maeve reached for her handbag, that rested reassuringly against her right foot, took out a new pack of paper handkerchiefs, ripped open the cellophane wrapper, and began mopping up the spilled beer. Balancing the soaking paper mass on top of the cigarette pack she got up and carried the full ashtray to the bar, where she pushed it through one of the rotating windows and closed it behind her. Before she had returned to her seat it had reappeared on the snug side of the bar, empty.

"All part of the service, Ladies."

Maeve retrieved it and placed it back in the centre of the table.

"Not that we'll be needing it now. They should really come round and clear the ashtrays once in a while, you know. For us that don't smoke."

"Bloody hell, Maeve. Why don't you use your eyes? Can't you see they're busy?"

At any other time Margaret would have gone on teasing Maeve about her fastidiousness, her killjoy spirit – if it couldn't be Doris then Maeve was almost as good a target – but today she hadn't the heart. Departures frightened Margaret and for once she had no desire to be alone, she needed the emotional support of her friends. It would be easy to drive Maeve away. It was simple to offend her high-minded principles, but to her surprise Margaret found she needed her, particularly now that Doris was so difficult to talk to. Margaret needed someone to stop her sliding alone into a terrifying future. Maeve was her last hope because, as Margaret was increasingly only too well aware, her natural vindictiveness had long ago hidden from view any of her other emotions beneath an angry and mean facade. At least Maeve knew her, had put up with her for all these years. Maeve, however, was too preoccupied with memories of her past to notice Margaret's restraint.

"You know it's not true that Barbara never cries, don't you?"

Margaret couldn't help herself. "You don't say! I could have sworn she was smiling when she stuck her head round that door a minute or two ago."

"But you know how she went on about never crying after

what happened to her? Well, I saw her cry before. More heard, really, if the truth be told. It was years ago."

"Maeve, what are you talking about?"

"I know she was crying just now, we all saw her, we were all crying, but then I heard her sobbing her heart out in the Ladies, all on her own."

Intrigued Margaret drained her glass of Guinness. Barbara was the only one of her friends who she'd never been able to satisfactorily bait, whose armour she'd never been able to pierce. But now she was hearing that there may have been a chink, it was just too good to be true, even if it was too late.

"Delicious! Doris, I think it's your round. I'll have the same again."

Doris looked up, confused, at the mention of her name.

"We'll be getting drunk."

"And why not on a day like this? Will you not be having one then, Maeve?"

"Oh, go on then, just the one."

"Not the first time you've had a few then?"

"No, of course not. You know, on special occasions."

"I'm sure."

They both looked at Doris, who smiled weakly, absolutely at a loss as to what they were talking about. Margaret held out her glass impatiently.

"Two Guinness's and whatever you're having."

Her lips quivering, eyes watering, Doris spoke softly, fighting to keep control.

"Barbara, we should drink to her. I'll get us another one. It must be my turn by now."

"At last! Doris you should pay more attention."

Barbara always got the drinks. She knew the barmen, could crack a joke with them, knew the rules, the etiquette. Doris was far from sure she could cope on her own. But Margaret looked determined, so viciously set, on her going to the bar that there was no alternative.

"Margaret, please. Here, Doris, I'll pay. I never like going up myself," Maeve put in.

"You're too soft, Maeve, you really are. Doris, are you going? If you don't get a move on, I'll be dying of thirst before you get back."

The voice of command came from a distance and Doris obeyed, moving to the bar clutching the money Maeve had thrust into her hand. She opened one of the small windows, leaving it positioned at right angles to the bar as she had seen her friend do many times before, and waited.

"Anyway, Maeve, I want to hear what you were saying about Barbara," Margaret pressed her. "You're absolutely sure?"

In an instant Maeve's concern for Doris had evaporated and she pulled her chair closer to Margaret.

"Certain. No doubt about it. It was Barbara and she was really upset. Crying her heart out, she was, in the toilets. In the one furthest from the door, you know, the one below the window. I peeped under the door just to check. It was her shoes".

Margaret nodded.

"Why was she crying, do you know? She was usually so tough."

"It was just after I was made a trusty and she wasn't. I liked Barbara and thought she deserved to be one, she'd been trying hard, but I was so pleased that I had got it. It was something I'd been wanting for such a long time. I should have liked to be a nun, you know, if things had been different."

Another silence. Margaret sniffed contemptuously.

"I felt guilty enough about it, I can tell you. It's not nice to win out over a friend. But when I heard her crying like that, I felt terrible."

Doris triumphantly placed a glass of Guinness down in front

of Maeve. The small circular metal tray she was carrying was swimming with foamy cream liquid. Margaret pulled a beer mat towards her and Doris carefully lowered a dripping glass onto it. As she did so her glass slid across the tilting tray, catching the upturned edge and almost toppled over. Reacting with a start, Doris levelled the tray and grabbed the glass, splashing her hand with beer.

"That was easier than I expected. What's his name was very friendly. What do I do with this?"

She stood looking round, still holding the empty tray with both hands.

"Take it back, then sit down and be quiet. Maeve is telling us about Barbara and when she cried."

"Thanks, Doris," Maeve said politely. Then to Margaret: "Well, after I'd heard her like that I went to see the Reverend Mother and I told her. I asked her if there was any way Barbara could be made a trusty, I even offered to let her take my place.

"You didn't?"

Maeve crossed herself.

"I said I wouldn't mind if Mother wanted to reconsider. I didn't want to give it up really, Margaret. But Mother was just looking at me, you know like she does. I had to do something."

"So what did she say?"

Doris sat down and raised her glass.

"Let's drink to Barbara."

"Shut up Doris we're talking. You should listen, this is interesting."

Margaret made no effort to hide the exasperation in her voice.

"Maeve … what did she say?"

"Well, she didn't say anything for a while, then just asked me why? It was embarrassing, us both just standing there."

"So what did you do?"

"Well you know how she gets sometimes – hard and sort of towers over you – she got like that. I knew I had to tell her. So I did. I told her everything. About her crying, about me feeling bad as she was a friend. She asked me if Barbara had put me up to coming to see her. I said no, but I'm not sure if she believed me as she got that determined look of hers and backed away from me and went and sat down."

"Is that all?"

"Wait will you. No, that's not all."

Maeve coughed, relishing the moment as the balance between them swung briefly in her favour.

"Mother's voice changed, became softer, more caring so it seemed. She said she'd thought about it all for a very long time and knew she had made the right decision. She would not be changing her mind, even though she appreciated what I had done in coming to see her. Barbara didn't know how good a friend she had in me. But, and she said this very quietly, told me I was to keep this to myself, Barbara was too mouthy by half and had a cruel temper to boot. She said Barbara was not at all suitable to be a trusted girl and never would be."

"It's lucky you made it then."

"Give over, Margaret."

Doris was staring at them, a strange knowing look that silenced Maeve, reminding her chillingly that memories could be dangerous things.

Chapter 5

Maeve's round – May 1949

"Come with me Maeve."

Father Brady's hand was cool and smooth to the touch, his skin tanned, the nails finely manicured.

"A nice walk in the garden is what's called for. The weather's lovely and the blossom is out. It's a picture."

A tall man in a dark black suit, he towered over Maeve, a diminutive attractive girl of fifteen, her long thick dark hair pulled severely back from her face and held in a pony tail by a red rubber band. She was drably dressed in a grey skirt, a white blouse buttoned to the neck, a green cardigan darned at the elbows, white ankle socks and sensible highly polished brown shoes that creaked as she walked. They could have been father and daughter, grandparent and grandchild, but there was no joy in their bearing. Their bodies seemed to pull apart and while he looked around at the delights of his garden, she stared at her feet. The priest said very little, but when he did speak Maeve would silently glance up at him her face wan and sunken, dark bags lining her brown eyes, one of which, he noticed, was slightly bloodshot. She was very pretty, he thought in passing, she needed looking after. He found he enjoyed being her protector and squeezed her hand gently.

For Maeve it was strange to have any form of physical contact. After all, it had been such a long time since she had even held hands with anyone. It had been frowned on at home, not something that you did at her age and certainly not in public. But you couldn't really argue with your priest, even Mother would have had to agree with that. She had been so strict about almost everything with her children: what they wore, how they behaved, how they spoke, the friends they could have. And it had got worse as she had got older and the family larger. Her mother had become so short-tempered and angry about everything Maeve did. She couldn't understand what she had done to deserve such God-less children, she said. Maeve was the oldest so she should know better; the young ones followed her example. She must try harder, confess all her sins and make herself a better person, it was the only way things would ever improve. They went to Mass every day as a family, neatly dressed, walking in line, their mother cheerily greeting all the neighbours. Then on their return a black cloud would descend upon her and for the slightest thing the blows would silently fall, the only sounds the occasional grunt from their mother's exertions and her hissing voice as she quoted the Bible at her cowering offspring.

Maeve believed she was a terrible daughter, a disgrace to her parents, although her father was rarely around these days. She couldn't do anything right and what shamed her mother more than anything was her lack of religious devotion. Jesus expected much better from her, she knew that. She deserved the beatings even though they hurt so much. You wanted to scream out, but that only made things worse and you then would have to spend hours on your knees upstairs in front of the Virgin Mary, praying for forgiveness, your whole body aching from the blows to your back and legs, and from the hunger gnawing at your insides. It was her penance and she would pay it. They spoke to her in the dead of night, when the cold wind was blowing in through the open window, the sheet gripped tightly around her neck, her teeth chattering. They would tell her about the children, who were playing, always playing. They never got any older, forever smiling and waving. It was paradise. She was sure.

Father Brady's grip didn't slacken until he had led Maeve firmly across the lawn to a wooden seat positioned under the shady canopy of a tall cherry tree covered in white blossom. He then let go of her hand, swept the bench clear of fallen petals and sat down.

"Join me, Maeve, won't you. I've something to say to you."

She hesitated, noticing the view for the first time. From where she was standing the lawn sloped gently down to a well-tended border of variegated greens and browns. Beyond she could see the spire of St Joseph's and the roofs of the town, the smoke from the many chimneys smudging the detail of the fields that stretched away to the undulating horizon. The hazy blue sky was dotted with clouds and the air smelled faintly perfumed. In an uncharacteristic moment of abandon Maeve reached up and pulled down an overhanging branch. On tiptoe she thrust her face into a cluster of white flowers and breathed in deeply. It was the scent of the playground, the children were running she could hear their laughter; it was impossible not to join in. She smiled and her dulled eyes brightened. Taken aback the priest shifted slightly as she sat down.

"It's beautiful, Maeve, isn't it?"

"It is, Father."

"I come out here everyday when it's fine. I feel close to God in a place like this. It's my Garden of Eden."

They sat for a moment, white petals loosened by the warm breeze, drifting past them like a gentle snowfall. Maeve raised her face and staring up through the branches let the fluttering shapes brush her skin. The priest closed his eyes. He was a holy man, he really believed that, and this was close to heaven. Earthly rewards he knew, but that couldn't be a sin, he refused to believe it.

"Maeve."

For a moment he couldn't bring himself to open his eyes.

"Yes, Father?"

He didn't want this to be a chore. He cared about this family, this girl, but the wind on his face, the dappled sun, were such temptations. He flung out his legs and let his clasped hands drop into his lap, his head lolled backwards. His muscles tingled in anticipation as he stretched his body, flexing his toes and squeezing his fingers. Finally he blinked several times as he hauled his body upright and turned to face the young girl sitting beside him.

"This has not been a happy time for you."

To show his concern he extended his arm along the back of the wooden bench towards her, but held back from any physical contact. Maeve glanced over her shoulder at him, the redness in the corner of her eye shocking in its incongruity, then turned away and looked down.

"You know your Mother has not been well for some time?"

Petals were gathering in Maeve's lap, she was counting – three so far, a fourth just fluttering past her bruised knee – these would be the number of children she would have when she was grown-up. She would love them all, but she would be strict and teach them the right way to do things. That was only right.

"Don't you, Maeve?" he pressed her.

"Yes, Father."

"Look at me child. I asked you to come here on your way home from school because this is very important."

Her mouth quivered imperceptibly and to the priest it appeared as if her small frame was collapsing as she exhaled heavily and hunched forward, only to snap rapidly upright again after brushing the blossom from her skirt.

"Sorry, Father."

"That's all right dear."

His arm grazed her shoulder.

"It's not an easy time for any of us."

She smiled feebly and for the first time he noticed that one of her front teeth was chipped. The jagged angle disturbed the equanimity of her face, the delicate features, the high hair line all part of an essential symmetry that was charming. She somehow appeared imperfect and damaged, which irritated the priest for he knew this to be unfair. Maeve was a pretty innocent in need of protection, not correction. She had been unlucky that was all and it was up to him to change that.

"Your Mother has been taken to hospital."

Maeve got to her feet, a concerned expression on her face.

"Sit down, child. There's not been an accident. She's gone to Mount Carmel. It's for her own good. They can look after her there."

"Why? There's nothing wrong with her."

"It all got too much for her. It's for the best, Maeve, believe me."

It didn't seem possible. Her mother had never been ill. Her children were always ailing, but not her.

"How long is she going to be there?"

"A long time, I think Maeve. The doctors say she is very tired and needs rest and quiet."

"When can I see her?"

She was beginning to have difficulty breathing. Her chest felt tight and she had to gulp air. She was suddenly very hot.

"Soon, soon. Now there is no need to worry. You'll be looked after."

As she began to shake, the priest grasped her firmly by the

shoulders. The harshness of his grip focussed her attention and she stared up at him, taking rapid shallow breaths.

"Calm down, Maeve. I know it's been a shock to you, but you're all safe and sound. You and your brothers and sisters. Your father doesn't feel that he …"

She began to cry and collapsed into the priest's arms. He patted her gently before continuing.

"He doesn't feel he can look after you. So the nuns will care for you all, for the time being anyway, until your mother is well. And, Maeve, they have a special job for you. They thought you were just right for it."

The only response from her was a faint tremor. Maeve found she was listening, the voice of the priest resonating through his chest a comfort, even though as yet she felt unwilling to stop crying.

"They want you to help in the Convent laundry. They have so much work, they're kept very busy. You'd like it, I'm sure."

Her head felt hot to the touch.

"I could look after them myself. I could".

Her voice was muffled and broken, the words indistinct.

"What's that, Maeve?"

She sniffed.

"I could take care of Brendan and Gavan and …"

"No Maeve. You were felt to be too young and, if I may say, too pretty to be left without any firm moral guidance, so the laundry was seen to be an ideal place for one such as you. You're a good girl, Maeve, sufficiently devout to draw all the necessary lessons from those less fortunate than yourself."

***

"Sister Elizabeth, I have your clean clothes."

"Ah, Maeve, come in, put them on the bed and close the door."

"Yes Sister."

Maeve glanced up and down the Convent corridor. It was deserted. Her linen trolley stood empty at the far end next to a tall dust-laden aspidistra. The early morning sun was shining directly through a window half-way along, casting its grid-like shadow on to the magnolia walls. The nuns had just returned from Matins in the chapel and Maeve always tried to have their clean laundry waiting for them in their cells when they got back. She was a little late today having slept badly the night before, but her final delivery was always to Sister Elizabeth. Her cell was the last one on the upper floor, on the corner with views of the gardens and the roofs of the houses beyond the Convent wall. A simple wooden crucifix was the sole adornment on the plain white walls. There was a narrow single bed and a small bedside cabinet on which Sister Elizabeth kept her Bible and a framed picture of Saint Teresa. It was very quiet, the only sounds were birds and the occasional drift of traffic noise from the main road. For Maeve, used to the bustle of communal living, this cell was a retreat. Sister Elizabeth didn't count as an annoyance, she was a friend, unlike the others she was always a pleasure to be with. A calm, cool presence, her soft whispering voice a balm for Maeve's tormented conscience, a confessor unlike any man she had ever met. The nun had saved Maeve from depression when she was sent to the laundry after her mother and her family had been taken away from her and had kept her afloat over the years ever since. For that reason her friend thought her beautiful, the delicacy of her features, sparkling blue eyes in a pale unlined face, her corn yellow hair cropped short, were punctuation in the letters of love that swirled through Maeve's mind. There was half an hour until Lauds.

"Sit down beside me."

Sister Elizabeth patted the bedspread with her hand. Maeve smiled and placed the pile of fresh smelling clothes on the end of the bed and sat down next to the nun. It was such intimacy, with their hips and thighs touching, that Maeve felt invigorated and charged her with a sense of well-being she had never known before. Hungrily, with eyes closed, she savoured the moment, briefly assuaging an appetite heightened by her emotional malnourishment. She gratefully rested her head on the nun's shoulder.

"Liz. Oh no."

The pile of washing teetered for a second, as the weight of their two bodies sitting side by side on the bed distended the ancient straw mattress, before toppling over and spreading an underskirt, blouses, vests and pants across the polished wooden floor. The bed creaked alarmingly as Maeve leapt to her feet.

"I'm sorry."

"It's not your fault, silly."

Elizabeth glanced nervously at the bed as Maeve got down on her knees and began gathering up the scattered clothing.

"Liz?"

Maeve giggled, for a second appearing carefree and abandoned. It was a sound Elizabeth liked to hear, a sight she needed to see, for though she loved Maeve, finding her neat, compact beauty overwhelming on occasions, there was a darkness that clung to her in her unguarded moments that even after all this time scared a true believer. In her laughter there was a light, the child had returned, it meant you could forget.

"Yes?"

"I've always wondered about this."

She gazed up at her friend over her left shoulder, amused that she could see through her own nose. It was such a very long time since she had noticed that, a time when there were brothers and sisters, a time when your body could still surprise you.

"What? You're looking very guilty."

"We've talked about it in the laundry..."

"What?"

"… but no one seems to know the answer."

"What? Come on Maeve, stop teasing me."

"It's a big puzzle to us all."

"Maeve?"

Maeve picked up a pair of Elizabeth's pants from the floor and placed them on top of the growing pile of laundry, then looked up again.

"Why do none of you wear a bra?"

"What?"

"You heard me Liz. Why do none of you wear a bra? You don't."

"How do you know?"

"I know."

Amused Elizabeth turned away, her face flushed.

"Don't go all shy on me Liz. We wash all your clothes, remember. None of you have any bras, not even the Reverend Mother."

"Maeve!"

The nun couldn't help herself, she began to giggle.

"You don't, do you?"

Maeve tickled Elizabeth's ankle.

"Own up. You don't, do you?"

"Stop it, please."

"Tell me. You don't have a bra, do you?"

The bed creaked as Elizabeth sat down heavily, her body shaking with laughter.

"No, I don't. I don't! Now stop it."

Maeve turned back to the scattered clothing.

"Why?"

"What?"

"Why don't you?"

"I haven't seen one in ages."

Elizabeth reached across and ran her fingers over the outline of the clasp of Maeve's bra, clearly visible through the taut nylon of her laundry overall. Maeve stiffened at the fleeting touch.

"'cept yours, of course."

Getting to her feet, Maeve turned holding the pile of washing. She wanted to hug her friend.

"Where do you want these?"

"Put them over there in the corner, by the cabinet."

Sitting down again on the bed, Maeve put an arm round Elizabeth.

"You still haven't told me."

"What?"

"Liz! About the bras."

"You don't give up, do you?"

She touched Maeve briefly on the end of her nose, then ran her finger slowly over the tip and down between the nostrils and the ridges on her soft upper lip, coming to rest on her front teeth. They both hesitated – the finger tasted faintly of carbolic soap – then Maeve kissed it. The silence was sublime, for an instant, they were the only living things on earth, then a distant voice and the slamming of a door opened their eyes, reminding them who they were and where they were. That smile would never leave her though, Maeve vowed, it was hers to treasure forever.

"You have them when you're a novice."

Dreamily Maeve gazed at Elizabeth. She had such perfect teeth, glimpsed between lips so pale they were barely distinguishable from her flawless white skin, the fine down above almost invisible, even when this close, except when it occasionally caught the light from the window as she spoke. And her breath smelled so sweet.

"You're not listening are you, even though you were so interested a minute ago?"

"I am."

"What did I say then?"

It was delicious – like waking after a night of deep sleep, her body resurfacing from some kinder more tranquil place – she could almost taste the cold fresh air of a new morning.

"Something about … I wasn't listening, you're right."

As they laughed, their foreheads touched and they held each other by the hand.

"You are a silly, you should pay more attention."

"It's difficult when I'm with you."

"Maeve!"

"But it's true."

"I know it is, but you shouldn't say it, that's all."

"Why? If it's true."

"You know why, we've been through it many times. Come on, don't look so disappointed."

She squeezed Maeve's hand.

"Don't you want to know the big secret?"

"Yes I do and it had better be good though."

Elizabeth could barely keep a straight face as she watched Maeve's hurt, petulant expression dissolve almost instantly, like a child's, into one of joy-filled playfulness.

"Only for the initiated."

"Good, I like secrets".

"I hope you won't be disappointed."

"I won't, now tell me."

"I just said that we all wore bras when we were novices, as far as I know anyway, and they get taken away after your profession. One day the laundry comes back and they are not there".

"Who takes them?"

"I've no idea. You should know more about that than I do, working in the laundry."

Maeve shrugged her shoulders.

"I don't know where they go either, if that's what you are thinking."

"Maybe we get them."

"Maybe. More likely there's a cupboard somewhere full of them. They're not really the sort of thing you can give away are they?"

"Oh, I don't know, I could do with a new one, this one's very worn."

Through her overall she stretched one of the shoulder straps of her bra with her thumb, then let it snap back, wincing as it stung her skin. The nun took hold of her hand again.

"Be careful, that's one thing we don't have to worry about."

Maeve laughed.

"That's not the only thing, but still."

"Anyway, losing your bra is all part of forsaking the world, leaving our past lives behind and devoting our new one to Christ…"

Their hands parted and both women crossed themselves.

"… giving up our worldly goods, shaving our heads…"

Maeve nodded knowingly as their fingers entwined.

"… the renaming, the…"

"The what?"

"The renaming."

"Your real name isn't Elizabeth? You never said."

The nun was genuinely surprised at the shock in Maeve's voice, she had always imagined that her friend was well versed in all things to do with the one big love of her life – the Church and all its trappings.

"No, no, I've always been Elizabeth, well Liz really, that's why I like it when you call me that. You're the only one that does you know".

Silently Maeve mouthed the words, "I know."

"I used to be plain old Liz Cullen, but when I took my vows they thought …"

"Sister Liz doesn't sound quite right, does it?"

"No, so I became Sister Elizabeth of the Passion, forsaking Liz Cullen forever."

"Until you met me."

"Until I met you."

She gently pushed a stray curl behind Maeve's ear. Instantly agitated, Maeve began fussing with her hair.

"Do I look a mess?"

"No, no. I'm sorry. Leave it alone Maeve, it's as lovely as always. Come on, you look tired."

"I didn't get much sleep last night. I just lay awake thinking."

"I know. You think too much for your own good. Let's lie down and have forty winks. I don't have to be in the chapel for another fifteen minutes or so."

Gratefully Maeve let herself fold into Elizabeth's arms and together they lifted their feet off the floor and fell back onto the creaking bed. Even though she was slightly taller than Elizabeth, Maeve always felt like a child when they lay together. Enveloped in a warm embrace, with her back hard against the cool wall, it was the safest place she had ever been.

Doris was annoyed. She should have been having a cup of tea with the others, now she was having to deliver clean towels to the Sisters because Maeve had forgotten to pick them up earlier. Admittedly, they hadn't been in their usual place in the airing cupboard – Bernadette had been late bringing them in from the lines and had only time to fold and stack them and leave them just inside the laundry door – but if Maeve had just looked. Now she was late coming back from her round and if Doris didn't take them, then there would be no time later.

It was a beautiful day, one that Doris had missed out on as she had been inside since opening the laundry in the semi-darkness of a misty summer morning. Her mood was dark. With the linen trolley missing, Doris had had to make several journeys to carry all the towels that were needed and they weighed more than she had imagined. It was hot work and to make matters worse all the Sisters were in their rooms after Matins and she had to apologize to each one for disturbing them. It was embarrassing and Doris swore she'd have a word or two to say to Maeve when she showed up from who knows where. She was doing this more and more often, just disappearing, maybe she'd taken up smoking and wanted to keep it secret, although that didn't seem like the Maeve she knew.

Sister Elizabeth's door was the only one that was closed. All the other nuns had left theirs open, as was the tradition, and it had been easy to catch their attention and hand over a towel; now Doris was uncertain what to do. You weren't meant to disturb the Sisters, not without a good reason, that had been made very clear right from the beginning. She had just the one towel left to deliver and didn't want to carry it all the way back with her to the laundry – she'd only end up having to bring it back when the Sister complained – but she was reluctant to leave it on the floor outside. Doris noticed the door was slightly ajar and leant forward, pressing her ear as close as she could to the narrow gap. There was not a sound coming from inside. Hoping the room was empty, Doris nudged the door gently with her foot and it swung silently open to reveal the slumbering couple. The bed was partly in shadow – the sunlight from the window falling fully on Sister Elizabeth dividing the pair into light and shade – and it took Doris a second to realize who they were.

Aghast, she stepped back into the corridor and stood, biting her lip, gazing at the intimate tableau, dramatically lit and perfectly framed by the door. It was so quiet and peaceful that Doris felt incapable of moving, unable to say anything, yet she knew it was sinful to have and to hold such a secret. It was shocking that she had never guessed about Maeve and it made her angry that her troubled friend, in all her years of unhappiness, should never have turned to her. They had spoken for so long about many things, but nothing about this, not a word.

Doris needed to tell someone, to scream and shout, to make a lot of noise, but instead she just stood there, knowing she would soon close the door behind her, creep away and never speak to Maeve again. But that didn't seem to be enough to Doris. Expectations were such dangerous things and when they failed there was only pain. She had believed in Maeve, she had been one of the certainties in her life, one of that small band with whom, back to back, she would face the world. Now with her defences breached, what was left but to flee?

"Doris Blaney, what are you looking at?"

The familiar voice, out of time and place, jolted Doris and she whirled round with a hissing intake of breath to face the Reverend Mother bearing down on her.

"That's Sister Elizabeth's cell, what do you think you are up to?"

A vestigial loyalty to her old friend motivated the mouthing of a few words in mitigation, but fear stifled the sounds. There was really nothing to say, only things to be done – shout a warning, slam the door shut, bar the way with arms outstretched and let them escape. But Doris' heart wasn't in it and she stood aside as Sister Beatrice approached. Briefly face-to-face Doris was no match for the withering eyes and expression of intense suspicion, history dictating that she look away.

"You shouldn't be here. Explain."

An imperceptible change in the atmosphere of the space behind them – a rustle, a murmur – led Doris to glance over the Reverend Mother's shoulder. Slowly the nun turned round until she stood gazing into the room. Doris peered from behind her back. Maeve and Sister Elizabeth were sitting up on the bed, terrified, their arms still round each other's waists. The Reverend Mother crossed herself, her lips twitched fleetingly, but she said nothing. Meekly, but in perfect unison, the two women on the bed swung their legs onto the floor, then helped each other to their feet, where they stood hands clasped in front of them and heads bowed. Their arms and shoulders just touched. The Reverend Mother stood motionless, which scared Maeve even more. Retribution should be physical, words would not be enough for what she had done, her punishment should rain down from on high. She was ready.

The words when they came were clear, concise and devoid of any emotion, save the icy neutrality of authority. Doris was surprised to hear her name, convinced as she was that safely on the outside, she was invisible, a bit player in a moral drama of such significance that her role of mere witness had been reduced to nothing and written out of the script.

"Doris, don't you say a word to anyone about this. Is that clear? I will talk to you later. You two, my office, now."

***

Events moved quickly after that. Sister Elizabeth was sent immediately to the Convent of St James and St Michael. She was given no time to pack her belongings and didn't argue, accepting her banishment as a just and appropriate punishment. For her, her friendship with Maeve had been of the "particular kind" that she knew had no future, for it was solely of the present. As she left she told herself she had no regrets. After all, no harm had been done.

For Maeve, the shock of losing her best friend, the fact of which was broken to her as she was leaving the Reverend Mother's study, was leavened by the unbelievable news that she was to be made a trusted girl, something she had yearned to be for years. A promise of silence over what had happened that morning seemed a small price to pay for such an honour, as was the demand that she never contact Sister Elizabeth again. They had sinned after all, but as Sister Beatrice said, those that truly repent get their rewards both in heaven and here on earth. And Maeve did repent. Afterwards, as the news sank in she had felt fleeting pangs of guilt over Barbara, who everyone had expected to be made a trusted girl, but would now have to wait for who knew how long. Her concern, however, was nothing to the happiness she felt at her own success.

The Reverend Mother never did speak to Doris. She seemed to assume that she would say nothing about what had happened, exploiting for her own ends the friendship that she knew existed between Doris and Maeve. This angered Doris and she never really spoke to Sister Beatrice again.

***

The laundry was closed; it always shut early the day before the Corpus Christi parade. The chemically sweet smell of detergent hung in the air. The floor was still damp, water ponding in the shallow dips in the concrete; the misted windows, tracked by falling beads of condensation, were clearing in patches high up near the vents in the roof, allowing the late afternoon sun to shine through and catch the motes of dust dancing lazily in the constricted beams of light. The high narrow room was deserted except for the sparrows in the rafters. They reappeared the instant the sound of the machines died away, rustling and chirping high overhead, until muffled by the encroaching darkness. The occasional ragged and broken feather, the tiny yellow, white and brown splatterings across the dull green finish of the presses, the greys of the floor, were the only evidence they were ever there.

Maeve tried hard to spot them in their gloomy aerial world, but the occasional twitch of light as wings unfurled and pale bodies hurtled across the void, was all she ever saw. She loved birds, fed them crumbs from her windowsill, felt she knew them well enough to name them, so wanted her friends to be up there, enjoying themselves as much as she was, looking down and sharing her joy of the place she had come to love. But her eyes failed her, misted as they were, moisture-laden and unfocussed. She had to make do with her friends' basic staccato birdsong as the unseen choral backing to her pleasure at being there with them on that particular day.

Maeve truly believed things couldn't get any better. The heavy sodden labour of the laundry was for others now; she was a trusted girl. Gone was the pain of the early morning; limbs, almost immobile, aching from the cold. No more breaking icicles from the taps in the freezing scullery, the numbing water on the face, that dull throbbing in the joints of your hand – that physical premonition from an early age, noticed more and more often, of worse to come. Maeve could now get up later than the others, take a silent breakfast in the refectory with the nuns and then work on the Convent door taking in laundry that others would fetch and carry. She would be meeting people. She had almost forgotten how to talk civilly to others, it was a revelation: Bingo, the weather, illness, His Holiness, the Pope, families and even sometimes children. Then going out shopping with the nuns, after only a week she loved it all, though sometimes – well often – she'd wonder how it would be sharing it with Liz. Curling up and telling each other everything they had done that day just like they used to. But better not think about that – Reverend Mother had told her not to. And now, best of all, she was to carry the Convent banner in the Corpus Christi parade through the streets of the city, where everyone would see her.

The anticipation had been almost unbearable, counting down the days in June until the first Thursday after Trinity Sunday – a holiday and one of the holiest days of the year. Maeve had always loved the crowds that flocked to watch the pageant, the songs and prayers, the decorations and the flowers. She had walked in such a procession every year for as long as she could remember: when young following her mother who would mutter earnestly about the Blessed Sacrament and the sacrifice of our Lord, her eyes forever searching the skies; more recently following the nuns who walked with eyes cast down, shutting out the world. She would hold her head high, now she had a leading role, marching close to Father Michael and the gold chalice with its precious holy bread. There would be blessings along the way and then mass at noon in the Cathedral… And they said it was going to be fine tomorrow – sunshine with the occasional cloud and a light breeze from the southwest. Her prayers were truly being answered.

A heavy iron was best for doing your clothes – skirt and blouse, cardigan if it got chilly, the long ankle length cape and linen head-dress – not forgetting your underwear. Maeve knew not everyone bothered. As Barbara said, "There's no one going to see them. Who'd be interested, more's the pity?" But Maeve felt strongly it said something about yourself, was important. So that's why she had come back to the laundry. You got the smartest results there, crisp finish, razor-edged creases, with only the minimum of effort. After all, she had been ironing for most of her working life. The calluses on her hand exactly matched the indentations on the handle of the iron, it all felt so natural. It was not like using that lightweight affair they had in the dormitory, which took lots of effort for very poor results. When Maeve had finished she folded the neatly ironed clothes and carried them carefully upstairs to get ready. She cared, even if no one else did.

***

The tense exaltation before the parade was thrilling for Maeve. She was flying with her birds, somersaulting through the air, short of breath and flushed. The bright light of the sun flashed before her eyes. Giddy giggling, it was all in her head. She was feeling faintly nauseous now, her mouth arid one moment, a flood of saliva the next.

"Is it hot in here?"

A feeling like a fist in her stomach, opening and closing. Bursts of chatter and a noise in her head were all she could hear. Exasperated looks.

"Give over, Maeve."

Her tongue, snake-like, dampened cracked lips, a little finger catching a dribble of moisture at the corner of her mouth.

"How many more times, Maeve? You look fine so you do."

Maeve's hand again touched that wayward curl of hair standing proud on the back of her head, unresponsive to her damping, combing and brushing. Why, on a day like this? Barbara was right, she knew that, it would be covered by her head-dress, nobody would see, nobody would know. But on this of all days she wanted it to be perfect. Just so.

It was her Mother who always said that, self-satisfied, herding her five children, youngest first, from the house to Mass in their Sunday best.

"You all look lovely, my dears. Just so."

Her Mother, Eilis, returning to her once more now she was back on the path to righteousness. Where had she been? Dreams, past and present, were disturbed by recollections of family life. The blank face of her Father, a physical presence without any identity, standing behind and to one side of her. Eilis's devotion to her family knew no bounds, her will strengthened by the knowledge of her mission on earth. As the blows rained down on her kneeling children, their knees scabbed and raw, she would berate them with biblical quotations – the words tumbling and sliding around and over their bare defenceless heads – screeds of them that Maeve could still repeat word for word years later.

Now was the day of the parade and at the age of twenty-four she was turning into her Mother. She could imagine what it was like to fill her very body, Maeve's slimmer form expanding to fit perfectly the plumper, more solid contours, their minds merging, a greater clarity of thought, a certainty sometimes lacking. And the Virgin Mary would stare beatifically down, her tears fatter, her smile that little bit broader.

"You look lovely, Maeve. It'll be fine."

"You sure?"

She had to look her best; all eyes would be on her.

"Like an angel."

"Give over, will you, you'll have me blushing."

Maeve's cheeks reddened at the attention she was getting, embarrassed that her efforts to prepare herself for this great honour should have become so public. It didn't feel right to her that on the day of the Corpus Christi parade, when they were supposed to be gathering to honour the ultimate sacrifice of our Lord, she should be getting all this praise. That she should be the focus of attention. She knew she would have to pay later, but then compliments were very reassuring. She waved them away.

"Jesus, it's true! Why hadn't I seen it before?"

"What?"

Everyone turned away from Maeve, ensnared by the tone of amazement in Margaret's voice.

"What, Margaret? Come on, tell us."

"You don't look like an angel at all…"

Maeve's ebullient mood faltered, Margaret could be so cruel sometimes and ecstasy was such a fragile thing.

"…you look like you're getting married. You look just like a bride."

There was silence.

In one brief sentence Margaret had conjured up the unfulfilled aspirations of almost everyone in that room – a sunlit dormitory with clothes scattered across neatly made beds, a wooden floor polished to a mirror-like brightness, the scent of cheap perfume floating in the air. Had conjured them up and dangled them over the bowed heads and resigned, sighing faces, then quickly dispelled them with a loud, undignified snigger.

"Only joking! I was just kidding. Forgive me, Maeve?"

The others muttered and cursed Margaret under their breath, before turning away. Maeve said nothing. She just sat down on her bed, smoothing out her white linen cloak beneath her. It tugged tightly at her neck and she had to stand again to release the pressure. As she sunk back on to her patchwork quilt she smiled. That was the nicest thing Margaret had ever said to her. She knew she hadn't meant it to be a compliment, of course, but a bride was all she had ever wanted to be, a bride of Christ. Her mother had wanted it too, her oldest daughter married into the Church.

"Trim your lamp wise virgins, behold the bridegroom comes; go forth to meet him."

They had talked about her becoming a postulant, had spoken to the priest, had discussed the vows of poverty, chastity and obedience. She had fallen in love with what seemed the most natural thing in the world. The black habit, head covered by a white band and a heavy black veil, the torque wound tightly and her hair cut to fit under it, the scapular hanging down almost touching the ground. At the age of eleven Maeve had started getting up at five o'clock in the morning to pray silently at the foot of her bed. The small statue of the Virgin Mary that Auntie Betty had bought for her during a pilgrimage to Knock, standing alone on her bedside table and slowly coming into view as dawn broke. A yellow light filled the room, the sleeping form of her sister, breathing heavily, was so familiar that Maeve felt alone. Watching the smoke rise from the neighbour's chimney into the navy-blue sky, cloudless except for dark shadows along the horizon, her devotion had felt complete. She had prayed and prayed, but it had not happened then. Maybe things would be different now?

She hauled herself to her feet and strode across the room to Margaret's bed, grasped her friend firmly by the shoulders and to the surprise of everyone, kissed her firmly on the forehead. Margaret's face was a picture to behold.

There was still one nagging doubt. Maeve had feared it would happen and it had. She was well and truly Cursed.

Women's trouble.

Maeve never really knew when it was going to catch up with her. At least she never ran out of sanitary towels as a result, was always very careful to keep well stocked up. The only good thing she could say was it didn't affect her that much, not like some she could mention. It came and it went, with only the very occasional stomach cramp to mark its passing. But now, on her "Big Day", the day of the parade, it did annoy Maeve. For a woman as fastidious as her, it cast a blight, but what could she do about it? There was no way she was going to miss the procession. It was just the cross she had to bear.

The banner was leaning limply against the wooden partition next to the inner door to the Convent hallway, exactly where Frank, the handyman had said it would be.

"No respect, that man."

Maeve crossed herself. The yellow cloth was crumpled, a deep crease obscuring much of Mary Magdalen's face and body, the gold brocade that ran along the top edge looked tangled and dirty in the dim light, the wooden pole scuffed and worn. There was barely time for her to register any feeling before the force of numbers at her back thrust her forward and without thinking, she had picked up the banner and stepped through the open doorway. The flag was heavier than she had imagined, the wood smooth and comfortable to the touch. Her forehead chilled instantly in the fresh breeze that blew rose-perfumed from the Convent garden. The fragrant air was invigorating and inspiring, banishing for the moment a creeping sense that all was not right.

Everyone was finally ready and in plenty of time, gathering behind Maeve in the hall of the Convent, searching out their partners as they had rehearsed the day before. The women's excitement was muted by the presence of the Reverend Mother standing alone on the third step of the stairway surveying the crowd milling just below her. The occasional whispered greeting was the only sound to rise above the shuffle and squeak of shoes moving across the highly polished floor. The grandfather clock standing in the alcove by the parlour door struck eleven, the chimes muffled by the unusual mass of bodies that encircled it. There was still ten minutes to go until the parade began, because as the marchers knew, all the clocks in the convent were fast. It was one of Sister Beatrice's little foibles.

"Punctuality is a virtue, ladies." A pause then a knowing smile. "One of those where I've found it does no harm to cheat a little." A forefinger briefly brushed her lips. "Don't tell a soul."

Maeve stared at the demure statue of the Virgin Mary, standing in front of her on the lawn, eyes cast down, hands clasped in prayer, surrounded by a bank of red carnations and pink and yellow roses. She was beautiful, her veil the purest white, her gown the palest blue. Maeve yearned to be loved by her, wished that she could in some small way be like the Madonna. She knew she would continue to try, but there was a certainty to the knowledge, which left a very bitter taste that only the little white pills could sweeten, that she was fit, and would always be only fit, to honour that other Mary whose banner she would be holding aloft today. That woman who witnessed the Resurrection, yet who was once as sinful as they come; a "redeemed whore" as Father James so emphatically put it every Easter:

"Now when Jesus was risen early the first day of the week, he appeared first to Mary Magdalen, out of whom he had cast seven devils..."

Maeve would hold that banner so high that it would hurt, her muscles rebelling against the pain. It would be her penance.

"You all right, Maeve? You looked to be miles away." Lily touched her on the arm. "Is that too heavy for you? I'd use that belt you've got for support if I was you. We've a long way to go."

Maeve nodded. She loved Lily, face flushed, long hair already escaping from her red headband, her enthusiasm infectious.

"You're right, I will. Is it time to go?"

"Yes, Sister sent me out to get Our Lady here ready, she has to lead the way."

"I know, I know."

For a moment Lily gazed quizzically at Maeve, taken aback by the look of her eyes, which appeared fixed and glassy. It was probably just nerves, but Lily couldn't be sure, sensing that it could be a forewarning of a much deeper malaise.

"Hey, watch out Lily, those are my corns you're treading on."

"I'm sorry, Barbara, I wasn't looking."

"No need to tell me. God that hurt."

"Sorry, I was ... I thought Maeve here was looking peaky."

"She does look a bit pale. You need some fresh air, Maeve."

A wan smile and a nod was all she could manage.

"I know."

"Come on, Lily, duty calls. Here's Helen and Pat – pall bearers extraordinaire."

"Give over, Babs, Sister will hear."

"She'd need bat's ears if she did."

Giggling quietly, the women stepped outside onto the lawn. Each moved to a corner of the floral plinth and in a mock display of military precision, nodded at each other, then together bent down and picked it up. The statue of the Virgin Mary swayed dangerously, almost falling as it rocked back and forth among the flowers. Maeve gaped at them wide-eyed.

"Watch it, she's going over."

Lily reached out a hand to steady the statue, almost letting the plinth slip from her grasp. It dipped unnervingly and one corner of the lace surround was dragged for an instant through a muddy puddle, staining the white embroidery an ugly brown. Embarrassed, the women stood to attention, eyes to the front, before glancing around, relief flooding their reddened faces as they realized no one except Maeve had seen a thing.

"Can you believe she's not screwed down?"

"It's that Frank."

"Will anyone notice that mark, do you think?"

"How bad is it? Sister Beatrice will only kill us."

"Helen, It's not that terrible. Now Lily, if you sort of stand in front of it no one will notice. It'll be all right."

"What about Maeve? She's looking very strange. She might tell, you know what she's like. Thick as thieves with the sisters."

"Don't worry about her. Maeve, you feeling better?"

Barely aware of the people around her, she was gazing up at the image of Mary Magdalen silhouetted against the blue sky. She squinted as the banner swayed gently across the face of the sun, alternately blinding then shading her eyes as it moved. Now unfurled above her head, it flexed in the breeze, the lead weights in the lining erasing the creases and holding the Holy image in shape, while the bright sunlight refreshed the vividness of the red, yellow and gold fabric. The glory of what she was about to do swept over Maeve and she again felt the excitement of being one of the chosen few. Hearing her name she smiled and nodded, but her attention was focussed elsewhere on the bright colours swirling through her mind.

"See she'll be fine, she's a friend."

"I hope you're right, Barbara. It would be bad to get into trouble on such a day as this."

Helen made a half-hearted attempt to cross herself, but the Virgin Mary began to move uncertainly again, and in mid-air her arm moved across to brace the statue.

"Give over will you Helen, you'll be getting us into even worst trouble if that falls over, just think of it."

"Stop it will you. I'll have to be putting this down."

The plinth began to shake – a pink rose petal fluttered down and landed at Lily's feet – as Pat fought to control her laughter. One hand covered her mouth and she bit hard on the soft flesh of her forefinger, but her body continued to convulse. Her amusement was infectious. Barbara and Lily, barely able to stifle their own giggles, tried to support the quivering platform with their free hands, while Helen held on to the statue and hissed frantically at Pat to get a grip, the desperation in her voice undermining the effectiveness of her pleas making them sound merely comic.

"Helen, please stop it. I've got to put this down. I've got to. I can't help it."

The plinth tilted alarmingly as Pat lowered her corner to the ground, the others given no option and fearing disaster, followed suit.

"You idiot Pat, if I hadn't been holding onto the Virgin, she'd have smashed to bits. Please."

Crouching on the ground and gripping her sides, Pat rocked back and forth, her flushed face grinning inanely at Helen. The illicit mascara she was wearing betraying itself in dark smudges at the corner of her eyes. She mouthed a silent apology, before turning away consumed by laughter.

"Never mind, Pat."

Barbara, grinning, placed a sympathetic hand on Pat's shoulder, signalling with a nod of her head for Helen to leave her alone.

The harsh exasperated tone of the voice was familiar but
unexpected. Pat instantly wiped her mouth and stood up,
turning with the others to face the Reverend Mother, who was
standing in the entrance staring at them. The tall thin figure –
hands clasped, as always across her stomach, fingering the black
cord of her heavy iron crucifix that dangled almost to the floor –
appeared to Lily, Barbara, Helen and Pat to float above them. The
slight hook of her nose and the narrowness of her eyes gave her
a bird like quality that transfixed rather than reassured. Her lips
barely moved, but her voice, clear and precise, carried cleanly
across the garden, causing others to turn and stop what they
were doing, out of fear that it may be them she was addressing.
In the silence that followed, Barbara imagined she heard a faint
echo, reverberating off the high Convent walls and bouncing
back to underscore Sister Beatrice's authority.

"Can't you see we are ready to begin the procession? And
you seem intent on messing around. It's not good enough ladies,
on today of all days."

"Sorry, Sister."

Outside the Convent gates uniformed police were drawn up
in two columns, one on each side of the street. A small crowd
had also gathered and stood around chatting and laughing in the
balmy early summer sunshine. Shouting loudly two young boys
in shorts, long dark socks, grubby white shirts and patterned
sleeveless sweaters chased a small flock of pigeons that had been
feeding on biscuit crumbs outside O'Connell's, sending them
wheeling into the air. The birds swooped once then twice over
the heads of the crowd, tracked by the grinning upturned faces
of the boys, before rising to settle in a row on the roof of the
Convent chapel.

Maeve felt nauseous – the fist opened and closed slowly in her
stomach – but exhilarated, as the Reverend Mother accompanied

132

by Father Michael and a police officer began to move forward through the gates into Arden Road. They were followed by the Virgin Mary borne aloft once again on the shoulders of Barbara, Lily, Helen and Pat, and behind them in pairs more than twenty deep the Magdalen women, all identically dressed in white linen cloaks and veils. Maeve with her banner took up her place eight rows from the front in the middle of the column flanked by two escorts – Doris and Bernadette – who each grasped a guy line tied to the top of the banner pole, their role to hold the heavy flag upright throughout the march.

Dipping slightly to manoeuvre the banner under the low Convent gateway, Maeve saw the policemen forming up on either side of the column, the crowds beyond standing and staring, children waving, a baby crying. She wished there was someone out there who knew her, had come to see her big day, to clap and cheer, a witness to the fact that something special was happening. There was always this yearning for contact with a wider humanity that the Convent couldn't deliver. Belief was nothing if it couldn't be put to the use of others. Devotion needed the warmth of the living to make it real, the intellect alone led only to cold barren places. Flesh and blood had been lacking for so long, but now she had another chance. The people were out there waiting for her and she had never felt so proud as she did right now.

"All these Gardai – they must be afraid we'll run away, given half the chance."

"They look dead handsome, don't they?"

"They sure do, very respectable."

"Don't spoil it, Doris, please. And you, Bernie."

Maeve ignored the look that flashed between her two escorts and stared ahead over the bobbing, covered heads to the statue of the Virgin Mary that appeared to be tilting alarmingly to the left. Sister Beatrice was saying something and she could see Barbara – the sleeve of her red cardigan gaudy among the pastel pinks and yellows of the roses – clutching the robes of the Virgin. Her flushed profile expressed concern but had not entirely lost the look, which increasingly marked Barbara out from the rest of the laundry women, that said she appreciated the essentially humorous nature of everything that went on around her. If she hadn't liked Barbara, Maeve would have been appalled at such a flippant attitude to something she held very dear, but Barbara was Barbara and got away with so much by simple force of character.

They turned into Tullamore Place and slowly made their way round two sides of the Square. The cobbles underfoot were painful to walk on after the smooth tarmac, distending and distorting the soft soles of Maeve's shoes and twisting her ankles uncomfortably. There was the occasional car parked at the side of the road and the marchers were forced to break out of their tight formation and bunch up together in order to get through the narrow gaps. A dog was barking, its young owner desperately yanking on its lead to get it to turn away, but it seemed incensed at the sight of so many people in the normally quiet street and continued straining, its teeth bared and neck muscles bulging. The elegant Georgian houses set back from the pavements and marked off by iron railings, tall windows open to the sky, seemed familiar to Maeve, although she had never been there before, as far as she knew. She felt uneasy.

On the opposite corner of the Square from the one they had entered was the Convent of St James and St Michael. Nuns were lining the pavement outside to watch the parade. Was Sister Elizabeth among them? Maeve realized she would be and felt sick to her stomach. It had been seven months since they had last seen each other and there had been no letters, just as they had said there wouldn't be. Seven months since Elizabeth had been sent away. It was impossible for Maeve to escape; she was trapped between the warm bodies of Doris and Bernadette, and the women in front and behind her – the smell of their perfume overpowering.

The parade inched forward, the congestion and the close physical contact enough to puncture the formality of the occasion. A policeman almost lost his helmet, catching it just before it was trampled underfoot, there was laughter and he smiled. Voices were heard shouting compliments from the crowd, heads turned and there were blushes.

"You're looking gorgeous, to be sure."

Barbara curtsied, the Virgin Mary bobbed, Sister Beatrice glowered.

"You're too kind, sir."

"Will I be seeing you tonight, then?"

"Hush up, Barbara."

The young man shrugged and elbowed his friend, who smiled and waved.

"Maybe another time then?"

A young girl gazed down on them from a first floor window, her face pressed hard against the glass, her breath misting the pane. Doris waved but the girl didn't move, her arms raised as if in surrender, palms open. Below at the open door stood her mother, hair a mass of red curls, a cigarette in hand, a baby sitting on the step at her feet.

Maeve tasted bile on her tongue. Her body was damp with perspiration and her head thumping. Out of the corner of her eye, she scanned the row of nuns as they drew nearer. Anonymous blanched faces, shrouded in white and black, moved slowly past. She could barely breathe. Her eyes were closing, feet shuffling forward, legs shaking – the anticipation of the inevitable was closing her body down – she knew it would not be long now. She thought she heard a whistle, high pitched, in the distance. Then she was there. Sister Elizabeth.

Liz. Her face, partly in shadow, was watching intently but with no sign of emotion, eyes flicking back and forth as the marching women passed by. Maeve had been waiting all her life for that flare of recognition. When it came it was blinding and lifted her clear off her feet.

She fell sideways into Doris's arms who, caught unawares, slumped against the policewoman beside her, knocking her backwards across the bonnet of a parked van. The marchers behind pressed forward, tripping over the collapsed bodies and stumbling one into another before coming to a confused halt. The banner of Mary Magdalen toppled slowly into the milling crowd, despite Bernadette's efforts tugging on her guy rope, and was trampled underfoot.

Maeve came to, lying in the road surrounded by women. Someone had slipped a folded cloth beneath her head. There was a brightness to the day and a clarity. She heard a voice above her that she only half recognized.

"I knew this would never work – the girl's a disaster. She'll never make the grade."

"Shhhh! Look she's waking up."

People were nudging each other and staring down at her, but Maeve couldn't identify any of them. All she could see was Liz and the look of love she had glimpsed on her face only moments before. For the first time Maeve realized she had lost the chance to be close to someone who cared, a terrible price to have paid for the trusted girl.

Chapter 6

The Snug – March 1996 – twelve minutes past one

"Are you all right, Maeve?"

Doris hated to see anybody cry, particularly on a day like this, their last together. Maeve smiled, her face blotched and red.

"I must look a real sight."

"It's nothing, no one will notice."

"Talking about me again? You'd better have been saying nice things."

Margaret placed the two glasses down in front of her friends – Maeve's sat unsteadily across the edge of a beer mat – and turned to fetch her own glass from the bar. As she did so her foot caught on the leg of their table, nudging it violently and toppling the glass, black foaming liquid poured into Maeve's lap. Attempting to stand up to escape the worst of the deluge, she found her chair was wedged against the wall and she couldn't move. Slumping back into her seat she let out a long drawn out moan as she tried to dam the flood with her hands.

"Margaret!"

"Maeve, I'm sorry. I didn't mean…"

Margaret turned away, unable to hide her amusement. Doris covered her smiling face with her hands.

"Look at you two, sniggering! I'm soaked."

"I'm sorry, Maeve. It's just so funny."

Margaret's body was shaking as she leant up against the bar. Maeve could be really stuck up sometimes, so worried about her appearance, it grated. She glanced over at the table again and couldn't stop herself laughing. The indignant figure, trapped, scarcely able to believe what had happened to her, was too delicious a sight for words.

"I'll ask if they have a cloth," said Margaret, "or maybe a bucket. You could wring your skirt out in that."

"Stop it, Margaret. Stop making fun!"

"Come on, Maeve, it was an accident."

"You stop it as well, Doris."

Maeve felt a tightening across her forehead and the familiar pulsing in the temples, accompanied, as always, by pressure behind the eyes. The smirk on Margaret's face was unbearable. She wanted to lash out, close that gaping mouth and make her think. There was a tense pain in her chest. She needed her pills, but they were in her handbag on the floor. The thought struck with force – her favourite bag would certainly be soaked and the brushed suede stained so easily. Maeve crossed herself. She didn't feel she could speak and was finding it difficult to draw breath. Margaret stared back at her dispassionately, slowly wiping the sodden cloth in circles across the table top, sending small waves of Guinness rippling outwards towards the table rim, where, breaking, they sent a shower of droplets raining down onto the sawdust strewn floor, Maeve's skirt and handbag and Doris' black shoes.

"Margaret, look what you're doing." Doris was concerned about Maeve, "She looks unwell. Help me carry this out of the way."

The two women gingerly lifted the table and moved it as far as they could towards the bar. At the last moment Doris tilted her edge of the table and sent the remaining Guinness and the drenched cloth cascading towards Margaret, but she didn't seem to notice, even when the beer darkened her skirt in a broken line where the table briefly rested against it, focussed as she was on Maeve. There was now just enough room in the crowded snug to allow Maeve to stretch her legs.

"Are you all right?"

The air seemed to be rushing into her lungs. She could breathe, it was very stuffy, but she wasn't suffocating anymore. Her heart though was still pounding. She could feel the blood moving round her body, veins expanding and contracting, the valves opening and closing, like lock gates, swirling on and on. It scared her, the thought of the ancient gates crumbling, beginning to leak, the liquid running the wrong way. She nodded at Doris and waved her hand at the floor. Confused, Doris looked around at the scuffed heaps of sodden sawdust – the bright amber fading to ochre – a lipstick stained cigarette end, a torn beer mat, her own bespattered shoes. She wanted to help but one glance at her friend was enough to stop her dead – the ageing strained figure slouched in her chair, legs thrust uselessly out in front, the dark stain in the lap, hand swinging lifelessly, lips moving soundlessly. She stood and stared with Margaret, the pair of them incapable of turning away from this painful image of a looming future.

"My handbag, is it there?" faltered Maeve.

Margaret and Doris got down on their knees. The bag, which had been pushed hard against the dark wooden partition of the snug by the leg of Maeve's chair, took them seconds to find, enough for the two friends to exchange guilty glances.

"I need my tablets. They're in the little side pocket."

"Which ones, Maeve? There's three or four bottles in here."

"Show me. Those."

"How many?"

"Just the one."

The pill sat on her tongue and the anticipation made her body tingle, then the bitter taste as it was washed down. It wouldn't be long now. The relief of her aches and pains, the sense of well being, the delicious warm summer glow, the end of anguish. Doris looked concerned.

"Are you all right, Maeve? I was worried for a moment."

It was an enigmatic smile, but reassuring nonetheless.

"I'm feeling much better, thank you. You know I get these turns, but they soon pass."

"We were both worried."

Margaret's hand moved tentatively forward, trembled in mid air, then withdrew. Maeve closed her eyes. A wave was cresting above her – a child on the sand standing gleeful in the surf, water foaming around her legs – building, lifting her up, sweeping her away, the roar in her ears, to break on some distant reef. She held out her hand. Margaret pleased, beyond imagining, took it and squeezed.

Maeve smiled dreamily then glanced down taking in the dark stain on her skirt and the sticky smears streaking her handbag, before easing herself past the chairs and tables and slipping out of the snug.

"Poor Maeve, she takes these things so seriously," said Doris.

"Always has done. Too many crosses to bear, that one. Enjoys being a martyr a little too much," retorted Margaret, unable to resist a dig at her absent friend.

"You should try to be nice to her sometimes."

"You're a fine one to talk, Dot. Anyway it's good to have a moment to ourselves without her, she always seems to be around and we can never talk privately. I was just thinking that we've had some good times together over the years, haven't we? Like the Bingo? Won't you miss our trips, Doris, when you leave us here for your niece's new place?"

Doris shrugged. She enjoyed Bingo, it was a game she could play without thinking – any potential sense of loss tempered by a delicious drunken befuddlement.

"I doubt any of your new lot will go, living where they do."

"You're right, Margaret, you're right, but I won't miss it as much as you would."

"You're right Doris, you're right."

They laughed together collegiately, their mutual history of fractured friendship enforced by an unnatural man-made union had held them together over the years; Bingo had recently reunited them. For Margaret could think of nothing she would like to be doing more than sitting in the fading splendour of the Machusla Hall, cards on her lap, stub of a pencil in her hand, sucking on a barley sugar and listening to the rolling, rhyming patter of the bingo caller. It was a comforting, perfumed, smoke-filled female world where the only man, sitting on a pedestal in a gaudy suit, had total control over your destiny. Time had long ago erased any trace of her youthful resistance to such inequality. Margaret now submerged herself gratefully in a society where luck was all, guiding you relentlessly call by call.

Winning was divine and Doris was there to worship at your feet, admiring and complimentary; losing was human and Doris, self-absorbed, ignored you. It was such company that brought Margaret back to take her chances week after week, not the money she lost or won.

"You know when we first started on the Bingo, don't you, Doris? It was that time when we ran away from the Convent together. Waved good-bye to the nuns and the bloody laundry, or so we thought. Little did we know they'd catch up with us, but it was still a great adventure while it lasted, wasn't it? Maeve going on just now about being a trusty and Barbara crying brought it all back. It happened around the same time, didn't it? When was that – the mid fifties?"

"It must have been."

Doris wasn't really certain she was hopeless with dates.

"Those were the best of days. Do you remember, Doris, climbing the wall and running down Gerry Lane in the dark, those kids cheering us on?"

She nodded. It was all coming back, but she couldn't see it, couldn't feel it like Margaret obviously could.

"I don't think I've ever felt so free as then. It was beautiful weather and there was everything to live for. God, we had some fun."

Doris didn't know about that so much, but she squeezed Margaret's hand. It seemed the right thing to do and she could think of nothing to say. The door of the snug swung open and Maeve appeared. She looked happier.

"What are you two talking about?"

"Running away. Have you ever thought of escaping, Maeve? Leaving it all and starting something new?"

Margaret's tone was serious and Maeve sat down before answering.

"No, I haven't, not even in the worst times."

She shrugged.

"At least here you know somebody will be praying for your soul."

"I'll always be praying for you Maeve, even when we're not together."

"I know you will Doris. I was never as brave as you two. I could never have done what you did."

Margaret touched Maeve on the arm.

"Now I've got to go to the Ladies".

A stillness settled over Doris and Maeve as Margaret swept out of the snug. They sat together in companionable silence, both fingering their glasses. Voices could be heard in the bar next door shouting orders above the hubbub of the late lunchtime crowd. The till rang, pool balls clattered, a door opened and in the distance a glass smashed.

"Know who I saw the other day?"

Doris looked up, startled, and shook her head.

"Frank's wife."

Maeve was surprised to see the colour fade from Doris' face.

"She looks much older than she did. Gone really grey, but I suppose we can't talk."

"Why d'you think of her?"

"No reason really. It was just I bumped into her and was shocked. I suppose you don't think about it until you don't see someone for a good while, then you notice. I hadn't seen her since his funeral. That seems a long time ago."

"It was years."

"She didn't recognise me though, walked straight past. Expect she must be on her own these days. How many kids did she have?"

"Four, I think."

The snug door swung open.

"I hope you two weren't talking about me?"

"No, about Frank's wife."

Margaret's left eye twitched. To Doris and Maeve she looked a little flushed. She could feel the tiny muscle tugging persistently, it came and went, a nagging reminder of how fragile her life had become. For she knew that her veneer of respectability was a lot less than skin deep. Barbara – it could only have been Barbara – had once told her that. It was a safer world with Barbara gone, you could never really like someone who could see through you like that, but a less interesting one nonetheless. She would miss Barbara and Doris for very different reasons and she was already missing Frank. Without him she could almost enjoy life.

"Funny thing to be talking about, I haven't thought of him in ages."

"He just came up."

Doris sat there expressionless, staring at her glass. Margaret was unsure whether to laugh or cry. After more than thirty years she still couldn't tell whether Doris was the most intelligent person she knew or the most stupid. Doris had always been everybody's fool.

Chapter 7

Margaret's round – June 1953

"What time do you call this?"

Margaret paused, panting quietly in the hallway. Her Father was still up, sitting in front of the flickering fire in the darkened parlour. He had laid a trap for her, waiting alone, his fermenting anger strengthening with each passing hour. Never a physical man, he now wanted to hit someone. He resented his daughter, her behaviour and attitude, her lack of respect, the very words she used. It was galling to him that she looked so much like her late mother, his darling Mary, one moment filling his life with joy at the fond memories she sparked, the next tearing it apart with her blunt insolence. Margaret's older sister, who her Father supposed looked like him, her slightly upturned nose the only trace of her Mother, never spoke to him like that. She was a good girl. His anger was making him ill, he couldn't sleep and he'd lost weight. Working in the fields exhausted him and there had been complaints that he wasn't doing his share, nothing formal yet, but it worried him that it was even a possibility he might lose his job. His father and grandfather had worked on the same farm; he'd always been a strong man, never a shirker. To be brought so low by a woman, by his own flesh and blood, was intolerable. He felt cold, even though he was sweating, and he kept throwing more peat on the fire.

She had hurried all the way back from the upper field, brushing straw from her clothes as she ran, had with relief slowed to a walk when she saw there were no lights on in her house, expertly raised the latch with barely a sound and slipped through the door, avoiding the creaking floor boards. She had almost made it to the stairs. Now she was caught. She should have realized, she'd seen the smoke rising from the chimney into the still moonlit night, and had smelled it's bitter tang cutting across the chill dampness of the air. It had been a warning, but exhilaration, the lateness of the hour and her Father's seeming incapacity for action had lulled her into a false sense of her own invincibility. The stairs loomed in front of her, offering one means of escape, the door behind her another. Her room was no sanctuary. Her sister was there and she always sided with their Father, her anger fired not only by a misguided sense of his injured pride, but also by an envy of the anarchic streak she saw in Margaret and the freedom it seemed to give her to do just what she wanted. The front door was Margaret's only option. Her breath reeked of cider and cigarettes, her hair was tousled, her clothes crumpled, muddy and covered in burrs, dried seeds, stems and straw – the aroma of the haystack was heavy upon her. There was only one interpretation and there was no way she wanted to explain that to her Father.

The popping of the fire was the only sound as she turned, arm outstretched, body alert and heart thumping. The boards creaked as she accelerated towards the door. The heavy iron latch was cold to the touch, cracking upwards, the door gave inwards. Then she felt the rush of a body, the impact knocking her sideways, sending her crashing into the coat stand, tangling her limbs in her Father's heavy overcoat. She could feel his firm grip on her wrist, see the fury in his eyes and hear the hatred in his voice.

"No, you don't, young lady. You're staying here."

Margaret felt a twinge of pain in her back as she landed heavily on the unyielding floorboards, coats everywhere, her Father kneeing her in the stomach and chest as he stumbled and almost fell on top of her. She screamed – she hadn't meant to, it was such a childish thing to do. She wanted to swear and curse and bring the wrath of God down upon his house and everything in it – but scream she did, high-pitched and piercing. Her Father hesitated, a vestigial parental concern a temporary brake on his anger, but then he was overtaken again and dragged his daughter roughly into the parlour.

"Da, are you all right?"

A light from upstairs illuminated the hallway.

"Keep out of this, Lucy. I'm with your sister."

His voice, authoritative and commanding, calmed Margaret's terror. This was so unlike him, he was play-acting, he wouldn't be able to keep it up and the man she knew, quiet and unprepossessing, the man she could bully, would return. He was hurting her wrist as they stood in front of the fire – the heat burned the back of her legs – facing each other, uncertain what to do next.

Already the encounter was settling into a familiar pattern and Margaret's confidence was growing. Without the lights he might not notice her dishevelled state and she would get away with a telling off about being out late. He had been smoking – his tobacco and papers were strewn across the floor beside his chair – and the room was so smoky that he wouldn't be able to smell her breath or smell her. He'd been drinking himself – look at him stagger – and wasn't thinking straight. He was half asleep – the dithering fool was getting old – eyes half shut, body stooped.

"Let go of me, Da, you're hurting me."

Love was such a strange thing. He was certain he had loved Margaret, could remember cradling her as a baby, had felt proud because she'd been such a pretty child, cheeky and full of life, unlike her sister. But then, Lucy was good to him, always had been, particularly since his dear Mary had passed on. It was true he had wanted a boy, but his wife had been so frail after Margaret was born that there was no way they could have tried for another, and they'd all said that as Maggie was just like a boy anyway he had the best of both worlds. When young she was good to her Father like girls often are and yet she'd loved running wild and playing games and all the boys had been her friends. He had tried to be proud of her but somehow Margaret had always let him down. He just couldn't understand her and, if the truth be told, didn't want to. He had loved her once, he knew that, he was not a heartless man, but people fell out of love and he couldn't bear to be reminded of that anymore. Life was difficult enough without all this shouting and upset; he wanted peace and quiet.

He hated his own daughter now, she filled him with disgust. Just look at her clothes all over the place, covered in straw, that smug look on her face. She'd been with that boy again. He wanted to slap her, wipe that smile away, but he would never hit a woman, couldn't bear to. She'd have to go though. People would not think ill of him, they would understand, they'd seen the way she'd been carrying on. They gossiped about her, he had seen their looks, the shakes of the head, he knew they talked about him, had heard the whispers as he passed by, was certain they wondered why he didn't keep her under better control and why he allowed her to do as she pleased. But he didn't, he had tried. With a ferocity that surprised even him he flung her hand away and saw her wince as it struck her hip.

"I'll hurt you... the things you've been up to!"

Clutching her wrist, Margaret stared at him in astonishment, unable to hold back the tears. The stairs creaked and they both glanced in the direction of the empty doorway.

"Is that you, Lucy? Go back to bed."

Alert to the slightest sound they stood together breathing heavily, eyeing each other. There was no movement, just the crackle of the fire and the ticking of the clock on the mantelpiece. Then the stand-off was suddenly over, Margaret's father lowered himself slowly into his armchair, watching his daughter, then angrily got to his feet and pushed her firmly into the chair on the opposite side of the hearth.

"Sit down and listen to me. I should give you a good hammering, the way you behave."

"What you talking about?"

Her voice was sullen, the sneer barely disguised.

"Don't talk to me like that."

She turned away, goading him.

"Look at me when I'm speaking to you. I said, don't talk to me like that."

"I heard. I'm not deaf."

"Look at me, Margaret, I mean it. Now, where've you been?"

"Out."

"I know that. Where?"

"With some friends."

"Which friends?"

"You don't know them."

"What d'you mean, I don't know them? For Jesus sake, I've lived here all my life, I know everyone."

"I don't know their names."

"Margaret!"

"I just met them."

"This is bloody ridiculous. You're telling me you've been out until gone midnight with people you've only just met and you don't know their names? You must think I'm stupid."

"You said it."

Angrier than he had ever been, he stood up, no longer able to distinguish between the abstract idea of a hated daughter, with which he'd lived for what seemed like ages, and the real thing cowering in front of him. He advanced and retreated, balling his fists, swearing silently.

"Don't speak to me like that, don't you ever. I'll …"

"You'll what, hit me?"

"Yes, I'll hit you. I'll hit you."

"Go on then. You don't scare me."

"Margaret!"

Fist raised, he towered above her. The tension was more than he could bear, he couldn't breathe and his eyes watered, then came the release. His fist thudded into the padded back of the armchair, tearing the perished material, a nail protruding from the wooden frame ripping the flesh of his hand. Margaret yelped as, arms above her head, she tried to slide out of the chair and escape.

"Da, don't. It won't do any good."

He stepped back, Lucy's voice a balm.

"Even though she deserves it."

"She just won't listen."

"I know Da, I know."

Dressed in a thin night-gown, with a cardigan draped over her shoulders, Lucy shuffled over to her Father and placed an arm around his trembling body. Together they stared at Margaret, coiled in the armchair and biting one of her knuckles.

"You know, do you?"

Margaret's voice was so low, they were uncertain they had heard what she said, but her Father was in no mood to let victory slip from his hands now that reinforcements had arrived.

"Yes, we bloody well do, and don't you speak to your sister like that."

The look of disdain on his youngest daughter's face, caught as she was in the shadowy glow of the dying embers, was such an incitement that without Lucy's restraining touch he would have hit her this time. He was not a violent man, he believed, he had hit very few living things in his life, but this girl was killing him.

"Margaret, for Christ's sake, you're only fourteen."

"So what? That makes no difference."

"You should show some respect to your Father."

"What, do as he says?"

"Yes."

"Just shut up, Lucy, will you?"

"Don't you talk like that. We don't want you here, you heard our Da."

"Be quiet, both of you. I can't bloody think with all this shrieking going on."

"Da, I was only trying to help…"

"I don't want your bloody help, leave me alone."

Dumbstruck and bitterly offended, Lucy retreated to the door. Margaret grinned and waved.

"You're both horrible. You're always ganging up on me. I hate you both."

"I hate you too, Margaret. Always have done."

"Stop it, stop it."

The sisters had not heard hysteria in their Father's voice before and they fell silent. He was shaking his clenched fists, glancing menacingly between the two of them and muttering unintelligibly. Not a tall man, he appeared diminished by his anger, threatening but also faintly ridiculous.

Lucy slipped from the room and headed for the scullery where she lit the stove in darkness, filled the kettle, set it on the blue flame and sat down to listen. Margaret was unable to resist the sight of her sister in full flight and shouted, "Stay away, it's none of your business, you old busybody."

Her triumph was brief. With a roar her Father leapt upon her, grabbing her clothes roughly and hauling her to her feet.

"I've told you – don't speak to anyone in this house like that." He began to shake her.

"You've been drinking, haven't you? I can smell it. You're disgusting. A girl of your age."

His words were clear, she heard everything as her other senses failed her. She could say nothing, her breath gone.

"What's this on your neck? Tell me, what is it?"

She wanted to tell him, she really did, wanted to explain, but her head was spinning, she was going to be sick.

"Look at this. It's a bite, isn't it? You little ... you've been with him, haven't you? You little whore. I don't believe it, a love bite."

Horrified, he could no longer bear to hold her and with all his strength flung her backwards into the armchair, the force sending it careering across the floor and crashing into the wall beneath the window, where it turned briefly before coming to a stop. Sobbing for breath, Margaret cowered in the chair, preparing for the next onslaught. She felt nauseous.

"Who was it, Margaret?"

The voice, at a distance, sounded calm and rational, if a little breathless.

"Tell me."

The menace was still there and she felt so tired. She didn't want to be hurt again.

"Tell me, Margaret, I won't ask you again."

It was hard to tell where he was, sitting or standing, his voice if anything sounded a little closer.

"Margaret?"

The anger was returning. She looked up and he was above her. She screamed. He grasped her by the shoulders, pinning her to the chair.

"Tell me."

His fingers were digging painfully into her thin shoulders. She started to cry.

"You little bitch!"

The weight was getting too much, pushing down, she felt as if her spine was about to crack.

"Da, please."

"Nice and polite now when it suits, eh?"

He pulled aggressively on one of her ears and she winced with the pain.

"Come on, tell me. I'm not going to stop till you do."

"Da."

"Da, what?"

He cuffed her hard across the top of her head.

"Look at all this stuff in your hair, it's disgusting."

"Please, you're hurting me."

"I'll hurt you. Now tell me, was he the first? I bet he wasn't."

Shuddering at the thought he pushed down with all his weight, waiting for her to cry out.

"He wasn't, he wasn't!" Margaret was shouting at the top of her voice. "Now get away from me."

Shocked he leant back, easing the pressure on her crumpled body, but not letting go.

"What do you mean, he wasn't?"

"He wasn't. You asked me, and he wasn't."

"What do you mean?"

Angry, vindictive, she broke free from her Father and turned on him, laughing bitterly.

"It was your brother, Uncle Mark, who started it. Been doing it for ages."

"What? How dare you. What's Mark got to do with it?"

"He used to do it to me. It was our little secret. All those times you left me with him."

"How dare you? How dare you?"

He lunged at her, but the chair blocked his way and she stepped back, taunting him.

"He used to take me into his bed to play little games. He said I wasn't to say anything to anybody."

Unaware her voice took on the teasing tone of her uncle, mimicking his every word.

"It'll be our little secret, nobody will ever need to know. Just you and me as special friends."

Her Father's hands tugged at his hair in impotent fury. He was unable to fully take in what was being said.

"You're a liar ..."

"I'm not. He did it, ever since I was little, you ask Lucy."

He looked straight at her, afraid for the first time.

"Lucy?"

"Yes, he did it with Lucy as well. Both of us, you ask her."

In the kitchen crockery crashed to the floor and Lucy began to scream.

***

Within a week Margaret was on her way to the Convent of our Lady of Mercy at the Magdalen Asylum in Dublin, on the recommendation of her local priest. His intention was to get her as far away as possible from her family – her poor Father still wasn't back at work and the sister was staying with an aunt. – and he was confident the heavy work in the laundry would soon settle her down. He had seen it happen before. Girls with too much spirit needed to have their energies redirected into more useful and Godly pursuits, for society's good as much as for their own.

To everyone's surprise Margaret appeared willing to go. For her it was as much an escape as it was for her family. She would be the first of her friends to leave that boring little town and where she was going she wouldn't stay long. A few nuns couldn't hold her. There would be ways of getting away.

When the time came for her to leave her Father couldn't look at her and neither of them said a word.

***

The zip was lowered slowly, an unmistakable sound, an uneven burr catching then running on. Margaret never looked at what was happening in front of her, never offered a helping hand, just stared at the cobwebs on the wall behind Frank's head. He was considerate, always laid out a neat pile of sacking on the floor for her to kneel on. Helped her off with her cardigan and hung it tidily on a wooden peg, for it was always warm in his small alcove – tools lining the walls – in the Convent basement, hidden away at the back of the boilers. He turned off most of the lights, leaving a single naked bulb casting a dim yellow glow above their heads. Washed his hands and face, then dried them on a grubby towel hanging on a roller on the wall beside the small washbasin. Placed a bar of Cadbury's milk chocolate just out of reach on the work surface and said, "For afters, if you're a good girl."

He would stand in front of her then and run his hands through her hair, while the bulge in his trousers would grow larger – at the beginning Margaret had looked on, wide-eyed. Now she glanced away, thinking, if she was lucky, of something else. Then he would ease back her head and open his fly. Frank's baggy brown corduroys smelled musty, not unpleasant, she was used to it, simply an organic addition to the atmosphere in which he worked, heavy with damp and the whiff of oil. There would be a moment when he would hesitate, his arms hanging down by his sides, hoping she would join in, but she never did and Margaret, her eyes still fixed on the ceiling, imagined he would shrug before beginning to rummage around with his hand, shifting slightly on his feet until his penis would break free from his clothing and stand erect before her. The foreskin would be slightly retracted revealing the narrow slit in the swollen tip – which he had said one time he would have liked her to have licked with the end of her tongue, but she never had. She knew this because she always kept her eyes open until, with one hand on the back of her head, he guided his penis into her mouth while with the other hand he pulled back his foreskin.

Frank would sigh contentedly and Margaret would know she was alone as he retreated into a world fantastically his own. He could never quite escape from his basement, as he would control his breathing and stifle his moans, but he was no longer interested in who he was with. Margaret didn't care now – there was no way of stopping it anyway – but she had done in the early days.

Frank was handsome. He had a wiry body and dark tanned skin, which glistened with sweat as he worked in the Convent garden in the summer, blue shining eyes and blond hair that would flop across his weather-beaten face when the wind blew. He would smile and wink at you and pass the time of day as he leaned on his spade, rolling a cigarette. He had told her she was the prettiest girl in the whole Convent. With her fine ash blonde hair, sea green eyes and crooked little mouth, she was "good enough to eat". Margaret had found him irresistible when she had arrived there, angry and rebellious. She saw in him a possible means of escape. If she gave him what he wanted, he would help her get away, she was sure.

Frank had promised to do what he could, but had not kept his word. Now her eyes always closed at the first bitter taste. Occasionally, if she was late arriving, he would have washed himself and the perfumed flavour would be overwhelming –

and she would swallow hard and try and remember when it had not been routine. As they each settled into position his head would loll back, his eyes close, and clutching onto one of the many warm downpipes that lined the walls he would ease his testicles out through his open fly, wincing occasionally as he caught skin or pubic hair on the serrated teeth of the zip. Then he would return to her, looking down angry and hurt, muttering a few unintelligible words, thrusting his fingers roughly through her hair as if he needed to make her suffer as much as he had.

It was at times like these, with her curls snagging painfully on his signet ring, that Margaret thought of doing him harm, of biting down hard, but the idea frightened her as much, if not more, than she knew it would terrify him if he could read her mind. She believed he could sometimes, he seemed to have such a hold over her, such an unnerving confidence that she would keep coming back. Being who she was she had rebelled once, stayed away, even told on him – on herself as it had turned out – but it had done her no good and here she was back on her knees.

"Come on, there's a good girl, say your prayers."

A placidity would settle on the statuesque pair finally motionless in the dim light. The thrusting would then begin, his hips moving slowly at first, before gathering pace until he found a satisfactory rhythm. The motion would ease Margaret backwards – Frank shuffling after her – until she was sitting back on her ankles, her head resting against the soft lagging of one of the boilers. It was uncomfortable and she constantly feared she would topple over, unable to resist Frank's determined physical pressure. Instinctively one hand would massage the growing pain in the small of her back, ready to prop up her falling body if she lost balance. The other would rest under her chin, giving support to her aching jaw. Margaret didn't move, she just listened to his irregular breathing – the sharp intakes of breath through gritted teeth and open mouth, the relaxed exhalation through pursed lips – her own lips locked firmly in place, tongue flattened against her front teeth. Frank would moan every so often and take the Lord's name in vain, slight little affairs, a suppressed whimper barely audible above the distant roar of the furnace, but Margaret was paying attention and would count.

"Three, four... five ...six..."

She had never got beyond eleven.

."... seven..."

Frank fumbled with the buckle on his belt, before pulling it free and letting it drop with a clatter to the floor. He undid the button on his trousers and the loose corduroys fell to the floor, bunching around his ankles. Margaret could smell the perspiration on his skin, the animal excitement of the chase. A tremor ran through Frank's body and he began to lick the air – the rouged cheek of Maureen O'Hagen, her knee, thigh, lips – dancing in front of him. He wanted so much more. With a frenzied waving hand he managed to push the seat of his underpants over his sweating buttocks, exposing them to the cooler air.

"... eight..."

Margaret knew what was coming next and sometimes she did and sometimes she didn't.

"... nine..."

"Will you do it, Margaret, like I like it?"

His voice was hoarse, barely a whisper. She reached up and touched his left buttock – it felt hot and faintly damp – his body tensed in anticipation, his thrusting briefly slowed then picked up pace. She walked her two fingers slowly towards the crack, pressing hard into his pliant flesh. He was very hairy. She had been growing her nails, although it was difficult working in the laundry, and she hoped she could hurt him. Suddenly his body stiffened and she quickly turned her head to one side.

"... ten..."

158

Hot semen spurted across her cheek and spattered her hair. She drew back, forcing herself against the boiler as Frank relaxed and appeared to crumple. She spat into her hand. He chuckled as he looked down at her, touched her hair briefly, then seemed suddenly embarrassed at his own nakedness – his penis wilting inches from her face – and he shuffled away from her, turning slightly, before bending down and hauling up his trousers. Margaret never looked back at him, keeping her eyes fixed on the concrete floor. She silently recited the rosary as she shifted into a more comfortable position, sitting bolt upright. Her scuffed red knees, raised in front of her, smarted painfully.

"Hail Mary, full of grace! the Lord is with thee; blessed art thou among women and blessed is the fruit of thy womb."

There was nothing more she wanted to feel, there was a numbing satisfaction to be gained from not thinking about anything at all and Margaret grasped it.

"...Jesus. Holy Mary..."

There was a box of Kleenex tissues that Frank kept high up on one of the work shelves, which he normally brought down and had close to hand, it was part of the routine. This time he had forgotten, for no reason that he could remember, and it irritated him. He was acutely aware of the indignity of stumbling around, trousers open, exposing himself in front of a woman, and it accentuated his sense of shame. He felt guilty enough, even with Margaret who he believed would never tell, without having to berate himself over his own fallibility. Firmly holding on to the top of his loose corduroys he stretched up, his penis trailing snail like across the surface of the work bench, and lifted the box down. It was a relief to wipe away all evidence, to cover up and feel clean again. He then handed the tissues to Margaret.

"Chocolate?"

"... Mother of God, pray for us sinners now and at the hour of our death..."

Margaret took the box and placed it on the floor beside her. She would never be able to do it, even with all the man size tissues in the world; she would never be able to wipe away her sins. Frank, satisfied and complacent, seemed to be able to. There he was sucking on chocolate, whistling as he tidied up – a thin reedy sound that could chill when heard in a corridor – ignoring her. There would be no words until she dragged herself stiffly to her feet, handed him back the box of tissues, and turned to go.

"See you again, eh?"

Margaret wanted to be discovered, needed it to happen, but knew nobody would ever find them.

"… Amen."

***

It was difficult for Margaret to face people after she had been with Frank. There was always a period of turning in on herself, of mental flaying, all of which got her nowhere. Her attempts to make sense of it had become routine, his attention which had once promised so much, had appeared to offer a way out, now seemed hopelessly inadequate. In disgust she would retreat to the common room and try to read.

"I said I'll go with you."

Margaret looked up. It was Doris.

"You mean it?"

"Yes, I told you."

"So what made you change your mind?"

"Oh, I don't know."

Margaret snapped shut the book she was reading – Black Beauty – tossed it on to the carpet and then crawled along the battered settee until her chin was resting on the arm inches from Doris who was sitting on the floor darning a hole in her woollen cardigan.

"Tell me. You've been saying no for ages."

"I'm feeling fed up."

"What's new? Go on, Doris, tell me, they won't hear."

Margaret nodded in the direction of a group of women on the other side of the room, seated round a radio listening to the Gaelic football match between Cork and Limerick. The commentary was muffled, indistinct. The nuns didn't like too much noise so the women huddled together, oblivious to all around them, beguiled by visceral memories of ancient rivalries.

"Well, it was you going on about running away all the time. Started me thinking about what you said about life passing us by. That we were still young, you know, and should go and live a little."

"But you always said that it was too risky."

"I know, but things have changed."

"What? Seems much the same to me: work, work, work, bed by eight thirty, listening to the radio, dancing with each other on a Saturday night to the music of the bloody Gallowglass Ceilidh band."

"Well, you know, Maeve becoming a trusty. Things have changed, they're not the same."

"You don't have to tell me! It was bad enough her being all religious and going on at me all the time, now there'll be no stopping her. Stuck up, she is. I don't know what you see in her."

"She's a friend. I like talking to her."

"That'll be a thing of the past."

"Suppose."

A cheer went up from the crowd around the radio. Margaret sneered at them and then squeezed Doris' shoulder.

"Dottie, let's go tonight. It'll be easy."

Doris leant her head against the arm of the settee and stared up into the determined face of her new-found ally. She had made up her mind to run away, but was quite happy to rely on Margaret to plan the deed.

"You know what to do. We'll slip away after lights out, then over the wall at the back where the old ivy trunk is thick almost to the top. It's not much of a drop from there into the lane and then we're free."

"Oh, Mary, mother of Jesus, that hurts!"

Doris gulped in air as she lay stunned on the damp cobbles, her right leg twisted awkwardly beneath her body.

"Margaret, I thought you said it wasn't very high? My ankle!"

A soft blue bag thudded on to the road beside her, closely followed by Margaret who also lost her footing on the slippery surface and crashed to the ground with a muffled yelp. She sat there, arms behind her, legs thrust out in front, grinning triumphantly.

"We've done it Dot, we've done it!"

Looking up at the street lamp above their heads, the saffron light diffusing weakly through the moisture-laden air, Doris was not sure. It was a long way back – she couldn't even see the top of the Convent wall from where she was lying – and the pain was intense. Sitting up and wiping the grime from her hands with a handkerchief, she shifted her weight, grasped her injured leg and eased it out from under her. Margaret in her excitement failed to notice that Doris was suffering and scrambled to her feet, slinging her black duffle bag over her shoulder.

"Come on, let's get going. We don't want to get caught here do we? That would be bloody typical."

Exasperated she turned and frowned at her friend.

"What's up?"

"I've hurt my leg, jumping down."

"Oh, no, don't say that. Come on. Here, grab hold."

Unwillingly Doris was hauled to her feet, expecting at any moment to collapse in agony and ruin everything. What would

Margaret think if she let her down now? She had rarely seen her so happy. This was her moment and she would never be able to forgive Doris if they had to hobble back defeated. Moving her ankle tentatively back and forth, she grew more hopeful as the pain eased.

"Doris, please. I'm sure it's nothing. Come on."

"I don't know, Margaret. I gave it a real knock when I came down."

"Come on, you old thing. I'll even carry your bag."

Margaret swept up the blue carryall and tugged on Doris's sleeve.

"Please!"

The pair moved off slowly, Margaret leading, Doris limping behind her. Two young boys, who had been watching them from the waste ground on the opposite side of the lane, whistled and then called out after them.

"Go on, you can make it."

"Hush up, you two. Shouldn't you be in bed?"

"Naaa."

"We'll tell your Mas."

Doris and Margaret laughed and began to run, raggedly at first, but then as they fell into step they gathered speed. They turned the corner into Railway Street with the boys' cheers ringing in their ears. The damp air was refreshing on their sweating faces as they raced through the anonymous streets. They were strangers lost in an unknown town in an unfamiliar age. Time travellers returning to a world they had both left years before. They gave no thought to injuries, tiredness or aching limbs. There was no time to think about the future – where they were to live or how they were to make any money. They were free. All they knew was that behind them lay the Convent with its rules, the toil of the laundry, Frank in his basement, Maeve and Sister Elizabeth. Things could only get better. The euphoria of their escape bore them on as they ran for their new lives.

***

Doris spluttered into her glass of red wine.

"And that's when he… Oh, Christ, look what I've done, all over the carpet."

Giggling, Margaret leaned over the laughing figure of her friend, who was sprawled across the large battered sofa, her legs resting in Margaret's lap. There was only a few years between them, but it mattered to Margaret that she was the youngest, the most vivacious, the most popular. She had grown her hair in the months they had been living in this small bed-sit and now wore it loose, the blonde tresses framing her delicate carefully made-up face with its slightly crooked mouth and dimpled chin. Margaret would never have run away with someone prettier than her. Doris was good company but no one could say she was beautiful, with her round, bespectacled face and blurred features, and even though Margaret had tried her best with her she still had no fashion sense, choosing as if by instinct the dowdiest clothes.

All the money Margaret earned cleaning went on clothes, make-up and going out. She spent her time wandering around shops, revelling in her new-found freedom to choose. Dresses in bright colours – peacock blue and hot pink – nylons and high-heeled shoes were the priority for her, while Doris was content with the clothes she already had. She made an effort to please Margaret and bought a new floral pleated circle skirt and a pale yellow fitted blouse with a small collar, but the uncertainty over money worried her and she was constantly nagging her friend about the lack of food and the need to pay the rent. It was an irritation for Margaret, but she was enjoying herself and chose to ignore it.

Together they stared at the floor.

"Don't worry about that, it won't show on that old thing. Look at the colour of it anyway. It's a waste, that's all. Here, let me top you up."

Doris straightened herself and held a shaking glass out to Margaret, who filled it to the brim with cheap red wine.

"Careful."

She drank deeply then set the glass on the floor.

"God, I feel so drunk, the room's spinning."

"It's your own fault, Doris."

Margaret's speech was slurred and Doris found it hilarious, rocking back and forth, clutching her stomach. Margaret pushed her feet aside and stood up uncertainly.

"You know what they say, don't you?"

She waved her arms in front of her as if conducting.

"All together now."

She began singing hoarsely and Doris joined in after the first couple of words, their voices growing louder as they repeated the single refrain, until they were shouting at the top of their voices.

"Beer on wine makes you feel fine, wine on beer makes you feel queer."

There was a sudden thumping noise on the ceiling and the sound of a distant voice calling out. Margaret clutched her mouth in mock embarrassment, before collapsing back on top of a giggling Doris on the sofa.

"That old bag upstairs never let's us have any fun, it is Saturday night after all."

"It's almost Sunday."

They hugged each other and sniggered hysterically before rolling apart, each flinging their head back onto the sofa and thrusting their legs out in front of them, bringing them down with a crash on a rickety coffee table which shook alarmingly and set off another fit of giggles. An unlit candle stuck in an empty milk bottle toppled over and rolled under the armchair opposite.

"It's lucky that wasn't lit or we might not be here."

It was such a release to laugh like this after working all week – cleaning offices and houses, mopping up other people's mess – that neither of them wanted to bring it to an end. They finally stopped, exhilarated and breathing heavily, sipped from their glasses of wine, and then turned their heads to stare drunkenly at each other.

"What did you say?"

"We could have been burnt to a cinder."

"No, not that, before."

"I dunno, I can't remember a thing. I'm too tipsy."

Doris tried to get to her feet, but Margaret held her back.

"I'm feeling a bit odd."

"You'll feel better if you stay just there. I'll open the window and let in some fresh air."

Margaret staggered across the room, bumping against the heavy standard lamp as she passed, knocking its floral shade askew and sending a shower of grey fluff drifting to the floor. The curtains were already open and she stared down into the street below. It was deserted, the drunks had long gone, weaving their way home, she could see a beer bottle upturned on the railings opposite, glinting in the street light. It had been raining when they had come back from the pub clutching their prize. Margaret never won anything, but Doris was much luckier and had chosen the bottle of wine – Mateus Rose – in the raffle over the forty Woodbines and the chocolates that had been left. But the rain had now stopped and the cobbles were drying quickly in the warm wind. The sash window was always difficult in damp weather and Margaret, straining as hard as she could, only managed to raise it a couple of inches before it jammed.

"Bugger."

The breeze moved the curtains gently back and forth. Margaret loosened her blouse and let the air reach her skin, while Doris, flat-out on the sofa, sighed her appreciation.

"Feeling better?"

"Mmmmmm."

"Then tell me what you were going to say."

Doris was feeling so tired that for a few seconds she had no idea what Margaret was talking about. She'd already told her about Maeve and Sister Elizabeth, it couldn't be that.

"Doris, I was telling you about me and Frank, and you said, "and that's when he" or something like that."

"Oh, yes."

"Doris!"

"I remember."

A salacious smile spread across her face and Margaret was taken aback. She'd lived alone with Doris in this bed-sit for the three months since they had escaped from the Convent, had had drinks with her and several boys, but she'd never seen her friend looking so sexually knowing before.

"That's when he, Frank, would ask you if you'd stick your finger up his, you know, bum."

Doris giggled to herself and gazed bleary-eyed at Margaret, who was horrified at what she had just heard.

"Doris!"

"Bum, bum, bum."

"Doris, how did you know?"

"Bum, bum."

"Stop it."

"Bum. I guessed."

"You couldn't have."

"I did."

Doris sipped her wine, never taking her eyes off Margaret, who had slumped on to the floor and was resting her back against the sofa.

"You did, didn't you?"

"I did."

"You actually did it?"

"I did."

"You did it with Frank. How could you?"

"How could you?"

"Why didn't you tell me?"

"Why didn't you?"

"I just did."

"So did I."

"I don't believe it. I thought I was the only one."

"Well, you weren't."

Margaret drained her glass and re-filled it. Her hand was shaking.

"In the basement?"

"Yes, same as you."

"How many times?"

"Only the once."

"Is that all?"

Doris blushed.

"Yes, I didn't like it."

"Neither did I."

"How many times did you do it?"

"I don't know. I lost count."

Margaret began to cry, long breathless sobs that chilled Doris. She slithered off the sofa onto the floor and flung her arms around the crumpled figure of her friend.

"Don't cry, Margaret. It's not worth it. He can't get you now."

"I couldn't escape, he kept saying he'd tell."

The tears flowed and her nose began to run, Margaret had never felt so bereft. The sacrifice she thought she'd been making had not been hers alone; she had not been the sole victim of his degradation. A community of suffering meant nothing to her.

"How did you get him to stop?"

Doris focussed drink-befuddled eyes, her head rocking gently from side to side, and tried to remember.

"It made me sick. Then he tried to make me eat chocolate."

Margaret let out a low wail.

"I used to like that! It made me feel better, took the taste away."

"Oh, no, it makes me ill to think about it."

Massaging her stomach, Doris looked around vainly for something to be sick in. The wastepaper basket was standing by the door, but it seemed a long way away. She thought she would get it in a minute if she felt worse.

"I believed it was just for me."

Doris was sweating. Margaret sobbed quietly.

"What?"

"The chocolate."

The furniture was moving, the armchair spinning one way, the lamp and the curtains the other. Margaret's face, still for a moment, drenched and red, shifted and blurred. She was leaving then she wasn't. It helped to stare at her own hands, which for a while seemed still part of her, but then they too would float left, waver right. Words were all she had left flowing out as she watched through a swirling, colourful space.

"I didn't go back and never said anything," Doris mumbled.

"Didn't he?"

"I suppose he must have done. I can't remember, Maggie. It can't have meant much if he did."

"He used to threaten me, you know."

"Yes, he was like that, but you always knew Frank was all talk and no trousers."

She began to hiccup.

"He wouldn't have done nothing."

Margaret was amazed they were talking about the same man. For her Frank had at the beginning been a possible means of escape. He had promised to help her get away from the Convent – slip her the key to the gate, find her somewhere to stay and give her some money – and in her desperation she had believed him. Later he became irresistible in an abject, self-destructive way, his allure reinforced by the threat of violence and exposure. Doris had succumbed to the same attraction but seemed able to shrug him off afterwards without a care. Such a revelation was no comfort to Margaret, she just felt even more desolate.

"He left me alone after that, but then I suppose he had others, didn't he? I was nothing special."

Doris was right of course, Margaret understood that. She had been the special one, but not, she now knew, the only one. Frank had been unfaithful to her with how many more besides Doris? That was the question.

"I was the special one, do you think?"

"No, Maggie – oh, my stomach! – he was just a bad man."

The room was spinning again, faster this time, and Doris knew she was going to be sick, she could taste it at the back of her throat.

"He used to say I was bad. You know, afterwards. I would be kneeling there as he buttoned himself up and he would speak to me like he was a priest."

Margaret coughed and dried her nose and mouth with her hand, then slipped a handkerchief from the sleeve of her blouse and wiped the mucus from her fingers.

"He would say I was a terrible sinner in desperate need of redemption."

Doris shook her head and lights flashed before her eyes. With one arm she steadied herself against the sofa, while her stomach churned.

"He would offer me absolution. He'd give me a sip of water from a glass, sometimes it would even be beer or something, then he'd get me to stick my tongue out and he'd place a square of chocolate on it and tell me I was absolved of all my sins."

Conjuring up a picture of Margaret on her knees in her basement confessional amused Doris; she could see it, feel the coarse sacking cutting into her skin, itching, but she was feeling too nauseous to tease. Her eyes watered as an acrid cocktail of bile, beer and red wine bubbled up from her stomach, scorching the back of her throat and fouling her breath.

"Should've reported him. Sorry."

Doris covered her mouth with her hand to mask the belch. For the first time Margaret noticed how pale her friend looked.

"I tried. Are you all right?"

"No, but talking helps."

"You sure?"

Doris nodded and attempted to smile.

"I told Father James once."

"You never?"

"I did. I was so angry one day I just went and told him. Didn't stop to think."

It was a sobering thought. Father James was a stiff-necked traditionalist, teetotal and deeply suspicious of the Convent women who were in his charge. Doris closed her eyes and rolled her head. Even the amusing picture of Margaret yet again on her knees in the semi-dark was not enough to steady the room.

"What did he say?"

Margaret shuddered at the memory of her resolve evaporating into the fragrant mugginess of the confessional as she spilled out the truth about her relationship with Frank, to be replaced by the chill that had never left her since, as the priest dispassionately gave his answer.

"He didn't even look at me. I could see through the grille. I'm sure he hadn't any idea who I was."

"Didn't he ask your name?"

"Yes, I'd told him that, Margaret Macready, but you know…"

The tears were flowing again, but Doris felt she could do nothing, her own eyes were watering and she had to concentrate on not throwing up.

"I know."

"He didn't hesitate, not for a second, that's what got me."

Margaret dabbed at her cheeks with her handkerchief, then despairingly dropped her hands into her lap and began to pull at the sodden cloth.

"He called me a liar."

Her voice was a whine, so out of character that it forced Doris to pay attention again.

"He said I was making it all up, fantasising. Can you believe that?"

Margaret stared at her drunk friend, who, when she finally noticed, nodded then after a pause shook her head.

"He said I was an evil woman to think such thoughts. Even he could see how good-looking Frank was, but that was no excuse for me to make such accusations against him. It was disgusting I should think that way."

Doris fought hard not to vomit. Her stomach was seething and she could feel the pressure inexorably building. She retched then swallowed.

"He said Frank had been with the Convent for years and had been a very good worker and that there had been no complaints. Everyone was very happy with him. He had green fingers and anyway he was married…"

Bitterly Margaret gulped red wine, spilling some on to her chest, the sight turned Doris' stomach and she leant forward, breathing deeply.

"… with two children, two lovely young boys, so how dare I say such things about him? Didn't I know that such lies were a far worse sin than anything I said he'd done? Didn't I? I was a sinner, but then I knew that."

"Is that it?"

"A sinner and he wanted to hear nothing more about it. If he did there would be trouble. He gave me my penance." Margaret laughed. "Then he got up and walked out before me. I could hear him tell those waiting outside he was sorry but he wasn't feeling very well and could they come back tomorrow. I couldn't stay in that place after that, I really couldn't."

She squeezed Doris's hand.

"I'd have gone even if you hadn't said you'd come with me, but thank God you did. I went with Frank one more time before we left. I think I was going to tell him, you know, put the wind up him. I wanted to see what he would say, but I didn't. You know what he could be like. Overpowering."

In a sudden moment of lucidity, Doris gazed childishly at Margaret.

"He was one of the reasons I wanted to run away, too, and then there was the business with Maeve... I'm gonna be sick."

She hauled herself to her feet and staggered towards the door. Grabbing the wastepaper basket she dropped to her knees and vomited violently. Margaret raised herself up and peered over the back of the sofa at the hunched figure. Doris was sick again. Within seconds the dark liquid began oozing through the woven wicker bands at the bottom of the basket.

"Come on, we both need cheering up. Let's have some music."

Margaret jumped to her feet, crossed the room and switched on the wireless.

"Who cares about her upstairs? Let her moan if she wants to."

She stared out of the window, absent-mindedly strumming her fingers on the wooden cabinet as the valves warmed up. Then squatting down she focussed on the glowing orange dial, turned the knob and watched the red needle move – voices and snatches of music fading in and out of the static – past Athlone, Budapest, Hilversum, Helvetia, until she found Luxembourg. There was a burst of jangling guitar, indistinct at first, then clearer as Margaret deftly tuned in. A bar-room piano picked up the refrain, then the voice. She listened intently, mouthing the words.

"Doris, it's Elvis. Do you hear?"

Excited Margaret turned away from the radio.

"Remember, I told you about him."

Doris was lying on her back on the floor asleep. Her mouth was open and she was snoring.

***

Margaret saw the policeman from a distance. He was leaning on the railings, smoking a cigarette and staring out into the street. He would have been more or less outside her house but he didn't seem to be paying any attention to her or anyone else, so she thought nothing of it. Just someone taking an illicit break from a boring job.

Anyway in spirit she wasn't really there, she was still at the seaside, her mind flitting across the vast sodden foreshore, bathed like everything else in the bright sunshine of late-April, breathing in the fresh scents of salty decay. The tide was way out and Margaret had felt ecstatic; she could see for miles, she was not hemmed in by buildings, people, cars and buses. Her life was out there, not behind her in grubby old Dublin. Over there was England, even America: New York, the Wild West, Boston. Her great-grandfather had emigrated years ago. There would be aunts and uncles, cousins, lots of them, she could look them up when she arrived. They wouldn't know anything about her, she could start afresh. Margaret Macready would be reborn. She had no ties now that Doris was gone, she could do what she wanted.

It was only a week since her friend had suddenly disappeared, but it was obvious she wasn't coming back. It had been a shock, but Margaret was getting used to it now.

She looked at Declan walking beside her. His hand crept into hers and gently squeezed and her heart lifted. He was a nice boy, not like the others. They only touched in private and then they touched everything; he was more tentative, but ever so much more intimate. They had sat close to each other on the bus, now he was holding her hand on the front at Howth. It was true there weren't many people about, but it said something about the way he felt. A kiss on the cheek was his reward, and a smile. She had a lovely smile, it never failed with the boys – he moved closer. Was he the one who would come with her to America? Throw it all in here and leave, cross the ocean with her and begin again? He probably would – he was only a waiter at Grogan's, working all hours and paid a pittance – but Margaret wasn't sure. She would give him everything he wanted, probably more, but not her life. That was hers and she would go it alone. There were always boys, plenty of boys, nice and not so nice. Declan was close to top of her list, he was fun to be with, but he was still just a boy.

A small flock of oystercatchers wheeled overhead, their cries bleak and forlorn in the warmth of the afternoon. The spell broken, they moved apart and walked hand in hand along the front towards the headland. Fishermen were mending their nets, working silently in pairs, the smell of tobacco melding with the ancient tar, the drying seaweed and rotting fish heads and bones that littered the shore, to produce an intoxicating infusion of the seaside. Their boats hauled up the beach across ancient sea-lashed logs, marooned clear of the waves, leant precariously, surrounded by halos of diesel drenched sand. Ragged flags of coloured cloth fluttered in the stiff breeze and a loose chain knocked rhythmically against the battered off-white, green tinged clinker-built hull of the St Patrick, Howth. Crab pots were piled precariously high, the rusting metal orange bright against the salt-encrusted black netting. Trapped in the mesh-dried twisted strands of seaweed, looked to Margaret at first glance like the withered skeletons of the many ensnared creatures that had scuttled to their deaths in those cages.

She shuddered. Eating such things had never appealed to her, crabs seemed so alien, from another world. The fresh fish lying gleaming and clear-eyed in boxes stacked waist high outside the ramshackle fishermen's huts was something else, though. She had always loved fish – fish and chips were one of the few happy memories from her childhood – but her landlady always complained if she cooked it, even on a Friday. It wasn't worth the trouble.

Another couple passed them arm-in-arm, heading home wind-swept, hair tousled, faces flushed, saying nothing but content in themselves. No one else was close by, the nearest people were way ahead of them, tiny stick figures in the shadow of the cliff. A dog was chasing his tail on the sand, sending up a shower of golden grains and yapping senselessly, his owner nowhere to be seen. The light suddenly dimmed, shadows disappeared, as a wisp of cloud passed across the sun. Both looked up, surprised, then Declan slipped a half-bottle of whisky from the inside pocket of his coat and passed it to Margaret. The liquid pleasantly burned her mouth and throat and she allowed the warmth to spread throughout her body before taking another sip and then another. It always amused her how generous the boys were with drink. She had never tasted whisky before, now she was always being offered it. It had taken a little time, but now she quite liked it. It seemed to make the day easier.

No one paid them any attention as they slipped from the path and climbed up through the blooming gorse – brilliant yellow on beds of dark green – the thorns catching Margaret's legs, laddering her stockings and raising a string of dark magenta beads across her pale white skin. Declan would lick them off, she would make sure of it, but that would be much later after they had climbed higher. They stopped, panting, to admire the view and sip again at the whisky bottle. The sun on the rippling water was blinding and, shading her eyes with her hand, Margaret stared at the distant hazy shore and imagined that it was America and she had just caught sight of it from the bridge of an ocean liner. She would see the Statue of Liberty at any moment. Declan had said it was only Portmarnock, but that didn't seem to matter. He was just a boy. She would see the Statue of Liberty.

They kissed to show she bore him no ill feeling, and he tried to get her to lie down. She said no and they climbed on, the path getting narrower, the drop below them more precipitous. It got colder and the wind stronger. She buttoned up her cardigan. The chill kept her sober.

Close to the summit they found a hollow, the grass close cropped by rabbits, sheltered from the wind by one of the few remaining gorse bushes, where they were hidden from all except those out at sea. Margaret had laughed out loud when an oil tanker steamed into view just as Declan had pulled down his trousers and bared his buttocks. She could imagine the captain scanning the shore with his binoculars and suddenly reeling back, unable to believe his eyes as he came across their naked bodies. She waved. Declan failed to see the joke and it took several minutes of fevered caresses before he forgave her.

They had made love as the seagulls soared and dived above them and Margaret's tanker captain steered his vessel due north across the mouth of the bay. The whisky bottle empty, they had shared a cigarette, lying on their backs staring at the sky. There was a chill in the air now as the sun slipped down behind the great bulk of the headland, casting a shadow out across the churning sea way below them, snuffing out the light as if a pall had been thrown over a glittering friend, leaving only a dull green corpse. It grew quieter; the seabirds had deserted them too. The only sound was the wind whistling through the solitary gorse bush, the last warm rays of sunlight retreating rapidly from its prickly thickets. As the light died, Margaret sat up. It was time to go. There was no reason to stay. Not for this – and she glanced down at Declan, lying satisfied, eyes closed, orange pubic hair poking through his still open fly.

She moved away, pleased to be alone, climbing into the light and warmth of the summit. Wind whipping her face, arms hugging her body, she stood and gazed at the horizon, tinged now with yellows, reds and purples. People were nothing to her, she knew that, just harsh words, angry faces, lies, betrayal, blows, a stickiness between the legs. She had seen it all, felt it all, but not anymore, not for much longer.

Her name could be faintly heard, drifting then gone. Way below Declan, his hair an orange full stop on a sheet of dark green, was stirring. She waved. He waved. It made her happy to see him. She loved a secret.

After that Declan chased her, slipping and sliding, down the steep slope to the shore. They walked back hand-in-hand along the deserted front, had a quick cup of tea in a cafe next to the bus stop, rode on the top deck back into town, briefly kissed as they said good-bye, Declan to go to work, Margaret to stroll contentedly back home.

She enjoyed walking. Her frustration and anger seemed to drain away then, flowing into the gutters and drains of the city she had come to know well. It was her time to dream. Drunk on the streets were her favourite moments, she loved the confusion of distance and time. One moment you would be outside Mulligan's the next across College Green, everything lost. Another moment and it would take forever to walk the length of

Kildare Street, your life stretching on ahead of you, people and places passing interminably slowly. The blurring of places and faces, the dulling of pain, the clarity of vision, familiar places seen anew – she drank it all in and cherished it, more than anything else in the world, for being her own.

There had been a long distance to walk to her bed-sit – the whole unbending length of Rathmines Street, slightly uphill, across broken paving stones and past gnarled tree trunks, their roots lifting the flags – but then she was there. Space had been erased without memory, she was happy; she had no need to remember. Her hand on the cool rusting iron of the ageing gatepost, she turned to walk up the steps to her front door. It was slightly ajar. The whisky dullness evaporated. In the brief instant before the policewoman appeared, Margaret's landlady at her shoulder, she knew there was something wrong. A trap.

"Margaret Macready?"

A male voice close behind her. It was the policeman. She should have guessed when she first saw him. It was getting dark. Looking up, the smoke pouring from the chimney was clear against the orange tinged grey of the evening sky. What a fool! If only she had stayed out longer.

Margaret lunged out of reach of the policeman, barging painfully into a dustbin, spilling its rank contents across the path before dashing down the steep slippery stairs to the basement well. Mrs Kilpatrick often left her door on the latch. Margaret would be lucky – she always was. Behind her she could hear the scrape of metal on concrete and a burble of voices, then the clink of iron-shod boots on stone steps.

The door wouldn't move, it was locked. The bitch! Pushing with all her weight barely shifted it and Margaret drew back her arm ready to strike the glass panel.

"I wouldn't do that, young lady," said a voice of booming authority. Then: "Margaret Macready?"

The policeman was not angry. She had expected him to be, but he sounded almost friendly. Even so she said nothing in reply. Her heart was beating fast and she needed to feel it. It showed she was alive. A vein in her temple twitched in sympathy, her head throbbed, the graze on her knee smarted, and her chest ached at the thought of all the trouble she must be in.

"Steady now, Margaret we know it's you. Why else would you run away like that?"

She shrugged.

"Margaret, don't play us for fools, your landlady pointed you out."

It was the first time the policewoman had spoken and there was a chill in her voice. She stood facing Margaret, about the same height and about the same age but devoid of sympathy.

"The old cow would say that. She never had a good word for me."

A shadow stepped back from the top of the stairs, shuffling footsteps could be heard then voices. Margaret was unable to contain herself and shouted out loudly, "Telling everyone all about it, are you? You old witch!"

There was for a moment silence. The policeman smiled.

"I'll not have you speaking to me like that in my own house!" came the landlady's shrill reply. "You dirty little animal. If I'd only known…"

"You'd have what?"

"I'd have thrown you out ages ago."

"Oh, yeah?"

"Come on now, you two, no more shouting in the street."

A gentle restraining touch on her shoulder.

"Stop it now, Margaret. Any more and we'll be taking you in."

The policewoman's steely eyes showed no pity.

"Not just taking you back."

For the first time Margaret understood what was happening, and almost collapsed as the realization hit her that this was not about some petty indiscretion – shoplifting, being drunk and disorderly, fornication – all of which she was guilty of, but something far more serious. Tears began to flow. She did not mean to cry, but it was impossible to stop.

"At last. Now, one more time, are you Margaret Macready?"

She nodded, her head hanging down, staring at her mud-spattered shoes.

"That's better. Now come with us and no trouble, mind."

A hand descended heavily on her upper arm, the firm pressure leaving her no choice but to move. The policewoman walked ahead, the policeman behind, constantly urging Margaret up the steep steps.

"Stand back now, please. No trouble."

People had gathered at the top of the stairs, jostling, necks craning, as the sorry procession emerged above ground. At the front, inches from Margaret, was her landlady, her face distorted by anger and disgust, restrained only by her respect for authority from lunging forward. The army at her shoulders, friends and neighbours mirrored her fury in their faces, but there were traces of amusement too. To have been harbouring an immoral fugitive from the Church – a Magdalen girl – was a blow from which God-fearing Mrs Cleary would take some time to recover.

"How dare you? After all I've done for you."

Margaret felt the blast of warm damp breath on her tear-stained face and, head held high, stared directly back. Inarticulate in her anger, Mrs Cleary stamped her feet and raged inwardly, the firm pressure of the policewoman's arm across her chest more than enough to hold her back. To her Margaret was evil personified – the devil's child – a fallen woman capable of anything.

The crowd parted as the prisoner and her escorts climbed the steps to the house, then closed behind them as they went inside. It was all so familiar, yet Margaret's mind was rapidly emptying. If asked, she would not have been able to describe the pale ochre wallpaper with the green vertical stripe, fading in places on the stairs where countless nameless people had rubbed against it, nor the balding red carpet with its gold, green and blue swirls; the picture on the landing opposite her room of a white-washed farm in the fog-shrouded wastes of Connemara, a mere blank frame. Soon she would never have been here, all traces of her presence wiped clean.

Her room was unrecognizable, too. She had kept it clean and well ordered, everything in its place. Now her clothes and makeup, all she possessed, were heaped untidily on the carpet. Scattered beneath the chest of drawers were the pieces of a small vase she had taken from her home that night her father had turned her out. It had been her only ornament and she had displayed it proudly centre stage. It had been her Mother's.

"How dare you? These are mine."

She turned, her anger against Mrs Cleary fired now by grief, straight into the strong arms of her captors, struggled briefly then sank to her knees. Released, she crawled over to her things, gathered them together then packed them carefully into her battered black duffle bag which the policewoman had retrieved from the top of the wardrobe and tossed over to her.

Her landlady, leaning against the doorway, watched in satisfaction. Silenced until then by a warning look from the policeman, she was no longer able to keep quiet.

"Make sure she doesn't take anything of mine. I wouldn't put anything past her, the little..."

"Mrs Cleary, please, I won't warn you again. We've got everything under control and will be leaving in a minute."

"What about the money she owes me? She hasn't paid me for this week yet."

"You should have thought about that before you turned me in," Margaret hissed as she got to her feet, hatred shrouding her eyes and baring her teeth.

"Should have waited until Saturday, but you couldn't, could you?"

"Wasn't me dearie, though I would have done if I'd known. Would have been a pleasure."

It was the cruel truth and Margaret knew it. It had seemed a simple case of cause and effect, but hatred was not enough to explain everything and now there was only uncertainty. The man and woman who currently controlled her destiny were no help either. One was almost bovine in his blank respect for the order of things; the other relished yet another sign of Margaret's demoralisation and confusion.

"We wouldn't tell you even if we knew."

"Couldn't reveal our sources."

"You needn't worry about it, either, as you won't have the chance again. If you think you can go and do just as you like, you need to think again. We'll be watching you from now on. Watching your every move."

Mrs Cleary nodded smugly as she followed the three of them down the stairs. Margaret's bag felt heavy, even though she knew there was very little in it, and she dragged it down step-by-step. In the dingy hallway the policeman took it from her and they swept through the silent crowd gathered outside and climbed into a black police car parked at the kerb. As she slid across the cold leather seat, it struck Margaret as strange that she hadn't noticed the blue light and white lettering as she'd walked home. If she had she might not be in this mess now, but she couldn't remember a thing. Her head throbbed dully. It was obviously meant to be.

A young boy pressed his face hard against the side window, his nose distorting grotesquely, teeth blackened from chewing liquorice, his breath misting the tinted glass. She covered him with her splayed hand and he stepped back, grinning. Through the rear window, Margaret saw his mother rush up and drag him roughly by the ear back on to the pavement.

"Right, to Our Lady of Mercy. Should take about fifteen minutes," the policeman told her, "They'll be waiting for you."

Chapter 8

The Snug – March 1996 – two minutes to two

Maeve was grinning idiotically. She wasn't a drinker, more's the pity. Of all her friends at the Convent, this was the one with whom Margaret would have to spend the rest of her life, the one with whom she had least in common. Just her rotten luck. All they could talk about was their shared time at the laundry. Margaret Macready was not going to have any family appear out of nowhere to rescue her – she had that in common with Maeve as well – no dreams come true. Or was it nightmares? She laughed. She'd never heard from her sister or any of the others in all the long years she'd been here. Had never gone looking for them either, even when she was on the outside. It had never occurred to her, till now. But she couldn't see it somehow. Her family had been smashed to bits as far as she was concerned when they'd cast her out. She could never forgive them, even if she was as lonely as hell.

It was almost two. Doris' lot were late. Maybe they had changed their minds, were abandoning her one more time. It wouldn't be difficult. There she sat looking so docile – this new habit of chewing the inside of her lip made her look like a sheep sometimes – it would be so easy to hurt her. After all, Margaret had done it often enough herself. Just say boo!

No, they would come. They were different, a new generation, the agonies of the past forgotten, they wouldn't let Doris down. She would go forever; let's face it, then Margaret would be alone. Or as good as.

"Doris?"

Her glasses flashed as she looked up, catching the afternoon sun as it streamed in through the misted windows.

"I've always wanted to ask you this … You are listening?"

Lenses flaring, Doris nodded blindly, her eyes sightless.

"Seeing as you'll be going soon, I wondered why did you go back to the Convent? You know, that time we ran away?"

Doris was paying attention but said nothing. She was thinking. This was a question she had never answered before even to herself. She knew exactly what Margaret was talking about. It was as if it was yesterday. It was true she had gone back to the laundry all by herself. She hadn't had to. Margaret and her had had a place to stay, they had work, more than enough, and money for what they needed. She had stayed away from the Convent quite happily for nearly three months but then one day, without telling Margaret, leaving her things in their room, she'd walked all the way across town, knocked on the gate and been welcomed back. No one had said a thing, but Doris had told them everything. Had freely confessed.

"I couldn't believe it, you know, when I found out. It took me some time as well. I thought you were staying over with one of the boys at first so I wasn't worried, but then when you didn't come back the next day or the next, I was scared."

"I did my penance."

"I'm sure you did. Didn't do me much good though. Couldn't go to the Gardai, could I? I thought you'd been murdered or something. I went spare."

"No."

"What did you expect? It happens."

"I don't think I thought about it."

"You're telling me! It took me ages to work it out. It was only when there was no body washed up on some beach somewhere."

Maeve shuddered, listening intently, drunkenly interested in a story that had scandalized the laundry at the time. They had never talked about it before, even when pestered. Doris always sank into a contrite silence, while Margaret viciously stared down anyone who dared mention it. She had been terrifying at the time, unapproachable, like a caged beast.

"No shallow grave uncovered, no head found in a dustbin in Drumcondra, no leg washed up at Clontarf, or bloody hand in a leaking carrier bag out at Blackrock."

A smile. Doris could manage a smile; Margaret did have a sense of humour. It had been one of the more attractive things about her in the early days.

"I'm glad you think it's funny, I was so scared! Eventually, though, you going back there was the only thing that could have happened. I couldn't actually check, of course, that would have been too dangerous, but I felt it was right. It sort of reassured me, then I discovered it was true and I couldn't believe it. That on top of everything else. How could you?"

"I...I..."

"We were having a good time, weren't we?"

"I'd wanted to see what it was like on the outside for a long time, I really had. And it was good, it was, Margaret. I enjoyed myself."

"But?"

"I got so lonely for the other girls, our friends."

Aghast, Margaret shook her head. She could not believe what she was hearing and made no effort to hide her disgust.

If there had been one time in her life when she had thought she had found a true friend it had been in those few months in the bed-sit with Doris. She had been a companion, a confidante, a co-conspirator and she had betrayed Margaret for others. Simple treachery.

"I couldn't bear not seeing them ever again, and I suppose I just wanted to go back. I felt I was an orphan again. It was like when I first arrived here and I hated it. I'd lost my real mother once, then I felt I was losing her all over again. The nuns were my mother."

Maeve, glass in hand, was nodding in agreement. She would never have dreamed of leaving and was reassured to hear Doris talking like this. Margaret's scarlet mouth twisted in derision.

"So that's it, you were lonely?"

It was difficult for Doris to add anything else. It was as simple as that for her, yet Margaret seemed to demand more. She could say that living with her had become increasingly unbearable, that her intensity and zest for life had been exhausting, that the risks she had been prepared to take, the men she'd been with, had made Doris sick with worry. But somehow loneliness said it best. It wasn't just a desire for the other people at the Convent, so much as the stability and security they offered, the routine. She knew Margaret would never understand that, however hard she tried to explain. In fact, she was sure she had tried in the past, one inebriated night or another, but had got nowhere. For Margaret, people were just a means to an end, never friends, and that included Doris. That was why she had gone back.

"You wanted your Ma, is that what you're telling me?"

"Sorry, Margaret."

"Didn't you think of me? How lonely I'd be…"

Doris looked at her, silently trying to be helpful.

"… because I was, Doris, you know that, don't you?"

She shook her head, scrupulously honest for the first time.

"You didn't know? More like didn't care. You've always been selfish, Doris Blaney, always out for yourself. I don't know why I asked you to come with me in the first place. I should've have known you'd let me down".

If she could have cried, she would have – anything to impress upon Doris the magnitude of her betrayal, because in Margaret's eyes, Doris had been a traitor since the second she had seen her, hand covering her mouth, standing at the back of the crowd of laundry women gathered in the refectory to welcome her back. She should have broken free then and attacked her, thought Margaret now, hit her hard, made her feel the anger she felt; but that wasn't really her style and she had got her revenge after all, over time. Margaret had verbally pushed, tripped, teased and confused Doris as the years took their toll. She now had her at her mercy and there was satisfaction in that. This was the last time they would meet, that was very clear, and it was time to have her suspicions confirmed.

"Did you tell them?"

"What?"

"Doris, you haven't always been so stupid! You know that, don't you?"

Maeve looked pained. She didn't want her friends to fall out, not now, not after so long.

"What, Margaret? What do you want to know?"

"Did you tell them where I was living? Did you?"

Eyes open wide, Doris stared at her.

"I told you, I told them everything."

"Our address?"

"I confessed."

"But why? I thought you were my friend?"

"It was for your own good."

"My own good? That's rich! You ruined my life, Doris. Do you know that?"

There was silence around the table.

"I was looking after you, Margaret. I did care. I told them about Frank."

"You did what?"

"I told Father James about Frank, when I got back. He said nothing at the time, just listened. But Frank never bothered you after that, did he? They made him move all his stuff out of the basement, didn't they? All he had then was the shed in the garden. I did that for you."

"Don't make me laugh!"

"I couldn't have you coming back and Frank still up to his old tricks, could I?"

"You think that makes me feel any better? I was free, Doris, and you took that away."

"I had to take care of you, Margaret. You were just too wild. You didn't seem to care."

"I don't think I'll ever be able to forgive you. How could you do that to your best friend?"

Margaret was aghast, but she found she'd overplayed her hand, as usual.

"No, you were never my best friend, Margaret," said Doris completely unembarrassed. "That was always Lily."

"Lily, Lily! You're the bloody limit, Doris, you really are."

"I wish she was here."

"What's the point of saying that? She's been gone an age." Margaret took a long draft of stout and stared malevolently at Doris.

"I really miss her."

"But she left without telling you where she was going, didn't she? Now that's not very friendly, is it?"

"She was my friend. She really was," Doris insisted stubbornly.

"Oh, was she? Well, I'm sick of you whining on and on about Lily. She left you in the lurch. No note, no message, no nothing. Some friend! I should know."

"Margaret, please. Can't you see she's getting upset?"

Maeve looked sympathetically across at Doris who was leaning forward onto the small bar-room table.

"She's upset. What about me?"

Determined not to be put off, Maeve spoke softly to Doris.

"It's all right, love. Lily was a friend to all of us."

"I know, Maeve, but she helped me so much, all those years."

"Aye, it would have been nice for her to have been here on our last day, the five of us all together again one last time."

"She wasn't very well before she disappeared. Do you remember? She wasn't herself. Maybe she died?"

"I don't think so, Doris."

"An' they didn't want to tell me, so as not to upset me. They knew I was her best friend."

"I don't think that's it at all, there was no reason for them not to tell us. They tell us when people die or leave or whatever, don't they?"

Maeve had been certain when she had started speaking, but grew increasingly uneasy as she went on, realizing that she actually had no idea what had happened to Lily. It was a mystery.

There was a cry from the public bar, some laughter then scattered applause. The fire in the corner of the snug settled, sending a stream of sparks crackling up the chimney, and a faint cloud of smoke puffing into the room. The coals glowed.

"I never stop thinking of Lily, ever," Doris persisted.

Maeve slowly shook her head. She desperately wanted someone to be thinking of her like that every day and every night, but her faith was slipping.

"I'm sure I'll find them in here."

A voice, familiar yet somehow distant, carried across the pub.

"Afternoon, Father."

"Seamus, what are you doing here? I thought you'd be at the races on a day like this?"

"I would, Father, but the wife has her brother coming round, and you know what she's like?"

"I do, Seamus, I do to be sure. Now, you can help me. Have you seen any of my ladies in here this lunchtime?"

The three women sat in silence, motionless, as if caught in the act of committing a petty crime.

"I thought so. Thank you, Seamus. I'll be seeing you and the wife at mass, Sunday?"

"I never miss, Father, you know me."

"I'll be talking to you about that, Seamus."

Laughter hung in the air like confetti as Father Michael swung open the door of the snug, drew heavily on the stub of a cigarette, then dropped it to the floor where it glowed briefly among the stained sawdust before being extinguished by the priest's grinding heel. He beamed at Doris, Margaret and Maeve.

"I thought I'd find you here."

He turned his head as he exhaled.

"I just bumped into Barbara outside the Convent, piling up her bags. She said you were still here. Been drinking all this time, have we?"

Maeve nodded.

"Come on, why the glum faces? I know it's a big day for you all, but there's no need to be so sad. Here, let me get you a drink. Then we can raise a glass to the future. Same again?"

"Thanks, Father. But things won't be the same though, will they?"

"To be sure, Maeve. But you'll keep in touch, I know you will."

As he made his way to the bar, the priest smiled benevolently at the three women.

"So what have you all been talking about? You've been in here hours."

Maeve glanced at Doris, who was sitting with her face cast down, then shrugged blankly.

"Old times, is it?"

"We've just been talking about Lily, Father."

Doris had flared into life, straightening in her seat, eyes staring straight at the startled priest.

"Oh, yes?"

"What happened to her, Father? None of us knows. We just keep guessing, going round and round."

To cover his confusion, Father Michael tapped the pockets of his tweed jacket, searching for his tobacco. He found it, took it out, opened it, slid the lid deftly onto the bottom of the tin and placed it on the bar in front of him together with his papers and matches.

"Do you know, Father? She was a friend of mine."

Margaret shook her head and blew out heavily. Maeve extended a comforting arm and Doris, relieved, briefly rested her head on it before looking up again, clearly distraught.

Lily's unexplained absence was a continuing agony for her, the loss tainted by the unwelcome suspicion of betrayal was difficult to bear at the best of times, but was made infinitely worse by the imminent departure of all her other friends. She was afraid of what was to come, the loss of the people she'd held dear, the severing of her collective lifeline to the past. She wouldn't be on her own, she would have her new family, but somehow they seemed outside time.

"Do you know what happened, Father? Because if you do Doris really wants to hear. It makes her ill sometimes just to think about it," Maeve told him.

A thinly rolled cigarette between his lips, the priest struck a match, the loose tobacco crackled and glowed and he inhaled deeply. Smoke eased your passage through this life, it really did, and knowing his luck would probably do it through the next as well. Father Michael smiled.

"I do know, yes."

The faces of the three women lit up expectantly.

"She told me everything."

"Tell us Father?"

Doris' voice was child-like and eager.

"I can't do that, Doris. You know I can't. Secrets of the confessional and all that."

And quite a few other secrets, he acknowledged to himself. Ones he never intended to let see the light of day. He handed the women their glasses of Guinness, which each accepted in silence, and then, double whisky in one hand, he drew a chair up to the table and sat down. Doris sipped at her drink then spoke up, ignoring the priest.

"Can you remember what Lily looked like?"

"Course we can, Doris, don't be so silly. It wasn't that long ago, you know," Maeve replied.

"I don't think I can. She was one of my best friends, Maeve, and now she's just a blur."

"Oh, come on, if she walked in here now you'd recognize her in a flash. Don't pretend you wouldn't."

"That's different, 'course I would. I'm not daft."

"Could have fooled me, sometimes."

"Margaret!"

"But she's not going to, is she?"

"What?"

"Come in here – into this pub – ever again. I won't ever see her again. And she was my best friend."

"You're forever telling us that, Doris, and we fucking know!

Going on like that, how do you think it makes us feel? You should think before you speak up. Lily probably just got fed up with you and wanted to get away. Start afresh with no ties."

"Margaret, please don't speak like that. Father Michael is here."

She looked angrily across the table at Maeve, who sat shaking her head.

"Oh, come on, Maeve, she gets on your nerves too, you've told me. Why don't you say something? Too scared people will think badly of you?"

Agitated, Doris stood up and glared at Margaret.

"Truth is you've never liked me, Maggie. Never, ever."

Father Michael felt as if he was slipping backwards, dissolving into the dark wood panelling and passing from view. So total was his disappearance that the women seemed to have completely forgotten about him. It was as if the absolute knowledge that he would tell them nothing had made him of no value to them, and as a result invisible. Here they were arguing about Lily thinking they knew her, when in fact he knew more about her than all of them. Lily's was not such a remarkable story, she was much like all the others in fact, except in one remarkable respect, and that would never have come to light at all if four years ago he hadn't given Lily and Doris the afternoon off...

Chapter 9

Father Michael's round – April 1992

Doris looked at the stain on the sheet, peered at it closely, but without her glasses things were not always clear. It was large, yellowish and ragged at the edges. She straightened up and stretched, arcing her aching back, pushing with her arms until she felt her chest muscles crack. This board was too low, she kept telling them, but it had done no good.

"Now should it go back?"

She really should wear her glasses. They would help her no end when it came to these sort of decisions, but they were next door to useless with all this steam. She peered at the stain again, smoothed it with her hand, then stooped down and read the cardboard label attached to the large dirty linen bag at her feet, filled with freshly washed sheets.

"Batch 17, Drumcondra Prison."

Her mind made up, she returned to her pressing.

"Who's going to check in there?" she sniggered. Doris was tired, she hadn't slept well, it sometimes happened and then she would pay for it for days afterwards. It always seemed to make her back worse and she'd get a terrible pain behind her eyes.

The ancient Stanley and Kennard steam press hissed venomously as Doris pressed down on the burnished brass bar and with eyes tightly closed she felt a hot rush of steam on her bare skin as it escaped under pressure.

"One, two, three," Doris counted, her eyes flickering open, "four, five, six". She wished she could see the clock on the wall above her head, but it was misted up. "Seven, eight, nine, ten."

Doris hauled up on the bar – first resistance as the pressure held – then the heavy counter-balanced press swung easily upwards. Clouds of steam rolled out, briefly enveloping her, as she stood again blind to the world, arms above her head. Swirling and spiralling in the many cross drafts of the old laundry, columns of mist would rise rapidly towards the skylights, open in all but the stormiest weather.

Squinting at the perfectly smooth white linen, Doris expertly grasped the sheet and with a flick of her wrists slipped the next creased section into position under the press. If you did it just right, then there would be no need to smooth out the material with your hand, you could bring the press down almost immediately.

Doris had it off perfectly, but it had taken her quite a while to achieve that exact balance between the forward flick of the sheet and the tension holding it back. It was amusing to watch people new to the laundry either pushing and sliding the freshly washed sheets into place, almost climbing into the press some of them, or else flicking them too hard and seeing the whole lot glide over the edge and fall in a crumpled heap on the other side. Newcomers missed bits as well and the rejected sheets would come back and have to go through again. It was often down to Doris to show them the ropes and it did make her laugh sometimes how useless people could be. It made her feel happy that she was good at something.

The steam was too much for some women, but Doris had got used to it. She liked the perfumed smell and the chemical edge that hung in the air. She could bear the tautness of the skin on her face that tingled after she had finished work, her ruddy complexion. Margaret always used to tease her, "who's been out for too long in the sun then?" but that was Margaret. She didn't even mind the burning at the back of her throat, the frequent soreness at night when she swallowed – she could take lozenges for that – and the sodden clothes at the end of the day. That was an occupational hazard, which almost everyone she worked with suffered from. You got used to the sweating, to the constant trickle of perspiration running down your spine and between your breasts, the beads of moisture on your nose, the dampness under your arms and the soaking handkerchief you kept in the top pocket of your overall for mopping your brow. Doris just couldn't imagine after all these years doing anything else and she was good at it. Doris was a perfectionist.

Today though she felt weary. As the steam cleared and she opened her eyes she saw the stain again – it looked far worse now the creases had gone – brown and mis-shapen in the centre of a vast expanse of white. As a girl when she first started in the laundry she had often been disgusted at the state of some of the sheets and clothes they had to wash, but had taken a strange pleasure in pondering what could have caused the stains, musing on lives so different from her own. The fascination had faded over the years as familiarity with people's dirty linen bred indifference. This stain had though for some reason rekindled her interest. It looked like blood to her. Tea was often the same colour but was more uniform, this stain was paler in the centre with a darker brown rim, that meant blood in her experience – and blood in a prison conjured up images of violence, petty jealousies exploding into savagery, out of control and primal, protection rackets, bullying, the sadistic razor slash, the arbitrary blow from a fist. The list was endless and Doris would let her imagination run free.

With a sigh she pulled the sheet from the press, tagged it with the prison mark, crumpled it into a bundle and walked over to the far wall before tossing it onto a small heap of assorted whites that were piling up ready for bleaching. Lily rubbed up against her with a tall bundle of sheets in her arms.

"Only ten minutes to go till elevenses."

"You always were a mind reader, Lily."

They both laughed. The press seemed strangely quiescent when Doris returned. Steam was barely rising from the many holes punched in orderly lines across its metal surface and it felt cooler than when she had left it. Doris shook her head and tapped at the pressure gauge on the side of the machine. The needle dropped dramatically. A loss of pressure, it had been doing this a lot lately. The whole thing was old and needed replacing. She knew what to do, but had been told she wasn't to touch anything. It was a job for Frank, but if you waited for him to repair anything you'd be here all day. Better to do it yourself.

Behind the steam press, painted red but covered in a layer of thick dust, were a series of valves and pipes that controlled and directed the steam from boilers in the basement. The rubber seal on one of the valves was faulty and would periodically leak, reducing the pressure and causing the regulator on the boiler to cut off the flow of steam. Doris had watched Frank deal with this problem many times before – he wasn't slow in coming forward in telling people about his technical know-how either – so she was confident she knew exactly what to do.

Closing the press, she crouched down and, taking special care to avoid hitting her head on the operating bar, she crawled under the machine. Heaven knew when they had last swept under there. The fluff and lint irritated her nose and she sneezed loudly, raising a cloud of dust that stung her eyes. Kneeling, she caught the crown of her head on a protruding joint in one of the steam pipes and cried out. Cursing herself for bothering with this problem and not calling Frank, she rubbed her head and gazed at the pipes that emerged through crudely cut holes in the floor.

There were three of them, each with a valve, two red and the third daubed with green paint. It was the last one that was hissing steam and leaking water – there was quite a puddle on the floor below. No longer as certain as she had been, Doris reached out for the green valve and tried to turn it clockwise. It was almost too hot to touch and wouldn't move. The spindle of the valve was rusty and she used all her strength to try and shift it, this time anti-clockwise. There was a high-pitched squeal as the valve turned suddenly in her hand. Scalding hot steam exiting at high pressure caught her wrist and forearm, instantly blistering the skin. Barely able to comprehend what had happened she rolled onto her side, clutching her arm and screaming. The hissing grew louder as the steam spurted out unhindered into the confined space below the press and then billowed over the edges of the press. For once Doris didn't close her eyes but forced them painfully open, staring ahead, a roiling whiteness blinding her. In panic she kicked out with her legs, pathetically trying to flee while lying down.

***

An animal thrashing in dread on the crowded, slippery, piss and shit-smeared ramp of the Dungannon slaughter-house. The smell of violent death heavy in the air. Her Father had taken Doris there one Tuesday afternoon on the way home from school – she'd been pestering him for weeks to show her where he worked. She had stood on the bottom rung of the metal fence that lined the livestock entrance to the abattoir and waited excitedly. She'd briefly held her father's hand. The smell of animals was heavy in the air – the manure reek of the farmyard touched with something rawer – Doris didn't find it unpleasant.

"The next batch will be along in a minute. If you stay here you'll have a good view and you'll be able to help the boys move 'em along."

"Da, can we go inside later. I want to see inside?"

"We'll have to see. If I can find Mr Tavistock I'll ask him if it's all right. It's not really the place for a young 'un like you."

"Da."

"All right I'll ask."

He had backed away, laughing.

"Don't you move now."

Her Father disappeared passing through the hanging sheets of opaque plastic that shielded the inner workings of the abattoir from those on the outside, just as a cattle truck reversed through the gates, its exhaust belching smoke. A young boy in a soiled tee-shirt and jeans, with muddy gumboots, ran ahead waving and shouting. Raising his hand suddenly, the vehicle shuddered to a halt inches from the top of the concrete ramp. A blond-haired man stuck his head out of the driver's door and called out. A thumbs up from the boy and the engine died. Diesel fumes, blue in the pale afternoon sun rose lazily upwards as Doris heard for the first time the lowing of the bullocks and the sound of their shuffling hooves on the wooden floor of the truck. Bits of animal protruded from the open slats that ran down both sides of the vehicle – brown fur, pale dripping noses, teeth gnawing the stripped wood, a shitty tail, its frayed creamy tip caught on a nail.

Several men wearing blood-stained aprons emerged from behind Doris, the plastic sheets slapping against each other as they walked through. They were smiling, one tossed a lit cigarette end into the yard and coughed, then he closed the gate, letting the heavy metal latch slip firmly into place, sealing off any means of escape for the cattle. The men moved up to the truck, one shook hands with the driver then climbed over the fence and readied himself on the other side.

"Watch yourself there, love. They can come down at a fair rate."

Without any ceremony they pulled out the metal pegs holding the tailgate in place and let it slam to the ground. The animals at the front, stunned by the sudden rush of daylight, blinked open eyed and for a second didn't move, then gravity and the crush of those behind sent them tumbling down the wooden ramp to crash heavily onto the wet concrete. The first bullock – his back to the gate as it opened, slid down on his side and failed to get to his feet as the others stampeded over him. He disappeared from view in the rush of black, brown and white animals, their bellows almost drowning out the cries of the men, who were now standing on the fence and lashing out at any part of any animal that came close. Most of the cattle quickly regained their footing, but appeared reluctant to move forward, the diesel fumes were clearing and the lead animals were beginning to sense what lay ahead. They tried to turn back, eyes bulging, nostrils flaring, but were forced forward by the weight of animals behind them. Muscles loosened in fear as panic spread through the dislocated herd and urine and faeces began to cascade down the ramp making it difficult for the bullocks to keep their balance. Hooves began slipping and sliding on the ridged concrete; the animals struggled to stay upright. The slaughtermen and the driver urged them on, voices loud and urgent, their hands slapping heavily onto quivering backs. The young boy screamed in glee and rattled a stick across the metal bars of the fence, his face wreathed in smiles. The human cries were matched by the panicked bellowing of the bullocks, growing more urgent as their mass squeezed the leading individuals along the narrowing passageway towards the grimy plastic sheeting that shielded them from seeing into the brightly lit interior.

Doris watched, stunned. Standing on the fence, she leant

back as the cattle brushed past her hands and feet. She had no desire to touch them, as she normally would have done at the farm, no desire to feel their terror, no desire to touch something she knew to be already dead. Seconds after the first bullock parted the plastic sheets and passed through the doorway, a sharp retort echoed clearly across the yard, and rippled through the straining column behind. She dimly saw a dark shape drop from view and shadowy figures close in around it.

"One, two, three…"

The bulging liquid eyes of a bullock, its head trapped across the back of the one in front, stared back over its shoulder, taking, Doris thought, his last look at the sky.

"…four, five, six, seven."

The retort again, followed by the tremor of the doomed herd. And so it went on. Doris stayed on the fence and did not go searching for her father, as she no longer had any desire to see what he did inside. At home she stopped asking him about his job and was never quite the same with him again. What stuck in her mind was the sight, as the numbers dwindled, of that brown bullock, the first to crash out of the truck, lying on his side in the filth, unable to get up and running, desperately running.

***

She began to feel the pain now, an intense burning in her hand. Tears streaming down her face, Doris cried out through clenched teeth, her lips pared back in agony.

"Oh my God, who is it?"

"It must be Doris."

"Get Frank, someone, for pity's sake."

"Doris, are you all right?"

"Listen to that screaming. Oh, Mary, mother of God, she's hurt."

As soon as she heard the commotion Lily rushed back from the drying yard, where she had been un-pegging and folding sheets. Instantly recognising Doris' cry she elbowed her way through the group of women gathered anxiously around the steaming press. For an instant she thought it had caught fire as the air was so thick and the room densely shrouded.

"Where is she, for God's sake?"

"Must be underneath, there's nowhere else."

"Sounds like it."

Thinking only of the valiant knights of yore, their heroic deeds and good triumphing against the odds, Lily covered her face with her sweat-stained handkerchief, got down on her hands and knees and reached tentatively into the steaming underbelly of the press. Her arm moved in a broad arc and found nothing. She crawled closer and reached in again. The others watched, huddling together as they drew nearer. An instant later Lily snapped back her hand and swore under her breath.

"She bloody kicked me! I think it's broken. I felt it snap."

"Move it around Lily, that's the only way to tell."

Lily weakly shook her wrist in front of the engrossed crowd and as the pain eased more confidently flexed her fingers. Again covering her face, she peered into the murk.

"Doris, it's me. Stop fannying about for a minute will you – and keep your legs away from me. I'm coming under to get you out."

Lily's familiar voice reassured Doris and her panic eased. Lily was her friend; you could rely on her to get things done. She lay still, waiting for strong arms to sweep her to safety, but instead a hand roughly grabbed her hair and pulled. Doris screamed.

"Lily, my hair!"

"Sorry, Doris. Oh, I'm sorry."

"Stop messing about, Lily. She'll be badly burned if we don't get her out soon."

"That's typical of you, Margaret. If you think you can do it better, you come down here and have a go. I don't see you."

"Come on, you two, this is an emergency. Keep at it, Lily, there's a good girl."

Aggrieved, she moved to the side and reached under the press again, grasped something solid and hauled Doris out by the arm. Her eyes were closed and she was curled up like a baby, damp hair plastered across a ruddy moisture-streaked face.

"She looks like a piece of salt beef," whispered Margaret, "pink like that an' all trussed up."

Barbara, despite being genuinely concerned, couldn't help smiling.

"Hush up, Margaret, it's not the time."

The hissing of steam from the faulty machine, an alarming symphony of gushing waves of sound and high pitched whines unnerved the women as they stared at Doris lying motionless on the floor. Lily held her hand, but was too shocked to speak even the most basic words of comfort. She feared for the damage that had been done and didn't want things to get any worse.

"This is ridiculous, let me through."

Her patience gone, Barbara pushed her way to the front, crouched down beside Doris and loudly called her name. Instantly her eyes opened and she tried to sit up.

"Take it easy, Doris, you're safe now, one thing at a time. How are you feeling?".

Lying back she croaked the word "hot" and smiled faintly. Then she raised her right arm.

"It bloody hurts."

The inside of her wrist was badly blistered.

"Don't worry, we'll take care of that. Doctor's on his way. It's lucky you had your sleeve down or it could have been a lot worse, strikes me."

Barbara touched Doris gently on the cheek. It felt hot.

"Does that hurt?"

She shook her head. Relieved, Barbara couldn't help herself.

"You were very lucky then. If it had caught your face... Good Lord, Doris, what an earth were you doing under there? You know Frank deals with all that sort of thing."

Bemused, Doris looked anxiously from side to side as if searching for the answer she knew was out there somewhere.

"Never mind, you old lummox. No real harm done by the look of it."

"By the look of what?"

Father Michael sounded angry. He had been showing a prospective client around the laundry and was irritated to discover no one working when he had flung open the door with a flourish. To find everyone gathered in a huddle at the far end of the hall had only made his temper worse.

"What is going on here? Why aren't you working? It's not break time yet."

Shrinking before him the crowd of women parted to reveal Lily and Barbara crouched over the prone body of Doris, the three of them shrouded in steam. Michael crossed himself.

"Doris has scalded herself on this old machine," Barbara called out without turning to face the priest.

"Never known this to happen before," he muttered to a smartly dressed man standing just behind him. "Usually runs like clockwork. Is she all right?"

"I think so, Father, shocked mostly. Just her arm seems to have caught the worse of it".

"Have you called for Doctor Trelford?"

"Yes... I'm not sure..."

"What do you mean not sure? You either have or you haven't."

A woman standing next to the priest meekly tried to come to Barbara's aid.

"Siobhan's gone to call a doctor, Father. Did so as soon as the accident happened. But I think she said she was going for Doctor Peebles."

"That old skinflint! We should never use him. I thought everyone knew that."

"Sorry, Father."

"I'd really have thought your Reverend Mother would have… Oh, well, never you mind. He'll be here soon, I trust?"

"I expect so, Father."

Sensing movement next to him Michael turned away from the woman. Visibly relieved, she retreated behind one of the nearby ironing boards.

"I really must be going, Michael."

"Sorry, Martin, we'll be in touch?"

"I hope so."

"Look, I'm sorry, we could have had a jar but I must deal with this."

"No, you stay and sort things out."

As the man passed out of earshot, Father Michael couldn't hide his annoyance.

"Damn, damn, damn!"

Noticing that everyone was watching him, he smiled and said, "No one heard that, am I right? Only joking, you know, ladies."

A few women nodded, the rest remained still.

"Now let me see. Lily, how is she?"

"Not too bad, I think, Father. Could've been much worse."

Michael crossed himself again.

"Where's Frank? We need him to switch off this infernal steam. And you lot should probably move Doris away from the machine just to be on the safe side."

The press hissed malevolently. Water was dripping onto the floor, pooling in places where the tiles were uneven and soaking into Doris' sweat-drenched overalls. She was starting to feel cold and a shiver ran through her body.

"Doris, you can't be cold after all that can you?" Lily said affectionately, her face smiling down at her prone friend. "It's one extreme to the other with you, isn't it?"

The dark silhouette of Father Michael loomed above them, his dangling crucifix the only thing that was clear to Doris.

"How are you?"

His voice reverberated from on high, echoing around the narrow canyon where she lay, between the crowding legs and the steaming press. Doris heard her Mother calling back to her from the kitchen of their house in Dungannon as she bellowed at her from the hallway.

"There's no need to shout, Doris, I'm not deaf yet. Soon will be, though", and she would laugh and mutter to herself, "No bad thing if it means not hearing your father ever again". Then she would return to her washing up with a grin on her face. It was a rare thing and Doris liked to see it. The room seemed lighter somehow.

Lily repeated the words more softly and Doris nodded.

"Help me up, Lily, there's a dear."

The faint words slurred indistinctly into a distant noise that was barely audible above the splenetic hissing of the press. It appeared to gurgle upwards from deep within her, breaking the surface like bubbles of gas disturbed by fish scavenging across the bottom of a scummy pond. It had the desired effect. A space opened up around Doris. Legs moved aside, the dark shape of Father Michael disappeared, there was light – a bright light – and the strong arms of Lily grasped her around her chest and hauled her upwards. Her breath smelled strongly of peppermint – Lily was always sucking on a sweet – and the blue blur of her bosom was mesmerizing. Doris felt very sick. A chair was brought in from the corridor outside – chairs were not allowed in the laundry itself, there could be no excuse for slacking on the job – and Doris was propped up in it, supported by Lily. The room was spinning and she now felt very hot. Sweat oozed, and the pressure in her skull intensified, her stomach began contracting convulsively, and leaning forward she vomited a torrent of brackish grey brown fluid, which gushed across the flagstones and spattered the shoes and stockings of the gawping onlookers.

A ragged gasp of disgust rose from the crowd as horrified they shuffled back, colliding and stumbling over those bending to inspect the damage or rapidly wipe away the offending stains. Even strong-armed Lily faltered, almost letting go of her charge as the warm spray tickled her bare legs and the acrid smell turned her stomach.

"Easy, Doris, you'll soon be fine."

The doctor arrived along with Frank and the men took charge. Doris began to feel better almost immediately. The steam was turned off and sanity returned to the laundry. The women began behaving normally again. There were offers of a cup of tea, a bucket and mop appeared and the mess was cleaned up around her. Frank had been angry, shouting that he had warned them not to touch anything and what could they expect if they took no notice of him? Father Michael had quietened him down and the pair of them had gone off together.

"Those two they know it's their fault really, guilty consciences if you ask me. If they maintained things better, accidents wouldn't happen." Barbara squeezed Doris's hand as she spoke. "You should sue."

Doris smiled. Barbara was such a card sometimes.

Doctor Peebles took her temperature, bandaged her up and said it could have been much worse, but she should still have plenty of rest.

"She'll be lucky! That's like gold dust around here."

That had raised a laugh, even the doctor had smiled and he promised to speak to Father Michael, to make sure Doris had some time off. It was wonderful, all the attention she was getting. She couldn't remember when that had last happened, it had been so long ago.

The priest had returned soon afterwards, looking concerned, and had had a quiet chat with the doctor. A minute later, all smiles, he had given Doris and Lily the rest of the day off. The doctor had winked at them as he left. Lily had winked back.

"Come on, Doris, let's have a cuppa, put our feet up and read our horoscopes. Every cloud, you know."

"'Dark handsome mature man seeks woman under 35, for friendship, with the possibility of a loving relationship. Trips to theatre, opera, restaurants compulsory. All enquiries answered. A photo please. PO Box 97.' Good Lord, bet he fancies himself, it's clear he only wants one thing. How old do you think he is?"

Doris looked up from her paper and smiled at Lily who was sitting in the broad bay window, leaning back against a large dull green cushion, her legs tucked up beneath her body and a copy of the Sunday Independent spread out in front of her.

"You what?"

Doris shifted her bandaged arm into a more comfortable position on the chair she was sitting in, her feet up on a pouffe and a mug of tea steaming on the small table beside her. The Convent common room was drab, furnished in browns and dirty greens, the heavy wooden panelling oppressive, a large aspidistra standing dustily in the corner. But relaxing here in the window with the light from a palely overcast day filtering in, with her best friend, she felt happy. She was lucky to know Lily who was always so full of life and brimming over with enthusiasm for everything she did. She was tall and slim but could lift more sheets in a pile than anyone Doris had ever known, her face completely hidden behind the sodden heap. She easily left the competition standing. The "laundry workhorse" was what Barbara called her. The best the rest could do was a pile high enough to rest their chins on. Flushed faces, cherry red on creamy white linen. Lily, though, was impressive. Mind you, her talent didn't help her much when she tried to find her way blind out to the many clothes-lines criss-crossing the yard. But it was impressive none the less. That was Lily all over – appearance before practicalities – and Doris admired her for it. Envy was what cemented Doris to Lily. It was not the destructive feeling she had met many times over the years, but a benign snare holding Doris fast, looking up to a friend she knew in her heart she would never come close to matching up to. Never be as popular. Never be as attractive. It had always been felt, and she had often been told, and who was she to argue, that she was the practical and down-to-earth one. Good with her hands. While others' heads and hearts were in the heavens, Doris would forever be down below doing what she did best. Lily was Doris' telescope to the stars.

"Mature – how old is that?"

Lily's voice sounded strange, husky and full of longing. Doris smiled as she replied.

"Must be at least sixty."

"Ugh, you don't think?"

Lily visibly shuddered.

"The perve! Going for young women like that. It's disgusting, it shouldn't be allowed."

"Makes sense from a man's point of view. If he can trap one. A young woman – pretty, slim, full of life".

"It's a horrible thought."

"Some men don't age too badly. Probably has money as well."

"Now you're talking."

"Lily, if Mother heard you."

"But she won't, will she? She isn't here."

They both laughed and took a sip of tea.

"Now this is more like it."

"You're telling me. Shame there aren't any more biscuits."

"Shhhh, we weren't meant to have those. No, I mean this: 'Blue eyes, blond hair, hockey player, in work, seeks fun-loving girl for carefree Saturday nights, no attachments. Photo please. PO Box 135.'"

Lily was silent for a moment.

"I wish."

"What? Oh come on, Lily. He's probably barely twenty, far too young for you."

"Doris, wouldn't it be lovely to meet someone like that? Go out for the evening. Have some fun. Nothing ever happens here."

"It's not really possible, is it? Things being as they are."

"No, but you can't help wishing, you know, that something might happen."

Lily rubbed her hand across the dirty windowpane and gazed out through the smudged glass at the starlings searching for grubs in the Convent lawn. In the distance a black cat moved stealthily along the line of shrubbery that masked the lower part of the high brick wall that surrounded the garden, inching his way towards the birds. Doris turned back to her magazine. It was way out of date but she didn't care; it was such a luxury to be able to read and unwind without someone bothering you about something or other.

"Maybe I should write in? You know, see what happens."

Lily was looking at Doris with an excited look on her face.

"I could write giving a false name, arrange a meeting, then go and see what he really looks like."

"You're mad, Lily. They'd never let you go. It's against all the rules."

"But I wouldn't go up to him, just look."

"Oh, yes, pull the other one. If you were there and he looked as good as he sounds. You'd be tempted Lily, you know you would."

Doris reached across and nudged her on the foot.

"Oh, but the thought. It's been so long since I went out anywhere in the evening and had some fun."

"It's the same for all of us."

"Yes, but I'm younger than you."

"Not by much".

"Ten years?"

"That's nothing."

Doris' laugh was infectious and Lily couldn't help smiling.

"It would be grand though, Doris, wouldn't it? You've got to admit it."

She looked expectantly across at her friend, lounging in the only comfortable chair in the room, and Doris hadn't the heart to disappoint her, even though she had long ago given up any idea of ever again venturing far outside their cloistered little world.

"It would."

Lily returned to her newspaper, satisfied. Doris continued to stare out of the window. Hazy memories came back to her of dark evening walks, stolen kisses, fingers intertwined, the fug of the bar-room as the door opened, heads turning, the babble of voices, giggles. They tumbled one over the other, spinning off into an ever more distant past, their colours fading, their scent hanging in the air.

The two women were silent, except for the occasional rustle of newsprint as Lily turned a page. Eyes closed, Doris swayed gently, her thoughts lulling her into a semi-consciousness which, fusing with the blackness that was never far away, brought on the welcome relief of the dead faint. She let herself go with a contentment rarely experienced. Lily looked up as Doris lolled back in her chair, her magazine sliding from her hands to the floor.

"Poor love, she must be dead-beat."

The paper Lily was reading was full of neatly cut out squares and rectangles. This routine act of censorship by the Convent made handling difficult, but for Lily what mattered most were the small ads and lonely hearts columns and she had turned there first, ignoring the rest. She would have been irritated if these had been cut to bits, but her luck had held, the nuns only being interested in excising controversial news stories, and she happily sank into this other world of petty desires, needs, wants and things for sale. Where did these people live? What did they do? What drove them to write in to the papers? What would their parents and friends say if they found out? She felt she had some answers to the many questions. There was loneliness – Lily was not lonely, she was never alone, she had plenty of friends – and there was yearning – an emptiness did creep up on her, particularly at night, but what could you do? It was fascinating but she couldn't imagine writing in, not like this. Lily tapped the back of the newspaper with her middle finger, almost causing it to fold over on itself. She shook it back into place. What were these people like?

"Lily Collins."

That was her name. Chilling. What was she doing there? She knew what she was like. She wasn't one of them. There was tightening in her chest, static leaping from fingertip to fingertip. It couldn't be? Lily glanced around the room. Doris was still asleep, mouth open, her breath an audible regular tick. It felt suddenly warm and stuffy in the room. She needed the lavatory, the only place where there was any privacy for her to think. Folding the paper over and over, Lily wrapped her name up like a surprise parcel and slipped down from the window ledge. Picking up her slippers, she crept barefoot – creeping was a way of life in the Convent – past Doris, crossed the room and with a practised air opened the door just enough for her to pass through, then let it close gently behind her. The polished black and white tiles were cold beneath her feet and she bent down to put on her slippers, accidently dropping the paper. It opened before her like some strange flower, fold after fold, petal after petal. Her name was still there. Flustered, she scooped up the crumpled pages and hurried down the corridor, flinging open the door to the cloakroom and dashing in. It was empty, and with relief she paused just inside. A glance in the mirror gave nothing away, her shoulder-length brown hair was in place, her face glowing radiantly, the usual picture of rude health. In the cubicle Lily closed and locked the door, then lowered the highly polished mahogany lid and sat down. Her only thought was, who could have done this to her? She knew then she didn't, it could only be, but she wasn't sure. The paper shook slightly in her hands.

"Lily Collins from Ballycraig, now believed to be living in the Dublin area. Your daughter would like to meet you. My name is Alexandra and I am 31 years old and have been living in the USA. Please, Mum, get in touch. If you have any information contact PO Box 275."

Mum, for Christ's sake. Ballycraig. Thirty-one years.

Lily's body shook uncontrollably. Salty drops spattered down, darkening the newsprint.

"Alexandra, Alexandra."

There hadn't been a day without some sense of her, a deep understanding that had insidiously permeated every cell of her body from the time her daughter had been dragged out of her. She had never really left her mother, Lily. A word to anyone would have been a betrayal of her own betrayal. She should have screamed, cried out, struggled like a baby. Like her baby had done. But she hadn't, she hadn't.

The Sunday Independent slid from her hands, the sheets of newspaper separating as they gently settled around her ankles. Hands hugging her empty belly, her mind was a blank. No images remained, not even the outline of a child, no sounds echoed however distantly; there was just emptiness. Her fingers ran obsessively over nylon overalls, tracing the only evidence that all this was true, the faint, ever so faint, stretch marks that branded her stomach. There was no doubt she was the one. Lily was "Mum".

Lily trembled with renewed terror when she realized she could have missed the advertisement, have missed her daughter's cry for help. How often did she read the papers? It was pure chance she'd seen this one. Only because Doris had burnt herself. She was lucky. Oh, God, so lucky. Lily could barely control her body, it was slipping away from her, her limbs agents all of their own, escaping from her, free. Breathing heavily through a parched mouth, open in startled amazement, she lowered herself to the floor, paper crackling beneath her, leant back against one cubicle wall, her feet firmly placed against the other, and grasped her bent legs with both arms and squeezed. Lily squeezed until the physical pain brought her body back to her, leaving her mind free.

There had been a baby she was sure, she could feel it somersaulting, stretching, but that had been Mary not Alexandra. A moment of doubt, the first and the last, but invigorating for Lily while it lasted. Life could return to normal, she could creep back into the room where Doris dozed and things would go on as before, she could live with her secret. But it lasted just a second.

"Are you in there?"

Lily opened her eyes. She felt so comfortable here on the floor, cradled by the walls. She could stay here forever. The door rattled.

"Lily, is that you?"

It was so hard, they would never understand how difficult it was to deal with people sometimes. You just wanted to be by yourself, somewhere safe, but in this place you were never alone. The air was cold on her forehead.

"Lily?"

Doris sounded concerned. This could never last. Doris was her ally.

"Yes."

"Oh, Lily, what's the matter? Are you ill?"

"No."

Her tone was harsher than she'd intended, almost angry, and Doris was taken aback.

"Lily?"

"I'm all right, now leave me alone."

As an afterthought she added.

"Please Doris."

"I'll be outside, I want to make sure you're not sickening."

Lily listened to the sound of Doris' footsteps slapping across the tiled floor, the faint squeal of the hinges, the click of the cloakroom door closing, and then eased herself from the floor. She felt stiff, her back ached and she had pains in her upper thighs and for the first time in an age she had a headache. Reaching down for the creased and flattened paper at her feet, Lily felt dizzy and had to quickly sit down. Arms on knees, head in her hands, her eyes searched for her advertisement in the swirling mass of newsprint. It was nowhere to be seen, but it was there. The date. What was the date? Again there was the sick feeling in the stomach. Oh God, the paper was over three weeks old. Was she too late? Was all lost, before it was ever found? Lily cried, quietly this time, because she knew Doris would be listening, but now her tears were for a double loss, for her baby and for her own innocence and it hurt all the more for that.

The only certainty for Lily was that she must save the one thing she had that was her baby's. Horrified that she had treated it so badly, she reached down and carefully picked up the newspaper, sorted the large unwieldy sheets into some sort of order, then searched through it, gently turning the pages until she found what she was looking for. Her advertisement – slightly smudged but not creased.

Dropping the rest of the paper Lily began to tear it out, at first giving the small printed paragraph a very wide berth, then with a growing confidence getting closer and closer until triumphantly she held in her hand a jagged edged piece of paper barely larger than the advertisement itself. She raised it up in front of her face, kissed it, then slid it carefully into the side pocket of her overall. Collecting up all the small tattered scraps of paper that were scattered across the cubicle floor, she crushed them into a tight ball, lifted the mahogany lid, tossed them into the bowl and as they rapidly disintegrated flushed them away. Folding the remaining pages of the newspaper together, Lily tucked them under her arm, unlocked the door, crossed over to the wash basin with its shiny brass taps, washed the ink from her hands and prepared to face Doris.

There was no way of escaping the inevitable questions. Doris was waiting in the corridor, arms crossed. Lily said she was feeling better, clutching her stomach as she did so, would like a breath of fresh air though before they went in for tea. And, please, Doris, a favour?

"Don't say anything to any of the others, will you, Dot? I don't want them making fun of me. I'd rather let it lie. After all, you're the one who needs the attention seeing as what you've been through."

"Don't worry Lily, I won't say a word. To tell the truth, I don't much fancy facing everyone either."

The two women hugged each other awkwardly, taking care to avoid Doris' injured arm, which she held out at an angle. She smelled strongly of perspiration and grease, but Lily didn't care and held on tightly, glad to have someone to comfort her, even if not to confide in. Towering over her friend, she rested her chin on the top of Doris' head, and in a very deliberate way reassured herself that if she told anyone about her secret it would be Doris. But, as she often found was the way with such contrived emotions, she instantly knew it was not true and felt pained at her own lack of sincerity.

Over the week that followed only one certainty grew for Lily out of the agony of never-ending, mind-numbing introspection, and that was that she had to do something. Her constant picking away at the partial memories that filled her head brought forth no solutions, no grand schemes, no relief. Alexandra was a sensation, nothing more. Try as she could she was unable to conjure up a picture that fixed in her mind and didn't fade when exposed to the withering light of her own basic honesty. Alexandra was an act of faith, only the second Lily had ever made, and it was as unshakeable as the first.

Her Mother came back to her, face screwed up with anger, red and inflamed, bawling streams of abuse, words too indistinct to mean anything now except rejection. Her Father, he could be any of a number of male faces, was there too: angry, leering, knowing, threatening violence, but emasculated by drink, falling over, snagging the tablecloth and dragging after him dirty crockery, the best teapot and much of what his wife held dear. The powerful rank smell of beer on his hot breath, regurgitating spittle close to Lily's face, was as fresh as the day before yesterday. Not so clear was Cormac, her lover, older by ten years and unobtainable. He resolved himself in Lily's mind into a mere handful of sensations, all erotic and most definitely, in different less stressful times, enjoyable.

Hatred was never something she had felt for Cormac and, try as she may, and she had tried very hard that Sunday afternoon in the Convent garden, she could not bring herself to blame him in any way. It was disconcerting feeling nothing much for a man she believed she must have loved and now knew she should hate. It was made even worse by the fact she knew there was nothing she could say to Alexandra about her father except that she had loved him and that he had not stood by them and that was that. He had disappeared from view. Their daughter went off to America, built a new life, made a fortune perhaps, maybe married a cowboy and was ever so happy. Lily had been a washerwoman in a laundry ever since, never known another man, was now uncertain if she really ever wanted to again. Men frightened her and she wouldn't have dared go up to one, even if she had summoned up the courage to reply to one of those advertisements. And she was a mother. Mothers should be with their children, that was only natural. No one disagreed with that. She should be with her daughter, it was obvious.

Lily felt so happy when she finally made up her mind that she cried out loud. She was standing at the clotheslines, pegging out white shirts, the sun was shining and there was a stiff wind blowing – a good drying day – her basket was almost empty and out of the blue she decided to answer the advertisement. Uncertain at first where this thought had come from, Lily stood completely still, a shirtsleeve flapping against her face, mulling over a fact that until now she had never seriously acknowledged as an option. The relief at the realization that it all made the most complete sense was physical in its impact and Lily screamed out her daughter's name. A pigeon, perched on the rusting iron pole supporting one end of the clothesline, rose into the air in alarm, flapping noisily away to settle again on the roof of the laundry. Maeve appeared suddenly from between the lines of washing, a wicker basket full of wet shirts in her hands, looking startled.

"Who's Alexandra?"

Embarrassed, Lily glanced away as she bent down to pick up another shirt, her left hand automatically selecting two pegs from her overall pocket. For a brief moment in the heady afterglow of a mind made up, Lily almost came clean and told Maeve the truth. After all, why not? Everyone had one secret if not more in here, it was that sort of place. But the problem was, people kept their secrets, they didn't talk about them even to their friends, or at least, Lily's friends didn't talk to her about theirs. Lily only had one secret, so she lied.

"Oh, Maeve, you startled me, I was miles away."

"Come on, Lily, who's Alexandra? And why are you shouting her name to the heavens. They'll have heard you in Dundalk Street".

Maeve had put down her basket and was standing with her arms folded, fixing Lily with her dark brown eyes. Lily smiled.

"It was something my mother used to do, name things, birds and animals and the like."

Maeve was looking puzzled.

"That pigeon."

Lily pointed to the guttering above their heads. Maeve turned and gazed upwards. The pigeon was still there grooming itself, head under one raised wing, a small white feather floated slowly downwards.

"Alexandra?"

Unconvinced Maeve turned again to face Lily.

"Yes, she's been there on the washing pole most of the afternoon. You'll think I'm mad, but I've been chatting to her, you know, about this and that. It's easier if they have a name. Alexandra sounds so grand and elegant."

Lily pegged the last shirt to the line as she spoke; Maeve pushed the other full basket over to her with her foot.

"Then it looked like she was going to do, you know, her business on the washing so I shouted out her name and she flew up there."

Lily shrugged.

"That's all, nothing really."

It was Lily, so it was probably true. It was Maeve's turn to smile.

"You're a funny 'un Lily. Pass over that empty basket."

As Maeve wended her way back to the laundry through the fluttering white linen, Lily blew Alexandra a kiss. It was, she recognized, the first contact she had had with her daughter, the first time she had actually expressed how she felt.

It was not easy, Lily discovered, to act on her decision. It was virtually impossible to get any time alone; there was always someone else around, who wouldn't let her be. It was rare for anyone in the Convent to sit on their own and even rarer for them to sit by themselves and compose a letter. Very few of the women there had anyone on the outside they kept in touch with, and if they did, then Mother frowned on them writing without letting her help. But Lily didn't need her assistance, it was the last thing she wanted and she was determined to do this unaided. She had been over it many times in her mind exactly what she wanted to say to her daughter, spoken it out to herself quietly so that no one would hear, but it was very different when it came to putting it down on paper.

Her friends were worried about her, she seemed distracted to them, preoccupied, not like her usual gregarious self. They asked permission to go to the shops so that they could sneak into the "Coach and Horses" on Saturday lunchtime to cheer Lily and Doris up after their adventure. Mother had agreed, provided they were away only two hours and weren't late back as there was plenty of cleaning to be done. Lily though had made her excuses, said she had to buy some sweets at the corner shop and would see them later. The others protested, but without passion. Better to let her do what she wanted.

She had bought a pen, writing paper, an envelope and a stamp and gone to the park in Fermanagh Street to write her letter. Her favourite seat was taken by a young couple who were holding hands and kissing, so she went round to the other side of the duck pond and sat in the shade under a tall sycamore tree. Leaning against the trunk, she felt invisible. Life went on around her in the sunshine, but she was totally alone. Lily turned to the first page of the writing pad and wrote her address in small neat letters across the top, added the date then hesitated.

She never had any problem finding the right words when it came to chatting to her friends, to people she had just met, in fact it was easy, words just spilled forth without even having to think about them. She was always being teased about "never letting them get a word in edgeways", "speaking nineteen to the dozen", her mother had called her "a chatterbox", Margaret was always saying that she "spoke before her brain was engaged", but then that was Margaret. Letters, she now understood, were different.

"Dear Alexandra,

I read your advertisement in the Sunday Independent and I thought I should answer it."

The right words just would not come. Her feelings for her daughter didn't translate onto paper in any way that Lily could understand, try as she might. They remained inky black scribbles scratched across pale blue paper. Three attempts, three crushed sheets of paper, balled at her feet, before she gave up. It was not clear what she should do next; Alexandra seemed further away than she had ever done.

Staring at the discarded letters now lying at the bottom of the rusty litterbin Lily had never wanted a drink so much in her life. She hurried across to the "Coach and Horses". Doris, Barbara, Margaret and Maeve were sitting in their usual seats in the snug. They looked up when Lily burst through the swing doors and pushed past them to the bar without saying a word.

"You're cutting it a bit fine, aren't you? We've got to be back over the road in ten minutes."

"I know, Barbara."

Lily appeared wan, her voice strained. The others exchanged glances.

"Two halves of Guinness, please, and do any of you want another?"

Only Doris nodded in assent, even though her glass was half full.

"I'll have one with you Lil."

The stout slid down easily. It gave Lily the courage to sit with her friends and lie to them. Vague mumblings of sickness, headaches, not sleeping very well, mere ripples on the surface as far below the resolution grew that all that was left to her was to consult a priest.

***

Lily was a regular at confession, as were all the women in the laundry, but Father Michael did not consider her to be one of the truly devout. She was dutiful, admitting to mundane transgressions, accepting her penance, but never opened her heart to him. She was one of his "in and outs", as he called them. He was surprised then when she sidled up to him in the Chapel one evening, just as he was getting ready to go home for his supper. He was thinking how hungry he was, musing on what he would be having, "if it's Saturday it must be beef pie, boiled potatoes and cabbage, followed by apple pie and custard" – Mrs Callaghan was nothing if not set in her ways – and thinking about the whisky he would be drinking afterwards. Lily took him by surprise, she was right behind him before he even realized.

"Father."

He jumped as he turned to face her.

"Holy Mary, Lily, you startled me."

His heart was thumping and he needed to sit down.

"You shouldn't go creeping around like that, look at me."

"Sorry, Father."

Lily was ashen faced and appeared close to tears. Father Michael imagined he smelled drink on her breath, but couldn't quite believe it.

"Oh, Lily, look at me – not as young as I was. But then none of us are, are we? Huffing and puffing like I don't know what. I can see I'll have to be cutting down on the old evil weed if I'm to keep in shape. Here, let me sit down. Take a seat yourself and tell me what's bothering you?"

Lily hesitated, her woollen hat clenched in anxious hands. She bit her lip. Michael felt his good humour returning; he was feeling more like himself again. He drew the brown paper bag that had just been delivered, closer to him along the pew, checked to see that the top was folded over and patted it reassuringly. It wouldn't do for Lily so see what was inside, but then she didn't look too bright at the moment. That being said, if she'd turned up a couple of minutes earlier she'd have caught him counting the money, then what would he have said? He'd have thought of something, he always did. Revived by that thought he turned his attention to Lily, smiling encouragingly at the standing figure.

"I'd rather not sit down out here, Father, I'd like to take confession."

Lily turned to stare at the darkened confessionals along the wall of the Chapel, avoiding the priest's eyes. Bemused, Michael dismissed his irritation over his delayed supper, sighed and got to his feet. "This better not take long", he thought, then, confused, was uncertain whether he'd spoken out loud. He realized how rude he would have sounded if he had, and blurted out the words again adding by way of mitigation, "I don't want you to be late for your supper. You know how strict Reverend Mother can be."

"No, Father, I've quite lost my appetite." Suddenly aware that her answer was somehow inadequate she added, "the worry you know, Father."

He was surprised and intrigued. Lily was not one of the women to whom he had paid much attention to before. Part of the reason was that she was tall, almost the same height as him, slim but solidly built, and that didn't appeal. That coupled with a bland openness of expression, the constant smile, the seemingly irrepressible exuberance, the thin wispy brown hair always tied back, the large hands, all meant she didn't conform in any way to Michael's idea of feminine perfection – petite, small frame, curly auburn hair. He had, after all, been known to be taken in by flame red curls on occasions, and large, bright hazel eyes. But in the dimness of the Chapel, head cast down, pale, the natural ruddiness drained from her cheeks, hair now hanging loose and falling beguilingly around her face where it curled slightly just below her chin, Michael had to admit for the first time that for someone in her early-fifties Lily did look … the priest searched for the word, before somewhat reluctantly settling on alluring. It wasn't quite right, but it was close. He did enjoy his job sometimes; it was these little surprises, setting, as they did, all your senses on edge.

Michael positively tingled as he closed the curtain, shutting out the feeble lights of the Chapel, and settled down onto the familiar cushion. Darkness engulfed him, the highly polished interior giving off its resonant aroma of wood, candles and beeswax. Lily shuffled around with her secret on the other side of the partition getting comfortable, then fell silent. After savouring the moment for a few seconds Michael cleared his throat, slid the grille gently aside and leant forward, praying he wasn't going to be disappointed.

He wasn't. It hadn't been what he called "a bombshell", there had been precious few of those in his time as a priest, but it had certainly been "startling". He hadn't guessed what was coming next and for that he was grateful. In theory he knew the background to all his women, why they were there and for how long, what their families thought about it all, but in practice he had never found the time or had that much interest in going back over their records to find out the sordid details. He had read the files on the few women who had been mentioned to him by Father James and by the Reverend Mother as having special problems, and had made the effort to seek out details on the women who interested him, but Lily had not fallen into either of those categories.

Lily had spoken softly, often hesitating, frequently repeating herself, but she held nothing back. For the first time in her life she told her story to another person in the fullest way possible for her. She even tried to articulate how she felt about everything, the hole that had re-opened inside her, the yearning that she was unable to shake off. Lily told him about the letter she had tried to write, burst into tears and couldn't stop, understanding then that she was completely at the mercy of this man, a priest, who she didn't totally trust. Catharsis offered relief, but at a price.

Michael had been taken aback at the flood of information that had poured out of Lily. He was used to inarticulate mutterings, half thoughts, dissembling, sometimes even outright lies, but not often heart-felt honesty served up in the true spirit of the confessional. It was rare and he was moved by it. And then, there was the startling aspect of it all, the thing he had not been expecting, which could have repercussions for them all. That had to be treated with a great deal of care and circumspection.

The existence of a daughter had not been much of a surprise – it was probably the same for most of the women in the laundry if the truth be known – the father rather more so. What had really set the alarm bells ringing was the fact that the daughter had not only found out about the mother and got hold of her name, but had also made contact with her. And this was in spite of the hidden, cloistered world Lily lived in, many thousands of miles away from America. Michael sensed a fault line shifting across a familiar landscape, threatening, but not yet dangerous. Where would it all end? How would it all end? The priest had no idea, but he was disturbed. He swore Lily to secrecy, "for the time being at least", and was pleasantly surprised to learn that that had been her natural instinct all along. He felt he could work with this woman.

The Chapel was cold when they emerged blinking from the charged air of the confessional, the dingy lights shining bright after the comforting darkness. There was a scampering in the roof space above, then an inner silence accentuating the sound of cars in the road outside. Father Michael placed an arm on Lily's shoulder and guided her down the aisle, picking up his coat, hat and the brown paper bag from the pew where he had left them.

Good Lord if someone had come along and picked that one up, I'd have been in trouble, he thought to himself with relief. The confessor and her priest paused in the Chapel entrance, Michael glanced back over his shoulder as he put on his hat, then switched off the lights, pulled the door shut and the two of them moved off into the damp murky night, both for different reasons uneasy at what had just happened.

Back in his room, following a scolding from his housekeeper, Mrs Callaghan, and an unsatisfactory supper of dried out meat pie, potatoes and cabbage, Father Michael reflected only briefly before pouring himself a whisky and making two calls. The first was to the Reverend Mother, Sister Beatrice, the second to his good friend, Bishop Donal. Both had been shocked at the news. Beatrice had let out a long drawn-out sigh – Michael could mentally see her crossing herself – and then listened in silence as he spelt out the bad news, only adding when he had finally finished, "You didn't waste any time, did you?"

"Someone has to move on this. Sit tight, Beatrice. Keep Lily happy – and most of all keep her quiet. We don't want this leaking out yet, if at all, especially to those friends of hers. There'll be no end to it then. I'm going to refer this one to a higher authority. I'll get back to you. Good night."

The Bishop had been more forthright.

"Bloody hell, Michael! This is a right unholy mess to be sure. Think about it."

"I have, believe me, it's a real can of worms."

"Dead right, if it gets out."

"Forced adoption?"

"And worse. Look, there's no doubt we'll have to keep this one quiet. It'll be a Godsend to the papers – which one did you say the ad was in?"

"Sunday Independent."

"Infernal rag! And those bloody campaigners, always on my back these days. You don't know the half, Michael, you really don't. Keep things under wraps for the time being, that's a good man."

"I understand. It wouldn't be good for anyone if this got out, least of all the women. Too many questions would be asked. It would open up old wounds unnecessarily."

The Bishop sighed.

"Yes, everyone starts wanting to know all the details. What happened to little X? Why can't I see little Y? There'll be no end to it. Sure and we thought we were doing the best for the children sending them off to good homes in the States – but will those lefty campaigners see it like that? Will they blazes!"

"Quite, Bishop," agreed Michael, all too aware of the recent critical reports in the press on the subject of the forced overseas adoption of Irish babies in the fifties and sixties.

"We are none of us lily-white in the face of media scrutiny," Bishop Donal continued. "Your own, how shall we say, "retirement home", for instance, Michael. Could be embarrassing if the wheres and whyfores of that ever came to light, hmmm?"

Father Michael's blood ran cold. In all the years he'd handled the laundry's finances, relieving Sister Beatrice of the burden, he'd dreaded this moment. Though to be sure he'd never looked on it as stealing exactly – the tokens of appreciation he'd received from several local hotels and nursing homes whose linen had passed through the laundry, but not its books. Over the years they'd been enough to buy a bungalow in Galway and swell his savings account nicely. He couldn't run the risk of the Convent coming under close public inspection.

"Keep a lid on it, Michael. It's for the best. Good night."

He had wanted to add one final reassurance, but had been abruptly cut-off. It left him feeling ill at ease and disgruntled with his friend. He'd always seen Donal as an ally, someone he'd watched with delight climb his way to the top with consummate ease. He must be feeling the pressure to talk like that. Michael had never been treated with such barely disguised brusqueness before. But then, he'd never appreciated quite how much his old friend knew about his financial arrangements at the laundry.

He slammed down the phone and drained his whisky in one gulp.

"The things I'm expected to do. The place would go to rack and ruin, it really would."

For the first time Michael was beginning to regret his involvement with the laundry. After all, he was just the local parish priest, it was nothing to do with him really. He had lent a hand to the Reverend Mother in some long forgotten emergency and had never gone away. It suited him and it suited the nuns to have him looking after their affairs, dealing with the outside world, negotiating the contracts that kept the whole enterprise running. He did all this while administering to the spiritual well-being of the laundry ladies, something the nuns felt needed to be sensitively done by a man, if possible, and Father Michael was nothing if not sensitive when dealing with their fragile egos. He was such an improvement over his predecessor Father James, if the truth were told. He had never taken much interest in the business, he was dutiful to the spiritual needs of the washerwomen, but that was all. Mass was held twice a week in the Convent Chapel – Wednesday and Sunday; confessions on Friday. Not like Father Michael who showed up most days for an extra hour or two, "beyond the call of duty".

The Reverend Mother would never say such a thing, but it was well-known that she had been very pleased when Michael had replaced Father James as the local priest. He had seemed so young, dynamic and full of life. Always willing to help, "not afraid to get his hands dirty", as the older nuns often used to say. This had been in the late sixties, but seemed like only yesterday to many, the collective memory of the Convent and its laundry was a long one. Almost everyone who was there now was there then. Father Michael had seemed like a breath of fresh air, a symbol of the changing decade, which had just begun to seep into the sheltered consciousness of the closed community on the corner of Carlow Avenue and Wexford Parade. He also brought with him a tang of the real world, a hint even of the corruption that would eventually touch the lives of many of the inhabitants of the Convent.

***

Father Michael had been beyond reproach in his dealings with the nuns. He had quickly gathered that this was an Order in turmoil. A genteel battle for the soul of the Convent was being waged between the relatively new Reverend Mother, Sister Beatrice, and some of the older nuns. Change was in the air and Beatrice was not afraid to face the challenge, diplomatically of course, ruffling as few feathers as possible, but change there had to be.

Father Michael administered mass to the nuns, took their confessions and quietly drank tea with the Reverend Mother every Tuesday afternoon. Her plans for the future, her understanding of Vatican Two, that quiet revolution that was seeping its way into the furthest outposts of the Catholic Church, her personal vocation as an ambassador of the modern Church had all come up and been gently discussed. Father Michael by his quiet compliance with her arguments, his personal decision not to challenge her beliefs, was seen by Beatrice as offering support for her plans and she quickly began to view him as an ally, even in the climate of the times as a co-conspirator. She began to go to him for advice, initially on spiritual matters, the interpretations of texts, the appropriateness of passages from the New Testament, topics for the nuns' weekly talks and discussions, but gradually their relationship had grown more practical. For him, Sister Beatrice was the only woman he had any sort of meeting of minds with, the only woman he unconsciously treated as an intellectual equal. For her, Father Michael was a reassurance, an insurance policy even, that she had a supporter, some sort of sympathetic emissary to a frankly male-dominated, often hostile world outside. Friendship, something Father Michael would have countenanced, was not seen by her as part of the bargain except in only the most rarefied, dilute form of the word. Her enclosed female universe fulfilled all her needs for companionship, moral support and spiritual love, it was only when her orbit swung into the real world, as unfortunately it often had to in her position, did she feel the need for a male ally.

As a result, over the years Father Michael became indirectly involved in much of the domestic running of the Convent, giving advice on everything, from food deliveries to which newspapers were appropriate for the nuns to read. It was, however, the Magdalen laundry in which he became directly involved. Sister Beatrice knew very little about the mechanics of the business and had no real interest in such things. She gladly handed the running of it over to Father Michael on the first occasion one of the boilers broke down. She never asked for it back and he'd been running it for over twenty years.

"A quarter of a century of whitening the public's dirty linen," was how he wryly saw his work at the laundry and he'd been good at it. The place had done well and the women who worked there had more than paid for their keep. Father Michael made his own investments, secretly, astutely, and had profited handsomely. The Convent had also benefited both financially and materially as well, as had the diocese. He had kept it going for all this time, so how Donal could speak to him like that? It was beyond belief.

Michael felt slightly nauseous and lay down on his bed to think. Two things were very clear to him: Lily wasn't going to let this drop and there was no way the Church was going to be happy if it all came out. That being the case, there was only one thing to do. Relieved, he sat up and poured himself another whisky, then leant back and absentmindedly fingered the mole behind his left ear. Get in touch with Alexandra, fix a meeting, convince her and Lily not to breathe a word – with God on his side, putting the fear into them shouldn't be too difficult. Michael had to smile. He was, he realized, making the assumption that Alexandra was still a Catholic. Maybe the women wouldn't be able to stand the sight of each other, and that would be that. And if it wasn't? Michael sipped his whisky. Then bugger it, dear Lily would have to go, and quietly. The Church was good at arranging things like that.

"A bit of good old bloody intrigue, as dear Donal would say, a bit of bloody subterfuge."

Michael raised his glass.

"You old bastard."

***

Alexandra seemed extremely amenable, and devout too, judging by her initial letter to Sister Beatrice in which she agreed that the Church was "the best conduit for dealing with this delicate matter". Father Michael, keeping a low profile for, as he put it, political reasons, couldn't have been happier. Lily remained in a state of benign shock, overjoyed to leave everything to him. She drank more than usual, suffered periods of intense apprehension, which silenced her for hours, followed as if to compensate by bouts of verbal fireworks that surprised her friends and raised their suspicions. But Lily said nothing about what was really going on. Even when pressed she lied, which was unusual for her and was to be a cause of great regret to her later; but Michael had sworn her to silence and for the first time in her life implicit threats from a priest scared her into obedience. It was chilling for Lily to understand that this wasn't just about her; she had responsibility, belatedly, for the soul of another person. The risk was too great. Eternal damnation had never seemed much to her, an abstraction at odds with her youthful appearance and natural exuberance, but when she tried to imagine what Alexandra may look like she found it easy to imagine her burning in hell, the flames licking around the strangely adult form of her screaming baby.

There were a number of surprises for Father Michael too. The first was the speed at which events unfolded, gaining a momentum that he knew would be impossible to halt if he was to maintain the aura of silence he so desperately wanted. The second was the unusual interest taken in Lily's case by his friend, Bishop Donal, who summoned Father Michael to weekly meetings to "keep abreast", as he put it, of events.

"What can you do, Donal? Americans only seem interested in instant gratification. The woman isn't prepared to write letters for a year or two, get to know her Mother that way. No she's coming over next month and wants to meet Lily. Can you believe it?"

"I bloody well can, Michael. It's all very fashionable over there at the moment, this rooting around in your past. Looking for ways to explain why your life is so meaningless and empty, looking for someone else to blame. That's progress, so they say. Regrettable, I know, but there's no reason why our little lady should be any different from all the others. She's on our trail, she'll have money behind her and she won't want to give up. Not yet anyway, not until the next fad comes along. I hear there's been the odd similar embarrassment over there – Chicago was the latest – so I hope you've got this under control? That child was the offspring of a Bishop, no less. At least Lily's was only a priest's."

He smiled mirthlessly.

"Donal, how long have we known each other?"

Michael was pleased that he was able to keep up an air of mock jocularity, even though he was growing angry with the way the Bishop was treating him.

"Long enough, Michael. Long enough."

Donal inadvertently shuddered. You old hypocrite, thought Michael, moving uneasily in his chair.

"If the powers that be want it kept quiet, that's how it'll be," he promised. "There's been too much nonsense recently about forced adoptions, cruelty in orphanages and … well, other things. This won't be going any further. But tell me, Donal, who was the priest? You have my word it'll go no further."

"Father Cormac O'Leary."

"Father O'Leary? I don't believe it!"

"Well, do, Michael. Believe it."

"I was at the Seminary with him – the dog. Where is he now?"

"Well, that's one blessing at least. He's dead. A heart attack."

"Good God."

"Exactly. But it's happened before and the Church has managed to keep it quiet. There is no reason why this should be any different. The last thing we need is a scandal, what with them starting to ask questions about the laundry and whether it's appropriate to be running such an institution in the late twentieth century. I ask you. It wears me out Michael, it really does. The upshot is a very low profile is the best thing all round."

Michael rolled his eyes and sucked heavily on his thin roll-up, which he held cupped inelegantly between nicotine-stained fingers. Smoke drifted up from the corners of his mouth as he spoke quietly, his lips barely moving. The laundry was a subject close to his heart.

"They've been talking about shutting us down for a while. It would be bloody typical if the irresponsibility of one of our own finished the laundry off. We have the ladies in our care – many of them have been there for years – and they offer a bit back for their keep. Tell me what's wrong with that? Some of them really enjoy it. I know for a fact that they'd be lost without it. Closing doesn't make any sense to me."

Least of all financial, he thought.

Bishop Donal was standing looking out into his garden, his back to the priest who was still relaxing in a deep well-worn leather chair pulled close to the coal fire.

"To me neither, Michael. Things aren't what they used to be, that's for sure. All it means is we'd better make damn certain we clean up this particular mess. Now tell me how it's going with Miss Collins?"

"I'll have to arrange a meeting between her and her daughter."

"Well out-of-sight."

"Of course, Donal, well out-of-sight. There's no way anyone'll get wind of this. I'm going along as well, just to keep things in hand."

"And Miss Collins, how is she bearing up?"

"Lily. Well, she's excited beyond belief. Frightened on top of that as well. But she's behaving more or less normally."

"Michael, more or less normally?"

"Donal, what can you expect."

Michael laughed. There was silence. Donal sat down in the chair opposite him, crossed his legs, and then smoothed his purple robes with his hands before clasping them together and letting them drop into his lap. His thin angular face grimly set he stared at his friend through dull brown eyes that watered slightly in the smoky air.

"Donal, no one will notice. Many of them behave strangely at times. Erratic. Nobody will pay any attention if one of their number starts climbing the walls, believe me."

"Michael, I want to. But reassure an old man will you. I need my sleep these days, more than I used to."

The priest smiled, but felt very uneasy.

"Seriously Donal, Lily is the weakest link that's true. But there's no way she is consciously going to jeopardize meeting up with her daughter. I've warned her about keeping it secret and she's got the message believe me. Accidents could happen, but I'm keeping a close eye and Sister Beatrice has put a couple of her most attentive Sisters on to the case. So we're pretty well covered. And if she does blurt something out, we'll dismiss it as the ramblings of a disturbed, confused mind. You know the drill."

***

Ethel Hannah died in her sleep. It had not been totally unexpected, she had long since given up working in the laundry – her legs just wouldn't carry her like they used to. Yet Doris had been shocked when Father Michael had stood up after breakfast one morning and announced that "dear sister Ethel had passed on peacefully" that very night. Seeking solace, Doris looked across the table at Lily who was sitting opposite her. Expecting a communion of tears and sympathy Doris was surprised to see Lily distracted, anxious looking, but certainly not upset.

"She can't have heard", thought Doris, waving to catch her attention. Mouthing the words, "Ethel's dead. Died last night", she expected Lily's expression to change, dissolve with the sadness she was bound to feel, until tear-stained, blotched red it would look like Doris felt, but it didn't.

Lily was thinking of her daughter – she had looked lovely in the photograph Father Michael had shown her: tall, like her, thin, with thick black hair like Cormac's piled high, a narrow face with petite, well formed features and a radiant smile. The picture haunted Lily at night. She could not escape it – it was eight days until her daughter arrived. Just over a week until she met her. It was such an overwhelming thought that Lily had found herself breaking into a sweat and trembling at the most unexpected times. The chill of her damp blouse as she stood in the Chapel for mass, a place she was spending more and more of her time, the salty liquid stinging her eyes at meal times, her bed drenched in the morning, hair plastered to the side of her face, were unpleasant features of her new life. Her friends noticed and were overbearingly solicitous, but she told them she was feeling bad and there was no need to worry as she'd seen the doctor – "time of life" – and they passed on nodding.

Lily was terrified she would let something slip if she spent too much time with them and ruin everything. She felt Father Michael watching her wherever she went and so she cut herself off. She felt guilty, of course, but it was nothing to the shame she was feeling at having abandoned her own child. She agonized over what she was going to say, how she was going to explain what happened. Alexandra looked kind and understanding, but Lily could in her mind clearly see her face contorting with anger as her feeble words failed to match up to the enormity of her crime, the vastness of her sin. She found herself tongue-tied, unable to say anything but, "Alexandra, I'm sorry. I'm so sorry, Alexandra. Sorry."

Father Michael had taken charge of the arrangements, giving Lily only the most basic information about what was going on, and from his point of view things were coming along very nicely. All his fears about Alexandra being out to stir things up, seeking publicity and keen to show the Church in a bad light, appeared so far unfounded. She wanted to meet her mother and that seemed to be all. She had plenty of money, that was clear; she was arranging everything on her side and was only interested in where and when the meeting could take place. Most importantly, she had agreed to Michael being the intermediary and had made no direct approach to Lily. What happened afterwards, once mother and daughter had met, did occasionally worry him, but he dismissed such dismal concerns with the thought that they would be able to work it out. He hoped so anyway.

A date had been fixed for the first meeting, but to Michael's initial annoyance, it clashed with Ethel Hannah's funeral. He considered putting it off until the next day, but decided that far from being a problem the funeral would provide ideal cover for him and Lily to slip away.

Members of the family occasionally turned up for the funerals. They would stand out in their black suits and dresses, heads sheepishly bowed, talking among themselves in whispers, hanging back. They would always sit in the rear pews, away from the rest of the mourners and never said a word to the other women, merely a nod at the priest. But no one came to Ethel's. It was a damp overcast day and the dark clouds threatened more rain. The laundry women gathered outside the Convent chapel, their best clothes hidden beneath heavy overcoats, ready for the half mile walk to the cemetery. Lily stood among them, wretched with anticipation. She had hardly slept or eaten anything for days. Looking in the mirror that morning she had wept at the sight of her drawn features and pale sallow complexion. The folds of her neck were red-raw, there were spots, whiteheads, on her cheeks and there were dark bags under her eyes. No amount of makeup could hide the fact that she was sick with worry. The pills they had given her to calm her down hadn't made much difference, just given her a dull headache. Lily despaired that her daughter should see her like this, but she had to go.

"Are you up to this, Lily, love?"

Barbara stood beside her. Doris and Maeve, also worried, were just behind.

"You don't have to go, you know. Ethel would understand."

"I'll be all right. The fresh air will do me good. I've been cooped up inside for too long."

"You'll take my arm if you need to, won't you? Don't be shy."

"Thanks Barbara."

The hearse carrying Ethel's coffin, which had been parked in front of the Chapel, now slowly moved off. Immediately behind were Father Michael, Sister Beatrice and six nuns from the Convent; following them the laundry women, who had formed up in two columns stretched out along Waterford Street. A passerby, who had just crossed the road to avoid the crush of mourners on the pavement, stopped and bowed his head until most of the procession had passed by. He whistled to himself as he walked rapidly on his way, happy to be alive.

The cortege climbed steadily towards the cemetery through quiet terraced streets, the road slippery under foot from the dampness in the air. Some of the women walked arm in arm, others took care where they placed their feet, breaking ranks around potholes in the road, disrupting still further the already ragged column, then stepping back into line. Lily walked on alone, feeling much better to be doing something, but try as she could, staring at the bobbing heads in front of her, she couldn't dispel the thought that her life was about to undergo a momentous change. She didn't want it to, but she didn't want it not to, either.

The large iron gates of the cemetery were open. The three gravediggers standing with caps in hand, bowed their heads as the hearse entered. The Convent plot was several hundreds yards off to the left, on the brow of the hill, overlooking the soggy mist-shrouded city. The air seemed fresher here and Lily breathed in huge chilling gulps. The view was breathtaking to women used to the limited horizons of the Convent and laundry, itself confined in the maze of narrow streets that surrounded and encroached on the hill. The expanse of the sky, patches of blue flecked with white and grey, fusing with the thick low-lying layers of early morning cloud and smoke that hung over the roofs below, was enchanting, a release for all but the most cloistered souls. Lily's heart was racing and she felt to be drifting away, her body stretching upwards, twisting and turning in the intoxicating air. Blindly she reached for Doris' arm, found it and relaxed, anchored, for the time being at least, to the earth. Doris smiled back at her, she was happy too in that perverse way that marks out those in the right place, a place they love, even in the most trying of times.

"It's grand, isn't it Lily? I always forget until I get back here."

She patted Lily's hand gently and stared out over the heads of the mourners gathering around the muddy, smeared hole in the ground. She was not expecting any reply.

Father Michael spoke a few words about Ethel that hung in the air, but failed to conjure up the old lady for Lily. The magic was not there and Lily felt absent. She was not interested in death, only in resurrection, the rebirth of her beautiful child and of her as a mother. She had died giving birth and been buried, along with all these people, now she was about to see the light of day again, breathe clean air free of history's fumes, touch and be touched by love. The truth made her joyful and she wept.

Her friends rallied round, the soft clucks of sympathy, the communal tears, encouraging words and the comforting arm, but what were friends compared to the tug of flesh and blood, wringing you out, and reforming you. Lily could not remember a kiss; try as hard as she could it was not there. A prayer slipped from her lips, over the grave of a woman she had loved in her own peculiar way, asking God for a kiss from her own family, an unconditional contact that would last her for ever. And today.

One by one the grieving women filed past the grave, dropping handfuls of cold earth onto the shiny wooden coffin. Each hollow thud dully echoing in a poor imitation of a military gun salute. The bunch of white roses resting on the crown of the coffin slowly disappeared, crushed beneath the muddy avalanche. Lily, who in her befuddled state, had given far more than she normally would have done when the collection for the flowers came round, remembered this act of generosity as she stared into the hole, noticing the smashed petals and broken stalks, threw her palmful of earth against the muddy walls, sending a small cascade of stones raining down.

Puzzled, Doris would have rushed after her if she hadn't been restrained by Barbara, who grabbed her arm and almost tipped her into the grave. The green grass-like matting laid unevenly over the bumpy earth was slippery underfoot and Doris had to grasp firmly onto Barbara and Maeve's arms to stay on her feet.

"Sorry Dot, but let her be. She's been acting funny for a while. This all must be affecting her more than we realize. Are you all right?"

Shocked into silence, Doris felt ill as she paid her last respects to Ethel. She had forgotten about Lily, who had pushed her way through the crowd and was at that moment standing alone and agitated by the empty hearse. Father Michael came up and took her gently by the elbow.

"Come on, let's go."

***

Father Michael and Lily were early, the traffic had been much lighter than the priest had expected and, to his surprise, he immediately found a parking space close to where they were to meet Alexandra.

"I've never been this lucky before, someone must be smiling down on us", he grinned at Lily, as he backed into the space, narrowly missing a young girl who ran diagonally across the street behind him. She turned and shouted, before hurrying on. Michael shrugged. Lily, sickly mute, sat apprehensively beside him, clutching her handbag with both hands. She wanted to smile, wanted to speak, wanted to return to her old life, where she could laugh and shrug off her worries. Father Michael had been so kind, had tried hard as they drove down through the bustling streets to cheer her up and reassure her. She had been rude and had barely uttered a word. Lily's head pulsed dully, her skin felt clammy and uncomfortable, her clothes ill-fitting and prickly to the touch.

"What would her daughter" – the very word made her nauseous – "think of her, such a dowdy old woman?"

She reached into her handbag, the strong smell of lavender briefly soothing, and took out a handful of barley sugars, each wrapped in clear cellophane. Lily offered one to Michael, who laughed.

"Thank you kindly Lily, but that's the third one you've offered me and a man can only take so much of a good thing."

"They help settle my stomach."

"Have one Lily. Don't mind me."

She dropped all but one back into her bag and unwrapped the sticky sweet, then greedily sucked it into her mouth.

"I'll have a cigarette if you don't mind. We're very early."

Lily shook her head and they sat staring out through the windscreen, saying nothing, as the small car filled up with smoke.

Alexandra was standing in a doorway across the street from Bewley's Oriental Cafe. She'd read about it in a Dublin guide book and it had seemed like a good place to meet – genteel, civilised, with plenty of Old World charm – for even now she wasn't sure if she wasn't going to explode with anger. All those years of pent-up frustration and pain pouring onto the greying stooped figure of the woman responsible for the disaster that was her life. Alexandra felt strongly that a place with waitresses in black uniforms with white aprons and headbands, lace doilies, bone china, hushed conversation and stained glass windows – she had particularly liked the sound of the windows, they set the right tone – could make all the difference. "Abandoned and shipped off", was how she described herself. She prayed that this woman had a "fucking good explanation" for why it had happened, why Alexandra Collins had ended up Al Hastert, living in the Bronx with two people old enough to be her grandparents.

She had got there early, determined to see the woman first. She had managed to use the word "mother" in her letters, but found she couldn't when thinking about her. If she was there first, she'd be able to size her up, get "the drop on" her, as her father would say, "calculate the angles". It had crossed her mind that she still might not go through with it, that she'd just slip away and forget it. The doorway was ideal, deep enough for the shadows to hide her, but wide enough to provide a good view of the street. The shop was also very quiet, with few people coming and going and she could smoke in peace, keeping watch.

She heard a girl swearing loudly in the street, a car honking, and smiled. For the first time something that reminded her of New York. Dublin, she had decided, was too quiet, people keeping themselves to themselves; it did get to you after a while. She felt like shouting out, pleading for something to happen to take her mind off the looming confrontation. Alexandra knew it was a shame to view her meeting with her mother like that, but she did and that was that. It didn't augur well, but then some of the best things that had happened to her had been surprises. She lit another cigarette and inhaled deeply.

Michael finally looked at his watch. He was feeling better now, a smoke and a few moments of contemplation worked wonders. Without thinking, he patted Lily on the knee.

"It's time we were going. You wouldn't want to be late, now would you?"

Lily, pale faced, glanced at him, her eyes damply blank.

"It'll be fine, she sounds a lovely girl. I'll be with you, remember."

Michael smiled reassuringly, hesitated then patted her leg once again, his good mood rapidly dissolving into a state of disgruntled unease. Lily breaking down on him now was the last thing he needed.

"I hope Alexandra smokes, my clothes will be stinking of cigarettes."

Michael couldn't help laughing.

"Oh, I'm sure she won't notice. Anyway you know Bewley's. By this time in the day you'll be able to cut the atmosphere in there with a knife. Believe me, Alexandra won't be interested in any of that. Come on, let's go."

They crossed the street and walked slowly arm-in-arm towards the ornate carved wood and coloured glass facade of Bewley's. Lily didn't know the Cafe, of course, had never been there. It was irritating that Father Michael could be so insensitive sometimes. Didn't he realize the laundry women never went anywhere and certainly not into the centre of town? This was a real treat for her. Then Lily remembered why she was here.

Alexandra spotted them the instant they reached the far side of the street. A strange mismatched pair clutching at each other and moving at a snail's pace, completely out of time with the people rushing by. Reflexively she drew back into the shadows, sucking hard on her cigarette, the glow illuminating her drawn face and hollow cheeks. The priest, all in black, overweight and greying, was smaller than the woman. Alexandra was taken aback. She'd imagined a short dumpy figure, white haired, beaten and bowed. This woman was tall, like her, elegant, her brown hair tied back in a bun and catching the sun, dressed in dowdy unfashionable clothes but then, what would you expect? She carried herself with dignity, despite the slight stiffness in her walk. Her hands betrayed her, though, clutching her handbag nervously at waist level, not exactly trembling, but there was a fearful tremor in the air as she moved. They went into the cafe and the door shut behind them.

To see her for the first time, so completely different from the person she had lived with for months, argued with, despised, fought with, hated, left Alexandra intrigued. Her Mother was someone else, a brave woman, she now realized, to come here and face her. Why hadn't she thought of this before? She lit another cigarette from the stub of the last one and leaned against the wall, unconcerned for the first time about dirtying her clothes. Mother had for so long been a round-faced, grey-haired woman almost a foot shorter than her with blue eyes and an accent that had never left the Bronx. The accent was the only thing they had ever had in common. Now Alexandra sensed she was going to meet herself, eye-to-eye, hear her real voice, touch her flesh and feel the warmth of her blood. In the sheltering shadows of her entrance she mourned for the time wasted and the love lost.

"She's not here yet, Lily, I've had a good look round. Hey, let's grab that seat in the window. She'll spot us easily there."

Lily followed his gaze and noted the small table with three chairs wedged up against the tall ornate stained glass window. The cafe was full and there was nowhere else to sit, but it seemed terribly public to her. But then, what choice had she got? He had been right, it was very smoky in here, Alexandra wouldn't notice a thing. Lily's eyes began to water.

"Father, I have to go to the …"

"Fine, fine, I'll see you in a minute. Take care now, won't you?"

A number of women nodded at him as he manoeuvred between the tables and sat down. The clock on the wall said 11.35, only five minutes late. He looked at his watch, a little slow. He hoped she would turn up, but you never knew with these people.

Please God, let this end happily.

Michael picked up the menu and suddenly felt very hungry. He was sure Mrs Callaghan was cutting back on his food. If she wasn't going to give him what he wanted he would have to forage on his own – a traditional fry-up would suit him just fine, washed down with cups of strong Assam. To give them their due they were very good at that in here, even if it was a bit pricey. You never knew, the lady might even pay. He stared at the waitress taking an order at a nearby table. She had her back to him, her white headband tied neatly in a bow around a mass of frizzy orange hair, wisps hung down over the white collar of her black uniform. Michael noticed her zip was slightly undone, the metal holder sticking up at right angles. His eyes followed the line of the zipper slowly down her back to its source at her waist, where it disappeared from view behind the frilly band of her apron. Her skirt seemed very short, but then again… at the back of her right knee there was a small hole in her black tights. She stuck her pencil behind her ear, turned, flushed, noticed Father Michael, smiled and sidled towards him.

"Morning, Father."

Michael felt his face reddening and looked down at the menu.

"Are you ready to order?"

He smiled up at her.

"Morning to you. I'm expecting some people, so I'd better wait a while."

"I'll be back then."

She was gone. Michael imagined the faint scent of spring flowers hanging in the air where she had been, but in fact there was nothing but the bitter fug of coffee and cigarettes and the tall figure of a young Lily. He was genuinely startled, his reverie instantly dashed. The resemblance was uncanny, black hair rather than brown and thinner more pronounced features than Lily's, but that could just be age. She was more elegantly dressed, of course, and pretty, very pretty. She seemed at first glance to be more serious than her Mother, but it was early days. There was no doubt about her credentials. Michael was relieved.

He stood awkwardly, wedged as he was in the corner seat behind the heavy cast-iron and mahogany table, and held out his hand. Alexandra, who had taken off her overcoat before coming into the cafe and had it slung over her right arm, had to transfer it to the other arm together with a heavy looking shoulder bag, before she could do the same. Her cold fingers barely touched his before she pulled them away.

"Alexandra Hastert, one time Collins. You must be Father Michael?"

Her brown eyes rested coldly on the priest, a slight smile twitching her pale red lips, her face otherwise impassive. Disconcerted, Michael made a genuine effort to remain civil but, not for the first time, he was suddenly consumed with an intense irritation at everybody and everything involved with this Lily affair. It was difficult for him to pin down, but he felt uneasy. So much was at stake. He had to keep a lid on this.

"Alexandra, pleased to meet you. Take a seat. It's all a bit cramped, I'm afraid. But that's part of the charm."

Throwing her coat over the back of one of the bent wood chairs, Alexandra sat down and picked up the menu. She smelled of vanilla, an icy fragrance that refreshed Michael even as it repelled him.

"Have you ordered?"

He was surprised she had not asked about Lily.

"No, I was waiting for you. They have a very good choice of teas or coffee. If you're hungry the breakfasts here are great."

"Thanks, I ate at the hotel."

Disappointed, Michael reconciled himself to a sticky bun. He would have to speak to Mrs Callaghan; it was not good enough for a busy man like him.

"How long have you been in Dublin?"

"I arrived yesterday."

"Good flight?"

"OK. Feeling a bit jet lagged today. But I'll soon get over it. I do a fair bit of flying on business."

"What line are you in? I don't think you said in your letters."

"Clothing."

"Must be interesting."

"It is."

"I've no head for business. Takes me all my time to sort out my own taxes. I couldn't be bothering with anything more complicated, except perhaps the parish petty cash and then of course there's the laundry. Who knows? Maybe there's a businessman hiding in here somewhere. You know what they say."

"Could we order? I feel in need of some strong coffee."

"Sorry, maundering on as usual. We could order, we certainly could. I've a good idea what Lily would like."

Alexandra started at the mention of her Mother, for the first time glancing away, scanning the crowded, hazy interior. Michael was strangely satisfied. Now all he needed was his red-haired, long-legged waitress, but she was nowhere to be seen.

Lily stood, door ajar, in the entrance to the "Ladies" and peered through the narrow crack. She couldn't see Father Michael, he was hidden by the corner of the bar, but she knew where they were sitting, and she could clearly see the back of the person talking to him. Tall, erect and motionless, dressed entirely in black – cardigan and Lily thought slacks but it was difficult to tell at that distance – thick dark wavy hair falling around her neck. Long thin pale fingers tugged abstractedly at one of her pendant earrings. A weak sunlight, filtered through the leaded glass above her head, dappled her shoulders with shimmering stains of red, yellow and purple. Lily crossed herself. She had worried about bringing Father Michael, but now it seemed right somehow. He was hearing her daughter's confession, absolving her of all her sins, leaving her soul clean, pure and open for the time, coming soon, when Lily would fling herself on her mercy. She felt sick but exhilarated. She had nothing to say to Alexandra but sorry, and now for the first time she felt it might just be enough.

"Excuse me!"

Startled, Lily opened the door and stepped through into the cafe, moving to one side to let the woman pass.

"Sorry."

Glancing ostentatiously at her watch the woman shook her head as she hurried towards the exit, apologizing as she did so to her waiting friend. Flustered, Lily backed towards the refuge of the "Ladies", reaching up once again to check her hair. Thinking this was foolish; she stopped and looked up only to see Alexandra staring straight at her. It was not clear that she recognized her, there was no discernible change in her stern expression, she remained seated, unmoving but Lily felt skewered, unable to wriggle free. All that remained was for Alexandra to reel her in.

"That's her."

Lily drew closer. She had not anticipated the intense pain of recognition, deeper than the mere physical similarities, which were unnervingly obvious, a natural sense of continuity that was irrefutable.

"She was in there a long time, she must be nervous. Look, her hands are really shaking now. God, she seems so familiar."

Standing for the first time in front of your daughter. Lily had thought about this, what to say, what to do, and had planned out, with the help of Father Michael, her every move. Play it safe with a handshake, bland enquiries about her flight, her health, what did she think of Dublin, the weather. "Don't push anything too fast", he had said, "take it easy, see how things work out. There's plenty of time."

The chair scraped noisily across the stripped wooden floor, almost toppling over, as Alexandra got to her feet to confront her Mother.

Face to face, immobile and tongue-tied, Lily stared into her daughter's eyes, thinking only how beautiful she looked. She had never imagined anything like this, she was so lucky.

Alexandra knew what she wanted to say to this woman, but the pale skin, the wrinkles at the corners of her moist eyes, the flecks of grey just beginning to show in her brown hair, struck her dumb. Her Mother was at her mercy, she could see that, and to Alexandra's surprise she found that was more than enough.

She said and did nothing, as beside her Father Michael rose with difficulty to his feet. The three of them stood silently. The couple at the next table glanced up at them, whispered a few words together, then turned again to watch. It amused them to see a priest so obviously at a loss for words, his arms hovering in mid-air, suggesting a coming together but lacking the courage to push the two women into the desired embrace.

The word had been there for more than thirty years, dormant, a witness. Lily knew it and sensed it was up to her. It was so quiet and she could barely see, the liquid colours fusing with the refracted sunlight merged with the fuzzy silhouette of her daughter to smooth away any detail. A vivid blindness that ultimately gave her courage. The word was there, submerged, as it had always been. Lily barely had the strength to cough it into existence.

"Sorry."

Uncertain, because nothing seemed to happen, Lily feared a mere word was hopelessly inadequate for such sinful dereliction – scared now that this might be true – that she had merely imagined saying it and that she had not said it loudly or clearly enough. The truth was she had nothing else to say, all she could do was shout it out again and again until Alexandra heard it, until she accepted it. Seconds passed, minutes, Lily's eyes filled with moisture, the word wouldn't, in the end, come to her rescue, her throat felt raw. As best she could tell no one was moving, not even Father Michael, whose black bulk shimmered nearby, silent. So this was it, the doorway to hell on earth, willingly held open by her priest and her own flesh and blood. Years of torment, alone, she deserved it. Killing your baby was not something you could ever atone for. The terror loosened her bowels – she had to go back, back to the Ladies where she had come from. Lily began to turn aside.

To the two witnesses, to Father Michael, it would have been difficult to say who moved first, who collapsed the triangle. The word "Sorry", hung there clearly for all of them, an expectation that was rapidly met. Barely a breath passed before some would say Lily flinched slightly as Alexandra gasped and flung out her arms to hug her, others would say there was nothing in it, the two moved together into a tight embrace.

The word, so unexpected, had stunned Alexandra, completely demolishing any lingering resistance to a relationship with her Mother. Her vow to remain dispassionate and detached until her story was satisfactorily told, to definitely avoid any physical contact with the woman until she gave up her secrets, was repudiated in an instant. The eagerness of the arms around her, the warmth of the firm body, the reciprocity of physical pressure – the atavistic pleasure she got from the long forgotten smell of naphthalene – brought a deluge of tears unseen since distant days in a Bronx bedroom, a broken doll at her feet. Happiness of such purity was a stranger to Alexandra, strictly raised in a faith she had guiltily lost long ago. A parent fixed you in time somehow, a before and now, without any doubt, an after. A history of the Collins' would include a future for her and that made Alexandra truly content.

Lily was overwhelmed, tripped up by the trickiness of time, beaten to the very door of despair, she was now holding her daughter. It had happened before, now it was more than a memory, it was a joy. Nobody else had noticed the gap in the story. She could cry happy for once, held tight against the bosom of her family.

For Michael, delighted things were going so well, he could only reflect that he had told her so. "You can never go wrong with an apology Lily, you think on that." He spotted his red-haired waitress coming their way.

"Shall we order?"

The two women kissed.

"Can I call you Mom?"

***

Lily was amazed at how little she owned now she came to look at it all packed and ready to go. A lifetime of work had not led to much, but then she wouldn't be needing a great deal where she was going, by the sound of things. What she had now was far more precious, so what did it matter that everything fitted into two small suitcases? She had another nagging little doubt though, that try as hard as she might she couldn't shake off. She thought she understood why she had to slip away to America and not tell anyone, it was "for the good of the Convent", but Doris, Barbara, even Maeve? Not to tell them didn't seem right. They could keep a secret, she was sure, but Father Michael was adamant.

"Tell no one, Lily, I mean it. His Holiness has given permission for you to go off with your daughter, but he has made it clear that this is a one off because of the special circumstances. He could easily change his mind if he heard you'd not kept your side of the bargain. Is that clear?"

She had agreed reluctantly, but had written Doris a letter full of optimism and lightness of spirit, explaining everything and pleading for her friend's understanding of why she had to leave secretly, and asking for her forgiveness. The letter ended with her new address in New York written out in block capitals and double underlined and a P.S.: Write soon, Doris love, write often.

She gave it to Father Michael, who nodded conspiratorially and slipped it in among other papers in the wooden bureau in the room he used at the Convent.

"Don't worry, everything will work out for the best."

A guilt-ridden Lily seeking redemption seized upon his words eagerly and she left reassured, believing that Father Michael would know the right time to deliver her letter to Doris.

The infirmary smelled strongly of disinfectant and Lily worried Alexandra would notice it on her clothes, she was used to it, even quite liked it, but she knew others were more fastidious. Alexandra was probably one of those people, she guessed, although she didn't know her that well yet, who always dressed beautifully and used expensive perfume. The infirmary had been Father Michael's idea; it was on the other side of the Convent from the dormitories, on the ground floor and close to the small "funeral" gate that opened from the garden on to a side street. "Ideal for a quick getaway", was how he put it. He had been going to add that "most people leave through that gate one way or the other", but had thought better of it as he looked up from his coffee into Lily's panic-stricken, bloodshot eyes.

The priest's own natural vanity made him sensitive to subtle nuances of appearance, not only in himself but also in others, and he was amazed how Lily had changed in just a few weeks. Where he would have expected her to blossom out in anticipation of her good fortune, she had visibly wilted, had lost weight, her features sunken and drawn, there was a puffiness around the eyes that had narrowed and dulled them, her normally translucent skin, that he had so admired, had tightened and dried. He noticed traces of eczema on the side of her neck, running up to her hairline, that she often touched unknowingly as he talked to her about their plans. They had spent many hours scheming and arranging the paperwork after Alexandra had, to everyone's surprise, invited her Mother to come and live with her in New

York, and he had had plenty of time to watch Lily as she slowly convinced herself it was the right thing to do. It seemed that the initial shock, and the subsequent effort in making her mind up, had exacted a heavy physical toll.

"I can see you need a good rest. You'll have plenty of time for that when you get to Alexandra's. Put your feet up, let your daughter pamper you. You deserve it, you really do."

Lily had been taken ill with "flu" the day before she was due to leave and moved into the infirmary, together with her clothes and belongings, while the others were at work. She was leaving, she knew it now, leaving her home of many years, the place where she had grown up, the only place she had ever worked, and for the first time she realized that it was a vital part of her – the high ceiling of the laundry, the blueness of the light, the chill of the early mornings, the heat and steam, the beads of sweat running deliciously down the length of her spine.

It had been a time of emotional turmoil on the previous day when she had to say good-bye to her laundry, and to her friends whom she loved even more, without any of them having any idea what was going on. Doris had been the hardest, she was so vague sometimes it was difficult for Lily to get her to pay attention to what she was saying. In the end she just kissed her and ran from the room.

They had all got used to Lily's recent strange behaviour and so thought little of it. Any doubters, and Doris was one of them, were reassured when they heard later about her fever. Lily was said to be too infectious for visitors and spent a lonely sleepless night worrying about what lay ahead.

Alexandra was a lovely girl, sympathetic and generous of spirit and money, of which there seemed to be plenty. They had talked and talked about the past and there had been little rancour. Her daughter had shown no desire to pinpoint blame, accepting Lily had had no choice about what had happened to her and believing she had suffered more than enough anyway with her years in the laundry. Lily loved her for that, knew that she had nothing to lose by going to live with her in New York, it was only for a trial period after all, she could always come back to the Convent, but she was plagued by doubts.

Alexandra's adopted mother was still alive, how would they get on? The Bronx was a strange-sounding name and she'd never really lived in a big city before. And she felt guilty, guilty as hell, there was no way she could escape it – about running out on her friends. Would they understand? Sleep came as Lily thought of Doris.

***

It was dark now. Lily could no longer see the statue of the Virgin Mary in the garden although it was only a few feet from the window. Alexandra would be arriving soon in a taxi to take her to the hotel – the first she'd ever have stayed in – before their early morning flight to America. Nervous of flying, anxious about leaving, even more scared at abandoning her friends, and exhausted, Lily was in a highly emotional state. Unable to sit still she paced the room, picking at her fingernails. It was hot. She took off her overcoat and flung it onto the bed. The statue was one of her favourites, standing in the shade of an ancient climbing rose – a damp and perfumed bower even in the hottest summer – marked with silvery grey and yellow lichens, its base a moss-covered green. She would never see it again, the Virgin's face gazing down at her from a halo of pink blooms, the grass wet beneath her back.

The door opened. Lily, briefly calm, stared out of the window. In the reflection she could see the black forms of Father Michael and the Reverend Mother, there was no sign of Alexandra, and

Lily felt a rush of indeterminate emotion. Her breath fogged the cold glass and she could see nothing more. It was very hot.

"Mom…"

Her finger streaked the misted window and she turned. Alexandra was standing there smiling, out of breath.

"…It's time to go."

They hugged.

"The taxi got held up in traffic. I'm sorry."

"Good luck, Lily, God go with you."

Sister Beatrice's hand was flaccid and cold.

"I'll remember you in my prayers."

Unexpectedly, Father Michael embraced her, his arms comforting and strong.

"I'll miss you, Lily. God bless."

They stood briefly together, cheek to cheek. It was a strange world, he thought. Having a priest's child had got Lily in here all those years ago, now it was getting her out.

"Those your two bags?"

She nodded and stepped back.

"Let me carry them out to the taxi for you."

She murmured her thanks and followed the priest out into the chill of the early evening. She felt Alexandra's hand resting gently in the small of her back as they made their way along the slippery path towards the high Convent wall. There was a nun, Lily couldn't see clearly who it was, standing at the "funeral" gate, the beam of her torch a yellow circle on the ground. Looking back the laundry was in darkness, looming black against the paler night sky. There were lights on in the refectory.

They'd be having their meal now. Who would Doris be talking to?

Chapter 10

The Snug – March 1996 – twenty past two

The whisky warmed Father Michael's insides. It was very stuffy in the snug, but he felt shivery, the aching chill of an imminent fever. He hoped he wasn't sickening for something serious. The priest ran his tongue over his front teeth, slightly lifting the upper plate of his new dentures. Gums rubbed raw, the stinging of the whisky distracted him, heightening his unease. The three women were silent for a moment and sat across the table from him, distractedly fingering their glasses.

The priest was beginning to feel both annoyed and uncharacteristically guilty about not having told them something about Lily. For the first time in ages he wondered if he still had that letter from Lily to Doris that she'd given him as she left. His desk was such a mess, it would probably still be in there somewhere. Should he have passed it on? It would have put an end to all this heart searching, before it even began, but what else would have come out? Father Michael shuddered at the thought and sipped at his whisky. He couldn't have risked that. Not then.

Now things were different, the world had changed more in the last four years than he could have possibly imagined. The laundry was closed, his women almost gone, scattered to the four corners of the earth, and the Church was a different, less familiar place. He had been thinking for a while that he didn't feel as at home there as he used to, but had put it down to creeping old age. Now he wasn't so sure. It occurred to him that there would be an address for Lily and he could at least pass that on. That should make Doris happy. After all, what did it matter now? He didn't want to be remembered as having turned up and spoilt their last drink together. Resolving to make one final attempt to bring them round, before slipping away to search his desk, he even considered buying them another drink, then Doris suddenly spoke out.

"I went back, you know."

They all turned to look at her. Michael waved a hand in front of his face to clear the cigarette smoke that hung around him like a shroud; Margaret smiled, while Maeve looked blank.

"I went back to the cemetery after Lily went."

The priest was puzzled for a moment, unable to fathom what she was talking about. Lily was a sensitive topic and he could see that the others hadn't been joking when they'd said that Doris was obsessed with her. Margaret couldn't hold herself back.

"Why, for pity's sake?"

"To see if I could find her. You know, a grave or a headstone."

"But she didn't die, she just went."

"We don't know that for sure."

"You don't know that for sure, you mean. The rest of us do."

Margaret looked across at Father Michael, seeking either confirmation or denial. She was still grinning.

"Oh, come on, Margaret, none of us knows what happened for certain to Lily."

Maeve smiled reassuringly at Doris.

Ignoring all of them, Doris continued speaking in a quiet monotone that had the other three unconsciously leaning forward to catch her words.

"It wasn't there, just some new houses. I was so confused. You know what I'm like – thought I'd got it wrong again. I almost cried, standing by the railings I could have sworn used to go round the cemetery. After all, I'd been there so many times, how could I have made such a mistake?"

"What wasn't there?"

Doris looked surprised at the interruption.

"Why, the cemetery, of course."

"Don't be silly, Dot, cemeteries don't just disappear. You must have got it mixed up."

"No, I hadn't. This one had gone. I was in the right place. A lady walking past asked me if I was OK. I must have looked a right state, standing there."

"Ooooh, I love a good mystery!" Maeve stood up. "Hold on Doris, I've got to go and spend a penny. Don't say another word till I get back."

She hurried away and Doris smiled at the others and sipped her drink. That was the strange thing about death, she thought, it was supposed to define a person. There was their life, complete, finished, a grave for their mortal remains and their soul was either in Heaven or in Hell. That was that person, nothing more was going to happen to change anything, that was them. But it didn't seem to work out like that for her. Dead people seemed even more elusive than live ones, always moving, escaping and disappearing. The others didn't seem to understand that. Things weren't clear at all.

Maeve returned slightly out of breath, wiping her wet hands on a small white pocket handkerchief.

"The towel in there is filthy, the people from the market must have been in. I'll mention it next time I'm up. I hope I haven't missed anything?"

They all looked at Doris, who picked up instantly from where she had left off.

"The lady said, could she help. I was so grateful. I could have stood there for hours not knowing what to do. I said, I thought there used to be a cemetery here. She said there was, but it was sold off and the graves moved to Glasnevin. Must have been eighteen months to two years ago. I probably looked upset, even though I was really feeling quite the opposite, because she took my arm and asked if I knew someone buried there. I said yes, and she said, poor thing – and they never told you? It's a disgrace, the Council."

"The graves have gone?"

Maeve was outraged.

"Yes, I couldn't believe it, Maeve. Houses and gardens, that's all there is now. They've kept the railings. It's like a little estate."

"How could they do that? It's not allowed. All those people buried there, their last resting place. It's not right."

Maeve shook her head then stared at the others incredulously, seeking support.

"They moved the coffins, all of them?"

Doris nodded at Margaret.

"So this lady said. She lives in one of the new houses. She gave me a cup of tea. She has that lovely view from her living room."

"It's horrible, moving people like that. Rest in peace they say. It's terrible."

Father Michael drained his glass and stood up and went to the bar.

"That means all the people from here will have been moved."

For the first time Margaret understood what Doris had been saying and it filled her with dread. Margaret's past worried her, more so now she was getting older. While she regretted very little of it, she knew she had never fully made amends for what she had done. Even though over the years she had confessed most of it to Father Michael, he had never, in her eyes, treated it seriously and given her a severe enough penance. She'd been too much of a coward to seek out a deeper, more profound redemption, always saying "next week". This uncertainty about her future in eternity had led her to find some small comfort in the fact that she knew where she was going to be buried, the exact spot, she had marked it out, always said a brief prayer when she was there. Now it was gone, paved over. She felt sick. This was a sign and Margaret was superstitious.

"What's up, Margaret? It looks like you've seen a ghost. Here get this down you. You'll soon feel better."

The priest placed two glasses of stout on the table and turned back to the bar. For the first time in many years Margaret began to cry silently, heavy tears carving runnels in her heavily powdered face. Doris and Maeve were shocked and uncertain what to do. A comforting arm, a reassuring hug, seemed totally inappropriate when it came to Margaret and she was left isolated in her pain. Even Michael returning from the bar with the last two drinks was surprised and could think of nothing but to light up another cigarette.

"Would you like one? I know you have in the past."

Such a small kindness was too much for Margaret and she covered her face with her hands. He shrugged and the three of them sat silently holding their glasses.

"It's nice up at Glasnevin – I went there, took the bus. Not the same day I went to the old cemetery, of course, but later."

Margaret raised her tear-stained face to look at Doris.

"It's right on the edge of town, fields all around. Big area, very big. But nice all right. Well looked after with flowers and the like."

Margaret smiled and wiped her tears with her hand. Maeve handed her her handkerchief.

"It's a bit damp, but clean. Only dried my hands on it."

***

Doris had to change buses twice to get to Glasnevin Cemetery. It had taken nearly an hour to get there, and she was glad she had told Mother where she was going. It was a beautiful day after the rain, with a clear blue sky and a slight breeze that gently moved the daffodils that seemed to be everywhere, a shimmering yellow sea that filled Doris with optimism. She was dropped off at the large entrance gates to the cemetery, the last passenger on the bus, and the driver gave her a cheery wave as she got down.

Peering through the ornate ironwork, painted black and gold but pitted and rusting in places, Doris could see lines of graves stretching away to the horizon, first dipping away from her to the left then curving up over the smoothness of the hill ahead, joining together in a shadowy line before disappearing from sight. A black gash of tarmac stood out clearly against the off-whites and greys of the headstones, but followed their line away into the distance, blending into the landscape. Yew trees, dark green and sombre, dotted the hillside, the only discordant colour a large bunch of dying red roses on a nearby grave. Doris imagined the stones going on forever, hill after hill, valley after valley.

Where could they be – her friends, Ethel, Lily and all the rest? There was no way she could find them here.

A "Visitors" sign, inside the front gates, pointed to a single storey brick building, covered in ivy. The heavy front door was wedged ajar with a highly polished brass boot scraper and Doris pushed it open and peered inside. A young man was dozing in front of an electric fire, its three bars glowing red, his feet clad in mottled green socks were up on the counter, a newspaper lying across his chest. The air was heavy with the smell of drying wool and warm rubber. Unwilling to wake him, Doris backed slowly away, but his eyes opened just before the door closed behind her.

"Sorry, love, you should have said something." His voice sounded muffled, "Must have dozed off."

He swung his feet to the floor, wincing slightly at the chill of the flagstones, and stood up. Closing the newspaper he tossed it onto the chair behind him, rubbed his eyes, then flattened his hair.

"Yes, love, what can I do for you?"

Both hands resting firmly on the edge of the counter as if he was steadying himself, he appeared to be concentrating on something else, but managed to smile at Doris as she re-emerged from behind the door and crossed towards him, anxiously clutching her handbag.

"I'm looking…"

She cleared her throat and started again.

"I'm looking for some graves of friends of mine, who were moved here sometime recently."

"Moved here? When was that?"

"Within the last two years or so, I think. The old cemetery …"Doris coughed again.

"Sorry."

"No matter, love. I'm in no hurry, you take your time."

"It was sold off by the Church, so I was told. They dug everyone up and brought them here."

"Been happening a lot in the last few years, what with the Church so short of money an all. What was the name of the cemetery?"

Doris felt weak, but there was nowhere to sit down. She wished she hadn't come.

"I don't know it was on Gallowglass Road. Is that any help?"

"Rings a bell. I haven't been here that long, but just after I started, which was about two years ago, there was a large number of people brought in. I'll have a look."

The man turned to a cupboard on the wall and took down a large heavy red leather-bound book. He dropped it with a thud on to the counter, dust rose into the air and he sneezed, rummaging unsuccessfully in his pocket for a handkerchief.

"My Mam'd kill me if she knew I was out without a blow rag," he laughed, wiping his running nose with the back of his hand. "This is the register, it'll be in here."

He opened the book then hesitated.

"Who are you looking for? Do you have a name?"

Without thinking Doris blurted out Ethel's. The man scribbled it down on a pad then with a grunt turned over the heavy volume and opened it at the back, scanning through the long list of names with his finger.

"Maurice Hancock, Ruby Hallam… no Ethel Hannah, I'm afraid. It's not a very common name."

"She must be there, I saw her buried. It wasn't that long ago. It was where all the Magdalen women went from our Convent – where they all ended up. Has been like that for years."

The young man sighed with relief.

"Ah, Magdalen women, I know where they'll be."

Turning the thick parchment pages until he found what he was looking for, he smiled crookedly at Doris.

"Here they are. What's the name of the Convent, do you know?"

To Doris it looked like his finger was resting on the last line of the last page.

"Should do, I live there. Been there for ages."

The young man, whose attention had been wandering – a flock of starlings was raucously tearing at the ivy that hung around the window that faced out over the acres of cemetery – looked at her again. An apology seemed to be forming itself on his lips, the muscles around his mouth quivered briefly, his brow furrowed, but he said nothing.

"The Convent of our Lady of Mercy at Magdalen Asylum."

"Ah!"

The finger moved across a list of tightly written names. Doris wondered if the address would be any help, was just about to spell it out as she had done so often before, when he looked up.

"Here it is."

He glanced at the page.

"The plot's a good way from here, though, right over by the railway."

There was a large map of the cemetery on the wall behind him – a dark black broken line marked the perimeter, thinner dotted lines carved up the vast area into sectors each given a letter and a number, these were divided grid like into numbered plots, the roads in dark black cut through this pattern disrupting the imposed order, arrows neatly placed beside them showed when they were one-way only. The man turned and stabbed with his finger at a black rectangle close to a break in the perimeter line on the opposite side of the map from the small "You are here" sticker.

"That's where they are, W7."

"That's where they are."

Doris couldn't help repeating what she had heard. It looked a long, long way to her. Having come so far she didn't want to go back without paying her respects, but something was worrying her.

"Thank you. Er, you said just then that there was no Ethel Hannah listed in the book? But I know she was buried there. It was the last funeral at the old place. It wasn't that long ago, I'm pretty sure."

"I know what it is. Transfers from somewhere else – you know, mass burials – are listed in this other book."

He pulled down another heavy volume from the shelf and let it thud on to the counter. The sharp retort startling the starlings in the ivy outside, the rapid whirr of their wings clearly audible as they spiralled away in panic. This book was only partly filled with names, the dirty thumbed pages standing out clearly against the clean cream of the untouched half.

"I'm sure they'll be in here somewhere".

There was a clock on the wall. Its cone-shaped pendulum swung dully back and forth at the end of a complicated series of chains – twenty to eleven. Doris knew she should be getting back soon. This was all taking longer than she had expected. In her mind it had been bright and sunny, there would have been lots of flowers, she would have walked through the gate and there in neat rows would have been her friends, their names clearly inscribed on pale marble headstones, going back over the years. Her life. She would have said Hello, sat for a few minutes on a nearby seat, looked at the beautiful view, then left.

"At last. Sorry about this. Here they are, Convent of our Lady of Mercy. No names, though, I'm afraid."

Doris looked puzzled.

"No names? But they all had names."

"I'm sure, but there are no names listed. It's all here apart from that – name of old cemetery, address, date of interment, name of convent, how many graves were moved. I'm sure this is the right one, the one you're looking for."

"How many were moved?"

Detail was the only way that Doris felt she could begin to understand what was being said to her. She knew there had been lots of graves at the old cemetery, she could remember that much.

"Er, let me see. One hundred and thirty two."

"And no names?"

"No, I'm sorry. Look, here, take a look."

He closed the first register and pushed it away down the counter, then spun the second one round so that Doris could read it. He helpfully pointed out the relevant section then backed away and began putting on his boots, which had been drying in front of the fire. The page had three columns of names running down it, all written in the same neat blocked handwriting. It took Doris several seconds for her eyes to focus and the letters to become clear. There were names each with a sector and plot number and a date, one after the other, hundreds of them. She could barely comprehend it. But the Magdalen laundry graves had no names, he had been telling the truth, they only had one of two plot numbers – W7, 19 or 20, and they all had the same re-burial date. Doris just couldn't believe what she was reading: Box 27 – unknown, Box 36 – unknown, Box 105 unknown and on and on. There was no one to recognize. There were no friends.

"Are you all right? You look pale."

Incomprehension had dried Doris' tears before they could even form. She just couldn't understand how this could be the case. She felt vaguely sick and the tautness that stretched painfully behind her eyes, from temple to temple, made her frown and squint even more closely at the page in front of her. To Doris, who could no longer see anything, her face felt as if it was folding in on itself, fold after fold, closing down.

"Here, why don't you take my seat?"

The young man was holding up a hinged section of the counter and motioning to Doris to pass through and sit down. Without thinking she shook her head.

"Thank you, but I must go and see them."

She had no idea where to go, but moved towards the door.

"Thank you, thank you."

"Hold on. It's too far for you to walk. Give me a minute and I can run you up there in my van. I need to go anyway to pick up the rubbish."

He unhooked a set of keys from a board in a small cupboard

on the wall, grabbed his patched green tweed jacket from the back of the chair, lowered the counter, then took Doris by the arm and guided her out of the room, kicking the doorstep out of the way as he did so. The door slammed behind them.

"It's very quiet at this time of day." And then to no one in particular he added, "I'll be back in less than half an hour anyway."

The battery-powered vehicle hummed its way sedately between the graves. The two metal bins in the back rattled together whenever they went over a pothole in the road, otherwise the world was silent. The sun shone ahead of them in the almost clear sky, the glare forcing Doris to look from side to side at the ranks of graves that appeared to drop away slightly from the road before climbing up and away over the sides of the valley. The headstones were a multitude of sizes and shapes, even colours, but were all neatly aligned with the muddy pathways that criss-crossed the cemetery, giving a deceptive impression of order. Line after line passed by, the occasional stone leaning at an angle, standing out, drawing the eye. Doris could think of nothing. The breeze on her cheeks was cool and refreshing, the presence of the young man, now whistling softly to himself, reassuring. They were climbing, the hum of the motor imperceptibly changing, straining now, more high-pitched. Ahead a row of yew trees marked the brow of the hill, a pile of black bin bags piled clumsily beside the road, the top one open revealing the brown withered heads and stems of dead flowers.

"I'll just stop and pick those up if that's OK, love? Won't take a minute."

Doris' silent compliance, mistaken by the young man for grief, was heightening the sense of intimacy between the two of them – she anxious for company, increasingly unwilling to complete this journey on her own, he only too aware of a more than passing resemblance, at least in manner if not looks, between this bowed old lady and his Great-Aunt Vera whom he had always liked but didn't see anywhere near often enough. He smiled as he climbed back into the cab. The air was heavy with the organic smell of rotting vegetation.

"Not much further now."

The railway was clearly visible below them in the distance, a straight green slash, topped with a ragged line of black, cutting its way at an angle across the cemetery, abruptly halting the lines of graves. The embankment backed by the low sun cast a long dark shadow, which was where Doris knew her friends were buried – she could see the finger jabbing at sector W on the map, just below the arrow straight stippled line that marked the track of the railway.

Halting beside a small white concrete marker, the letter W neatly painted on it in black, the young man touched her lightly on the arm.

"Plots 19 and 20 will be just over there, down that path."

He pointed. Doris turned and looked at him. He leant forward onto the steering wheel and gazed out through the streaked windscreen.

"Would you like me to come with you?"

Doris nodded, then stepped carefully out of the cab. It was surprisingly muddy underfoot, even though it hadn't rained for several days, the clay holding the water in low-lying yellowing pools. The young man came round to join her, jumping agilely over the puddles.

"I'm so sorry, I don't know your name?"

"That's all right, it's Peter."

"Mine's Doris, Doris Blaney."

She smiled at her saviour, knowing there was no way she could tell him how important he was to her, how vital. Peter returned the smile.

"Let's go, it's this way."

He took her arm and guided her between two moss covered graves; Jesus hanging on the cross gazed down upon them, bathed in green light. As they slithered along the muddy path, their shoes instantly wet from the long lush grass that sprouted between the stones, and passed into the shadow of the railway, the atmosphere suddenly turned frigid, the savour of decay hanging damply in the air, cutting to the lungs, raising a pain in Doris' chest and throat. It seemed several degrees colder, autumnal even, when they reached plots 19 and 20. They were at the end of the path, tight up against the rusting fence that marked off the cemetery from the steep rise of the embankment. Young nettles, dark green, flourished in the soggy no-man's land, snuffing out the chances of any other plants growing there.

"This is it. Here we are."

Peter respectfully stepped back, drawing his jacket close around him. Doris stood there alone at the foot of the two narrow, overgrown and unkempt plots. At their head were six small grey stones, tightly positioned one against the other, each covered in lettering and numbers that were already disappearing under the ubiquitous green, despite their relative youth. Hands clasped, head bowed, handbag firmly under her arm, Doris felt relieved, for she had found them and some at least were remembered. Her eyes weren't good enough to make out exactly what was inscribed on the stones, but she was certain they were names, the names of her friends, her family. Edging carefully sideways along the thin furrow between the plots, Doris began to cry, selfish tears streaming down her face. This was where she was going to end up and she didn't like it. The cemetery smelled rotten, was cold and there was no view, not like the other place. She had liked it there. Now this was all she had to look forward to. It was true she would be with her friends, but that didn't seem enough somehow.

For the first time in many years Doris prayed – pleading to be spared an eternity in this spot of perpetual shadow, friends or not. As so often in the past, she felt nothing, but this time she didn't blame herself. Her mind was clear, she knew things, Ethel had prayed all her life and she had ended up here. From that moment Doris knew she no longer believed. It had never seemed possible in the laundry to own up and face it, it was too much part of the routine, but here, face to face with her future, it was different.

Finally she felt able to wipe away the tears and meet her friends properly, say hello again after all these years.

"Lady of Mercy at Magdalen Asylum, In loving memory of C. Kearney – April 1858, M. Maher – September 1903, B. Fitzgerald – May 1921", and so it went on. Doris read all the names, stepping gingerly over the grassy mounds as she came to the end of each stone. "P. McQuaid – November 1946, D. Robinson – July 1956, T. Gallagher – March 1975." That must be Teresa, she remembered a petite, vivacious women, always singing. And then she found her, the last name on the sixth stone: "E. Hannah – December 1994". Ethel was the final name of the long list, but there was plenty of room in her column for a good few more names to be added. Doris tried to imagine her own name carved into the stone, the lettering fresh and untainted by age, but the image escaped her and she turned her head away.

The sun was lower now, the light more orange. Peter was still there sitting on one of the stones, hands in pockets, his head down. He looked up the instant she moved his way. One thing pleased Doris, there had been no L. Collins, she was happy about that. The thought of Lily lying here didn't seem right; she'd been too full of life for that. It was time to go, but one final question was troubling her.

"Peter, you said that over 130 women were moved. How did they fit them into this small space?"

For a second he was nonplussed, then he replied.

"They'd have been cremated, I expect. Only way they could've done it. Cost too much otherwise."

***

Margaret handed the handkerchief back to Maeve.

"Thanks. You say it's nice up there at Glasnevin?"

Margaret was feeling even more bitter. Everything Doris said or did seemed to make things worse.

"Yes, the area is. But the cemetery is horrible. It's very well looked after mostly, but it's so big you get lost. You can't find anyone. It's got no soul and it's very damp. It's not a place I'd want to be buried in."

Margaret nodded, drinking it all in. Doris surprised you sometimes, she really did, even now she was still capable of turning the knife.

"Thanks very much. Because you're getting away, you can say that. You realize, don't you, that that's where me and Maeve are going to end up? You really are spiteful."

"Me, spiteful? That's a bit much coming from you. You're full of it, always have been."

Father Michael appreciated he was escaping all the awkward questions that should have been coming his way – about Lily, the graves and the laundry – but he also understood sadly that the women had got away from him too. He would long ponder how it had all come to this, how he had lost control, but in the end would decide that maybe it was for the best. This was the moment for him to take it easy, if not to retire then at least give more consideration to his own spiritual well being. Humility was about to re-enter Father Michael's own personal lexicon, or so he hoped.

"Ladies, thank you for your company."

His voice, loud and unexpected, punctured the tense atmosphere.

"Looking at the lateness of the hour, I think I'll just go and check Doris' niece hasn't got lost. She should have been here by now."

Maeve adjusted the cardigan around her shoulders and reached down to pick up her handbag. The priest raised his hand.

"There's no need for you to move. Stay and finish your drinks. I'll bring her across, when she arrives."

Maeve didn't sit down but edged uncertainly towards the bar. "It's my turn isn't it?"

"No, Maeve, it's mine. You've bought us one already."

"Sorry Doris, I forgot."

"Doesn't matter. Seeing as you're up. Could you get them? I'll give you the money."

Doris held out a folded five-pound note and Maeve took it gratefully. Margaret glared at Doris.

"Full of spite, that's rich coming from you. You're one of the most spiteful women I've ever known. You pretended to be my friend, Doris Blaney, and then you ruined my life. You wrecked it more than you can ever know."

Doris just sat there. Father Michael's departure from the snug had been just a brief interruption in a dialogue between Margaret and her that had been going on for years. Now none of it seemed to matter, there was nothing new in Margaret getting cross with her, and anyway she was leaving soon for good. She didn't dislike Margaret, it was just that her behaviour always failed to match up to the image you carried around of her in your mind. Living together for so long meant you had to make allowances and she suspected they all had for Margaret. In fact, she knew it. Margaret Macready was a friend in theory only; in practice she rarely was. It made it easier to say goodbye.

Margaret wanted to leave the pub and get away. Doris' treacherous placidity was driving her wild. It was like children playing in the park – their squeals and shouts cutting right through you – you wanted to hit out to make them go away. You don't, of course, you are in control, but what if all constraints, moral, legal and human, were gone? What if there were no consequences to your actions except personal satisfaction? What if whatever you did, nothing changed – the outcome was the same? Why not strike that blow? Doris would still leave, they would go their separate ways, but the feeling of satisfaction would stay with her forever. She would lose Maeve, of course, but that was a price she could afford to pay. There would be one less sanctimonious voice droning on.

Time for once was on her side as Maeve struggled at the bar and Doris sat passively beside her, large eyes open wide, looking as if her head was on the block. Margaret had the luxury of considering what she wanted to do with the rest of her life. She could be true to herself or not? Strike the blow or not? Leave or not? How much time did you need?

Maeve lurched back from the bar clutching two glasses of stout.

"That's right, isn't it, Margaret? I thought I could remember. Paddy there helped me out."

Margaret nodded, she needed a drink.

"I think I'd lose my head if it wasn't screwed on," Maeve maundered on.

And she was curious. Doris had a family and she wanted to see them. They would be here soon. No need to leave just yet.

"Cheers."

Maeve slumped back onto her chair, her glass waving unsteadily in front of her.

"I'm tipsy, Maggie. You're my best friends, aren't you?"

She looked blearily from Margaret to Doris and back again.

"Cheers, I'll miss you, I really will."

The glass moved alarmingly in front of her face as she tried to drink from it – her body near paralysed by drink allowed her briefly to focus her senses – and she carefully set it down on the table, which seemed to move as well.

"I must go to the Ladies."

Doris smiled and raised her glass, as Maeve stayed seated, grinning stupidly at both of her friends.

"Oh, this is ridiculous. Come on, Maeve, I'll go with you. We don't want any more accidents, do we?"

Margaret got unsteadily to her feet, rolling her eyes as she knocked against the table, rocking their glasses of stout alarmingly.

"We're getting too old for this, eh, Dot? Could've drunk you all under the table in me glory days, now I'm nearly as bad as her. Ah, well."

"Some way to go yet, Margaret, some way."

Maeve had turned her swaying head and was looking anxiously up at Margaret, her face pale and clammy.

"You going."

The words, a slurred statement of unhappy fact rather than a question, amused Doris, who in her drunken reverie was finding the world a clearer and more comprehensible place.

"We're all going, Maeve dear, it won't be long."

"Stop it, Doris, you're scaring her. Look."

Lips quivering, luminescent skin now tinged green, eyes brimming with tears, Maeve was trying to lift herself out of her seat.

"It's just the drink."

"Yeah, well, she's had too much, that's for sure."

"Like all of us."

"No. You can never have too much. I've always told you that, remember, Dot? I've never had too much and never will."

Barging past chairs and tables Margaret came up behind Maeve, grasped her under the arms and hauled her to her feet.

"There now. Come with me. You'll soon be feeling better."

Supporting each other, the two women swayed out of the snug, leaving Doris alone, for the first time in what seemed like an eternity. It felt wonderful. She could stretch out her legs, her arms, without having to say sorry. Her thoughts were her own, words could stay unsaid. She could stand or sit. Stay or go. Do what she wanted without anyone – and they had been friends, good friends – having an opinion, telling her what to do or teasing her. She could be herself. Her life had not been hers, it could so easily have ended up like many of the laundry women's had, in a hidden grave at Glasnevin cemetery. A barely remarked end to a wasted life. She had been responsible for destroying her own family and should have been more careful. Nowadays, if what Doris read was true, people would take a much more relaxed view of her behaviour, but it was a very different world then. She had paid for her mistake and now she was being given a final chance. Her past was out there, where it had always been. The difference was she could now reclaim it for herself, without any fear of discovery, without any chance of retribution. Doris breathed in the smoky air with relish.

Chapter II

Doris' round – February 1948

The hot water lapped at her chin and she could feel her hair billowing out behind her every time she moved her body, tickling her neck and cheeks. As the rippling surface stilled, wisps of steam would rise again, dispersing into the cold air, misting the windows and mirror, droplets running in erratic rivulets down the walls. She closed her eyes. The light through the window, the curtains only half pulled, was bright and painful for sensitive eyes, even though she knew the day outside was overcast. She thought of the hours stretching ahead, her family away until evening, the house empty, the enjoyment to be had. It happened so infrequently that Doris could never really believe it, not until it was all over, and then the memory would soon take on the quality of a dream. She was happy, she knew that much. The knowledge was a lurid multi-coloured certainty that never left her, illuminating the dullest moments of her day, raising a wry little smile, suggesting a snatch of song, vividly spurring her body on – running, skipping – delighted by everyone and everything. They joked she must be in love, teasing her, asking who he was, "what a lucky lad." – her mother, only half in jest, reminding her that there was "plenty of time for boys, you should finish your schooling before you start on that nonsense". And Father Martin coming to her rescue: "Leave her be. She's in love with life, isn't it lovely to behold?" It was true, she was in love, but they had no idea with whom and Doris was determined to keep it that way.

She stretched out her arms, then folded them behind her head, cushioning against the hard enamel. She loved the bath like this, filled to the brim and every move a potential danger, with the water slopping over the edge, running down the cast-iron sides, washing over the white painted lion's feet and ponding in the runnels between the uneven stone flags. It angered her father to waste hot water like that, he just couldn't see it, but it would be all mopped up well before he got back. He would never know.

Doris opened her eyes. Her pale body stretched before her, its shape comically distorted by the refraction of the water, nipples just breaking the surface ahead of her, then her knees, drying now and spattered with a few beads of water, her feet hidden beneath Brigid's body. Her friend was almost completely submerged, only her nose visible above the surface, the taps looming above her – they swapped ends each time they shared a bath together – her body fitted comfortably around Doris, her legs passing under hers, feet resting under Doris's arms. Every movement tingled, skin sliding against skin, the intense intimacy exciting the still waters.

Doris thought Brigid had a beautiful body, her skin darker than Doris', the breasts larger, her waist narrower. Her legs were longer and a perfect shape. She admired that figure now, following its lines beneath the sparkling choppiness of the bath water. Possession of that body made Doris jealous, anxious to protect all that she had, to keep for herself something that another thought was his. She sought reassurance.

"Brigid?"

Her glistening face breached the surface.

"Yes."

A voice, sleepy and relaxed, whispered in reply.

"Do you know how long we've been together?"

"What?"

"Do you know how long we've been together?"

"No."

Doris' legs squeezed Brigid, bath water slopped back and forth, covering Brigid's face. She rose up seconds later spluttering and spitting furiously, face streaming and hair dripping.

"My mouth was open, you silly. I nearly drowned."

"That wouldn't do, now would it?"

"You'd have some trouble explaining it to your Ma."

Doris laughed.

"Don't!"

"The only good thing is, I wouldn't be around to catch it."

Water splattered noisily on to the flags as Brigid sat up and tickled Doris under the arms with her toes.

"Stop it, I hate that."

A perfectly aimed jet of water caught Brigid full in the face and she recoiled, coughing. Doris waited, poised. Explosively Brigid burst upwards and flung handfuls of water, drenching her and the wall behind, then collapsed back with a yelp. Wiping her face, Doris gazed in amusement as her friend writhed in the bubbling froth, gurgling unintelligibly and clutching her elbow.

"Are you all right?"

"No, I'm not …"

She was smiling.

"… I caught my funny-bone on the tap. It hurts."

"Poor baby, rub it better."

"Pax?"

"Pax."

Soaking wet, with her curly black hair plastered to her head, Brigid was transformed in Doris's eyes, no longer the voluptuous temptress, more the grinning pixie with her round face, delicate nose and pointed chin. It was perfect; she loved the first and was best friends with the second. It would last forever.

"Why do I always get the tap end? It's not fair."

"You don't. We take it in turns."

"You sure?"

"Yes, I'm sure."

She blew a kiss that spun through the air and caught a grinning Doris on the lips. Satisfied she watched as Brigid ran a hand – the damp flattened curls beneath her arm briefly exciting – through her sodden hair, strands springing free, changing back to her more carefree, dishevelled self.

"What were you saying?"

"Oh, nothing."

"Could you pass me the towel? My eyes are really stinging. Thanks."

"I wanted to know if you knew how long we'd been together?"

"Well, it depends."

Brigid wiped her face and handed the towel back to Doris who threw it across the bathroom aiming at a green painted wooden chair in the corner. She missed and the towel landed on the floor, soaking one end in the encroaching puddle.

"Bugger. Depends on what?"

"When you count from."

"What?"

"When we first saw each other, or when we first held hands, or first kissed, or… you know."

"When we first held hands and when we first kissed were the same time."

"An hour or so's difference."

"Yes, but that's the same."

282

"So is that when you're counting from?"

"Yes."

"Let me see... Two and a half months by my reckoning."

"More."

"More? Three months."

"Less."

"Seems longer."

"Stop it. You don't know do you?"

"I'm pretty close."

"I've been counting the days."

"Go on know-all, tell me."

"If you count today it's eighty-seven days since we first kissed. That's two months, three weeks and five days."

"I was lying."

"What?"

The word frightened Doris and she was momentarily stunned, fearing the worst.

"It doesn't seem longer at all. I can't believe it's been that much time. It's passed so quickly."

They each leant forward and kissed on the lips, Brigid's hand tentatively stroking Doris on the cheek.

"Do you know how many times we've kissed?"

"Don't tell me you've been counting that as well?"

"Yes, go on, guess."

"Doris!"

"Two thousand, four hundred and twenty-five times ..."

"No."

" ... that's on the lips. If you include everywhere else then ..."

"Doris, stop it."

"... you get up to nearly five thousand times. Four thousand eight hundred and seventy-seven to be precise."

"You're mad, Doris, keeping count like that. You haven't been counting anything else, have you?"

"Maybe."

"Oh, my God."

Seconds passed, Doris relishing her friend's incredulity.

"That got you, didn't it? I'm only teasing."

Brigid splashed out, hiding her fleeting embarrassment. Doris just smirked, ignoring the shower of water that rained down upon her.

"It's worrying, Doris. I just thought it was something you would do."

"Don't know me at all then, do you? The days are right though, I have been counting those."

"I was only half wrong. You can wash my back to make amends."

Brigid tossed the soap to Doris – who grabbed at it, before losing the bar among the tangle of limbs – then raised herself up, water streaming from her body and turned round, lowering herself slowly into the bath, her back towards Doris.

"All yours."

"I think you're sitting on the soap."

As Brigid slightly lifted her body, looking back over her shoulder, Doris thrust her hand beneath the raised buttocks.

"Hey, that tickles."

"Just looking for the soap, it must be here somewhere."

"Doris!"

"I almost got it then, now I've lost it. Keep still."

"I can't. Stop it."

"I've got to get it. If you stopped splashing around I might be able to see it."

"Doris, please."

"Got it."

Triumphantly she pulled her hand from the cloudy water and thrust the smooth orange bar into Brigid's face.

"I knew it was down there somewhere."

Brigid's body relaxed, sinking into the bath, her back arching forward in anticipation.

"I bet you did."

The soft soap foamed easily in Doris' hands, the clinical fragrance infusing the moist air. She deliberately placed her fingers together in the centre of Brigid's back, between the shoulder blades, and then eased them outwards in broad arcs across the smooth skin. The body tensed. Circling again and again until the blood red welts merged into one radiant ruddy whole. The soft down on her shoulders standing erect, the skin pliant to the touch. Lathering again, then slippery hands following the contours of rib then breast, face drawn close to foaming back, tongue tracing the line of Brigid's spine, vertebra by vertebra.

"I love you, Doris."

The voice, husky and deep, barely audible, seeped through the skin, exciting a body vibrant with expectation.

"I love you too."

They held each other tightly, erasing for a moment all constraints, all obligations, all vows, cutting them off from everyone they knew, everything they knew they should be doing.

"What can we do, Brigid?"

"We can do this, silly".

"I know, but I'm so happy with you, I want more."

The soap was bitter in her mouth and she silently spat, the spittle, bubbling, passing between her lips onto the silken sheen then sliding away into the milky vastness. Doris wanted them to be one person, didn't want to be herself, she needed them to merge completely, peel back their skin and refashion it anew. Brigid wanted it too, she believed that, but she was older, more experienced, had emotional ties that Doris could never fully chart, was far more complicated than she would wish, was a person Doris still didn't know.

"You'll get it, my love."

"I know."

"It's getting cold in here, we should get out."

They washed in silence, passing the soap back and forth, watching each other, rinsing those hidden places – the back of the neck, the armpit, the top of the legs – that the other couldn't reach. Sharing one large green bath towel, they rubbed their damp bodies together, drying each other, laughing as the water gurgled away. Naked, their bodies tingling in the raw air, they mopped up the puddles of water, wiped clean the bath, then ran to Doris' room and leapt gleefully beneath the covers of her single bed. Body piled on shivering body they lay, breathing heavily, their tentative caresses bringing warmth to chilled limbs. Wet hair cold to the touch, darkening the white linen pillowcase, spurred them on to a greater physical intimacy. Sucking the ends of moisture-laden curls, touching, rubbing, kissing on the cheeks, then the lips, perfunctorily at first then with increasing passion. Tongues flicking here and there, bringing to life, warming, charging, exciting the body.

Doris kissed the dimpled chin that she loved so much, briefly taking the pointed tip fully into her mouth, then with deep sighs of contentment she slithered down to the neck, teeth nipping at the folds of loose skin as she passed. Brigid swallowed hard, her throat twitching as Doris kissed it. Leaving behind a moist trail of saliva she buried her face between Brigid's breasts, breathing deeply before rubbing her nose and mouth into the fleshy mounds, searching for the nipples, which when found hardened and stiffened as she sucked. Then on to the broad expanse of the chest, skin stretched taut across an exposed ribcage, heart beating fast, breathing rapid, kisses evenly spaced, then sinking into the softness of the belly, the deep well of her navel, searching for the bottom with her tongue – the giggling, hands faintly pushing on shoulders – moving on across bare flesh, the first downy hairs softening with the moisture of her tongue, then an abundance, thicker, wirier, resistant, still damp, the strong fragrance of coal tar.

"Doris, look what I've got for you."

Surprised, she turns, her head resting comfortably between Brigid's legs, to find her mother standing in the open doorway, dress material falling from her hands. In that brief instant she understands her horror for this was never meant to happen, she sees the agonised expression and hears the ear-piercing scream, the thud from downstairs, the sounds of her father and brother, Kevin, running up the stairs and knows she can change nothing.

***

It always smelled of piss in here, some people had no respect. You had to stand at the door sometimes just to be able to breathe. It didn't seem so bad today, but then her nose was running and she had been crying. Anywhere was better than that house at the moment. The rain was pouring down outside – the sky leaden and overcast – and looked like it would continue forever. Doris was soaked to the skin and needed somewhere to shelter. She often came to this small dark room at the bottom of the monastery tower for a cigarette. You had to duck to get in and then you would disappear and become invisible to the outside world. If you spoke in whispers nobody would ever know you were there. It helped that hardly anyone visited the ruins, except the odd local boy, it was very quiet and out of the way, even though it was just on the edge of town. You could even see the roof of her house from here, but they couldn't see her. A person could think.

Did she feel guilty?

No.

Did she regret it had happened?

No.

Any regrets at all?

Yes.

What?

That they'd been found out.

Her family had come apart in front of her eyes, there was no other way to describe it. Doris had been scared at the violence developing in front of her, about her but not of her. A member of the audience, when she should have been the star. It was as if for each act she moved further from the stage – first the stalls, then the dress circle and finally the gods – the actors diminishing as time passed, their words becoming more indistinct.

Her lovely God-fearing Father had been angry beyond reason, his fury releasing a stream of expletives that demeaned all who heard them. His face the colour of well-hung beef, he raged back and forth, overturning furniture, fists raining down on walls in savage bursts of bone-splintering brutishness, spittle flying from his open mouth. He was beyond control, his family cowering in corners. Malcolm Blaney stopped only once briefly, out of surprise, when he bit his tongue, the blood running between gritted teeth to drip onto his heaving white shirt, then he was off again, fighting his own way into a very personal damnation.

Doris had to get away.

Strong willed and moral, her Mother had been a good friend. Doris had loved her more than anything and they had always been close. Now she couldn't have been further away, pressed against the wall, crying, fists in her mouth, gasping for breath. Doris would remember her eyes – wide-open, staring, brown spheres ringed by white, cow's eyes at the point of death – and would dream of them over the years, their significance waning but the sense of regret never leaving her, even though she often couldn't quite remember what it was for. Her Mother had said nothing in the end, her wailing that of a mute who had lost the power of speech long ago, but still had the sounds of the words reverberating in her head. Her silence had hurt the most.

Doris had to leave.

Kevin, her brother, had collapsed onto his knees, head in his hands, and was in danger of his rampaging father colliding with him but seemed oblivious to his peril. Doris liked her brother – loved had always seemed a bit strong to describe what she felt about him – and they had grown closer since he had got married. He had been calmer, more considerate, prepared to sit down and talk and even listen sometimes. There was less friction, fewer arguments, even though the small three-bedroom house they shared with their parents now had an extra person living there. She felt enough for him that she should have been moved by his angry curses and desperate uncomprehending moans, but she wasn't. Kevin was invisible. The horror she felt blinded her to all but her parents, breaking up before her eyes. There was nothing to say and nothing she could do to change things.

She must escape.

Brigid had played only a very small part, scrambling from the bed, a crumpled sheet wrapped round her naked body, silently running from the room, barging aside all obstacles. As she dressed, body shaking, fingers fumbling, Doris had called out her name, but there had been no reply. There was nothing left to do but flee.

The heavy rain was sheeting across deserted streets as she ran to her tower. Her thin summer dress was drenched in an instant, her brown curly hair plastered to her face, her glasses spattered with drops of water. She could barely see and found her way by instinct. It angered her that they had let her go, had offered no resistance as she brushed past their grieving bodies. They were impotent, her family, they really were. They should have done something, she expected it, but they didn't do anything.

She was alone at last, sucking the rank air deep into her lungs, desperate for a cigarette. She had remembered to bring a packet, grabbing them from the bedside table as she left, matches too, but they were sodden, the soft cardboard coming apart in her hands. There would be no salvation for her now. Standing alone on ground made holy by the passage of ancient saints, Doris seethed with contempt.

***

The Reverend Mother wouldn't look at her. She was talking, but not communicating. The words soft and low, matched the dim lighting of the study, and seemed to travel away from Doris as if they weren't really for her.

"All meals will be eaten in silence."

Why was no one talking to her?

"Work in the laundry starts at six thirty in the morning."

Her whole family had been struck dumb.

"Everyone gets ten shillings pocket money a week…"

The couple who had driven her this evening from her home all the way to Dublin – it was her first visit and the dread she had been feeling was tinged with excitement, she couldn't help it – had not said a word to her, just whispered to each other in the front seat, with only the occasional furtive glance in her direction.

"… and we'll look after it for you."

Her new priest, Father James, she thought that was his name, had been silent, just sitting there waiting, so she told him everything. She felt he knew it all anyway, but spilling it out again, for the last time, helped.

"No one is allowed to leave the Convent without express permission from me and that is rarely given for any of my girls, not until we can trust them. That is very important. Trust is the basis of our little community and I will not have that trust broken. Anyone who challenges … "

Now she was standing in her best clothes, suitcase in front of her, and listening to rules and regulations laid down by a woman she had never met before, who had total control over her life, but wouldn't speak her name.

"Lights go out at eight-thirty in the evening. No talking after that."

Her disgrace seemed like it would never end.

"Finally, and most importantly, you must not talk about why you are here with anybody. Is that clear?"

A nod.

"If you behave, we'll get on just fine."

Doris never had told anybody why she was there, not even her best friend, Lily.

Chapter 12

The Snug – March 1996 – ten past three

Doris would buy another drink, before the others got back. It would be the first time she had ever done that, gone to the bar on her own and ordered something just for herself. There was enough money in her purse. Maeve was too drunk to notice anything, Margaret might, but then who cared? It was over between them. The snug door swung open. It had been too good to last.

"I was sick."

The pale figure of Maeve stood there, face forlorn but voice triumphant. A grinning Margaret loomed behind her, nudging her forward.

"Was she sick! I've never seen anything like it."

Maeve concurred.

"I feel much better now."

"Went everywhere, that's why we've been so long. Had to mop it up."

"Margaret, please."

"Maureen was very good about it. Said she'd deal with it when I told her. Said not to worry."

Doris squirmed with distaste, but Maeve was not paying attention.

"Just need a sit down."

"A glass of water, Maeve? It usually helps."

"That'd be nice, thanks, Doris."

Settling into her chair Maeve looked frail, uncertain in her movements, her confidence shaken. For the first time she seemed too thin to Doris, her brown hair, barely flecked with grey, no longer enough to ward off the impression that she was an old woman. Doris had always envied Maeve's lithe figure, had wished she herself had been taller, as over the years her stocky frame had thickened and filled out. Maeve, and Barbara as well, had seemed immune to the wrinkles and creases that beset everyone else they knew. Now suddenly everything had changed. It was disconcerting for Doris to be reminded that they were all getting old, just as she was discovering for herself a growing faith in the future.

"And thanks, Margaret. If you hadn't been there, I don't know what I'd have done."

"It's all right. I know what it's like. Three glasses of water, is it?"

They all laughed.

"So they've not arrived yet?"

"No. Can't see them anywhere, can you?"

"They're late."

"Only by about half an hour. I'm sure Father Michael'll find them."

"Maybe they're not coming."

"Margaret, I haven't been in touch with my family for over forty years, now they say they're coming to get me."

"For a trial run."

"Yes, for a trial run, so they'll be coming. Probably held up in traffic somewhere."

Margaret wouldn't give up, Doris realized, it would continue until the very end.

"So you could be back. If it doesn't work out?"

"Could be, Margaret, but not if I can help it."

Maeve looked genuinely disappointed, while Margaret just smiled.

"They better turn up soon in any case, or they'll be throwing us out of here. Then where'll we go?"

"They will be, Margaret, don't you worry your head about that. And anyway if they don't arrive I'll just wait across the road. My case is there."

"Well, while we're waiting, any more secrets you've got hidden away you want to tell us about?"

"None. I've no secrets."

Margaret snorted.

"If you believe that…"

"If I have, I can't remember them."

They all laughed again, drawing closer together. Maeve was visibly cheering up, the colour returning to her cheeks, her body straightening in the chair. Unlike Margaret, who thrived on discord, she just wanted them to be friends. She needed kind words to take her on into a future made uncertain by its reliance on her, at times, frightening friend.

"That's your excuse is it?"

Margaret's smile hid her grim determination to hound Doris to the bitter end. Her mission made urgent by the pressure of time and the growing conviction that once again she was being duped in some way. To be short-changed by a failing old woman, one she had known for most of her life, was unbearable to her. Sensitive to the signs Maeve tried her best, as Barbara had in the past, to place herself between the bickering pair.

"Margaret, I'm sure Doris is telling the truth."

"You are, are you?"

"I am. Who needs secrets at our age?"

"Why don't you ask her? I notice she's not saying anything."

The need to respond was gone. Silence had bought her respite in the past, and it would work again now. Time was on her side, after all, but the cost had been high. Years lost in a haze that Doris, in this moment of drunken clarity, feared would never dissipate.

"This way. I'm sure they'll still be there, I only left them about ten minutes ago."

It was him again, the voice of authority that had punctuated their conversations over the years and once again brought everything to a full stop. The door of the snug swung open and the tall figure of Father Michael appeared, silhouetted in the bright sunlight streaming through the mirrored windows behind him in the public bar. His face was in shadow, and the voice, disembodied, sounded to be coming from high above them.

"Success."

There was a moment when Michael almost believed the three women blinking up at him had no idea what he was talking about. But it passed in the time it took him to inhale deeply on his cigarette and he felt a load lift from his shoulders.

"I have someone here I think Doris has been waiting to meet."

He stepped aside, holding open the door. Light flooded in, dazzling them. The women glanced aside and when they looked again Doris' niece was standing there, smiling nervously.

It was hard to see anything at first, the sun glinting on her glasses, heart thumping, but even in silhouette she was so familiar. The fuzz of dark curly hair, cropped short, the elegant thin neck, the narrow sloping shoulders, thin body, not too tall, shapely legs.

"Hello."

The fog seemed to clear that little bit more, just a brief glance followed by one simple word reverberating across the decades. It could be her sister-in-law standing there, Doris was certain, a little older but otherwise she had hardly changed at all.

"This is Kathleen… er, I'm sorry."

"Cowan."

"That's right, Kathleen Cowan. I do apologize, I've a terrible memory on me sometimes. Cowan née Blaney."

Kathleen nodded demurely.

"Come in and I'll introduce you."

Stepping into the shadows of the snug, the door shutting out the sunlight, Kathleen came clearly into view. Short of breath Doris followed her every move, eyes intimately fixed on the detail of her face. The high forehead, pencil thin eyebrows, brown slightly hooded eyes – beacons for a sly hidden sense of humour that, Doris knew, could flare like a spark in a dry meadow and die away just as quickly – the narrow nose broadening slightly at the nostrils. The high cheekbones were there, the wide mouth with delicate lips parting tentatively to reveal strong white teeth, the pointed chin, hair tucked behind tiny head-hugging ears, the pale skin gleaming. It was all as Doris remembered. A sign from almost half a century ago carried by a messenger with the same smile and dimpling cheeks. The memory was now so vivid and precise – Kathleen's mother had never pierced her ears and worn gold and pearl ear-studs, but then times had changed – that Doris revelled in the detail.

"This is Margaret Macready and this is Maeve Kennedy."

"Pleased to meet you. Don't get up."

A delicate arm was extended – a white short-sleeved linen blouse, her shoulders draped with a black cashmere cardigan, a pewter art nouveau brooch pinned at her breast – and shook their hands.

"And this is your aunt, Doris Blaney."

Doris rose to her feet and edged her way round the table, steadying the glasses as she went. Kathleen's hand was cool to the touch, light and insubstantial, her skin soft and perfumed, the flickering kiss brief, and much to Doris' surprise repeated seconds later on the other cheek.

"Auntie…"

Her breath misted Doris' glasses, for a moment obscuring the tears.

"… I'm glad to meet you after all this time."

"So am I. I."

There were so many things Doris wanted to say, so many things she wanted to ask, but couldn't. Emotionally overwhelmed, she was crippled by an inability to make sense of the memories swirling into her mind. Try as hard as she could, the words were not there.

"Father Michael told me so much about you when we spoke on the phone."

The priest nodded as he slipped another roll-up from his cigarette case, accepting the credit.

"I'm so glad you agreed to come and live with us."

"I'm happy to."

"We've got plenty of space. There's a room for you and we have a lovely garden overlooking open fields. You could imagine you were really out in the country. As you know, there's just the two of us, me and my husband Mark. He couldn't come today he's at work – he's a solicitor – so we won't get in each other's way. It'll be grand."

"No children then?"

The words had finally come and Kathleen smiled.

"Come on, Doris," chided the priest. "Not so many questions, there'll be plenty of time for that."

"It's all right, Father. No, we haven't any children and no plans either. Getting a bit late to tell you the truth …"

Doris' heart warmed to the whispered intimacy.

"… anyway Mark's got quite a large family – lots of nieces and nephews – and many of them live nearby, so the house is never empty of children."

"I didn't mean…"

"I know, and we also live very near to my mother. You remember her, don't you? I see her most days."

"You look just like her."

"Do I?"

Kathleen laughed out loud.

"A number of people have told me that. You're not the first. Don't see it myself, but then who am I to say?"

"The spitting image."

"Well, thank you. She's kept her looks, I can say that for her. If I'm only half so lucky."

"They're calling last orders. Would you like a drink, Kathleen?"

"I won't, thank you, Margaret, I have to drive, but let me get you one?"

"I will Kathleen, thank you."

"Maeve, Auntie?"

They both shook their heads, Doris marvelling at being called an aunt for the first time in her life, something she had never expected to hear.

"Father, you sure? So what's it to be, Margaret, a stout?"

Turning at the bar, while she waited to attract Patrick's attention, Kathleen gazed at Doris.

"Speaking of family likenesses, Doris, you look a lot like my Da. Bet no one's told you that in a while. Not surprising, though, I suppose, brother and sister. Yes, thank you, a Guinness, please."

"How is my brother Kevin?"

Discomfited for a moment, Kathleen said nothing. She paid for the drink, handed it to Margaret and then sat down beside Doris.

"Da's dead, Auntie, you knew that surely?"

Doris shook her head. Kathleen took her hand and glanced up at the priest.

"You did Doris."

Father Michael spoke softly.

"I told you all this after I'd spoken to Kathleen here. Last month wasn't it? The time when she agreed you could go and live with her. You must have forgotten in all the excitement."

"He died over two years ago."

Doris nodded.

"It was in his sleep. He'd not been well for many years. It was the same thing that took your Father ..."

It was coming back to her now.

"... and your Mother. Oh must be ten years ago or more. Grandda died just before Christmas ... when was it? "83 or 84?" 83, that was it, and Grandma followed him in the spring. It was a sad time for us all. Da took it very badly. He was never the same after that – we should have told you at the time. I'm sorry, Auntie."

Her words trailed off into nothing as Doris shook her head. Grief was an elusive emotion, she'd always found. She'd lost her family once long ago and felt little but anger. Now they were dying on her once again and it left her unmoved. It was inappropriate, though, she could see that by the sadness in Kathleen's eyes, so she squeezed her niece's hand affectionately, took off her glasses, placed them on the beer-stained table then turned her head away to stare myopically at the brown wood panelling on the wall. Kathleen reached across, placed her arms gently round her shoulders and gave her a hug.

"I'm sorry, Auntie. I really am."

The whispered words tingled, her breath hot on Doris' ear.

"I'm sorry too, Doris."

A hand touched her shoulder; Maeve's voice an echo from a distant past.

"We'll make it up to you, you see if we don't."

The moment held, as the years seemed to drop away for Doris. She grew stronger as if drawing energy from the young body that clung to her. Kathleen seemed reluctant to let go and it was wonderful to be held again after such a long time, to feel the embrace of someone who cared for you.

There was a final fleeting kiss on Doris' cheek then Kathleen pulled away, smoothing the back of her hair with her hand as she settled back in her chair. Father Michael reached across to stub out his cigarette in the overflowing ashtray on the table, he was smiling.

"Well, Mrs Cowan, thanks very much for agreeing to take care of Doris. I hope it works out well for you all. I'm sure it will."

He looked from one to the other, beaming.

"You seem to be getting on like a house on fire already."

Kathleen nodded at him, her face unsmiling, as if for the first time she was experiencing doubts about the responsibility she had taken on. The priest got to his feet.

"I'll say good-bye then. Doris, don't get up."

Father Michael leaned across the table to shake her hand. His crucifix, dangling free, clinked against one of the glasses.

"You be good now."

He winked. The grip was firm and warm and with his rings cutting gently into Doris's hand, slightly painful. As he let go she felt him slip her a tightly folded piece of paper.

"And don't be a stranger. Come and see us, won't you? God bless, Doris. Mrs Cowan. I'll see you two on Sunday. Oh, by the way, Doris, the Bishop asked me to give you that. Goodbye, all."

The snug door swung closed behind him, and the women looked at each other with relief. They could hear Siobhan whistling as she swept up in the public bar.

"What, Doris? What's he given you?"

Margaret was consumed with curiosity.

"Show us."

She slowly unfolded the paper, adjusted her glasses, and then stared in astonishment at the words written in large block capitals.

"What does it say?"

"It's Lily's address …"

"What?"

"… in New York."

"I don't believe it! He had it all the time, the sly bastard."

Kathleen looked at Margaret, surprised at her use of such language.

"Who's Lily, Auntie?"

"An old friend."

"That's nice. Well, we ought to be going too, Doris. We must be the last ones left in here."

Kathleen smiled at her aunt, a kindly look that Doris knew she would be able to live with. It was strange that she had only known Kathleen existed for less than a month, had had no idea her brother and his wife had a daughter, until that day when Father Michael had called to her almost in triumph to say that her niece had replied to his letter and was prepared to consider taking her in for a "trial run". Things would be fine, she was sure.

"You off then, Doris?"

The barman was peering through one of the open windows on the bar.

"Good luck to you. I wish you all the best. My profits will be down, to be sure, as I'm losing one of my best customers. But never mind, I've still got these two."

He nodded at Margaret and Maeve, who were standing awkwardly now, uncertain what to do.

"You take care."

Smiling he shook her hand across the damp bar, then disappeared.

"All set?"

Kathleen was on her feet.

"We should miss the worst of the traffic if we get going now."

She stepped aside to allow Maeve, pale and tearful, to squeeze past. They hugged.

"I'll miss you so much, Doris, I really will."

"I'll miss you too, Maeve."

"Please come and see us – please! I'll write as well."

"I will."

"God be with you always, Doris."

Hunched, looking no one in the eye, she scurried from the snug. Margaret was standing in front of Doris before she had time to register Maeve's passing, her mind on other things. A brief silent embrace. Neither woman could think of anything to say, then as Margaret left she turned, grim-faced.

"Goodbye, Doris, I'm on my own now."

Fresh cooler air flooded into the snug as the door swung shut.

"That just leaves us two."

A gentle touch on her shoulder.

"You all right?"

Doris nodded.

"You sure? We could have a cup of tea before we go, if that would help? There must be somewhere round here."

"No thanks. I was just thinking…"

"All right then. I'll go and pick up your bags from the Convent. The car's parked outside."

Across the road from the Coach and Horses the laundry where Doris and the others had worked for so long was silent now, cold but not damp. The floors were dry, the windows streaked with dirt and grime, not steamed up and running with water as they would normally have been on a Friday lunchtime. Light streamed through the still air, flecks of dust hanging immobile where once banks of roiling clouds had scudded across the open spaces in impudent, small-scale mimicry of the real thing racing in from the West high overhead; above the grey shining slates and chimneys belching smoke. Dust sheets covered the washing machines, the copper boiling pans, the steam presses and the rows of irons. Sparrows scuttered high in the roof, perching now and again on the black iron rods that had once opened and closed the slatted windows, before flitting back and forth through the cracked panes of glass. The doors were locked.

As they pulled away Doris looked out for the last time at the high dark walls that surrounded the Convent. She was beginning to understand how it would be from now on. The past could be rewritten. Her best friend, Lily, would come back to her. Her parents were gone, her brother was dead. Her lover was alive and waiting for her. Doris wondered if this was the time to tell Kathleen how much she loved her mother, Brigid.